'Such a terrif... ...elly

BLUES,
...w what
you did

TWOS
and
BABY
SHOES

the Further, Further Adventures of
Constable Mavis Upton

GINA KIRKHAM

BLUES, TWOS and BABY SHOES

I know what you did

Urbane
PUBLICATIONS

urbanepublications.com

GINA KIRKHAM

First published in Great Britain in 2019
by Urbane Publications Ltd
Unit E3 The Premier Centre Abbey Park Romsey SO51 9DG
Copyright © Gina Kirkham, 2019

A CIP catalogue record for this book is available
from the British Library.

ISBN 978-1-912666-54-6
MOBI 978-1-912666-55-3

Design and Typeset by Michelle Morgan

Cover by David Hallangen
HALLANGEN ART

Printed and bound by 4edge Limited, UK

URBANE

urbanepublications.com

**For my wonderful grandchildren,
Olivia, Annie and Arthur**

*'You make the world a little softer
A little kinder
A little warmer'*

BLUES, TWOS AND BABY SHOES

CORA

The little brass bell sitting above the glazed door tinkled as Edna Flaybrick shuffled her bunioned feet into the shop. A draught of bitterly cold air took the opportunity to sneak in behind her, whipping up several brown crusty leaves that eventually settled on the dark grey corded carpet.

Cora May Spunge looked over her half-moon glasses and sighed. At a very sprightly 72-years young and the only still flexible OAP volunteering in Junk & Disorderly, Westbury's one and only charity shop, she knew she would be the one that would have to bend down to pick them up.

"Morning Edna, chilly one today isn't it?" Cora carefully folded the wool blend jumper on the counter, patted the sleeves across and straightened out the collar. Edna didn't reply, she sniffed the air, swiped her handkerchief under her nose, nodded and ambled over to the bookcase. Cora tried again. "Looking for anything in particular? We've just had a couple of bags dropped off, think there are a few of those Mills & Boon type paperbacks in one of them if you want me to have a look for you," she helpfully offered.

Edna carried on tracing her gnarled fingers across the spines of the books already on display. "Can't abide sloppy stuff. I'm looking for a good murder today, something I can get me teeth into." She sniffed again but this time used the sleeve of her coat to catch the offending sliver.

Cora smiled to herself. The last time Edna had got her own teeth into anything worthwhile was back in 1954, before dentures and before Cyril Hislop had done the dirty on her with Clementine Perkins.

Oh, my goodness, Cora May Spunge, you're such a naughty girl! What dreadful, unbecoming thoughts for a lady of your age.

She subconsciously berated herself whilst trying not to giggle, imagining Edna's clackety false ivories clamped around Cyril's manhood. That was the thing with people of her generation, they forgot.

They forgot where they had come from.

They forgot what they had done.

They forgot who remembered.

She clipped the coat hanger clamp onto the waistband of the tweed skirt, brushed it with her hand and looked around for the best place to hang it. A place that would show it off to its full potential.

It was so very true; youth really was wasted on the young. She had the experience that came from the heady days of her own youth but a failing body and mind that couldn't do it justice. Some days she remembered with clarity, other days it was just a tantalising wisp of the echoes of her past. Oh, how she missed her Harold. He had been a good husband in his own way. He hadn't set the world on fire, but he had loved her, cared for her. She absentmindedly rearranged the shelf behind her, shifting two china ornaments to the back and bringing forward a small pink teddy bear with a satin bow tied loosely around its neck. She brushed the soft fur between the ears, momentarily holding it against her cheek. They had never been blessed with children, that part of marriage had eluded her, it was just Cora and Harold against the world. No giggling little ones, their faces softly lit by tree lights at Christmas, no sleepless nights, no damp nappies hanging on the drier in front of the fire, no chubby hands to hold or cuddles to feel.

She quickly pushed the bear back onto the shelf.

What's done is done, Cora my dear. No point in crying over what never was.

There had been so many nights when Harold had taken to his study to read, smoke his pipe and generally while away the hours leaving Cora to sit quietly on the small, three-legged milking stool in the kitchen, darning his socks. She had accepted this way of life, she had never believed that she was worthy of anything more than a regulated pattern to her days and a sense of loneliness to her nights.

And then one day Harold chose to drop down dead.

Just like that.

With absolutely no thought whatsoever for Cora.

She had stood looking at his lifeless body splayed out on the small tufted lilac bathmat. Electric toothbrush in one hand, still vibrating with gusto and his flaccid Bertie Brewster in the other. She had felt nothing. Absolutely nothing. No sadness, no melancholy, no anger, no disappointment, nothing…. apart from the obvious horror of wondering what he had been using his toothbrush for at the time of his sudden and selfish departure.

In truth he had never excited her. She had secretly read one of those Mills & Boon books herself during her lunch break a few weeks ago. Harold had never made her tingle from head to toe, not even *that* important lady bit in the middle, like the hero on those pages did. Harold was just…. well…. he was just Harold! She certainly couldn't imagine herself doing to him what Edna had reputedly done to Cyril behind the boiler room of the local open-air lido in the summer of 1954; with or without teeth. She giggled loudly, which made Edna proffer the *Westbury Widow Death Stare* in Cora's direction.

She tried to look suitably chastised, but in truth, she couldn't even be bothered to feign it. Neither church attendance, of which she was a regular, her stints in *Junk & Disorderly*, or her weekly line dancing classes, could haul her out of the current dissatisfaction she felt with her lot and what lay ahead.

When had her life become so ordinary, so expected, so mind-blowingly, bloody boring?

THE REVEAL

Things That Make Me Nervous – Part 1....

That thought makes me snigger in a very unladylike fashion. It sounds like an excellent title for a self-help book, propped up in our local supermarket against *Bungee Jumping for Beginners* and *50 Ways to Use Feminine Hygiene Products in a Manly Manner* (I just know you're going to Google that last one!).

I'm not only nervous, I'm actually bloody terrified too.

I, Mavis Jane (Blackwell) Upton, or better known to my colleagues and bosses over the last twenty years as Constable 1261 Mavis Upton, ace police driver, apprehender of naughty people, lover of crisps (any flavour) and hater of big knickers - is currently contemplating how to tell my hubby that I'm also going to be a geriatric incubator for his first child.

The box sits on the breakfast bar in the kitchen. Waiting for the kettle to boil I wonder if my great idea of a surprise reveal is the best way to do it, but I truly can't think of any other way, except to blurt it out and probably give him a coronary in the process. I absentmindedly pour the boiling water into the two mugs and watch the tea bags bob up and down. Mr Grumpy on the side of Joe's mug glares back at me; this bright blue, square man with a downturned mouth makes me feel very blue too. How am I going to manage at my age? Although wonderful and the best thing that had ever happened to me, it was hard enough the first time around as a single mum with Ella. I was so much younger then too.

Oh well, it's now or never... or at least until I start waddling like a duck and I can't see my feet!

I take the stairs two at a time, slopping tea onto the carpet.

"Bloody hell Mave, I wouldn't get me big toe into this!" Joe held up one of the delicately knitted white bootees, pinched between his finger and thumb and swung it from side to side. The paper I'd wrapped them in had been excitedly discarded on the bedroom carpet. He ran his free hand through his hair, causing spikes to spring erratically into action.

I half-expected him to pull his ridiculous Stan Laurel face as he paused, his mind processing the hint my gift held for him.

I daren't breathe, I just waited. The fluttering in my chest a mixture of anticipation and apprehension. Knowing the precious treasure I held inside me, I carefully placed my hands gently over my tummy as his eyes darted from the bootee still dangling between his fingers, to me and back to the bootee.

After what seems an eternity, I think the penny has finally dropped.

"Oh Em Gee...!" Flinging the duvet back he leapt out of bed and grabbed me around my waist, dancing me around the bedroom. "Italy.... we're only going to bloody ITALY!!" Laughing, he flopped back down onto the bed, double punching the air in unbridled excitement.

I sighed, blowing my fringe upwards, away from my eyes. This seriously wasn't going to plan. "Joe, no.... I... oh dear, I'm... we're..."

Pushing himself up onto his elbows, he searched my face. "Err, boot, I get it, the shape of Italy; holiday, sun, beer..." he paused, the Stan Laurel face making a tentative appearance, ".... you know, beer, more beer, a bit more sun?"

Jeez, just how stoopid can one human being be!

(That is definitely an exclamation - not a question)

"No Joe, not Italy."

"Not Italy?"

I shook my head. "Not Italy..."

"Spain... is it Spain and you're just a bit shit at geography?"

"No Joe, not Spain."

"Oh..."

I waited, the silence palpable between us.

Blimey, did he want me to act it out like a ruddy game of charades?

"Dearest husband, somehow I think the moment has passed, don't you?" I picked up the bootee he had dropped, pressed it against the other one and folded the satin ribbon into a neat bow. Popping them back together into the little box, I bit back bitter disappointment. "Thank goodness you didn't take up that post in CID, their detection rates would be marginally shittier than they are now!" I snapped.

He tilted his head to one side, scratching the back of his neck. A fleeting wisp of realisation sparked in his eyes. "Feck me Mave; you're not are you?" he snorted.

"Not what? You can say it you know, I think the word you're looking for is *pregnant*.... with child, bun in the oven, harbouring a fugitive, on nine month standby!"

Never had such a romantic, break-it-to-him-gently plan gone so completely off the mark.

"Oh dear." He vigorously scratched the top of his head this time, his eyes darting from the box, to my face and back to the box, his mouth opening and closing like a cod fish.

I bristled. "*Oh dear!* Is that it, just *oh dear*?" My voice automatically went up several octaves.

"Gosh, no, not at all my little turnip!" his fingers nervously plucked at the crumpled duvet. "Erm, wow, how fantastic, I didn't see that coming...... especially at your age!" he spluttered.

Funnily enough, he didn't see his Mr Grumpy mug hurtling towards his head either!

"Good grief Mave, just how much crap can one person accumulate?" Sergeant Beryl Scully held the double fire doors open for me as I nudged around her with my battered cardboard box. The old tin caddy marked *Dunkers* wobbled precariously from its lofty position on top of two box files and a plastic mug, which at one time had sported a rather nifty lid until Petey had decided to use it to feed the station mice his butty crumbs. Rather than risk some dreadful illness, I'd declined its return, preferring to live dangerously with a mug that occasionally slopped tea dregs onto my combats.

"This is the last one Sarge, they've cleared a space for me in the office, I've even got my own desk and support chair too..." I tried to sound positive, even a little excited. "... it adjusts, swivels, tilts and it's got padded arms." I grinned.

Beryl gave me a look of understanding mixed with a trace of sympathy. "A desk job is not really for you, is it?" she smiled, whilst repositioning my treasured biscuit caddy. "It's only for a while, you'll be back out there in the thick of things before you know it."

I screwed my nose up and sighed. "I know but this just seems so weird, so wrong. I should be out with the Section, chasing the

BLUES, TWOS AND BABY SHOES

naughty boys and locking them up, not driving a desk on the second floor of Westbury police station dribbling with boredom whilst looking out of the windows." Ambling backwards, I pushed open the second set of doors with my bum.

"Hey, watch where you're going HMS Broadbeam…"

If my hands hadn't been full, then whoever that insult belonged to would have felt at least one of my fists. I marvelled at how hormones and pregnancy had produced a rather aggressive streak in me, whilst guilty remembering the look of incredulity on Joe's face that morning when the mug I'd launched at him had bounced off his head.

Bob Cairns squeezed between the small gap that remained between me, the box and the door. "Don't go getting big-headed lass, but I think I just might miss you on the Section." He went to ruffle my hair but quickly thought better of it.

"Oh Bob…" all thoughts of randomly punching him gone, "… that's such a lovely thing to say!"

He harrumphed and grinned at Beryl before he continued. "I mean, who else is going to make the tea and clear up after us?" Holding the door open for me, he winked. "To be honest *Tubby*, we didn't know if we were supposed to congratulate you or buy you a gym membership for your birthday!" he guffawed loudly before disappearing up the next flight of steps, his distinct, guttural laughter echoing around the stairwell.

Jeez, I'm already starting to feel nostalgic, so much so I want to cry, what the hell is wrong with me?

Beryl caught me. "Now, now Mave…" she wagged her finger, "…we'll all miss you, of course we will but for now it's a no deal situation. There's no bargaining to be had, office job until that little one makes an appearance, okay?" She pointed to the swell of my stomach, my combats straining at the zip making it more obvious than I thought. She didn't wait for a reply as she let go of the door, being friends as well as my Supervisor, she didn't need one.

I stood alone in the corridor outside the brown painted door, the sign informing me that this would be 'home' for the next few months, a place where I would forge new friendships and hopefully learn new skills....and maybe even find that all elusive, much desired, dunkable biscuit!

CRIME MANAGEMENT & VICTIM SUPPORT UNIT

MOTHER CARES

"**M**uuuuuum…… Muuuuuuum….."

Ella's voice. My little girl, my daughter. Is it the absence of toilet roll again, a shoelace undone, a missing spotty wellington or some other disaster that has befallen her? It's not time for school is it? Or Brownies or after school club? I groggily open my eyes, take in my surroundings.

Beamed ceiling, log burner fire, squishy sofa. I stick my tongue out and then clack it against the roof of my mouth. It's like Gandhi's flip flop. *Bluuurrrgh.*

"Muuuuuum, for goodness sake wake up!" Ella's voice proceeds her as she bursts through the door into the lounge.

"Whaaaat? I've not been asleep, I was just resting my eyes…" Swinging my legs down from the arm of the sofa, I check out my puffy ankles and sigh. Great, that's all I need, Oedema of the lower extremities, just like old Phyllis from next door. Dear Phyllis has reliably informed me on numerous occasions that she is a martyr to her fluid retention and has been for over thirty years. I've been known to snigger behind her back, maybe this is payback time for me!

I look at Ella, my beautiful daughter. Not the little girl of the drowsy dream I have just had, but a young, confident, intelligent and funny woman. Married and embarking on motherhood herself. I still marvel at how I have created such a perfect creature, another human being. I subconsciously place a hand on my tummy and feel a slight flutter.

And here I am doing it all over again, virtually side by side with my own daughter.

Once Ella had got over the initial shock of her own mum being pregnant at the same time as she was, we had sailed along together with ante-natal appointments, comparing notes, me giving out old-fashioned and out of date advice whilst Ella imparted to me much needed updates on what was termed as my *Geriatric Pregnancy….* all obtained via that trusted on-line source, Mr Google!

"I'll put the kettle on, I've bought a packet of custard creams and we can have a little browse through the Mothercare catalogue." Ella dropped the glossy brochure onto the coffee table. I gave it a cursory glance, flicking through the pages whilst she clattered cups and rattled spoons in the kitchen. "How did your antenatal check up go, sweetheart?" I turned to page 6, enviously eying up the stroller and pram systems, sighed over the colourways, drooled over the fabric and then moved down to the price.

Feck me, I'd have to re-mortgage the house or sell myself on Corpy Road to afford any one of them!

Ella breezed in with the tea tray, a radiant grin lighting up her face. She plonked herself down on the sofa next to me. "It was good Mum, no issues. Baby is doing well; my blood pressure is fine, and we even discussed my birthing plan."

I laughed. "Birthing plan? Believe me, when it comes down to it, you'll just lie back and alternate between puffing and grunting with a few choice swearwords thrown in for good measure!"

She handed me a steaming mug of tea. "There's so much you can have now Mum, water births, different types of pain relief …. in fact, they said it's not really pain that you feel when you're in labour at all, it's more a sort of pressure, is that right?"

I think the look on my face gave the game away before I had even opened my mouth. "Seriously? Ella, that's like saying a tornado is merely a breeze!"

She giggled, popping a custard cream into her mouth, she tried to speak, spluttering crumbs over herself. "Bloody hell, what have I let myself in for then, got to admit I didn't even think about the end bit and the less romantic and embarrassing parts of becoming a mum." She proffered the packet of biscuits towards me.

My tummy did a flip as a wave of nausea swept over me. "Ooooh, errr... I think baby says a big fat *no* to custard creams." I burped loudly. "If you think that's embarrassing, wait until you're the size of a rhino and then everyone will know what you've been up to to get that way!" I sniggered.

Ella's face turned a beautiful shade of pink as she groaned. "OMG Mum, nooooooo don't even go there.... you and Joe.... I mean, oh my word, how absolutely gross.... don't tell me you've been doing *it* at your age, that's disgusting!"

I hoped she was joking.... if she wasn't, I'd seriously consider asking for my money back from the extra biology classes she'd taken at summer school in 1994.

RUB-A-DUB-DUB,
WHO'S IN THE TUB

"**A**R12, AR12, can you start making to a report of sus circs, concern for welfare of an elderly male resident?" To an untrained ear, anyone would be forgiven for thinking that Heidi in the Control Room was starting to panic, but to Bob and Degsy, they knew differently. This was Heidi's natural tone, underneath the high-pitched squeal of her voice coming across their radio's, she would be the epitome of tranquillity itself.

"Show us making Heidi, what's the location?" Bob turned on the blues and twos of the patrol car and grabbed his A to Z.

"22 Balmoral, voters show a Sydney Tindall living at that address. Informant is his niece, says he's 78-years old and hasn't been seen since last Friday, newspapers are poking out of the letterbox and all the curtains are closed, she'll wait outside for you."

Degsy knocked on the indicator and accelerated onto Werrington Road. "Well that's going to be just a little bit smelly if he has croaked it…." he graciously observed. "Right before scoff too, it'll put me off eating it, always does."

Bob gave him a sideways glance and sniffed. "Feck me, you're full of sympathy today Degs, has the ever ready and willing Lillian been keeping you up late at night rummaging in her cellar?"

"We don't have a cellar, mate, you should know that, you've been to our house enough times," he snapped back.

"It's a euphemism you divvy. What I'm asking is, has Lil been ravaging your body and wearing you out? You don't have to go into the gory details..." he grimaced, "…. just a simple yes or no will suffice."

"Bugger off, Cairns and don't be so nosey!"

They drove the rest of the way in a mutual silence.

"This is it." Bob jerked his head towards the run-down end terrace. "Blimey, it's defo seen better days…." he paused momentarily before adding in exasperation, "… oh jeez, what the feck is he doing here?" The figure emerging from the back jigger, a confident swagger in his stride, was none other than Petey Thackeray.

Frustrated, Bob barked at him. "Why didn't you shout up, soft lad, would've saved us a blue light run if you're already here."

Petey stopped in his tracks, transferring his Custodian helmet that was used for foot patrol, from underneath one arm, to the other. "I did Bob, really I did, but I don't think my battery's much good on this, they weren't receiving me at first when I told them I was in the area…" he paused to take breath, "…. but it's all in hand, CID are on their way, Coroner's officer has been notified along with CSI and I've even given his niece the death message too, she was upset but very understanding, she's having a cup of tea with the neighbour." Looking very proud of himself, he eagerly awaited Bob's response.

Bob shook his head. Petey, the sections very own dozy melt, years of experience but still acted like a proby, faarked up everything he touched but had a heart of gold. He would drive everyone insane on the one hand but endear them on the other. "Okay, okay point taken, a bit quick, but well done son. I take it from all that you've been inside?"

"I have, oh yes, I had to." He nodded his head excitely. "I had to force an entry too, I was just coming out to tell you. I found him and I'm afraid he's dead, very dead indeed. Can't be hundred percent sure, but in my opinion, I'd say he drowned." He nodded his head again, but this time as an act of authority.

"Drowned!! What do you mean drowned?" Bob started to push past Petey, just as the CID car pulled up. He watched as DS Jim Shakeshaft heaved himself out of the driver's door.

"Bob, Degs…" Jim nodded to the two older officers and turned to Petey. "What have we got?"

Petey puffed himself up to twice his normal size. "A body Sarge, a dead body… in the bath… in the water. I forced an entry and found him, I called up because he was in his clothes, so that's not normal is it?" he looked to Jim for approval of his actions. Jim gave nothing away, his silence forced Petey to continue. "Erm, yes, so I erm, I made the decision that erm… that it was probably suspicious, people don't take a bath in their clothes now, do they?"

Bob quietly sniggered, well it was Poulton Sands, a rather strange little corner of Westbury, so who knew what the locals got up to in their spare time. It was akin to living in Royston Vasey.

Jim had an uneasy feeling. The same feeling he always got when one of Petey's crime reports crossed his desk, or a witness statement he'd taken found its way into his post shelf in an internal orange envelope. It was true what everyone had been saying for years, if Petey Thackeray had a guardian angel, it was probably following him around hitting him over the head with a wand shouting, *'turn to shit'*.

"Right okay, we'll boot up, the DI's with me, he'll want to take a look too before forensic get here." Jim opened the boot and pulled out the scene kit, taking two pairs of blue over shoes and two white suits from the box. Passing one set of each to DI Roger Shone, he briefed him on the circs that Petey had given him before they disappeared into the back entry leading to the rear of the terraced house.

Kicking his boot into the kerb, Petey shoved his hands into his pockets and wistfully imparted, "D'you know, if there is such a thing as an afterlife, I bet old Mr Tindell is looking down on us right now, wishing he'd had a shower instead of a bath."

Degsy, his temper getting shorter by the minute was just about to impart a bit of worldly-wise advice himself when his thoughts were abruptly interrupted by DI Shone's booming voice bouncing off the brick walls and the cobbles.

"What the fuck are we letting loose on the general public these days, Jim? I mean, for crying out loud, a proud and disciplined service, lateral thinking…."

Bob, Degsy and Petey stood in silence, straining to hear the rest of the DI's rant. They didn't have to wait long before he emerged into full view.

Beckoning Petey towards him, he went nose to nose with him, his voice loud but controlled. "Right son, tell me this, how was *he*, our victim, when you checked for signs of life? Any output, anything that could be resuscitated?"

Petey, his eyes darting from side to side looked to Bob and Degsy for reassurance, when none was forthcoming, he took a deep breath. "Well, I think it was quite obvious he was dead, Sir…. I mean he was under the water and not moving at all, Sir."

The DI's eyes almost stood out on stalks. "Ah, I see, not moving then. Right, so no signs of *him* doing the breaststroke eh? No sign of *him* doggie paddling his way to the deep end of the roll top bath to let the plug out then?" he sarcastically growled. Beads of sweat were starting to form on Petey's top lip. He still had absolutely no idea as to what the DI was on about, but he most certainly wasn't going to be the one to point that out. He decided there and then that he would just nod enthusiastically and hope for the best.

Roger Shone turned on his heels, a pink flush disappearing under his collar. "Jim, get me out of here, will you? And you…" pointing at Bob, "… sort this mess out, speak to the niece and I expect a report on my desk confirming Constable Thackeray's urgent and very much overdue First Aid Course."

As the silver Ford Fiesta disappeared along Balmoral Road, comically hitting a speed bump, Petey let out a sigh of relief. "Well, that's a turn up for the books, maybe they didn't think it was suspicious after all, boys!" He turned to hopefully find camaraderie in what had been an uncomfortable ten minutes, but Bob and Degsy had already disappeared inside to get a better understanding of the DI's instructions.

Bob dunked his biscuit into the murky mug of tea whilst simultaneously unclipping his tie. He launched it across the night kitchen, it skimmed the top of Petey's head and hit the fridge door before settling on the edge of the bin. Several sniggers did the rounds of the large table. Sergeant Scully was quick to intervene.

"Okay troops, it was one of those things. It happens, no harm done, I'll sort out the report to the DI, let's move on, shall we?"

"Move on! Hey Sarge, we can't let this one go, it's one of the best feck-ups he's ever done, it's a little bit more than just a cake fine too." He animatedly jabbed what was left of his half-eaten biscuit towards Petey. "Constable Thackeray's dead body…. that actually wasn't a dead body!" Bob lost it, laughing until the tears rolled down his cheeks, which in turn set everyone else off.

Degsy held a checked tea towel over his face, snorting unceremoniously into the grubby fabric. Petey's crestfallen expression was a picture as he nursed his thermos flask, hoping to find at least some comfort in its warmth.

"Washing! A bath full of Mr Tindall's dirty skids and shirts left to soak whilst he was out at his *Soup & Butty* church meeting." Bob howled, shaking his head. "Mind you, judging by the stains on his Y-fronts I think it was them that died a death years ago!" He paused getting his breath back. "And to top it off, I had to go and see his niece and undo *his* death message...." he poked a finger at Petey, "...you should have seen her face when I told her Uncle Sydney was still very much alive and currently enjoying a bowl of tomato soup and a ham batch. Thank god she had a sense of humour."

Beryl surveyed her troops, desperately trying to resume order whilst holding down a very unladylike snort that was threatening to release itself into an uncontrollable fit of the giggles.

"It was the bubbles and the air, it filled out the shirt...and.... and the trousers, they'd blown up too, it looked like a real, live dead body!" Petey wailed, looking at everyone in turn for just an ounce of sympathy. The sniggers and guffaws told him there was none to be had.

Degsy grunted and threw the tea towel at him. "Just face it, yer melt, you faarked up ... again!"

SHORT BACK & SIDES

"**F**or god's sake Mave, how much longer are you going to be in there? I'm desperate!"

I could hear Joe pacing up and down on the landing outside the bathroom and seconds later the door handle rattled. "Bloody hell Joe, can you not use the downstairs one, I could be in here for some time, give me a bit of peace, hey!" I flicked the plastic cover from the Bic razor and inspected the blade as Joe's muffled grunts became more urgent.

Grunt away my little pea brain, this woman ain't getting out of the bath just so you can point Percy at the Porcelain!

"I'm in the process of creating and should not, under any circumstances, be interrupted...." I yelled, ".... a woman with a sharp cutting object in her hands whilst fat and 24 weeks pregnant is not a woman to be irked, Joe!"

"Fine!" he huffed.

I listened as his heavy footsteps hit each stair on the way down. Jeez, at times he was like a petulant child, even Ella had stopped stair stomping when she'd finished puberty. I looked down at the large curved bump of my tummy and gave it a little pat. "Okay Spud, it's time for a quick trim, just in case a little bit more than your heartbeat is being checked today." Although I couldn't see how badly overgrown it was myself, in fact I hadn't seen much of anything below my waist for weeks, I certainly didn't want Alison, my midwife being forced to fight her way through a jungle.

Gone were the days of heart shapes and landing strips, a basic tidy up was all that was needed, particularly as I was flying blind.

The first two gentle sweeps of the blade seemed to go well, I swished the razor around in the water and set about positioning myself for the next stage. The ultra-edge trim...

Taa Daa.......

With a flourish I yanked the blade in a curved upward motion.... and....

Yeeeeeooooooow!

"Joe, Joe, Joe.... oh, shit Joe!!" I screamed, flailing in the water, trying desperately to heave my bulk out of the bath. "Shit, shit, shit, I think I've severed my.... oh bugger, my.... oh gawd, whatever it is I've got down there!"

The bathroom door burst open, and a red-faced, panic struck Joe flung himself towards me, gathering me in his arms. "Feck's sake Mave, what on earth have you done, you daft mare?" Grabbing the bath towel, he wrapped it around me whilst frantically searching for something to stem the flow of blood.

"It's my lady bits, I think I've chopped them off..." I wailed, "... oh my god, does this make me a eunuch, Joe, does it? I can't be a eunuch, I'm too young!" I looked at him pleadingly as he disappeared below to check. I sat on the edge of the bath, my hand dramatically gracing my forehead, as I waited for his diagnosis.

"It's a small cut my little dumpling, nothing major. No artery severed, no missing bits..." his head disappeared under the towel again, "…. nope, definitely no missing bits, it's all there - well at least from what I can remember before you became a cuddly hippo!" He started to laugh uncontrollably. "Stay there, I've got some blood-clotting spray stuff in my kitbag, that'll help, just keep pressure on it." He wiped his eyes and kissed the tip of my nose. "You know I love you even if you are a rhino!"

I sniffed. "You said hippo! Huh, I do wonder Joseph Blackwell, sometimes you can be such a twa…."

"Ah, ah, now then, no bad language in front of our innocent little baby, you naughty girl." He quickly disappeared into the spare bedroom.

I sat looking at the mess I'd made, toilet paper strewn on the floor tiles, puddles of water mixed in with splatters of blood and a hastily discarded Bic razor, which was definitely the Devil's implement. I vowed that as painful as I'd heard it was, I'd only ever wax my fun bits in future.

Joe's disembodied voice bellowed along the landing. "Can't find it, it was with all my toiletries the last time I went to Public Order training, they've all gone, have you moved them, Mave?"

"Try the big basket in the airing cupboard, it's got all sorts in there, moisturisers, toothpaste, deodorant, cleaning stuff…you name it, if it's anything to do with the bathroom, it's in there," I helpfully offered whilst angling Joe's shaving mirror to my nether regions to see what damage I'd caused. I grimaced.

Jeez… even a vajazzle couldn't make that attractive.

"Here we go, found it. Right my little turnip, steel yerself…. it's gonna be cold!"

With a flourish that Liverpool's own flamboyant hairdresser, Herbert Howe would have been proud of, he shook the canister and sprayed copiously.

"Faarking hell, matey…" I clamped my legs together quickly.
"What?"

"Are you sure that's not anti-freeze?" I squealed, grabbing for my clean knickers on the radiator.

"What, like a special sex aid treatment for the eternally frigid woman in your life, alongside Viagra and Durex?" he guffawed.

Once again my fringe did the Mexican Wave, as it always did when the air I blew upwards was measured against his bad jokes and crass stupidity.

"*PRICE RIGHT* tacky glue carpet spray, you bloody idiot!" Exasperated, I spat the words at him whilst he sat, suitably chastened at the breakfast bar. I slammed the kettle down and chucked a dirty spoon into the sink.

"Do you know what it was like in there, standing behind the curtains with half the ante-natal staff at the clinic sniggering behind my back. '*Pop over there and remove your panties, Mavis.'...*" I mimicked Alison's voice and exaggerated her manner by waving my arms around, almost knocking Cat off the window ledge.

"... only I couldn't could I Joe? And why couldn't I?" I waited for a response, my head tilted. He just sat there looking sheepish, mumbling something inaudible.

"I'll tell you why I couldn't take my panties off... because the bastard things were welded to me like bloody industrial Velcro because YOU..." I jabbed my finger at him, ".... YOU sprayed my foo-foo with *PRICE RIGHT* tacky glue carpet spray!"

Joe went to open his mouth, thought better of it and clamped it shut whilst cosseting the offending canister in his hand, pretending to read the label, rather than look me in the eye.

I squeezed the tea bag out and hurled it towards the bin, not even bothering to open the lid. It hit the wall, splattered and dropped to the floor. "So now not only is it unattractively shredded, it's bald too and I'm a pair of maternity knickers down as they had to be cut off!"

I waited, breathless from my outburst. "It's a bit late to read that now, don't you think? Correct me if I'm wrong, but that level of intelligence might have been handy before you practiced doctors and nurses on me?"

He shrugged his shoulders and smirked. "Well, you can't blame me entirely my little turnip; it does say on the label that it's suitable for *rugs*!"

CORA'S SURPRISE

Cora opened the barn-style door just enough to let the tabby furball slink into the warmth of her kitchen. Barnaby was the love of her life and he gave unconditional love back to her; just so long as his blue ceramic bowl was replenished regularly and kept full of kitty treats.

"Good morning my handsome boy," she positively purred as Barnaby curled himself around her legs. "Just let me put the kettle on and then we'll have a cuddle." Her sheepskin slippers with the non-slip sole tapped gently on the red quarry tiles, fell silent as they shuffled across the threadbare rug, and tapped again as her feet once again found the tiles by the sink. She filled the old-fashioned whistling kettle by the spout, lit a spill and allowed for a short hiss of gas before finally igniting the ring, the temporary blue flames dancing in a circle before they were smothered by the bottom of the kettle.

"Right, come here my boy…." Cora picked Barnaby up, tittering to herself as he awkwardly elongated himself, so his back legs were almost touching the floor. "…my goodness Barnaby Spunge you're almost as tall as I am!" she exclaimed. At a mere 4' 11" in her support stockings, that really wasn't a difficult task for Barnaby to equal. She knew her treasured cat companion was not the least bit interested in anything she had to say, but in her book, it was a damn sight better than talking to the walls.

Sitting in Harold's old armchair by the fire with her welcome morning cup of tea, the ticking from the clock on the mantle mesmerizingly punctuating the silence, Cora once again drifted off into her memories. She had remained in the neat little two-bedroom terraced house that Harold had first taken rent on a week before they had married. In the ensuing years and with his first promotion to store manager of the local supermarket, they had, or at least Harold had, secured a mortgage with an option to buy, to own their own home, to be masters of all they surveyed. She smiled to herself, remembering him coming home with the news and a fine bottle of Harvey's Bristol Cream sherry which they eagerly devoured in celebration.

Ah, that had been a happy time, a time when the chinking of glasses had heralded a future for them, a time before her dreams had crumbled.

Shaking her head to dissipate the worst of the memories, Cora ambled into the hallway, pulled on her coat, carefully placed the felt camel bucket hat on her head and checked herself in the mirror. There had once been a youthful, vibrant young woman in that mirror, a woman with clear, smooth skin and blonde hair that sparkled when caught in the sunlight. A woman with an edge, an excitement. The reflection that now stared back at Cora was weary, defeated and.... old!

"This will never do, will it, my dear Barnaby?" she tutted. "I think your mummy needs to find something to bring a little bit of adventure into our lives, don't you?"

Barnaby yowled in agreement before settling himself down in front of the fire, tucking his head under his tail, he gave Cora one last haughty glance before he fell asleep.

"Be a good boy whilst I'm gone, won't you? It's sardines for tea, a special treat for my pussy," she cooed as she closed the front door. She suddenly threw her gloved hand to her lips, "Oh my goodness, what a wicked thought..." she sniggered as she eyed up one of the refuse collectors manhandling a large bin, his muscles flexing wildly, "...what I wouldn't do to have a little treat for my own pus......"

The timely metallic clanking, banging and whirring of the bin wagon as it swallowed up next doors trash, drowned out the rest of Cora's saucy life observation and wanton desire.

"Ah, Cora glad you're in today, we've had a large donation and it's all just been dumped in the back for the time being." Freda Wainwright the other volunteer who gladly and willingly gave her time and window dressing skills to *Junk & Disorderly* fussed around Cora as she tried to hang her coat up in the staff room. "It's from that old dear, Martha whatever her name is, you know her, used to come in here every Tuesday after picking up her pension." Freda waited expectantly.

Cora had to smile. '*Old dear*', that's what Freda had called her, an '*old dear*'. Quite ironic really considering how old they were too. "Martha Mackenzie, I think that's who you're referring to," she helpfully offered.

"Yes, yes, that's her." Freda carried on flicking the yellow duster across the glass shelving unit in the window.

"What about her then?"

"About who?"

"Martha Mackenzie!" Cora almost spat the name in frustration.

Freda looked momentarily puzzled and then the penny dropped. "Ah, oh yes...... she's dead."

"Maybe you'd like to break it to me a little more gently, Freda?" Cora smirked.

The seconds ticked by as Freda continued to busy herself with her cloth and the non-existent dust. Cora could tell she was desperately thinking of what to say next. She didn't have long to wait.

"Well, you see…. Martha had been a bit off colour for a while, indigestion she thought, so she went to the Doctors and they gave her some pills…" Freda reached across the junk jewellery display to flick at an imaginary cobweb, "…anyhow, she takes the pills but doesn't feel any better so she's thinking maybe it was something she ate, but it wasn't and now she's just a little bit dead!" She stopped dusting, tilted her head and gave Cora a smug look. "Is that gentle enough?"

Cora tilted her head back, waited until Freda resumed her dusting, and childishly pulled her tongue. She could endure Freda for short bursts, but after a while they would get on each other's nerves and then their little niggles would start. There was something about Freda that made Cora's skin prickle, she couldn't put her finger on it, but it was there. She was all sweetness and light, stalwart member of the Townswoman's Guild and baked cakes on Saturdays. Cora wouldn't have been surprised if she had a bloody halo stashed somewhere that she regularly polished with the damned duster! She grabbed at the first black binbag from the pile that had been donated from Martha's house.

How terribly sad that this is all that is left of someone; a pile of clothes, a few trinkets, some well-worn shoes, a pair of Sunday Best and a collection of handbags.

Cora felt like crying. A lump formed in her throat and tears pricked at her eyes as she carefully sifted through Martha's possessions. She held up a pretty pink hat with a dainty cluster of flowers on the band, she remembered Martha wearing it at the Summer Fair only a few short months ago, she had admired it then. Plonking it on her own head, she spotted a pale pink handbag peeking out from under a pile of shoes.

Oh, it's so pretty, and how very daring compared to my navy accessories.

She made a conscious decision that a small donation would cover the items and she would begin to become daring herself. This could be the start of her new adventure, out with the *Colourless Cora* that had been her lot for far too long and in with *The Stupendous Ms Spunge.*

Yes, she liked that very much.

Sitting almost cross-legged on the tiled floor she set about checking the handbag for compartments and any treasures that may have been overlooked inside but she was disappointed to find it empty, not even a ha'penny piece or a thruppence. She loved to find old coins in forgotten purses, wallets and handbags, but Martha had left nothing. Her fingers probed the silk lining until they hooked themselves into a large hole in the corner. Digging deeper, the tip of one finger touched something, something hidden in the lining, Cora's heart skipped a beat as she grasped the item and pulled it, with some difficulty, through the hole. A small tearing noise heralded the making of an even bigger hole that she would have to repair when she got home.

Turning it over in her hands, she marvelled at it. It was a small notebook, leather bound, embossed with flowers and a blue velvet string wrapped around it, tied in a bow. She tentatively pulled on the loop, the cord fell away, allowing her to excitedly open the first page. Her eyes darted from side to side following the neat, elegant writing. She turned another page, her breath catching in her throat, and then another page until the realisation of what she was holding in her hands hit her....

"Well, spank me on the bottom with a Lipton's cheese paddle...." Cora breathlessly uttered, "...*The Stupendous Ms Spunge* might just be embarking on the most exhilarating adventure of her life after all!"

NEW BOOTS

"**E**ight seconds, I got eight seconds!" Pip held her oatie crumble in triumph and then commenced a juggling act trying to stop the dunked section hitting her paperwork as it drooped and dropped off. "Damn!" She licked the side of her hand and then wiped the remaining gunk on the edge of her chair.

Klaxons starting up in the rear yard broke my attention, oatie crumbles forgotten, I heaved myself up from my desk and waddled over to the window. "Urgent job broken out, what I wouldn't give to be back out with the Section," I wistfully observed. As if on cue Spud decided to give me one hefty kick from inside. I looked down at the swell of my belly straining against the maternity top I'd only just bought the previous week. At this rate I'd be spending more on clothing for this pregnancy that I had in my entire, non-pregnant life. I gave a gentle pat to where I thought Spud's feet would be. "You feel the same way, don't you? You can't wait to be out too." Another boot, this time in the ribs, was a sort of affirmation that Spud was getting impatient.

Crunching the remainder of her biscuit, Pip joined me. "Look on the bright side, it's not for much longer, you'll soon be on maternity leave. Just think of all those lie-ins, no dealing with other people's shit reports and… err actually, talking of which, DS Shakeshaft has put a file in your tray AND there's a sticky on it."

She pulled a 'don't ask me' face.

'Sticky's' normally meant a shed load of crap was going to befall whoever touched one. A bit like accepting a demonic parchment, one touch and the curse was on you before it even got chance to fizz, burn and destroy itself. Grabbing a pen from the holder, I eased myself back into the chair. The manila file was tied at the side with standard green loops. The yellow sticky was neatly written, probably by Jim Shakeshaft himself, and simply stated *'Blackmail – Incident Report'*.

I felt a surge of excitement. Blackmail, now that was something different, it could even brighten up my remaining weeks here, something to get my teeth into. I turned to the first page, a brief resume of what had so far been taken for the incident report and a complainant interview request from Jim. He'd included his anticipated joy at me obliging by adding two smiley faces and a gushing line on how fabulous my interview skills were. His belief that flattery would get him exactly what he wanted from colleagues was legendary around the nick – and to be honest, it usually worked. I was already running an interview plan around my baby-brain. I began to read his notes.

'The Complainant is Edna Flaybrick, 78-years. Ms Flaybrick has lived in the Westbury area since 1953. She previously owned Peek-A-Do Hairdressing salon between 1960 and 1987 which had a subsidiary Beauty Spa in the basement of the shop.

On 12th February this year, Ms Flaybrick received typewritten correspondence that was hand delivered by unknown persons, through the letterbox of her home, 71 School Lane. It outlined information that the author claimed to have acquired regarding certain irregular activities undertaken by Ms Flaybrick between the dates of 1961 and 1985 and although not graphic in detail, does

provide a certain trigger word which has left Ms Flaybrick in no doubt that the threat is real, hence her contact with us. She would prefer to be seen at Westbury, rather than her home address and will bring the letter with her. She has been advised re forensic preservation.

The demands to keep this information confidential by the author and not to be disseminated for public consumption is the sum of £1,000.'

Jim had included the original call taker log, a search on Edna, her home address and shop premises and an appointment date for her to attend Westbury Police Station.

"So this is what you get up to now you're no longer a rufty-tufty street cop...." Bob's distinctive voice cut through my concentration. "..... biscuits, tea, comfy chairs and a feckin' rubber plant on yer desk, what's the world coming to?" he snorted, ruffling my hair. He was clearly amused that my large bulk made rapid movement impossible so any chastisement I wanted to offer for messing my hair up, would certainly go unfulfilled.

Nothing made my heart warm more than to see him and his wobbly belly clad in an over-washed, over-worn NATO jumper that was sporting various remnants of his canteen breakfast down the front. "Bob! About bloody time you came for a visit, I'm only two floors up, you know." I shoved the biscuit tin towards him as he plonked himself down on Pip's chair. Pip looked on in amusement as he threw his feet up on the desk, unclipped his tie, and settled back.

"Blimey Mave, that's bloody enormous!" He prodded a finger at my belly. "Have you got a whole herd in there?"

"Yeah, very funny, as if I haven't heard that one before!" I made an exaggerated yawning motion. "So, what's the visit for?"

He grinned. "To tell you how much we love you, how much we're missing you and how much Petey is faarking up without you being there to look after him."

"I'm not his mother, Bob, he's a grown man and capable of more than you think, he just a bit of a dork, and that's something we can't change…" I shoved what was left of the oatie in my mouth then quickly regretted it. "…. must admit though, the body in the bath job will haunt him for the rest of his career, it's bound to become legendary." I spat crumbs across the desk in my haste to finish my sentence. Closing Jim's file up, I quickly jotted down Edna's appointment in my diary. "Come on, real reason for the visit then?"

"A Section night out Mave, it's Degsy's birthday and we're all proper pissed off with the shift changes, rest days being cancelled and general shit being thrown our way, so Beryl suggested a night out, boost morale a bit." He made an air quote with his chubby fingers emphasising the word *morale*.

My face lit up. "Ooooh a night out, count me in, I could do with a bit of a laugh and the chance to get myself glammed up a bit, maybe a new outfit."

Bob unsuccessfully bit down on a smart-arse answer; the hiatus was all of two seconds before it burst from his mouth. "Excellent, I'll let the section know you're all for getting glammed up whilst you're knocked up… should make for interesting attire, Mave, think Degsy's got a tent in the garage if yer struggling!" he guffawed.

"Feck off, Bob!" I cheerily replied.

Boots. New Boots.

It was like a mantra as I found my seat on the train bound for Liverpool. I might not be able to fit into slinky, skimpy dresses or butt-squeezing jeans but that was no reason for me to not at least try to make an effort for our night out. I'd already bought a pair of black sparkly maternity leggings with a waistband that promised to expand comfortably to accommodate two hippos, three rhinos and an elephant, and a pretty floaty top in a vibrant shade of ochre. The top also promised to tether out of control, pregnancy affected, Dolly Parton bazookas.

I was looking forward to seeing how that turned out!

The train rumbled into Central Station, the strangely addictive smell, a heady mix of creosote, tar and Jeyes fluid, forcing itself into the carriage through the open windows. I inhaled deeply. It was comforting and gave me a fleeting memory of being taken to see Father Christmas and his Scouse grotto with my Nan. The hilarity of the Liver birds dressed as reindeers standing in the fake snow outside a cardboard cut-out of *The Grafton Ballroom* had been completely wasted on the 8-year old me, not so on my Nan who had been mortified at missing the '*Warning notice for minors*' on the way in. She had frantically grabbed me by the hood of my duffle coat, dragged me under the blue braided rope of the queue barrier, which had then given her a second chance at almost strangling me, before hauling me outside onto the pavement. Years later she had confided that the next Christmassy 'scene' had been a skimpily dressed Tinkerbell pole dancing inside the Grafton with the Elves leerily watching on, waving £1 notes. Her other admission was that just maybe the billboard advertising '*F.F.C and His Alternative Scouse Grotto*' might have been the great, big, feck off clue for her.

I couldn't help but smile, she was a complete one-off, her passing had left a huge hole in my life, but I knew she'd be dancing and partying with my mum on a cloud somewhere causing mayhem and madness, as they always did. It was also highly amusing to learn that the extra *F* in F.F.C didn't stand for *fabulous*!

My first stop was Debenhams. Their advert had promised me the perfect pair of boots amongst their vast selection. Making my way to the shoe department, I fought my way through the Melanies, Traceys and Cassandras who were desperate to shower me with their latest fragrance. As lumpy and large as I was, I still managed to deftly duck each cloud of mist as it was eagerly squirted my way. A shower of *Midnight in Bootle* narrowly missed the sleeve of my coat, falling in fine droplets to the tiled floor.

Edging through the open plan areas, squeezing between rails of clothes and handbags, I excitedly emerged into the Shoe Department. I felt like a kid in a toyshop, every shelf held a delicious colour in leather, patent, glitter, satin and canvas, they were scattered on the floor too, discarded by shoppers who had tried them on and then moved onto another style, another hue. I took in the Stiletto's, ballet pumps, flatties, brogues, courts, sandals, ankle boots, calf boots, knee boots and….

OMG…. F.M.B'S!!

I hadn't seen or even owned a pair of those since my 30's when I'd tripped the light fantastic in Leighton Court on the Debbie Does Disco nights. They must be back in fashion…. oh happy days! I ran my fingers across the beautiful leather boots sitting rigidly like soldiers to attention on the rails, searching for my size. There were 5's, 6's, 2's and 3's but no 4's. I could feel a hormonal rage building inside.

Don't they know I need a size 4? Don't they know I want a size 4? Don't they know I must have a size 4?

As my blood pressure rose, Spud have me a warning kick. I *oofed* loudly and doubled up as his footballing skills forced me

BLUES, TWOS AND BABY SHOES

to sit down on a nearby chair…. and that's when I spotted them. Crumpled to one side against the foot measuring stool, the most delicious pair of black suede thigh boots beckoned me. Discarded, undesired and exactly what I was looking for. I picked one up and checked inside.

Hallelujah, a size 4!

Grabbing the other boot, I held them aloft like a trophy. I tried them on, slowly sliding the zip from my ankle to above my knee and then up to my lower thigh. They fitted beautifully.

I had found my perfect boots, and as an added bonus, they were FMB's!

I giggled wondering what Joe would make of them.

Parading up and down, checking them out in the full-length mirror, I held my hand up to eye level, closed one eye and blocked out my huge bump to get a better view of them. Being the shape of a dumpling was sort of detracting from the sexy image the boots were begging me to portray. I sighed.

*I **would** be sexy again, once Spud made an appearance and I'd shed this baby weight, I'd get back to the old me…. so, in anticipation of that day, these boots would be mine!*

I was still floating on a cloud of euphoric boot bliss when I was rudely interrupted.

"Err, excuse me, those boots…."

A rather flustered looking woman wearing fluffy pink socks stood directly in front of me in a quite menacing manner. I paused, taking in her expensive leather jacket and tri-highlighted hair. I tried to raise my eyebrows, hoping the pencilled-in job I'd done that morning had held long enough to give me an expression of anticipation. A quick glance in the mirror made me groan. I'd already subconsciously wiped one off during my meltdown trying to find the right size boot. Not to be deterred, I gave her the one eyebrow I had left, secretly amused, it struck me that it was almost the equivalent of a middle finger salute.

"Mmmm, I love them…" I preened whilst flicking an ankle to show them to her at their best angle, smug that another shopper could be so envious of my choice that she felt the urge to comment on them. "They are divine, aren't they?"

"That's exactly what I thought when I purchased them last week…" Fluffy Pink Sock Woman snarled, "… they're actually mine you stupid bint!"

My remaining pencilled in eyebrow shot up to somewhere near my hairline as I hastily removed, then quickly mourned my beautiful, but fleeting FMB's, as Fluffy Pink Sock Woman snatched them from me and stormed off in a cloud of Dior J'Adore.

Gutted!

EDNA

"**Y**our 3 o'clock is here Mave, I've put her in the side room with a cup of tea..." Pip grinned waiting for me to acknowledge her, before laughingly adding, "...I think someone's going to have their work cut out today if first appearances are anything to go by."

I groaned. I was hoping Edna Flaybrick would be easy on the brain and not one of those interviews where I had to frantically try to keep them on track to the task in hand or suffer hearing about their haemorrhoids, the latest episode of EastEnders or the extortionate price of a loaf of bread. Still, I suppose when you get to that age, those things become important. I wriggled in my chair.

Dear God, if my haemorrhoids and an episode of EastEnders became my sole topic of conversation when I reach that age, please shoot me now!

Reaching for Edna's file, I plastered on my best professional smile, whilst resisting the urge to give myself a very unladylike scratch just to check I wasn't already cultivating a bunch of grapes in anticipation of my dotage.

"Mrs Flaybrick? Good afternoon, I'm Mavis Upton from the Crime Unit." I held out my hand in greeting.

Edna sniffed loudly, her rheumy blue eyes narrowing. "It's Ms, not Miss or Mrs or any other combination, thank you very much," she grumbled.

Great, what a crap start, this wasn't going to be easy. Breathe Mavis, breathe.

My smile became impossibly tight, my top lip stuck to my teeth giving me an air of Les Patterson, Cultural Attache, without the extra saliva. I ran my tongue around to free it up so I could speak. "My apologies Ms Flaybrick, if you'd like to come with me, we can get ourselves settled in one of the interview suites, the chairs are a lot more comfortable there."

"Mmmmm looks like you need it with an arse that size," she muttered under her breath.

"Sorry, what did you say?" I was absolutely dumfounded; did she really just say that?

She defiantly tilted her head. "You'll thank me for it later, if your friends and family aren't going to tell you, then you'll blithely carry on travelling through life overweight and unhappy!" She took off her coat and plonked herself down in the chair nearest to the window, setting her blue leather handbag on the coffee table, she carefully removed her gloves.

"I'm almost 8-months pregnant Ms Flaybrick, hence the excessively large bump at the front." I stood sideways to show her, just in case she had somehow managed to miss the total eclipse of the coffee machine.

"That's as may be, dear but it doesn't excuse the size of your bottom, now does it?" she smirked.

I couldn't make up my mind if she was being frivolously humorous or just plain bloody mean. "Right…." I sat down across from her and opened the file, secretly hoping my obviously large bum wasn't splaying itself out like an oil slick either side of the seat. "…I've been asked to obtain a statement of complaint from you Ms Flaybrick in relation to the letter you received demanding monies."

"Please dearie, call me Edna, I'm actually quite nice really, it's just these places…" she waved her arm, a tsunami of wobbling bingo wing encompassed the whole room, "… well, they do set me on edge." Her smile had become warmer.

I smiled back. "Yes, I suppose police environments, if you're not used to them can be very daunting. Okay Edna, I'll just start off by us having a little chat, from that I can make notes and then we can prepare your statement, is that okay?"

Edna nodded, settled herself into a comfier position on the chair, and waited.

"It says here that you were owner of *Peek-A-Do* Hairdressing salon, 42 Market Street between 1960 and 1987, is that right?"

Edna shifted in her chair, her eyes darting around the room until they finally settled on the handkerchief that she had pulled from the pocket of her coat. She began to wring it into a ball. I waited, giving her time to compose herself.

Years of experience is telling me there's definitely a lot more to this than meets the eye. I seriously hope there are no bodies buried in the basement at Peek-A-Do. Blimey, I'm going to have to caution her if she decides to straight cough to that.

"It's okay Edna, you take your time."

After what seemed like an eternity, she clicked the clasp on her handbag and pulled out an envelope. She fixated on it for a few seconds before she finally spoke.

"It was when they referred to *Peek-A-Do* and a *blow-job* in the same sentence…." She pushed the envelope towards me.

Blow job! Oh gawd, please don't let me start laughing.

"Ah, I think you mean blow-dry, Edna." The effort I was putting in trying not to giggle was killing me. Poor Edna, she must be really nervous.

"No, I mean what I say, it was *blow-job* and then they mentioned *short back & sides*... well, that was it, I mean, that was me speciality back in the day." She wistfully looked out of the window and sighed. "I was young, had all me teeth then although I didn't always do the services myself, that was just the early days before I expanded the business."

Spud gave me an almighty kick in my side which made me jump. Grateful for the distraction, I stood up, feigning discomfort, giving myself time to think.

Noooo, I'm mishearing this, please, please not 'icky's' from an old dear, OMG can this day get any worse?

The next words out of Edna's mouth proved it could.

"Do you want me to explain *short back & sides* my dear, just so you know where I'm coming from? I'm sure you've cottoned on by now. Back in the day I was known as Madam Diamond D'Light of *The Open D'hore* bordello that was housed in the basement of *Peek-A-Do*."

The silence between us gave a vacuum to the room as she waited for my response. I knew if I opened my mouth to speak, I'd choke with laughter. Edna broke it for me.

"So you see, the blackmail letter is spot on, whatever comes next will only serve to further prove my youthful misdeeds and unless I pay up, it will be all over Westbury and beyond..." She jabbed her gnarled finger at the envelope. "... and believe me, if whoever is doing this goes public with it, I'll take some very interesting public figures down with me!" She sat back in triumph. "Something I'm sure your Chief Constable wouldn't embrace, my dear if you get my drift."

Oh jeez!

"Right, erm, okay.... well, if we... I mean, I... err...I'll just get some evidence bags, back in a minute."

... and with that I made the hastiest exit my bulk could manage without getting unceremoniously wedged in the swing door as I scurried out to find Jim.

Bloody hell give me haemorrhoids and EastEnders any day!

I know
what
you did

IT'LL BE ALRIGHT ON THE NIGHT

The rain pattered against the glass of the French doors, bubbled momentarily giving a magnifying glass effect to the willow tree outside, before sliding slowly to the bottom, catching in the black rubber of the double glazing.

My eyes welled to the point of brimming before I caught myself, stoically refusing to let a tear fall. Far from being as romantic as the rain, what I was about to produce from my left nostril if I didn't sniff it up quickly would end up elongating itself into my cleavage. I grabbed another Kleenex from the battered box at the side of the sofa and gave my nose a good blow.

"Hormones running riot Mum?" Ella's soft voice broke my reverie. "Felt like that myself last week, nothing a chocolate éclair won't cure." She shoved the open box across the coffee table towards me.

I sniffed again. "It's says 'four Belgium Chocolate Eclairs' on the box." I peered inside at the solitary pastry squished in the corner, prodded it and then swiped my finger along the cream. "What happened to the other three?"

"Oh erm…. mmmm, well errr… it was the temporary traffic lights on Heron Road, baby was a bit peckish." She grinned as she patted her huge stomach. "Baby comes first, especially where chocolate is concerned!"

  BLUES, TWOS AND BABY SHOES

I slowly heaved myself up from the sofa to face her, our respective bumps almost touching. We simultaneously snorted at the ridiculousness of the situation.

How on earth had this happened. Mum and daughter. Me carrying Ella's brother or sister, Ella carrying my grandchild. You couldn't make this up if you tried, it was like a storyline in a cheesy low budget soap opera.

"I haven't seen my feet for weeks; my back aches, my hair's falling out and I've got zits. I'm 48-years old and I've developed teenage acne…." I wailed whilst exuberantly pointing at the offending pimple on my chin.

Ella began to snigger. "It's one bloody spot Mum, in fact I thought it was a bit of dried up breakfast muesli, it's hardly an outbreak of festering pustules for goodness sake!" She flopped down onto the sofa, thrusting her legs out in front of her. "Be grateful it's only a zit look at these bloody trotters, I have cankles Mum, puffy, fat, swollen cankles…" she sighed. "…how on earth will they ever go back to normal?"

I plonked myself back down next to her and shoved my left foot up to join hers. "Snap!"

She giggled. "One foot! Is that all you can manage?"

I looked on sheepishly, the reality of my ridiculous outburst hitting home. "Yup, 'fraid so, I was expecting moments of 'glowing', I had lots of glowing when I was pregnant with you, this time it's been so different, I'm more flowing most days, I think Spud is using my bladder as a beanbag. I just feel fat, fed-up, ready to pop … with odd ankles! How's Luke taking it all with you?"

She grinned. "He's so laid-back Mum, nothing seems to faze him, he's even been coming with me to the childbirth classes…" she paused to think. "…mind you he did go a bit green around the gills when they demonstrated a nappy change on a real baby!"

I laughed, imagining Luke dry barfing at what a diaper could hold after a decent 4oz bottle of formula. "Joe's been reading up on it virtually every night…" I pointed to the well-thumbed copy of *Mother & Baby* on the coffee table. "…. he feels his role will be more important once Spud is born." I gave a wistful smile.

Ella grabbed the magazine and plumped the cushion up behind her. "We'll be okay Mum, I know we will, anyway…. ooops!" She quickly grabbed the pages as the inside of the magazine dropped out from the cover. Holding it up to examine it, she tutted and shook her head, a shiny beast of a Harley Davidson adorned the first page. "Bloody hell, he's hidden a *Motorcycle Monthly* in it – he's learning how to change oil not nappies, no wonder he's been so engrossed!"

"Joe…." I waited, swishing the rapidly cooling water over Spud who gave a fist bump in appreciation. The majority of it had all but disappeared down the plug hole before the realisation hit me that I was stuck. Shoving the plug back in, I'd managed to save some of the water before wailing like a ridiculous damsel in distress.

"Joe, I need yoooooooo…" Spud gave a flurry of kicks, clearly unimpressed with my high pitched, dulcet tones. *Alien* sprang to mind as the skin on my tummy undulated left to right and then the outline of a foot appeared.

Where the hell is your dad, hey? We need Daddy to come to the rescue don't we Spud?

"Joe, I'm stuck!" No frantic footsteps preceded the appearance of Joe's head around the bathroom door, just his pink face bearing a smirk of epic proportions. "You've been there all the time haven't you, you absolute fanny, how could you leave me like this?" I howled.

"Easy, it's amusing Mave, no matter how you look at it, it's funny." He tried to grab my arm but the copious amount of Baby Oil I'd not only poured in the bath but slathered all over myself in the hope of avoiding stretch marks, had turned me into a slippery whale. "Faarking hell, my tub of lard, whose bright idea was this?" he snorted.

"Don't laugh at me, this is…." I didn't get the chance to finish my howl of despair as I lost my grip on the side of the bath. Executing an ungainly roll, I slid forwards, bobbed for two seconds, my face pushing under water so my nose hit the bottom of the bath and then my whole body unexpectedly swivelled and self-righted like an inflatable Lilo in the shape of a hippo with its legs akimbo. Water splashed over the side, drenching Joe.

"Oh my God, so that's what they mean by a mufftash…." he roared, tears rolling down his cheeks. "…I've just seen your mufftash, Mave!"

"It's not a mufftash," I indignantly wailed, pushing my wet hair out of my eyes as water dripped from my nose, "You know that's where I had my little accident with the glue that was actually ALL your fault, I just lost more than I thought I had and it hasn't grown back yet!"

"I'd say that was a bloody big accident my little sprout, even RyanAir's got bigger landing strips than that!"

"I hate you Joseph Stephen Blackwell…"

I know I should be happy, ecstatic even. I have everything I could ever wish for, so why am I crying? I'm sitting here on our bed, butt naked, my once pert nellies wedged under my armpits bawling my eyes out like a 2-year old. I feel lost, out of my depth. I'm going to be a rubbish at this, I know I am. People look at me, 'She's old enough to know better...' that's what they are thinking.

I am old enough to know better.... but it still happened anyway.

My hands gently stroke the bump that is Spud. My Spud. My baby... our baby, and I weep just that little bit more.

I wish you were here Mum, even a cuddle would help, I just need to know it's going to be okay.

Then I hear her voice in my head, soft and reassuring.

'Oh Mavis, my love, calm down, please don't cry. Just remember what I taught you right from when you were a little girl; patience really is a virgin!'

.... and suddenly I'm laughing. Laughing at the ridiculousness of it all, the memory of her wonderful malapropisms and a sense of gratitude that my name isn't Patience.

BLUES, TWOS AND BABY SHOES

ASHES TO ASHES, DUST TO DUST

"**S**he was a hooker, Jim…" I dropped the Flaybrick file on his desk. "… the owner of a brothel, here in Westbury! Anyway, statements attached, letter and envelope have gone for forensics." Shifting a pile of paperwork from the chair, I sat down. Dropping my elbow down on to his desk, I propped my chin on the heel of my hand and waited.

"So I heard, beggar's belief doesn't it? Mrs-Fine-and-Upstanding of this Parish flaunting the flange for cash." Jim grimaced. "Mind you, she was probably a looker in her day," he quickly added. "Did you manage to get a decent statement, don't want the D.I picking holes in it, he's on a mission lately."

"Cheeky sod, you can take them yourself in future if you don't trust me." I playfully cuffed him over the head with the flat of my hand. "I get the impression after taking her statement, that she was actually quite high class in her dealings. Solo for the first five-years and then took on a succession of experienced girls from out of town for the remainder of her 'career', and all carefully run and managed from her pretend Beauty Spa in the basement." I picked up the grey metal file punch that had Jim's name proudly scrawled on the top in black Sharpie pen.

Everything in this nick demanded a stamped ownership or it went walkabout. The most popular were cap badges, pens, staplers, file punches and the most important piece of kit in any police station throughout the whole world... *The Fork!* You couldn't claim to be a police officer unless you'd eaten a pot noodle with a folded up HazChem card in the absence of that all elusive piece of cutlery. Over the year's donations had been eagerly accepted from charity shops, the estate of someone's dead grandmother/aunt/sister (as long as they didn't die from something catching), BOGOF's from the Tesco Value range, even 'borrowed' from the local truckers café on the Dock Road, so many that we should be drowning in bloody forks, but no sooner had they hit the cutlery drawer, they were gone, never to be seen again.

My eye suddenly caught something bright poking out from underneath the elastic bands and pencils in Jim's half open drawer.

"Jim, is that a fork?" I leant forward, my hand almost touched the chrome handle of the drawer before he beat me to it and slammed it shut. "It was wasn't it? You've got a fork!" I excitedly squealed. "I was just thinking about them and you've got one..."

"It's mine..." he childishly pouted. "...I got it from home so keep your hands off it, I can prove it's mine, it's got my name on the handle."

The panic in his voice was almost palpable, the sheer terror at the thought of losing his fork had sent him into a meltdown. I giggled. "Chill, I promise I won't tell anyone, there'll be no ninja attacks on your office by the night section screwing your desk, honest!" I heaved myself up from the chair, arched my back and gave Spud a rub, more as a distraction. Jim's gaze momentarily left his drawer containing his beloved fork and settled on my bulk. Feeling obliged as a gentleman would, he quickly leant forward to help me, his psychedelic kipper tie dangling in front of him.

I just couldn't resist, quick as a flash I pounced with the file punch.

Hearing him wail in dismay as two holes peppered the fat end of his tie, I burst out laughing. "Let's see if the D.I can pick the holes in that then, shall we?"

58

"Have you heard of this place before, lads?" Petey skitted the sheet of paper across the table in the parade room. "Just taken a phone call in the Cons writing room, Licensee is reporting a burglary overnight, so I've created a log and sent it to the Control Room, said we'd go Degsy."

Degsy groaned and gave Bob a sneering smirk. Being paired up with Petey was bad enough but now he was hand picking his own jobs to go to as well. "Give it here, let's have a look." His eyes quickly moved from left to right, taking it all in. He passed it to Bob, shaking his head.

Several seconds passed before Bob spoke. "You took this down exactly as she said it, son?"

Petey nodded enthusiastically. "Don't know why the call came through there, but I listened, I took it all down carefully, then typed it up on the system, then I phoned through to the Control Room, told them the log was on the way and said to tag us as going." He seemed mightily pleased with himself. Beryl cupped her hand in a 'give me' motion. Bob passed the printout along to her, his finger pointing to the first section. She smiled, then just as quickly bit down on her bottom lip before passing it back to Degsy.

Degsy had already dissolved into rambunctious snorts of laughter. "*The Coarse Hair Pubic* house! You absolute feckin' melt!"

Petey strained over Degsy's shoulder, squinted and sighed. "Doh, trust me, I've missed the '*l*' out of public, haven't I? Oh, what a dozy sod I am!"

"It's not just the missing '*l*' Petey, my boy… have you, in all the time you've been working this patch, heard of a premises called The Coarse Hair Pub? Come on, son!" Bob scoffed.

Petey thought for a moment, the wheels and cogs clearly having a difficult ten seconds as they tried to engage. "Err, now I come to think of it, nope."

"Nope, that's right. It's a great big fat nope because it's *The Corsair Pub*, you know, the one we went to last week for the full-scaler, the big kick-off, the fight where you lost your glasses…. not some intimate residue left on the bog seat in Trap 2, you dipstick!"

Shona Lawrence was a career barmaid, having known no other profession since she had reached the age of eighteen. She'd worked some dives in her time, sticky carpets, beer-swill lino and the smell of nicotine which never left her clothes or hair, no matter how many times they'd been washed. There were days when she'd wiped her feet on the welcome mat when leaving some of the dumps she'd managed, and too many nights to count when her hoarse voice had called time on the stragglers, the dickheads, the lonely and the plain drunk.

She looked in the mirror; her red, chapped fingers traced the lines on her face. She tried to smooth them away with her hand, her nails catching in the yellow-grey of her hair.

"Bleedin' hell my girl, you're looking as rough as a badger's arse this morning." She laughed at her unladylike observation, which set off a rasping coughing fit. Once she had hacked up yesterdays forty Benson & Hedges, she lit up her first of the day, clicked the kettle on and checked her watch.

No longer a barmaid, she was now the widow of George Lawrence and the proud licensee of The Corsair Public House which serviced the 1960's grey concrete housing estate and beyond. Granted it wasn't a top end pub, in fact it wasn't even a mid-range one, more of a spit and sawdust affair but for once she could walk the carpets without leaving her stilettos embedded in

BLUES, TWOS AND BABY SHOES

the tacky tufts, and best of all, it was hers.

That was what made it all the more galling - some bastard had violated her pub and her boundaries, had stolen from her. The small cash float from the till, a few bottles of whiskey, her brasses had gone from the walls along with the *Dick Braynes Darts Trophy* that the pub team, the *Projectile Dysfunctions*, had won last year. Twenty-four years they'd been completing in that, never even made the semi's because half the team were permanent pissheads and couldn't see the board. Keeping them sober for the final had been challenging to say the least, that was what had made it so special.

"Pah, if good old Dick Braynes were alive, he'd be rolling in his grave knowing that our lot are the current title holders," she bitterly spat.

They'd also stolen her Nan's beautiful matching pair of Imari Porcelain Vases. Sitting each end of the mantlepiece in her living quarters above the pub, they had become such an important part of her life holding sentimental memories and were worth a few bob to boot. She hadn't heard a thing, nothing, not a bump, creak or a bang. She had got up after a pretty decent sleep and had immediately noticed they were gone when she'd shuffled into the sitting room in her best fluffy pink mules. The more she thought of them, the more it brought her closer to tears. Ever since the loss of George, they had come to mean so much more to her.

"Bastards…" she muttered to herself as she made her way down the back staircase into the pub to let the Bizzies in.

"Quick, jump in, if we're quick, they'll still have the spoils and we can nab 'em in the act." Degsy excitedly revved the engine as Petey jumped into the passenger seat. He had barely clicked the seat belt into place, when AR12 roared into life with an impressive wheel spin, leaving The Corsair Pub in the distance, along with Shona Lawrence and her fluffy mules.

"CCTV was bloody good, wasn't it Degsy? They hadn't even bothered to hide their faces or anything, this is going to be sooooo cool." Petey was on a roll, his knees involuntarily knocking together in excitement. "She was dead nice too, wasn't she, Mrs. Lawrence, I felt very sorry for her, I mean can you imagine after losing your husband like that, and then to lose …."

"Shit!!" Degsy braked hard at the junction. Petey shot forward, the seatbelt taking the strain, forcing a rather loud 'oooof' from him. "Sorry matey..." Degsy's apology was sincere for a change. "… here we go, Twickendale Road, salubrious abode of Jackson Paul Kenwright and his bezzie mate, Barry Kewley."

There wasn't anyone at Westbury nick that hadn't at some point in their career, come across or had dealings with Kenwright and Kewley, either for drugs, stolen property or on some occasions physical combat, as Kewley never, ever came quietly. Kewley, better known as Uncle Fester was a hard man, Kenwright a good burglar, but only when he wasn't wired on cocaine. The near perfect CCTV images of them bumbling around The Corsair like the Chuckle Brothers was prime time viewing. Degsy knew that at some point, the stills would become posters around the nick with hilarious smart-arse comments attached. Kenwright, with Shona's vases tucked under each arm actually glanced at the camera and grinned at one point, before Kewley quickly pulled the hood of his jacket up for him.

"Don't go off on one Petey, we all stick together for safety. Surprise is our best tactic, if Kewley wants to fight, it's all hands, remember what happened to Mavis and Beryl, it wasn't a pretty sight."

Petey nodded. "I feel a bit sick Degsy, are Bob and Don backing us up?"

Degsy jutted his chin towards the communal garden of the flats. "They're already in place. "Okay, count of three and we go in...."

"One..."

"Two..."

"Three..."

The door to Flat 3, 87 Twickendale Road popped with one touch from Degsy's shoulder.

"Well, well, well what have we got here?" Bob crunched over the discarded cans of Special Brew littering the floor, before greeting the sprawled figures of Kenwright and Kewley by the battered, grimy, floral sofa.

Kenwright was kneeling in front of the stained grubby coffee table, slumped over, face planted in a mound of fine powder, the residue spread around his nose and mouth, the two ornate Japanese vases belonging to Shona Lawrence in front of him, one upright, one tipped on its side. Kewley, his arms resting on his thighs, almost toppling off the sofa could barely keep his head up as he smirked at the pile of dust in front of him. A plastic gas meter card had been used to separate and cut and two straws were discarded next to an empty packet of cigarettes.

"You been snorting the Devil's Dandruff, Barry?" Bob laughingly enquired.

Kewley was more inebriated that wired. "It's shite, been whizzing that up me snout all morning and nowt, no buzz, nuffink." He wiped his hand across his mouth, a string of saliva catching on the sleeve of his hoodie, "We had to get pissed instead. Jackson's a soft twat, swore blind she had good booger sugar in her pub, that's one dumb broad stashing that crap!" He flicked his hand in a show of disdain towards the two vases, his voice lost as he mumbled into his chest.

The utter brilliance of the situation was not lost on the lads, apart from Petey, who, hands in his pockets, remained baffled by the root cause of the laughter that was now filling the seedy flat.

"Before we caution them, d'you want to tell Kewley?" Degsy grinned at Bob.

"Aye, why not, think it's me public duty don't you?" Sniggering, he positioned himself directly in front of the two slumped figures. "Kewley, Kenwright …." Bob swept his hand in polite introduction towards the two mounds of powder spread across the table, "…. I'd like you both to meet the recently deceased Mr. George Lawrence and Buster the dog, his faithful companion."

"Jeez, you're joking, they'd been snorting the remains of poor Shona's hubby and his dead dog?" I screwed my face up, desperately trying not to laugh too much, since Spud had decided to reposition itself, it was now permanently headbutting my bladder. Any giggle control I'd previously held had now deserted me completely. "Who had the job of telling her?"

Silence.

I looked around the night kitchen table. It was like looking at the Three Stooges… but as a rare appearance of all six of them at the same time. Bob, Degsy, Petey, Don, Jim and Beryl, their eyes wide open in feigned innocence, clutching their mugs of tea.

"You didn't tell her, did you?"

Silence.

"Oh my god, you just swept what was left of them back into the vases, didn't you? I don't believe it; how on earth did you know who was who?"

Six sets of shoulders shrugged in unison. Bob pulled his lips back across his teeth and let out a long sigh before finally piping up.

"Well, that's the bummer…. we didn't."

THE VISITOR

The kettle let out its distinctive whistle. Cora marvelled at how it could cheerily herald a new day, but always gave a more weary, gentle emission at bedtime when she was preparing her nightly Ovaltine. She reached up on tiptoe, her fingers probing for the orange tin on the top shelf. Hugging it to her, she prised the lid off, the rich, malty aroma brought back memories of Harold humming to himself, standing in this exact same spot in the kitchen…

'*Two level teaspoons, mixed to a paste with a little boiled water and then topped with hot milk, Cora… just the way you like it,*' he would always say. She would smile kindly, nod and accept his offering.

Only it wasn't the way she liked it, for over forty years she had yearned for an extra spoonful and one that wasn't flat but piled high. She had often yearned for other things from Harold too, but he always had an excuse. His decision to change to single beds had been the bombshell that had ended any hope she had held of further romantic liaisons with him.

'*Good grief, Cora…you've squashed my Moby Dick!*' he had barked when she had passionately jumped on his new 2'6" bed, her winceyette nightie billowing as she straddled him. Suitably chastised she had returned to her own bed to nurse her bruised inner thigh caused by the sharp corner of Harold's rather large hard-back edition of Herman Melville's masterpiece.

Oh my… large, dick, hardback and Harold had been four words she would never have visualised being said together in a month of Sundays.

She giggled at the memory. "It's three heaped teaspoons, Barnaby, three… not two!" She dug her spoon deep into the tin with gusto and a hint of defiance.

Barnaby cocked his head to one side, studying her, his amber eyes unblinking. She often wondered what he was thinking or if he did think of anything important at all. In her humble opinion, cats only ever thought about food, sleep and the occasional belly rub, not dissimilar to Harold's needs. "You can take that look off your face too, young man…" she berated him, "…I had enough of Mr Spunge's frequent disdain for little luxuries for far too long, I certainly don't need it from you."

She chuckled to herself as she dampened down the fire in the sitting room, carefully replacing the fireguard. Things were going to change in this household, in fact her whole life could change if everything went to plan.

A lovely little cottage in the countryside with Barnaby, an orchard, maybe grow her own vegetables and best of all, she could have the kitty sanctuary she had always dreamt of for the lost, the unwanted and the cruelly treated.

Picking up her tiny tray holding her precious Ovaltine, she made her way upstairs to bed. She couldn't wait to read the next instalment in her wonderful charity shop find.

The Little Book of Misdeeds, Sins & Mishaps she had decided to call it.

Once ensconced in her marshmallow bed of brushed cotton sheets, her pink counterpane pulled up to her chin and pillows plumped up behind her, she made sure her Ovaltine was at the ready on the oak bedside cabinet before picking up the notebook.

BLUES, TWOS AND BABY SHOES

The warm glow from the old 1940's rose glass lamp gave ample light in which to read.

Barnaby had snuggled up to her in his usual place. She dropped a hand down to stroke him. "My oh my Barnaby Spunge, I think Mr Cyril Hislop has been quite a naughty boy in his day if this entry is anything to go by..."

"It's okay, I'll get it." Joe's voice was followed by the sound of his footsteps hitting every other step on the way downstairs to answer the door. I held my breath. For some inordinate reason, every time he did that, I half expected to hear a hiatus in the regular foot pattern with an ensuing bump, bang and a curse telling me he'd completely missed a step and fallen down the rest.

I heaved myself up from the bed. My quick lie down had turned into two hours of snoring and slobbering into my pillow and I was still absolutely exhausted. I gave Spud a little pat.

C'mon my bean, don't be keeping me waiting...

Even though my due date was three weeks away I'd already reached the epic proportions of a whale and had now got to the point where my belly hid everything from the waist down. Some days I didn't know if I was wearing knickers or not. I'd already wandered around our local Tesco car park au naturel under my tent-like smock whilst carrying a box of Typhoo Teabags and a dishcloth under my arm. It had taken a gust of wind for me to remember my knickers were still warming on the radiator in the bathroom at home, proving without a shadow of doubt that it's not only Typhoo that gives you an *'OO'*. I was seriously considering serving an early eviction notice on Spud if this humiliation continued. Ella had definitely fared better, she was due any day and had taken everything in her stride. I was so proud of her but disappointed in myself. I wanted to be the one she ran to for advice, but instead it was the other way around, I'd been such a wimp with this pregnancy. Shuffling my feet into my slippers, I slowly made my way to the bathroom. In my youth I'd loved Gene Kelly's 'Gotta Dance' from Singing in the Rain, now I was humming and mouthing 'Gotta Pee' every twenty seconds - and don't even get me started on sneezing!

"Mave, think you need to come down, there's someone here to see you."

I heard the front door close and muffled voices coming from the lounge below. I checked myself in the mirror, creases from my pillow were still imprinted on the side of my face and one half of my fringe was stuck out at an odd angle. I breathed into the palms of my hands. *Bleurrrrgh*. Definite case of dragon breath. A quick swill of mouthwash wouldn't go amiss. "Coming, won't be a minute!"

Lumbering each stair, feeling for them with my feet rather than being able to see them, I eventually made it downstairs, only to be confronted by Joe in the hallway, frantically flapping his hands with a look of bewilderment on his face. The first thing I noticed was a small, battered suitcase near to the front door. I looked at him and mouthed '*who is it*?', my index finger pointing wildly towards the closed door of the lounge.

Joe ran his fingers through his hair, an action he always did when he was thinking of what to say. "Erm, it's a woman, an old woman. She says she's your Aunt, something to do with your mum's side. You've never mentioned having an aunt before, Mave!"

My heart dropped, well as far as it could considering Spud's bum was in the way. I felt the colour drain from my face, my lips parted, desperately trying to find the right words. But there are no right words, not when you're trying to tell your hubby about the black sheep of your family. Someone you hoped would be dead and if by some miracle they hadn't snuffed it, they would never, ever darken your doorstep, let alone bloody cross over it with a ruddy charity shop suitcase.

AGATHA

"**M**avis, my dear... just look at you!" Agatha Hortensia Winterbourne, her cupid-bow lips gaily painted with a liberal slick of dark red lipstick, quickly pursed them together like she had just sucked on a lemon.

I stood rooted to the spot taking in this ridiculous caricature of a woman who was now standing, flamboyant, in the middle of my Moroccan rug. Small and rotund, her heavily powdered face was topped with an unruly mop of curly dyed ginger hair. What resembled a multi-coloured Bedouin birthing blanket was casually flung across her shoulders, a sarong style olive green skirt skimmed a pair of tangerine floral T-bar shoes that had curled up Velcro straps.

I wanted to laugh but didn't dare.

"Aunt Agatha... I... we...erm ...gosh, we thought you were dead!"

Joe gave me daggers, his eyes almost popping out of their sockets. I shrugged. Once again, a stupid head thought had somehow found its way out of my mouth.

"Not quite dear child, not quite..." She flicked the end of the blanket across her shoulder, one of the beaded tassels smacked Joe on the nose. I sniggered.

"How did you know where I live Agatha, we haven't seen sight nor sign of you for over thirty years and then you just turn up out of the blue?" No point in holding back, I'd already let her know that we thought she was six-feet under and of no consequence to us, might as well go the whole hog. She pursed those ridiculous lips again. I couldn't help but notice the bleed of the lipstick into the smoker's lines that spidered their way around her mouth.

Flashing her heavily hooded blue eyes, she tilted her head towards the door as Alfie, Dad's dog came bounding in. "It was a chance meeting with your dad, Arthur, before he passed on…." she bent down to stroke Alfie's head. He flattened his ears back, the wag of his tail dropped to an agitated tremor. "…it was actually very four tortoises that I got to speak to him, considering."

I looked at Joe, Joe looked at me. *Four tortoises!*

We were none the wiser for our mutual glances.

"Considering what? When did you see Dad?" A knot formed in my stomach, for all we had been through, the closeness we had fought to nurture between us, overcoming his demons and mine for that matter….and he hadn't told me he had spoken to Agatha.

Agatha prevaricated, delving into a large tapestry shoulder bag that was limply slumped on the sofa. "Now let me see, I'm sure I had it in here somewhere…" The first fistful contained a mint humbug that had seen better days, two pens and a used tissue. The twisted wood bangles on her wrist rattled as she tried to shake the sticky sweet from her fingers. "…no, no, no that's not it!" she impatiently grumbled. Two more attempts produced a packet of paracetamol, one hooped earring, three costume rings and a pair of orange bloomers complete with lace edging.

Joe actually began to blush as Agatha made a huge deal of shaking them out and holding them up with a flourish. "Mmmmm, well these have definitely seen better days, can't think why I've still got them." Shafts of pale sunlight from the window poked through the multitude of moth holes in the orange fabric. She flung them to one side with wild abandonment. They landed on Alfie's head, hanging from his left ear. He gave Agatha a look of pure indignance before shaking them off.

"Ah, voila!!" She triumphantly held a glass ball in both hands. "My orbuculum." She proffered it towards me, stroking it gently with her fingers. The glass carried a slight blue tinge, small sparkles of light burst from the sphere. "I was scrying for a client and he just popped up, Arthur Albert Upton appeared without even being called…." she again made a dramatic play of caressing the glass. "…quite impatient he was, said it was his last chance to speak before passing on."

I drew a sharp intake of breath and hiccupped, which made Spud kick me sharply in the ribs. "When you said you'd spoken to him before he passed on Agatha, surely you meant before he died?"

"No dear, he was quite dead and had been for some time… hence him appearing here. It's only for the departed you know, it's not like texting or sending emails. It's for the spirits and the spirits alone to communicate with the living. He was preparing to pass on to the next plane, quite excited about it too from what he told me."

"Agatha, Dad is dead, and in my condition…." I exaggeratedly pointed to my tummy, "…I certainly don't need your nonsense, bloody communicating with the dead, for goodness sake. Your fairground stuff from years ago won't wash here!" I angrily spat. "Mum told me all about you!"

Agatha sighed and looked to the ceiling, hugging her crystal ball to her chest. "Ah my dearest Josephine, a woman who had extra-century perception herself but denied it!"

"Extra-sensory, it's extra-sensory and no she didn't have it…. she was… err…. normal, just normal, now please, what do you want Agatha?" I was verging on bursting into tears. Joe put his arm around my waist and gave a gentle, reassuring squeeze.

"Maybe a nice cup of tea will help calm things down, Mave." He ushered me to the sofa. "Right Agatha, put your balls away and sit in the chair over there. There's absolutely no point in everyone getting wound up and upset."

"I know my voice can be a little gruff at times, son - but it's ball; in the singular!" Agatha started laughing as she flopped herself backwards onto the cushions. "Mind you, I did hear about your cousin Frank at the wedding…"

"Right, that's one less biscuit for you with your tea, Aggie, now start behaving!" Joe's admonishment was gentle but firm.

I looked at him, my kind, warm, sensible Joe. The man that was going to be Spud's daddy and I knew that everything would be alright.

Joe clicked off the bedside lamp, vigorously punched his pillow a few times, and snuggled down next to me, pulling the duvet up to his chin.

"She's as nutty as a fruitcake, isn't she?"

"Yep."

"Look, if you don't want to talk about it my little sprout…"

"I do Joe, but I just don't know where to begin."

"Mmmmm, well I always find at the beginning is a pretty good place to pick up from - unless it's boring, if it's boring, just skip that and get to the juicy bits."

In the half-light that was seeping through the gap in the curtains I could just make out his face. A slight smirk held, before worried he'd upset me, he quickly found his 'serious' face.

"Well, let's see…." I rolled onto my back and stared at the ceiling, blocks of orange from the streetlamp outside the bedroom window scattered across the white plaster, giving an eerie glow, "…. Agatha Hortensia Winterbourne is my mum's sister, as you've probably already gathered. She is the black sheep of the family, the one that nobody talks about. She is self-centred, cruel, mean, a fraud, corrupt, nasty…"

"Whoa my little chickpea, don't hold back will you?" Joe snorted.

"I'm speaking Joe, you wanted to know!"

"Sorry, go on."

"So, Agatha did a mean line in fakery in her day, started with Tarot Reading, Crystal Balls, Fortune Telling, that sort of stuff. She had a little cottage not far from Westbury, it was all done from there, called herself Gypsy Sybella-Simone. She transitioned into Clairvoyance, claiming she could speak to the dead. Long story short, she caused a lot of grief within our family, she ripped off a lot of innocent people, I'm amazed that she was never caught and went to prison! So, it was no surprise when the family didn't want anything more to do with her." I paused, reliving Mum's frequent conversations concerning Agatha and her 'misdemeanours', as she had called them.

"I can understand the family being embarrassed, Mave, but don't you think it was a bit harsh to cut her off completely, she must have been devastated?"

I sighed. "If she'd been any bloody good reading her crystal ball, she'd have seen it coming, wouldn't she? She's a cow Joe, she was mean to Mum and the final straw was her being caught with Dad in the coal shed on New Years Eve."

"Aww Mave, maybe she was just grabbing a lump to bring the New Year in…"

"Nice try, the only lump she was grabbing was disgustingly my Dad's!" I felt sick just thinking about it. "So, she was banished, not just from the family, but from Westbury and beyond. Nobody has heard from her for over forty years, in fact we all thought she was dead." I muttered under my breath about wishing she was.

"So, what are we going to do with her? We can't just ignore her, you heard what she said. She's only got months left, if that." Joe nuzzled into my neck, his breath warm and comforting. "She's dying Mave, we can't abandon her now."

"I don't know, I really don't know."

Silence reigned, the bedside clock hypnotically played its tempo as we both stared at the ceiling, deep in thought.

Tick, Tock, Tick, Tick, Tock, Tock, Tick....

Joe sniggered. "Fortuitous...."

"What?"

"Fortuitous! That's what she meant by four tortoises...."

Oh for fecks sake.... not another one in the family!

WHITE RABBITS

I watched Degsy and Bob, hands laden, juggle the pints, shorts and several packets of crisps as they wove their way through the tables in The Ship Inn. Beryl and Don were deep in conversation and Petey was still sitting forlornly staring into the glass of Lime & Soda that had been his companion for the last hour.

I readjusted the cushions I'd pinched from the comfy chairs in the side bar, propping myself up so I didn't slouch sideways like poor old Liberty Lil used to do after a night on the voddie. Actually, talking of which, I knew chatting job was supposed to be off limits on a night out, but the suspense had been killing me.

"Degs, just a train of thought, what happened to Lil after the drugs bust last week, she was carted off to A&E wasn't she? I didn't see anything come through on the Intel reports as to why." I took a sip of my drink and crammed a handful of cheese and onion crisps into my mouth.

Wiping the beer froth from his top lip, Degsy paused, gave Bob a conspiratorial look and started laughing. "She was so gatted on her Limited-Edition Vodka from Indian Joe's brewing vat, it addled her brain," he snorted. "It started when the lads from the squad used the universal key with a bit more gusto than necessary and the door completely shattered. Joe shit himself and shouted for her to hide the '*buzz*'."

Taking up the story, Bob dissolved into a fit of very unmanly giggles. "So, Lil does no more than leg it into the bedroom, slams the door shut and shoves the bed against it, trying to block the lads from getting in, but it wasn't stopping Regan, remember him from B Division? Well, he shoulders the door, caving it in, pushing the bed and Lil ten feet across the room. He goes to grab her and she's lying there spread-eagled on the bed in the throes of ecstasy, legs akimbo...." Another snort and Bob's beer sprayed across the table.

"Oh my god, I know she's legendary as a nymphomaniac, but what a time to decide to pleasure herself, I'd have died laughing." I crammed another handful of crisps into my mouth, this was so good I should have brought popcorn.

Bob continued. "Anyhow, there on the dressing table is a large bag of the Devil's Dandruff, out in the open for all to see, fortunately she hadn't had time to hide it, or so we thought. Lil's cautioned and cuffed and as she strolls out the bedroom with Regan, she's walking all funny like. She straight coughs to Indian Joe in a high-pitched voice that 'everything's okay, she's hidden it'. Regan's puzzled like, as the package is still on the dressing table ready for photographing." Relating this epic tale was thirsty work, he quaffed the remainder of his pint in one gulp. "Just then, Lil decides to have a little kick off, starts struggling against the cuffs, lets out a massive fart with all the effort and sets off a faint buzzing sound. We all go quiet listening and suddenly matey boy here..." he jabbed a finger at Degsy, "...bursts out laughing and shouts that it's coming from her hoop!"

Degsy smirked and threw his hands up, giving rabbit ears with his fingers. "So, cue two hours later and we're stuck in A&E with Lil in total vaginal spasm whilst they try to figure out how to extricate a large *Rampant Rabbit* vibrator wedged between her right ovary and her tonsils!"

Even Beryl couldn't stop the flow of tears from laughing, wiping them away with the heel of her hand. Spud not impressed with my cackling, gave me a sharp pain that ran the width of my tummy. I grimaced. "I had heard that Regan has a sort of coochie-clamp effect on women, must be all that muscle and manly pheromones he gives off." I gave my belly a discreet rub. "I know Lil's a bit on the dense side and Joe has his own vocabulary, but really?"

Bob nodded. "Really, true story, apparently she thought he'd taken the batteries out and hidden tabs inside it…. and it was an easier option than trying to squeeze a Sainsbury's carrier bag and half a kilo of cocaine up her chuff. What she hadn't counted on was the excitable gusto in which she'd rammed *Roger Rabbit* instead!"

Another sharp pain made me jerk forward, I puffed through it until it ebbed away and that's when I noticed Petey, lost in his own world, silent amid the backdrop of our raucous laughter. "You okay Petey?"

His sad eyes were magnified ten-fold by the lenses of his glasses. "It must be great to be like Regan Belshaw…" he spat the name with venom, "…all masculine and sexy, no wonder he turns heads."

The laughter quickly died to be replaced by a sudden mutual awareness.

Oh shit, he knows!

THE ARRIVAL

"Joe, Joe…" I gently tapped him on the shoulder.

"Ugh, what?"

"It's Spud…. Spud's …. oooh owwwww eeeeeeeeeeeeeeeeeee…"

Joe exploded from the bed, tripped over the duvet still wrapped around his leg and headbutted the wardrobe. "Oh my God, it can't be, it's too early…. oh my God what do I do now, shit…. where's my skids, my shoes, I need my shoes."

I watched him hare around the bedroom, opening drawers, grabbing armfuls of his own clothes and throwing them into his rucksack.

"Calm down, for goodness sake, just chuck some underwear and socks in the bag for me."

"I'm ready, it's done, let's go…" he breathlessly gasped as he grabbed hold of my hand and started pulling me towards the bedroom door.

I yanked my hand back. "It's okay, chill, I need…" Another contraction hit, I held onto the end of the bed, panting through it, the art of conversation lost.

"I'm ready, hurry up, get your coat and we can be on our way." He was like an excitable child, standing there, rucksack flung over one shoulder, hand on hip, grimacing.

As the pain subsided, he took the opportunity to disappear, I heard him jump two stairs at a time, with a jarring thump at the bottom. I checked my watch. Regular, six minutes apart and that one was just under a minute long. Still plenty of time to get there, I kept two mental fingers crossed.

"Mave, come on, hurry up…" I could hear him in the hallway, jangling the car keys, huffing, puffing and chunnering to himself as I eased my way down the stairs. I paused halfway to get my breath as a more low-key contraction hit, which in turn gave me time to take in the vision of my darling hubby, my sometimes fuckwit of a soul mate, the love of my life.

Standing by the open front door with the ready baby bag clenched in his hand, wearing a T-shirt, hoodie and his best trainers accompanied by a fabulous line in bright orange ankle socks… and no trousers!

I despair, I really, really do.

"It's coming, my baby's coming…. I'm having a baby!" Joe burst through the double doors of Westbury Maternity Unit, arms flailing, his rucksack and the baby bag swinging either side of him. I waddled slowly behind him, rolling my eyes whilst giving an embarrassed grin to several expectant dads standing outside on mobile phones or puffing away underneath the *No Smoking* signs.

"Joe, it's me that's having the baby and I'm fine!" I hissed as I caught up with him. "This is going to be a bloody long labour if you don't take a chill pill."

The receptionist on the admissions desk gave me an empathetic smile. "Mrs Blackwell?" I nodded. "And this will be Mr Blackwell." That was more of a statement than a question. "Right, let's get you booked in and someone will come to take you to the labour ward."

She took my notes, skimmed her fingers across the keyboard. "This seems to be a very popular day for our babies to want to arrive, we're filling up nicely." She appeared to be genuinely happy at the prospect. The seconds ticked by before she looked up again. "Are you alright Mr Blackwell?"

I turned around to see a vacant space where Joe had been standing.

"Mr Blackwell?"

Oh no Joe, not now…. now is definitely not the time to faceplant the linoleum.

"He's fine Mavis, don't fret. He's having a cup of tea and a biscuit in the side room, once he's levelled out a bit, we'll bring him back to be with you." Alison Waterfield, my midwife, gave me a reassuring smile.

"I just can't understand him, he's in the job like me, he's always the cool one, can cope with anything, never faffs or panics. You don't think he's ill, do you?" My concern for Joe was starting to outweigh any trepidation I had about the imminent arrival of Spud.

"Promise you, he's not ill, he's just got himself so excited and worked up at meeting this little one, it's pushed him over the edge a bit." She laughed as she adjusted the back of the bed. "Don't forget, you've done this before, he hasn't." She made a few notes on the file and checked my blood pressure again. "Are we still going with the epidural?"

Mmmmmm, that was the million-dollar question.

So far I was doing really well, granted when a contraction hit, it was bloody painful, but up to now I'd coped, and I hadn't had an epidural when Ella was born. No, Mavis Jane Blackwell-Upton isn't a wimp - I could do this without voluntarily giving myself a dead foofoo in the process.

"No, thanks Alison, I think noooooooooooooooooo… eeeeeee……" My squeal went up several octaves. "…. yeeeeeeeeeeees purleeeeeeeeeese." And just like I had all those years ago on my first date with Joe, I had managed to change a *no* into a *yes* in 2.2 seconds flat.

"Right, I'll take that as an affirmative…" she grinned, "…I'll go and get the Anaesthetist, we might as well get it done now and then we're good to go whenever baby decides to make an appearance. I don't think it'll be too long now."

I sat on the edge of the bed, Joe, now fully recovered, was standing in front of me holding both my hands. The deed had been done.

The very young and handsome anaesthetist, Dr. Jack Edgeware, after successfully killing the top of my legs, bum, tummy and foofoo, was busily writing up his notes.

"Can you feel anything at all Mave?" Joe whispered, in part reverence and part fear.

I wriggled my toes, or at least I thought I was, even shifting slightly on my bum felt weird. As though it was there and my bum but not there and someone else's bum at the same time. "No, nothing, I can still sort of move my legs, but I'll wait until a contraction comes to let you know for sure."

I tried to adjust my position slightly, I knew I was putting some effort in, but my muscles weren't registering.

"Try to stop wriggling, surely that's not going to help…." Joe kissed the tip of my nose, "… I read in that Baby magazine that at this stage you should be…"

I interrupted. "Baby Magazine! Now would that be the one that teaches you how to ride a crotch rocket.... and no, it's not a euphemism before you ask!" I started to laugh, which under the circumstances was the worst choice I could have made.

Paaaaaaaarp.

It came from nowhere, no warning, no lower belly rumble - nothing. If I'd had any feeling whatsoever on the lower decks, I could have clenched my cheeks together, but it was pointless, no matter how much a squeezed, a second fart loudly escaped. A heatwave of epic proportions enveloped my face. "Oh shit, do you think he heard that?" I frantically pointed to the corner where the delectable Dr Jack was sitting.

Joe couldn't speak for silent laughing, tears streaming down his face, his shoulders heaving up and down, but no sound escaping from his lips. "Oh Joe, please, just cough loudly or something, it's the epidural, I can't control it." I looked over in desperation to where Doctor Edgeware was still blithely scribbling his notes, making no acknowledgement to my predicament at all.

Paaaaaarp, phffftt, brrrraaapp, fwaaaap....

"Oh God, that's it... just kill me now!" I hissed. "...thanks for nothing, you twonk!" I began to hum Land of Hope and Glory with increasing crescendo in the absence of Joe coming to my rescue by coughing. "What is wrong with you, help me out here!" I spluttered.

By now, Joe had face planted the bed, head buried in the pillow howling fit to burst. His muffled voice just about audible. "I c-a-n-'t b-r-e-a-t-h-e...."

I sat forlornly, legs hanging over the edge of the bed, resigning myself to the fate of a further five minutes of uncontrollable bouts of flatulence intermittently broken by the sound of Joe almost choking with laughter each time I inadvertently dropped one.

After what seemed like an eternity, Dr Edgeware closed his file, tucked it under his arm and gave me a polite nod of his head along with a disarming grin. "I usually look to giving a few words of encouragement at this stage Mavis, so just look on the bright side, it never stays windy for long!"

And with that he was gone.

He's here.

At 05.56 a.m pink and with a hefty set of lungs on him, Spud made his way into the world weighing an eye watering 9lbs 9oz.

Exhausted, I look at my darling Joe, weeping with joy holding his son, his first born and I just know that all is good in the world according to me, Mavis Jane Upton… who, at this moment in time, is simply known as nothing more wonderful than *Mummy*.

The best title in the whole world.

SURPRISE, SURPRISE!

"**R**ight, let's get you onto the ward, Mavis, textbook delivery, so just an overnight stay, I think." Alison picked up my notes. Joe trudged behind, bogged down by bags, clothes and his trusty rucksack. He was still shell shocked, a glazed, half-drunk look in his eyes as he wandered like a lost soul along the corridor.

"Here we go." She manoeuvred the fish-tank cot into the curtained off cubicle alongside my bed. "Have we thought of a name for Baby Blackwell yet?"

"I think he suits Alfie, don't you Mave?" Joe looked gooey eyed into the cot. "He looks like an Alfie."

I shook my head in disbelief, I would have preferred a comfort blow of my fringe but most of it was still plastered by sweat to my forehead so no matter how much I puffed, it didn't move. "Are you saying our son looks like a dog? How can we call him Alfie when our dog is called Alfie? We can't have both of them rushing down the hallway when you shout, '*walkies*' or taking a dump together in the back garden can we?"

"Oh yeah, I thought it sounded familiar when I said it," he mumbled.

"Pass me the bag please, I could do with a couple of Face Wipes." He happily obliged and heaved it onto the bed. I set about rummaging around in the depths, pulling out various oddments, toothbrush, deodorant, polo mints and….. "What the hell are these doing in here?" I held up a tatty looking jockstrap, a pair of underpants and some rugby socks.

He sheepishly took them from me. "You said grab some underwear and socks, so I did."

"From my drawer Joe, not from yours!" I rolled my eyes and blew him a kiss. "When have I ever asked to wear your smelly old jockstrap?"

He shrugged, stuffing them into his own bag. "You don't know what you're missing then."

I lay back on the pillow, tired but elated, thinking of names for our son as Joe, besotted, gazed at him in the cot. "Freddie Blackwell. Nope. Nathan Blackwell, maybe. Sebastian Blackwell. Definitely not. Logan Bla……."

"How about Benjamin Blackwell?" A familiar disembodied voice shouted from behind the curtain of the neighbouring cubicle. Joe, briefly taking his eyes from his son, gave me a look of puzzlement. He quickly turned and pulled the curtain to one side, revealing my next-door-bedmate.

I gasped.

Joe snorted.

"Ella!"

"Hello Mum…"

Holding a tiny bundle, little fingers peeking out from the folds of the blanket, Ella serenely smiled at me. "…meet Daisy Jane Gilbert, your granddaughter!" she softly whispered.

Cyril Hislop shuffled along the hallway, kicked the threadbare rug back into place and bent down to pick up the two envelopes that

BLUES, TWOS AND BABY SHOES

had clattered through his letterbox. Scratching under his armpit, he had a quick sniff of his fingers.

"Must be nearly Christmas, Thomas..." he rubbed behind the ear of the big ginger cat as it sat regally on the bannister post, ".... I can feel a bath coming on!" Chuckling to himself, he ambled back into the kitchen, dropped the letters onto the stained tablecloth and noisily scraped the wooden chair backwards, so as to allow his bulk room to sit.

Cyril plucked at the dried egg stain on his vest and wistfully remembered better times, times when Clementine had been alive. He wondered what good is a wife if the one you choose decides to flee this mortal coil prematurely and leave you to fend for yourself.

"She was a good egg though, wasn't she?" He laughed at his choice of words as he scraped the dried, yellowing mess from under his fingernails onto the hem of the tablecloth. Looking at the twisted corner of the checked material, he examined the disgusting blob of orange wax adhered to it and made a mental note to stop using it to clean his ears out. Maybe he'd even give it a wash before the end of the week if the mood took him.

Dear, sweet Clementine. She had been standing by the cooker waiting for her famous Victoria Sponge to complete its baking cycle when he'd left her to nip to the bookies that fateful day. Returning some two hours later, he had spotted her through the glass in the half-glazed kitchen door, still bent over one of her cookery books. Admiring her still fairly pert rump he had given it a resounding slap and a few words of encouragement to get her in the mood. She had chosen to ignore his sexual advances, remaining silent and engrossed in her book. Not to be downhearted, he'd friskily danced into the morning room to read the paper and have a smoke, happily consoling himself that there would always be time later when they retired to bed. When 6 o'clock had been and gone and she hadn't shouted him for his tea, guts-a-grumbling, he had gone in search of her.

"Stiff as a board, she was, Thomas - stiff as a board and still bent over her cookery book…" he guffawed. Thomas looked on with complete indifference to his master's story. "…must have been stone cold dead when I'd given her me love tap on the arse and there's me thinking I'd lost me touch!"

Thomas the cat sniffed the air in disgust and silently disappeared through the cat flap.

"So, I'm talking to meself now, am I?" Cyril leant forward and grabbed the first of the two letters. "I'll be talking to the bloody walls next like the woman in that ruddy film Clementine watched all the time, what was her name, *Shirley Turpentine* or summat!" He began to laugh, coughing as he caught his breath, the torn envelope in one hand, the letter in the other. His eyes scanned the typewritten words, his heart missing several beats as the colour drained from his face.

"What the absolute feck….!"

"It's another one Boss…" Jim held the telephone between his left ear and shoulder, his right hand holding the clear evidence bag containing the letter. "…yep, 75-year-old local man, Cyril Hislop." He listened intently. "No, nothing, same as the other one, no prints but a small fibre which has been catalogued, he's taking our advice so far. Yep, right, thanks Sir. No, it doesn't say exactly what information they're holding, just the 'buzz' words only Cyril seems to know what they mean, and he's not talking."

Settling the phone back in the cradle, Jim gathered the file together, pinned the box and pushed it back into the 'Active'

section on his desk. He needed this like a hole in the head amongst the rest of the crap that had fallen on his desk lately. Another blackmail report. The investigation into Edna Flaybrick's job had come to a grinding halt when, against police advice, she'd sneaked off on the quiet and paid up, later withdrawing her complaint. At least that's what they believed, but without proof, they were stymied. Frustrated, he shook his head. He couldn't understand why Cyril Hislop had reported his letter and kicked up such a fuss in the interview room but was refusing to discuss what 'sin' the blackmailer was alluding to. How the hell did Cyril expect them to solve it with only half the information and no forensics.

He'd run the words over and over again in his own mind, hoping it might jog something, a sort of eureka moment which would slot everything into place and he'd be able to have another go at Cyril.

Easter Surprise in Fifty-Five....

Easter Surprise in Fifty-Five had sounded like a song title. Jim had Googled the exact words and then different combinations of them, and nothing had come back on the searches. It wasn't a poem either.

Unless Cyril Hislop decided to be more forthcoming or a further demand was received when he didn't pay up, Jim had no more to go on for this investigation than he had on Edna's.

Cora chuckled as she counted out the money. Some crisp new notes fluttered amongst those that were well used, passed from purchaser to seller, shop to store, store to bank and then from Sinner to Redeemer. She was the redeemer, quietly sealing their fate.

Oh gosh, yes... I like that, I can be Miss Celia Fate, Blackmailer Extraordinaire!

"I'm redeeming their souls before they pass on to another realm. We're all getting so very close to that light aren't we, Barnaby?" she dolloped a large forkful of tuna into the small bowl, Barnaby softly wound himself around Cora's legs, waiting. "We have extra pennies coming in now so only the best for Mummy's little boy." She put the bowl on the mat and watched him perform his intricate dance before sniffing it and finally taking a mouthful.

She set the little wooden tea tray with her china cup and saucer and a dainty side plate for the piece of cake she had bought from the local bakery. Such a treat. Treats that would become more frequent if things went to plan. She was still waiting to hear from Cyril Hislop, he had been number 2 on her list, she was sure he'd pay up eventually. Settling herself down in the armchair, she stoked the fire and threw on an extra log. Picking up her *Little Book of Misdeeds, Sins & Mishaps*, she gently flipped the satin bookmark over and turned to the next page. "They need to repent, pay for their sins, it'll make them so much happier in the long run, I'm sure." her rheumy blue eyes scanned the handwritten words.

Oh, my oh my, how absolutely, mouth-wateringly delicious....

..... and for once, Cora wasn't talking about the cake!

WHEN THE WIND BLOWS

"It's a Code Brown, Code Brown….. I'm calling a Code Brown, Mave!!!" Joe came flying out of the nursery, hands flapping in a mad panic. "It's everywhere and it stinks…" he suddenly went into barfing mode, dry retching, his face turning several shades of red, eyes watering.

"Oh, for feck's sake, it's a bit of poo, stop being such a bloody wimp…" I threw a nappy at him, "… fold up the poopy one, wipe his bum, cream and change, it's simple. You can't just deal with the wet ones, what are you going to do when I go back to work?"

"But he's got… err extra bits, where am I supposed to put them?" he wailed.

Jeez!

"Where do you put your *extra* bits Joe, I bet you don't tuck them into your socks or tie them around your neck, do you?"

He grinned. "Oh my, to be such a big boy, my little turnip." I hit him with the bag of toilet rolls I was holding. "Ooof!! Okay point taken, but just stay here so I know you're there if I need you." He tried to give me his melting dog-eye look.

I stood back by the door, watching him place everything he needed with precision at the side of the changing mat. Picking Benjamin up, he gagged again. "Bloody hell, that's disgusting, what on earth has he been eating, it's all down his legs?"

"He doesn't eat, he only drinks milk, just get on with it, I've got so much to do and Ella is due in half an hour with Daisy." My patience was wearing thin but I did have a smug smile. Looking at our tiny mite, I was amazed that he could produce so much, it definitely was the worst nappy I'd ever seen – or smelt. Oh well, in at the deep end, Joe would have to learn. Holding Benjamin by the ankles, he lifted him slightly, ready to slide the dirty nappy out from under him.

"Wait a mo, you haven't wiped his bum, you need to wipe his bum before you put the clean one underneath otherwise…."

"I know what I'm doing, I'm getting the hang of it now," he sharply interrupted.

I shook my head; if experience was anything to go by, I knew exactly what was going to come next.

Both hands full, little ankles in one, nappy in the other, Joe bent down to closely check what needed wiping, at the exact same time Benjamin let out a truly tremendous trump….

Ella squealed with laughter. "Nooooooo, I don't believe it, poor Joe!"

I clicked the kettle on and grabbed a couple of teabags. "Yep, it was everywhere, he was pebble dashed right in the kisser!" I started sniggering again. Every time I thought of Joe's bemused, poo covered face and the horror when he realised what had just been expelled from Benjamin's bum, I dissolved into uncontrollable laughing.

"Where is he now, having a lie down to recover?"

I listened for running water. "Nope, think he's on his third shower if I'm not mistaken. D'you want a biscuit, got some lovely

BLUES, TWOS AND BABY SHOES

shortbread on the go?"

Nodding, Ella followed me into the lounge. Daisy, her beautiful blonde curls just peeping above the blanket, was fast asleep in the carry cot. Benjamin, after his explosive start to the morning had not long been fed and was sleeping it off in the nursery.

"So, what's the score with Auntie Agatha?" Ella asked through a mouthful of biscuit. "Have you heard from her lately?"

Oh dear. Auntie Agatha!

How I wished she wasn't figuring so heavily in our family life. The woman was a bloody menace, but she was my mum's sister. Joe had been right, I couldn't turn my back on her. Since her visit, she had spent a week in a local B&B finding her feet and then we'd secured a rented flat for her, not too far from us on a short-term lease. There was no point getting anything more as from her last hospital appointment, it was made quite clear that she wasn't long for this world. She was stoic and seemingly unconcerned by her imminent death, and I could hardly shed a tear for a woman I barely knew and really, if I was honest, didn't particularly like. "She's okay, driving everyone nuts and from what I can gather, there are a lot of people in Westbury that wish she hadn't returned."

Ella raised her eyebrows. "In what way Mum, was she really that much of a troublemaker in her day?"

Taking a long swig from my mug, I prevaricated, trying to think of the right way to explain Agatha. "Well, she wasn't one to beat about the bush when it came to men. They didn't have to be hers, she wasn't that fussy. She didn't want them, she just needed them for a short while, it was only fun to her but it broke a lot of relationships, caused a lot of upset and pain." I thought back to the stories that Mum had told me whilst puffing away on her cigarettes, wistfully remembering Dad, Agatha and others that had figured in her life.

"Old Agatha certainly wasn't shy at obtaining money by deception either. Usually with that bloody crystal ball of hers or the tarot cards. She knew everything about everyone's business around here, she was so nosy, so she used it to her advantage."

"Oh dear."

"*Oh dear* is just about right, there were quite a few sighs of relief when she suddenly upped and disappeared in the mid 1950's. She was gone for a couple of years, then turned up like a bad penny, stayed long enough to cause more turmoil and then vanished again, until she suddenly appeared on our doorstep." I gathered our empty mugs and waved them at her. "Another cuppa?" She nodded.

"So it's just a case of keeping an eye on her until the inevitable then, and make sure she doesn't find the energy to get up to her old tricks?" Ella smirked as she tiptoed to the carrycot to check on Daisy.

"I think it's more of keeping an eye on certain members of Westbury's church circle, if they get their hands on Agatha it won't be Christian goodness they'll be bestowing on her…" I had visions of them turning to the black arts, making a rather plump wax effigy with ginger hair to stick pins in. "…that crowd have very, very long memories!"

HAIRY MARY FROM THE DAIRY

Bob pushed the remaining chunk of sausage around his plate, mopping up the egg yolk and brown sauce. Westbury nick canteen was buzzing with stories, banter, gossip, snippets of intelligence and the occasional outburst of raucous laughter. Huddled in groups over mugs of tea, coffee and various combinations of what stood for breakfast once Maggie had slopped it out onto the plates, were a balanced mixture of uniform, CID and civvy staff.

"Beans, bacon and a bap…." her gravelly voice echoed through the serving hatch. "…you've got to the count of three to get it, ONE…. TWO…."

DC Jim Shakeshaft was on his feet sprinting across the chequered tiles, eagerly grabbing the plate proffered by Maggie's rough hands through the small wooden opening. Returning to his table, he was greeted by a unified roar of derision from just about everyone in the canteen.

"Feck me, a Detective that can run - put that in yer notebook lads!" Degsy snorted through a mouthful of toast.

Another rousing cheer went up. Jim's cheeks flushed as he dropped his plate onto the melamine table. "Yeah, yeah, very funny lads, you seem to have conveniently forgotten that I've got my name down for the next Marathon."

Bob squeezed past him, taking the opportunity to prod Jim's overhanging gut. "….and a Snickers, Dime Bar and a KitKat by the looks of it, mate!"

Cue another round of laughter at Jim's expense but he took it in good humour. Grinning, he gave Bob a dead arm with a friendly punch to his upper bicep. "When's Mavis back, anyone heard anything?"

"Couple of weeks I think, she's decided to come back early. The little one has settled well, her and Joe have arranged their shifts and to be honest, I think that bloody weird Auntie of hers has got something to do with it…" Bob pulled at his tie which had been clipped to the pocket tab on his shirt. He checked it for anything untoward before he continued. "…the barmy old fart is hanging on longer than they thought and driving Mave nuts, said she needs to get back to work to get away from her."

Jim shovelled in another mouthful of beans followed by a slurp of tea. "Mmmm, well, when she does get back, can you let me know? We sort of started on a job together before she went off on maternity leave, need to speak to her about it."

Bob nodded. "The blackmail one?"

"Yep, gone quiet of late but it's still sitting in my pending, need to have a pow-wow and see if there's anything more, if not it'll be filed until something else comes up." Jim didn't look happy at the prospect, but with that many active investigations on the go, temporarily dumping one was hardly the worst he could do. Having got Bob's assurance, he went back to finishing his breakfast.

Bob ambled back to the table. "Off to the bog, see you downstairs, Degs." Scoff almost over, taking the opportunity for a comfort stop before heading back out, was a given after two mugs of tea.

Pushing the door open he spotted the forlorn figure of Petey at the urinal, barely holding himself up. Leaning forward, his head on the tiles above, one arm supporting himself, the weight of the world on his shoulders. Bob positioned himself next to him and unzipped in what he hoped was a very manly manner. Having only two stalls made it impossible to have the usual obligatory one stall gap between him and a fellow piddler.

There was something about communal wizzing that always brought out the macho side of him, Christ knows what he thought he had to prove, but over the years he'd perfected the art of the quick zip, fast draw, streamlined wizz with a deep baritone voice if he had to speak to anyone whilst carrying out his deft combo.

"Alright matey, didn't see you in the canteen, everything okay?" He waited for Petey's response.

"Not really, long story…"

Bob marvelled at Petey's ability to wee in staccato.

"…. it's Betty."

Bob's heart dropped nearly hitting his testicles, which were currently overhanging the blue serge material of his pants, enjoying the breeze from the open top window.

Feck me, not in here, not now….

After his barbed comment in The Ship several months ago, they'd all reached the conclusion that Betty's indiscretions with Regan Belshaw was not just their knowledge, but Petey's too, although he hadn't expounded on it since. Maybe this was it.

"What about Betty?" he waited with bated breath.

"We're having problems in that department…" he jerked his head towards Bob's own todger. "…. I seem to have lost it Bob, you know, the urge. Well, I get the feeling but nothing happens, it sort of wil…"

"Right son …" Bob harrumped, "…erm are you sure this is something you want to be talking to me about? I mean, you know

I always take the piss, lighten it a bit, you might need, say a Doc's help, someone to take it seriously," he helpfully offered as he tried to hasten the flow.

Jeez, being a shoulder to cry on for personal stuff was okay in the canteen, in the bar or the pub, but not in the bogs!

Petey was undeterred, his Sherman Peabody eyes once again magnifying behind his glasses. "She called it erectile disfunction, can you believe that? Erectile disfunction! I tried to sort of play it down a bit, I was dead embarrassed. I said to her, now look Betty, it's no biggie…."

Smirking, Bob glanced down at Petey's todger still on display and couldn't help himself. "Aye, apparently not, son…!"

Cyril Hislop broke out into a sweat. Standing in the queue, impatiently waiting his turn, he had an overwhelming urge to scratch under his armpit again. There were only two old biddies ahead of him now, so hopefully he wouldn't have to wait much longer, he just wanted to get his money and get the hell out of there.

His bulbous eyes scanned the mahogany wood panelled interior of Westbury Loan & Savings Bank. He wiped his forehead and top lip with a grubby, off-white handkerchief before shoving it back in his pocket. Could they be watching him now, right this very minute? He knew Mrs Jones, it definitely wasn't her, she was a blind as a bat and could hardly string two words together let alone write a blackmail demand. His head snapped to the side so he could glare at the middle-aged man filling out a withdrawal slip at the back counter.

This is a bloody nightmare.

BLUES, TWOS AND BABY SHOES

'Pay up or face the consequences...' that's what the latest letter had said, and he knew only too well what the consequences for him would be. He shuffled forward.

'*£1,000.00 in twenty-pound notes, in a plain brown envelope before 1pm on Friday*'.

That wouldn't make much of a dent in his savings, but it was the principle of the matter, someone getting his hard-earned dosh for doing nothing more than digging up the past. What galled him even more was the drop-off location. Westbury St. Nicholas church of all places, during the Save the Roof Bring & Buy sale.

Cyril cringed at the thought of having to enter a church again, the last time had been on his wedding day to Clementine in 1958. The years of debauchery, drinking, smoking and foul language that followed from their blissful reunion had prompted her to warn him of the fire and brimstone retribution by Him upstairs, should Cyril ever venture over the threshold of a sacred sanctuary again. He hadn't even bothered with a church service for Clementine's passing, opting for the budget *Bag, Burn & Bury* mode of despatch.

"Morning Mr Hishlop, what can we do for you today?" Hairy Mary McIntyre had been with the bank ever since she'd been made redundant along with a herd of Jersey cows and two milk floats, from her accounting job at the local Dairy. A little woman with greying hair, large owl-like glasses and a very unfortunate top set of dentures. Her carefully cultivated upper lip hair was legendary too, talked about in the nooks and crannies of The Ship pub on nights when there was no gossip to be had. Cyril couldn't drag his eyes away, the bristly hairs undulating as she spoke.

"Mr. Hishlop *peep*…shir?" Her denture whistled the 's' in both words before dropping down onto her bottom lip. She hastily pushed them back into place with her tongue.

'*Dignitash*…. a Support Group for women with facial hair!' That thought popped into his head from nowhere, making him laugh out loud. He quickly caught himself.

Mary glared at him. "Ish *peep* it a deposhit or a *peep* withdrawal, Mr. *peep* Hishlop?" she waited, head cocked to one side.

Three whistles this time, he didn't know if he could carry on with his poker face, his giggle muscles were starting to spasm. "Withdrawal please Hai…err Mary." He slid the cheque underneath the glass partition into the shiny metal money bin. "How are things with you?" he needed to pass time, look normal.

She slid the drawer over and swept the cheque towards her. Cyril watched her face as she took in the amount he'd scrawled in the top right-hand corner.

"Very good, Mr Hishlop *peep*, it'sh *peep* all shwimming along nishely *peep, peep*." Four whistles that time, she'd actually incorporated the 'c' in *nicely*. She grabbed a thick wad of notes from her side drawer and slipped off the paper band, ready to count them. "I've been shecretary *peep* of the Weshtbury *peep* Shoroptimisht Shoshiety *peep* shince *peep* Sheptember *peep*, you kn…."

That was just one 's' too much, without further warning, once *September* had been uttered, Mary's top set of dentures gave up the ghost, toppled out and dropped with a resounding clatter onto the shiny brown blotter in front of her, they teetered, rolled and then plopped into the money bin. Cyril thought he was going to burst if he couldn't find an outlet for his laughter. Spluttering, his mind racing to think of anything he could say to diffuse the situation, he came out with the first thing that entered his head.

"That's nice Mary, always good to be involved and get your teeth into something…" he guffawed as she frantically tried to retrieve her gum-beaters from the tray, a look of horror quickly masked by annoyance crossing her face.

"You could at leasht have the deshenshy to pretend you hadn't notished!" she growled, as her hand scooped the offending dentures up.

Cyril chortled to himself, he'd actually quite fancied telling her not to *bristle* with indignation but seeing the way she had just rammed her teeth back in whilst giving him a glacial stare, he thought better of it.

BLUES AND TWOS

"Well Mum, your gorgeous grandson is giving Joe the run-around, I don't think he can cope with anymore poopy nappies, I've never known a baby produce so much!" I pushed the stem of the red rose through the brass hole in the bowl and used the edge of my hand to wipe away a leaf that had fallen onto the black granite. "We've given him Dad's middle name so he's now called Benjamin Arthur, you'd adore him, I know you would, he's growing into a right cheeky little chap."

As I arranged the last of the roses, carefully making sure they didn't hide Mum's name, the first tear fell. I angrily brushed it away with the heel of my hand. Surely after all this time I shouldn't be crying over her grave.

I miss you terribly Mum, the world is so dreadfully quiet without you.

"Your great-granddaughter Daisy is just adorable, but I suppose you already know that, hey?" My voice wobbled, I tried to smile, but it was more of a grimace as I desperately tried to stop my own version of Niagara Falls from making a show of me in the middle of the churchyard. I gave a furtive glance around the tilted headstones, towards the path and arched gate, relieved to see I was still the only one here. "I'm going back to work, I have to, I'll go insane if I don't. Honest Mum, I've tried but your Agatha is driving me nuts, her malapropisms are worse than yours and Dads put together!" I wrapped the cut off stems in the cellophane, ready for the bin. "Can't believe for all these years I thought she was up there with you causing total mayhem, driving God to consider a transfer down below, but all along she was alive and biding her time to come and bloody torment me!"

I waited for her answer, not in the physical world, but in my head, my promise to keep her with me.

'I will give you the words you need, for then you will always be alive in my heart.'

The warm sun dappled through the trees resting on my face as I closed my eyes, a wood pigeon, loudly flapping its wings echoed through the churchyard, the ripple causing a flock of starlings to take flight.

….and then she was there.

Oh Mavis, she is truly a dreadful woman, full of naughtiness, wrongdoings and suppository remarks to people….

And suddenly I'm laughing, just as I always did when Mum had imparted her worldly advice and musings.

…I'm not gone Mavis, as long as I'm a pigment of your imagination, I'll always be here.

"Joe, quickly I need your help!" I took another deep breath and tried again. Grabbing the metal clasp on my trouser zip, I pulled. Sweat was starting to form on my forehead from the effort. It didn't budge, not even a centimetre. I'd managed the buttons, but try as I might, the rest of the material wouldn't meet, my grossly wobbly mummy-tummy was flopped, squashed and on display through the gaping hole, beautifully framed by the brass teeth of the zipper on either side. I prodded. Somewhere in there was a belly button.

"Hurry up or I'm going to be late for my first day back…" I sat down onto the bed, trying to find relief, but quickly realised my mistake. The strain was just too much for the waistband.

Snap… pop…. ping….

One button would have been unlucky – but two at the same time was actually quite funny. They propelled themselves through the air just as Joe walked through the bedroom door.

"Owwwww Jesus, Mave…" his hand flew up to his eye, "…what the feck was that?" he checked himself in the mirror. "Look at that, it's swollen and red, I could go blind!"

"Oh, grow up, it hardly touched you, you're such a wimp," I snapped, all humour in the situation gone. If it wasn't bad enough that I couldn't fit into my combat pants, the strain on my XL shirt was even worse. I looked like a badly stuffed cushion. Each boob was vertically divided in two by my bra and the middle shirt button was barely able to contain the avalanche of flesh that was straining to escape.

Joe sat beside me and gently took my hand. That one show of affection was the final straw, I started to cry. "I'm worried about leaving Ben, I can't fit into anything… and not just my clothes…" I blubbed. Blowing my nose, the snort ricocheted from the four walls. "… I mean, where will I even fit in on the Section when I get back to work, I've been gone that long?" A sob caught in my throat as the tears fell.

"Oh Mave, Ben will be fine, wasn't Ella always fine?" He tilted my chin upwards and kissed the tip of my nose. "You were a single mum in the early days of the job and you did it, and as for work, they can't wait to have you back, it'll be just as it always was. Don't ever forget, we're a family here at home and we're a family at work; we got this from every angle."

I sniffed like a petulant child. He was right, I'd had tougher times, I'd fought to get this far, why on earth was I giving up so easily? This wasn't the strong, resilient, albeit slightly nutty, Mavis Jane Upton I'd carefully crafted and created over the years.

Right, you old boot, pull up those big girls knickers and let's kick ass...

"Big knickers!!!" It was like a eureka moment.

"What?"

"Big, humongous, hold-it-all-in knickers," I breathlessly squealed, jumping to my feet, leaving Joe sitting opened mouthed on the bed.

My head disappeared into the wardrobe as I launched a tsunami of clothing from the depths of the fitted drawers. Flinging them around, my heart skipped a beat as my fingers gently caressed the familiar material.

"Voila!" I waved them in the air.

"Feck me, we've just had a total eclipse..." Joe doubled up laughing as the massive expanse of cloth obscured the window.

Hopping around the bedroom, I kicked off my combats, felt around for the dental-floss sides of my old thong and quickly discarded those too with a flourish. They landed on the bedside lamp, I squealed in delight, it was like winning hoopla at the local fairground. Joe looked on in awe as I disappeared into the bathroom.

"Wow, you haven't flung your underwear around the bedroom for me in ages..." he breathlessly panted, "...have you got time for a firkle?"

The seconds ticked by in silence.

"Mave, firkle... a bit of rumpy-pumpy, fancy it?" His excited voice went up a few decibels, unsure if I'd heard him the first time.

"Taaaaa daaaaaa..."

I slinked into the bedroom, shimmying my now beautifully

contoured body, tightly held together by an elasticated pair of *HOLYSNOW Butt Lifter Magic Knickers.*

Joe freaked as soon as he saw the two large, specially tailored holes in the back for each cheek to poke out of, the sling effect pulling them up to a nice, pert level.

"Feck me, Mave… do you know your ass is hanging out?" he spluttered. "…you'll get frostbite in them there wobbly cheeks!"

I gave him my perfectly crafted death stare, cocking my head to one side. "Firkle Joe? Isn't that what you fancied a few moments ago?"

A look of sheer panic crossed his face. "Think I've changed my mind, my little pumpkin…." He started to make his escape, lunging for the bedroom door. "… in fact I think I'd rather have a do-it-yourself moment and really risk going blind than cavort with you wearing that!" he snorted as he disappeared onto the landing.

"Yeeeeoooooooooow…"

Oh gosh, I haven't lost my touch after all….

Amazing how far you can fling a SWAT boot AND still find your target.

"Yay, welcome back chick!" Marion Dewsbury threw her arms out, offering me a welcome hug.

"Maz! I thought you'd retired." I slammed my locker door shut and reciprocated, my chin resting on the new and very different epaulet she was wearing. "What happened? Please don't tell me you've come back as a civvy just so you can solve the *Dunkable Biscuit Quest*!" Laughing I hugged her tighter.

"Managed six months out and was bored to tears and having to endure 24/7 with the old twat at home was just too much." She exaggeratedly mimicked a look of horror. "So as soon as this came up, Call Handler in the control room, I was up for it. Been back two months now."

I lifted my body armour up to my nose and gave it a sniff. Not too bad considering it had been in storage in the tiny locker for nearly twelve months. I'd either washed or dry cleaned the rest of my kit and was good to go.

"Must admit, as much as I loved having time off with Ben – and Ella and Daisy too, it's great to be back." I hoisted my utility belt over my shoulder and checked my handcuffs were still running smooth through the ratchets.

Sirens suddenly set up in the back yard, their howling melody drifting through the open window at the bottom of the locker room. The hairs stood up on my arms as goosebumps prickled their way across my skin. This was what I'd been missing, it never failed to bring me alive.

"Cuppa before we start shift? We've got plenty of time," Marion offered, pushing the door to the night kitchen open.

"Yeah, why not!"

It was nice to be back in familiar territory. Nothing had changed, for all that concern I had felt gnawing away it me, it was still the same. A dirty, damp tea towel that nobody could be bothered to pick up was crumpled on the floor by the fridge, pools of tea, coffee, milk and probably bodily fluids knowing this lot, decorated the large table. A half-eaten biscuit had been left teetering on the corner of the draining board, the sink full of chipped mugs that had no doubt been accumulating since I was last here.

Picking up the dishcloth, I smiled. Dry, crusty and threadbare in places. I filled the kettle up and set out a couple of clean mugs that were almost hidden in the back of the cupboard.

"Surprised Beryl has let this happen..." I nodded towards the sink.

"She didn't, haven't you heard?" Marion looked surprised. "Beryl's been seconded to a serious crimes unit over the water. Temporary posting, but they needed her expertise."

I saw that spark in her eyes, a flash of anger quickly followed by a sadness. I recognised it only too well and knowing Beryl's specialist training, my heart also sank. "Child Protection?"

"Yep, the worst kind." Marion poured the boiling water into the mugs. "You've got a new Sarge on your section now..." she grimaced and rolled her eyes, "...still no sugar?" Giving a sideways glance to my combat pants, she smirked. "Had a bit of a struggle did we?"

"Jeez, don't even go there, it was more of a bloody battle if I'm honest. You don't lose baby weight as quickly when you're a geriatric; I had to borrow Joe's spare combats, nothing else would fit me." I took a swig of my tea. "Is it that obvious?"

She grinned. "I think it's the 10" turn-ups on each leg that gives it away. Bit of a difference between 6'3" and 5'3", Mave." She shoved a plate towards me, a mixture of digestives, ginger nuts and fig rolls were randomly piled high.

I shook my head. "Definite diet and some gym time to boot, it's horrendous what having a baby does to your body, you'd be howling if you knew what I was wearing underneath this lot."

"Oh come on, you look amazing, girls half your age couldn't boast looking like you after having a sprog," she giggled. "It'll all snap back into place soon enough."

I loved her optimism. "Maz, my lovely friend, after expelling what was akin to a bloody bowling ball, my poor vagina looks like a Bloodhound in a wind tunnel. Believe me... that'll never *snap* back!"

Our laughter could be loudly heard winding along the corridors of Westbury nick.

It was so good to be back.

BLUES, TWOS AND BABY SHOES

FATHER FORGIVE ME

Cyril had parted with his money.

Just like that. £1,000 of his hard-earned dosh, gone. And now he had that bloody detective whatever his name was, sniffing around. He'd left the money exactly where he'd been told to, wrapped in a brown paper bag, next to the knitted tea cosies and crochet doilies on the middle table in front of the church organ. He had wanted to wait and see who would pick it up, but circumstances beyond his control meant he had to beat a hasty retreat.

He scratched his groin, went to sniff his fingers and quickly changed his mind, Christmas was still a long way off for the bath he'd been promising himself. Armpits were one thing; sniffing an excitable crotch scrape was something totally out of the ballpark. He bent down to fork the jellied cat food onto the plate.

"Thomas, come get it…" he huffed, chinking the side of the plate as a calling.

Clementine had been mistaken over the fire and brimstone bit, he hadn't self-combusted on the threshold of Westbury St. Nicholas church, but he had spotted something pretty evil draped over the font that had almost made the arse drop out of his pants.

Agatha Hortensia Winterbourne.

The cat slinked into the kitchen, curling himself around Cyril's left leg. He gave him a cursory rub behind the ears. "Blast from the past, eh Tom? That was a woman you'd happily ride into battle..." He snorted at his own joke. "...trouble with a capital T that one, there's gonna be a few unhappy faces around here, I can tell you."

He couldn't help but wonder if Agatha's unexpected return from the dead had something to do with his current predicament.

"If that's the case, then I can tell yer this for now't Tom, I won't be the only one parting with money!"

Once again, he heard the cat flap rattle in its frame.

So much for that bloody cat being company and listening to his woes, he'd actually got more satisfaction talking to Clementine that fateful day until, much to his disappointment, the Undertakers had arrived to take her away.

Cora patted a stray piece of hair back into place and gently pinched both her cheeks to bring a slight glow to her complexion. Funny how having something exciting in your life, something to look forward to each day – other than her stints at *Junk & Disorderly* – could change how she viewed herself.

No more the wilting wallflower. Cora May Spunge was making waves!

She sat down at her little desk, rearranged the silver-plated frame which held the aged photo of her beloved Harold. Beloved he truly was, after all, she had loved him even though she had been a little disappointed in what he had offered her, how he had allowed her to live her life. A life where she had spent each waking day agreeing with him. She slid her diary towards her and opened it at the *Things to Do* page, pressing the sheet down, the words already written making her secretly smile with delight.

Edna Flaybrick.......... £1,000

Cyril Hislop............. £1,000

Picking up her Parker pen she carefully placed a neat tick against Cyril's name, it matched the one against Edna's. She liked things to be balanced.

"I truly thought I was going to have problems with him, my dear Barnaby, he didn't settle his debt straight away, did he?" She opened her *Little Book of Misdeeds, Sins & Mishaps* at the next marked page. "I suppose in this day and age it's not the worst sin is it, cheating on Clementine and fathering a child with a teenager? But it was what came after, that was the bigger sin, don't you think?" As expected, Barnaby didn't reply, he just gave her a lofty look of indifference from the bookshelf where he had found a comfortable spot between the warmth of the table lamp and a large, musty tome.

Oh yes, Cyril had been quite the one in his day, what was it they used to say?

Cora wagged her finger, knowingly. "That was it, he couldn't keep it in his pants, Barnaby, old Cyril was quite the womaniser back then. So sad to think because of his bullying ways and threats, that baby was horribly abandoned and then given up for adoption, according to my little book." She could have more from Cyril if truth be known, since discovering further information about the infant it could all prove quite fruitful to her endeavours.

"Right, less of this slacking, let's get back to business…." She placed the single sheet of lavender paper into the feed roller of her pale blue Smith Corona typewriter.

Turning to her book, she started to read.

"My, oh my Barnaby, another juicy one!"

DRESS TO IMPRESS

"**I**t's Private Benjamin, get the best biscuits out!" Bob grinned, the remnants of the pink wafer he was eating were glued to the front of his teeth. "Welcome back, we've saved the washing up for you," he guffawed.

I pulled the chair out from under the parade table and plonked myself down next to him. "So I see…." My elbow shoved the discarded internal envelopes, screwed up bits of paper and yesterday's Intel Report into the middle. "…nothing's changed then?" I teased as I started to underline the day and date in my pocket notebook. "It's great to be back though!"

Silence.

I looked up to see the suddenly miserable faces of Bob, Degsy, Don, Charlie Falmer, Mark Wallington and Petey. Petey looked as though he was ready to burst into tears.

"What's the matter with you lot, is me coming back so bad?" I was starting to feel a little bit unwanted, a bit like a fart in a spacesuit. I searched each of their faces in turn. Degsy was the first to speak.

"Not you, Mave…" he jerked his head towards the open door, "…we'll tell you later." He brought his index finger up to his mouth, hushing me.

I did my usual and blew upwards at my fringe, wondering what on earth could be so awful that it could reduce this shower of

  BLUES, TWOS AND BABY SHOES

normally loveable, loud and funny guys to a miserable version of the seven dwarves minus Happy.

I didn't have long to wait for an answer.

One look at Sergeant Alan Ballcock as his bulk filled the room was enough for me to suddenly develop an unnerving twitch to my left eye. No wonder the lads were subdued, his reputation went before him, and part of that reputation was his intolerance of female police officers. I say *intolerance* as a kindness, he actually despised us.

Oh gawd, first day back and I've got a twatbadger for a sergeant!

He threw his paperwork on the table and grunted loudly. "Right, Bob, Derek – AR12 Refs 1800 hours, Don, Custody Suite needs an extra pair of hands, get AR12 to drop you off, don't want a car sitting there for the whole shift. Charlie, you take Petey, AR11, and don't let him fuck anything up for a change, hey?" He intently examined the sheet of paper in front of him. "Take your refs at 1900, Mark, Mavis AR13, refs 2000 hours." His eyes, bulbous, swept the table.

Scrawling our call sign and refs in my book, I caught Mark's eye, giving him a sheepish grin, I curled my lip and rolled my eyes.

"Don't know what your smirking at Upton, thank your lucky stars we're short on drivers or you'd be walking the beat or the best place for women, covering the front office!" He rammed his folder under his arm and disappeared through the door, not even bothering to give a backwards glance.

"Oooh you've got a fan there, Mave..." Degsy chuckled, "...you'll be on his Christmas card list in no time." He tipped his chair back onto two legs and craned his neck, making sure the Sarge wasn't in earshot. I found myself doing the same, more out of incredulity than anything else whilst giving my famous death stare to his back as he disappeared down the corridor.

"Did he really just say that?" I was gobsmacked. "We're in the twenty-first century of policing not the dark ages, what the feck have I done to upset him, I know he hates women in the job, but my feet are barely back under the bloody table."

"Calm down, calm down, Mave…." Mark gave his best Scouse impression, wobbling his head so the curls on the top bounced backwards and forwards, "…he's just living up to his nickname, that's all. Don't take it personally."

Jeez, how much more personal could it get, this is only the start, I know it!

"And what nickname would that be?" I waited with bated breath, indignation still bubbling under the surface.

"Thrush…"

"Thrush…. why?" Half expecting what would come next, my mouth twitched, stifling a giggle.

Mark started laughing. "Oh, just because he's an irritating twat!"

"Ah, correct…" I grabbed my briefcase, shoving the shed load of paperwork that had accumulated during maternity leave into the inside pocket. "…so that must mean he's the only man in history to have all three parts of both the male and female anatomy to his name!" I snorted, "Suits him, he's such a fecking bellend!" I kicked down hard on the door stop to free the open door as I made my way into the corridor.

"Mavis Upton!!" Bob jokingly gasped, "Well, I never, our Mavie's vocabulary is at last getting more colourful."

Petey's face lit up as he joined in the banter. "Yeah, that just about sums him up, you're right, testicles, todger and err…. toes?"

The collective groans followed by laughter were proof that our mutual camaraderie, even with the horror of Ballcock being our new sarge, was still alive and kicking.

BLUES, TWOS AND BABY SHOES

Mark initialled the petrol column, shoved the Vehicle Logbook back into the glove compartment and threw his flat cap onto the back seat. "Was it hard leaving the little one to come to work, Mave? I remember Di feeling out of sorts for a few weeks when she went back."

I pushed the car into first gear and edged out from the rear yard onto Manor Road, the windscreen wipers smeared an arc across the glass as the screen wash went to work. "A little bit, but to be honest because Joe's with him, it doesn't feel as though I've abandoned him to a childminder, think it's going to be tiring juggling the shifts and motherhood again though."

He nodded in agreement, pensive in thought. After a few minutes, he sighed. "Don't let *Cockbollocks* get to you, he's a dinosaur. We all know what he's like, he can't get away with it much longer, someone's bound to dob him in."

Pulling into Cutters Camp Site, the full beam of my headlights picked up the single track, bouncing back from the hedgerows, lighting an arc into the tall oak trees. "I know, but who is going to stick their neck out and report him, none of the girls want to do it. Who wants to be the one that shouts '*discrimination*' and if the true facts don't get passed around the other nicks, you suddenly become a pariah!"

Mark grunted. "Aye, I suppose you're right, but everyone knows what he's like, Christ, even the bosses must know, he makes no secret of it. We'll always stick up for you, Mave, you know that don't you?"

A fox bolted from the greenery on my offside, I gently braked, giving him time to get across. He disappeared into the dense undergrowth. "Thanks, I appreciate it, but nobody would want to work with me through choice after that, they'd be terrified I was a career complainer to climb the ladder and that they'd be your next victim." I gave him a wry smile. "Nope, I'll handle it myself if needed, no need to go making an issue of it just yet."

The natural silence that we often shared between us when 'hunting', enveloped the car. I dipped the lights, bringing the car slowly into the first car park. The tyres crunched on the cheap crush & run the council had thrown down. A full circuit, picking out the bushes with the roof bar side beam was completed with a negative search.

Mark unwrapped a mint humbug and popped into his mouth. "Did you hear about Petey when they sent him up this end to look at the Dogging problem? Nobody thought to explain the 'public sex with an audience angle' to him…" He made air quotes with his sticky fingers. "…I mean for crying out loud, he's an adult, you shouldn't have to, should you?" He started to choke on the sweet, coughing and spluttering.

I gave him a hefty slap on the back. "I'm surprised they let him loose up here, to be honest."

"Yeah, me too. Well, anyway, he comes up here, catches quite a few of them at it, a real coitus interruptus. He tells them to put their clothes on and then bugger me, he does no more than produce with a flourish a handful of *Bonio* dog biscuits from his pocket and asks where their dogs are!" Another lung crushing bout of coughing followed, along with a snort of laughter that sounded like a donkey braying.

"D'you know, as much as Ballcock is praying on my mind, you guys never fail to lift my spirits, thanks matey!" I hit the headlights again to take us to the next car park. "It's pretty Q down here, maybe the cold is keeping them inside tonight."

"Can't think of anything worse than flashing your bits and

chancing frostbite for a quick shag, can you?" He shoved a half-eaten flapjack into his mouth. "Having said that…" he coughed again, splattering crumbs all over the dashboard and the centre console, "…it could be worse, you could be the one that's watching doing a bit of DIY without yer gloves on!" That set off another bout of laughter.

"Jeez, mate, don't you ever stop eating?" I chided. "Hey up, what have we got here?" I swept the headlights towards the far corner, a solitary car glinted out of the darkness. "Get the reg just in case it does one." I pulled in at an angle across the front of the dark coloured Mitsubishi Animal. The lights picked out a solitary, startled occupant, the whites of his eyes acting as beacons in the darkness.

I started to snigger.

When will they ever learn?

"Good evening Sir, just checking that you're okay, we've had various reports of untoward activity around this car park." I could hear Mark taking the mickey out of my use of 'untoward activity', mouthing the words and making rude gestures at the rear of the Mitsubishi. Ignoring him, I kept a straight face and carried on. "So, whilst my colleague makes a check on your vehicle, I can run your details, and if all's well, you can be on your way as soon as." I paused, waiting for his response. He seemed a fairly decent chappie, and from what I could see through the high driver's window, he was well dressed. Red and black tartan brushed cotton shirt with a black leather waistcoat, designer stubble, neatly cut hair. No alarm bells were ringing yet.

"Oh dearie me, gosh erm…. yes, okay erm…oh dear," he squeaked, beads of sweat appearing across his top lip. He nervously brushed them away with the back of his hand, his voice quickly dropping a few octaves with his next sentence. "Yes, my name's

Desmond Alexander Ashford date of birth 27th April 1978, miss."

He'd just finished his sentence with 'miss' - now that did ring an alarm bell.

I shouted up the details, including the address he'd provided, Heidi's response in the control room was pretty instant. "Yep, thanks Heidi…" I clicked off. "Okay, Desmond, now if you'll just step out of the car for me, please." I waited.

"Why? I haven't done anything, why do I have to get out, I've got rights you know?" He was becoming more and more flustered, perspiration dripping down the sides of his face.

"Well according to the details you've just given Desmond, you've got a no bail warrant outstanding for you, fail to appear for theft from last year, bad luck mate!" Mark unclipped his handcuffs. "Now if you'd just like to do as my colleague asked, and step out of the vehicle…"

Slowly the driver's door to the Mitsubishi opened, a hiatus of several seconds passed before one hairy leg clad in fishnet stockings gracefully unfurled itself from the leather interior. The foot was encased in a size 11 bright pink patent leather stiletto shoe that crunched the gravel as it tentatively touched terra firma. It was quickly followed by a second leg and foot attired the same, making a matching pair.

What the actual fuck…….

Mark looked like he was going to expire on the spot from laughing, whilst I struggled to stop myself from actually howling like an idiot.

Desmond stood in all his glory, hand on hip, his black suspenders kissing the lace edge of a pair of black silk crotchless knickers, the whole lower ensemble flying in the face of his masculine upper half. I tried to drag my eyes away but couldn't, I was morbidly drawn to his ample tackle dangling through the gaping hole of what I could only describe as Primark's best *Secret Possessions* boudoir range of lingerie.

"It's Primark…!" I spluttered, which made Mark laugh even more. Poor Desmond was left standing in the middle of the car park, lit by my car headlights like a star turn at the local Social Club on a Saturday night, his previously semi-erect todger now miserably pointing South.

"Desmond, just get in the car…." Mark held open the rear door to the marked police car.

"Nooooooooooooo…" I squealed, making Desmond jump so high with fright he almost fell off his stiletto's.

"What do you mean, no?" Mark looked baffled.

Desmond just froze.

"I'm not have his meat and two veg slathering themselves across the upholstery in my car, it's disgusting, haven't you got anything to put on Desmond?"

He shook his head.

"Jumper, coat, sack, dirty magazine…. anything, even a bloody newspaper to sit on?"

He continued to shake his head, almost on the verge of tears.

"Get hold of him." I disappeared into the boot of the patrol car. "Voila, this will have to do." Holding up a reel of blue and white 'Police' tape I began to unravel it, fluffing it up until it covered the back seat. "Now you can sit down, but don't you dare fart…." I wagged a finger at him, he just looked more embarrassed by the minute. "…and I hope you wipe properly too, I can't be doing with skid marks."

Now it was Mark's turn to look mortified. "Mave, behave!!"

"What?"

He jerked his head towards Desmond, hunched in the back.

"Okay, okay…" I put my hands up, easing myself back into

the drivers seat. "...but just in case you hadn't noticed, his hairy chakras have fallen through the tape and are currently nestled inside your hat!"

Marks face was a picture, all empathy for Desmond's predicament gone. "Jesus lad, pick 'em up and find somewhere else to rest them, will you?"

I bit down on a snigger, there was no way that hat would ever grace his head again after Desmond's bits had been cupped in the lining. Something told me that once back at the nick all evidence of Mark's ownership would be erased from the inner headband before being sneakily swapped with someone else's.

"Custody has already been cleared and a marker put on his vehicle, he's happy for it to stay there, aren't you, Desmond?" Mark half turned waiting for confirmation.

Desmond didn't reply, holding his head in his hands, he stared at the floor.

"Come on Des, it's not all bad, you'll be kept in overnight, breakfast in the morning and straight to court." Trying to make a stay in one of our cells sound like a stay in a Premier Inn was difficult, but I kept on. "You'll even have your own en-suite bog!"

He groaned, shaking his head in disbelief. "Me name's not Desmond, it's Barry, Barry Fortune, check me out, I gave you me mates' details because I'm a disqualified driver..." he let out a guttural grunt, acknowledging his own stupidity, "...it's his car too, can't believe soft lad never told me he was fecking wanted for thieving!"

There you go - Fortune by name but not fortunate by nature!
Gosh I love my job!

SECRETS

Joe checked the alarm clock. "Mave, it's eight-thirty…"

I moaned, barely able to open my eyes. My head felt like it would explode with the dense heaviness of sleep deprivation, courtesy of Benjamin and his nocturnal playtime. Every time he'd been soothed to sleep, I'd barely managed thirty seconds back in bed with my head on the pillow, before he was off again.

"I'm too old for all this," I whimpered, hoping for sympathy. When none was forthcoming, I threw back the duvet and half rolled, half fell out of bed. "I'll never cope with Auntie Agatha today…" I checked my hair in the mirror and stuck my tongue out to see if anything disgusting had fermented on it during the night. "…could being tired, hormonal with a baby-brain be a defence for murder, Joe?" I had visions of suffocating Agatha with one of the pink and orange cushions from her sofa.

"What, like a lapse of sanity, a moment of madness?"

"Yes, yes exactly like that!"

"Nope, you don't have moments of madness my little turnip…"

"Aww, even after all these years, you're so sweet, Mr Blackwell," I cooed.

"…you're just mad full stop, so there's no defence in a temporary breakdown is there?"

I hit him with the pillow, knocking him backwards so his head bounced off the wooden bedhead. "Right, might as well face the old boot, get it over and done with and then we can enjoy the rest of our day off together. How about taking Benjamin to the park and then a pub lunch?"

"Sounds good to me, chickpea."

"Here you go Mavis, a nice cup of tea." Agatha set the cup and saucer down on the psychedelic tablecloth in the small kitchen and pushed a side plate laden with buttered toast towards me. "Thought you might like a little nibble to start the day." She busied herself returning the butter tub to the fridge, shutting the top cupboard door as she passed it.

Her dress sense hadn't much improved. Todays ensemble was a red, highly patterned full-length skirt which undulated each time she changed direction, topped by a purple velvet jacket and a green scarf that was pinned at the front by a silver brooch in the shape of a pentagram. A small amethyst bead sat at the head of the pin. I looked down as she shuffled back to the table. Those ghastly tangerine T-bar shoes were still clinging pitifully to her feet too. I wistfully thought back to Mum's favourite poem, *When I Am an Old Woman I Shall Wear Purple*, she had loved the idea of growing old and becoming acceptably outrageous. Just the thought of her dressed as Agatha was, brought out old Larry the Lump. I swallowed, trying to dislodge it and stop the onset of tears, but they pricked and sparkled all the same.

Gosh Mum, would this have been you, would you have looked this way if you had been allowed to grow old?

Pulling my emotions into check, I forced a smile. "Thanks Agatha, I was in a bit of a hurry this morning, toast would be lovely.

So, how have things been, are you still happy here?" I wanted to sound interested, enthusiastic even, but in truth, I was just passing time with her. I was trying my hardest to be the type of niece she wanted me to be and failing dismally. I just couldn't forget how much hurt she had caused Mum all those years ago.

"Oh, you know, happy as I'll ever be I suppose…" she paused, looking around the kitchen, "…oh yes, that was it, would you like something on your toast? I've got some lovely lemon turd."

I almost choked on the mouthful of tea I'd just swigged. "Err, no thanks, think I'll give that flavour a miss, buttered is just fine." Nibbling at the end of the triangle, I watched her more closely. The defiance and spark in her eyes had gone, the vibrant colours she was wearing betrayed her heavy spirit. She quickly averted her eyes and looked down, her hands began to brush imaginary crumbs from the tablecloth.

"Agatha?"

She looked up, just as the tears began to fall onto her powdered cheeks. She pulled out a yellow handkerchief and dabbed under each eye. She truly was a rainbow.

"I'm sorry Mavis, I didn't intend this to happen, I was hoping I could manage on my own, but I can't, and time is running out…" she leant towards me, placing her hand on top of mine, "…" I have such a terrible secret and I need your help before I depart from this life."

"A secret love child, Joe!! Can you believe it?"

Joe manoeuvred the pushchair over the cobbles and down the slope. I followed behind him, flailing my arms like a windmill as I explained Agatha's 'terrible secret' to him in all the gory details. I was still gobsmacked that nobody, not even Mum, knew.

Joe, his head wobbling as the cobbles vibrated through the pushchair stayed silent.

"I mean, how can you do that? You carry a baby, give birth and then..." I took a deep breath to enable me to get the rest of my words out without expiring on the spot, "...she just gave it up, just like that. Left it in the foyer of The Winter Gardens Picture House whilst The Belles of St Trinians was playing!"

Leaning forward, Joe checked Ben hadn't succumbed to concussion from the cobbles, satisfied he was okay, he stood waiting for me to catch up before he spoke. "I don't know, desperation maybe, it was different in those days, the stigma was terrible back then."

"Not half as bad as it used to be in the 30's and 40's, still no excuse Joe, but my heart did break for her. She's distraught and wants to find them and say sorry, explain why she did what she did before she dies." My fingers felt for the notebook I'd hastily stuffed in my bag when I'd left Agatha's. Sitting down on a nearby bench, Joe put his arm around me. I watched Ben, his long lashes sweeping his cheek as he slept, one tiny hand peeping above the blanket, chubby fingers curled over the crochet edging.

I could never abandon you, my beautiful boy.

I opened the book Agatha had reverently pressed into my hand. Unfolding the aged yellow newspaper cutting, I spread it out for Joe to see and pointed at the relevant paragraph.

WINTER GARDENS BABY ABANDONED
'Only hours old, the child had been found by Norma Pattinson, 19-years, who worked the ticket box at The Winter Gardens, Alderney Road, Westbury'

Norma had apparently taken the opportunity whilst the film was in full flow to nip outside for a quick ciggie and a tryst with her boyfriend. Pushing open the inner doors, she had found the tiny baby wrapped in a white blanket in a cardboard box, left by a potted Areca Palm in the foyer.

I read out the next part of the article to him. "*The infant, a girl, was deemed to be a healthy weight and full term. She was taken to Westbury Cottage Hospital.*"

The date was Saturday, 17th April 1955

"Agatha wants me to help find her, I have to do this Joe, you understand don't you?"

Not another word was said between us. He gave my hand a gentle squeeze and softly kissed my cheek. I had his blessing.

BEATRICE

Jim Shakeshaft looked at the murky, brown mixture in his personalised *Mr Reet Wazzock* mug, a gift from his cousin in Yorkshire. Stirring it didn't improve its appearance, nor did three sachets of sugar, he actually wasn't sure if it was supposed to be tea or coffee. He bit into the cheese & onion pasty, catching the flaky bits in his hand before they landed on his trouser leg. In the absence of a bin, he threw them over his shoulder. He had nine investigations on the go, two could be filed pending further evidence, three were being passed back to uniform to deal with, which left him four cases to work on.

"Dave!" He waved one of the blue files above his head, shouting to the other end of the C.I.D office where Dave Aldred's desk was tucked away in the corner. He was relatively new to the department, an ideal candidate to take at least two of the four cases. Dave's head appeared above his computer screen. Standing up, he ran his hand through his hair. Jim wished he'd get it cut, or at least do something with the bloody floppy fringe he was sporting.

"Yep, Sarge."

"S.18 assault, uniform have taken first account statements, photographs of the injuries are in there too and there's a copy CCTV disc from the scene, it's worth looking at. Just waiting on forensics but we've got a name, yours for the taking." He handed the file to Dave, mentally ticking that one off his list.

Somewhat distracted, he didn't see me come in until the door banged shut. "Yo, Shakey, you wanted to see me?" I dragged a spare chair from the desk next to Jim, it wobbled precariously as I sat on it. "How are you enjoying the promotion?"

He grinned, wiping a sliver of cheese from his chin. "A lot more responsibility, but yeah, it's good, and less of the Shakey in front of the others, if you don't mind!" He winked and reached for a familiar file leaning against the side of the cabinet. "It's the Flaybrick/Hislop job, remember before you went off, the blackmail letters?"

I nodded. "Yep, what are the developments, anything come of it?"

"No, Edna Flaybrick aka Diamond D'Light, she definitely paid up, although we've still got no proof and Hislop went bandit on us. Refused to make a formal complaint, said it was all sorted and it had been a misunderstanding, a joke gone wrong, but we suspect he paid up too. We still don't know what the black was on him."

"This is Westbury, there's nothing, and I mean nothing you can discount, I've just discovered a member of my own family has a skeleton in the closet, well a huge one to be honest..." I snaffled a handful of crisps from his open packet and crammed them into my mouth. "...and I've got Sergeant Thrush on my back already, I've hardly been back five minutes."

"Good old Thrush, what did you lot do wrong to get him, hey? They actually had a leaving party at Moorcroft nick when he left to come here you know." Jim rolled his eyes.

"Really!" I was amazed that anyone could like him enough to give him a decent send off.

"He didn't go to it himself like; they waited until his car had left the yard and then the balloons, poppers, sausage rolls and flags came out!" We both doubled up laughing. It was nice to know that even the jacks thought he was a complete tool as well.

"Right, fun and laughter apart, I'll keep this job with me, it'll get filed, but just wanted to know if anything does come in that resurrects it, would you be interested in giving a helping hand, if needed, it's right up your street?" He flashed what he thought was a smile to charm the birds out of the trees.

"Jim, mate…. if you're trying to flatter and charm me, you really do need to remove the chunks of onion between your front teeth, it's seriously not a good look!" I pointed at the offending tooth.

He frantically rubbed his tongue underneath his top lip. "Better?" he grinned like the Cheshire Cat waiting for my approval.

"Yep, better, now all you need to address is the heavy fall of dandruff on your shoulders, it shows up a bugger on a dark suit."

He flicked his hand across his left shoulder. "It's flaky pastry; it's from my pasty, I chucked it behind me before you came in."

"Yeah, yeah, yeah, that's what they all say. Head & Shoulders Shakey, Head & Shoulders!" I danced around his desk and grabbed another handful of his crisps. "Seriously, no worries, of course I'll help, you'll just have to clear it with Thrush first, he'll listen to you," I shouted before disappearing through the double doors.

Jumping the stairs two at a time, I made my way to the floor below and the night kitchen. Bob and Degsy had nipped to the chippy for scoff and there was a portion of Salt & Pepper chips waiting for me.

Passing the noticeboard, I stopped to read the latest postings and role applications. C.I.D were looking for Trainee Investigators again. They had quite a turnaround, those that couldn't stick it and those that went on to bigger things in specialist departments.

I sighed.

As much as I loved being uniform and out and about in the

thick of it, if things panned out badly with old Thrush, then that might be an option I'd have to consider.

Beatrice Higgins finished plumping up the cushions on her bed and gave one last sweep of her hand across the quilted counterpane. Satisfied her pink and white haven was spick and span, she tightened the belt on her cream satin couture dressing gown, slipped her toes into the extra-large fluffy mules and pattered out through the french doors onto the veranda that serviced her bedroom. Gracefully settling herself into the chair, she crossed her legs at the ankles, turned them ever so slightly to the left and haughtily stretched her neck.

The early morning sun cast dancing colours and shadows through the trees in the garden below, two white doves romantically locked heads in the dovecot. This blissful scene awaited her each morning. She took a sip of the Darjeeling tea that dear Maddie, her live-in, had brought her. Carefully replacing the china cup onto the saucer, it barely made a sound as it settled back into the small round dip.

Beatrice loved days like this, when the world was at peace, when nature promised….

Oh my goodness!

Suddenly all hell broke loose, her perfect little world was, in the blink of an eye, about to be destroyed. She jumped up, her hip brushing against the little table knocking the cup and saucer onto the wooden decking with a clatter. A scream caught in her throat as her delicately manicured hand clutched her breast, threatening an attack of the vapours.

"Get that fucking cat out of my garden!" she bellowed, in a

voice several octaves down from her initial squeal. Grabbing the turquoise and orange Master Blaster Super Soaker water gun from behind the potted aspidistra, she took aim and fired towards the dovecot where the dastardly cat called Biff from next door, was creeping up on its prey. Her darling doves.

Pulling hard on the trigger, she hollered with triumph. "Take that you bastard…" as a forceful spurt of water sailed through the air, hitting its target.

Biff hadn't known what had hit him, he just knew that the one white feather he'd managed to retain in his claw was all he'd got from his early morning foray before he'd been gifted an enema of epic proportions. Lying on the grass he could do no more than watch two pairs of wings fluttering off into the distance.

Beatrice kept her eye on him for a while, wondering if she needed to reload. She didn't. Biff the Bastard Cat, wet, bedraggled and embarrassed, slunk off into the nearby hedges and jumped the wall. The temptation was there to give him another blast up the arse, but she resisted.

"A lady must never show too much exuberance should they, Maddie?" Beatrice fanned herself, trying to tame the flush of pink that had rushed to her cheeks. Maddie herself had flown to her aid on hearing the ear-piercing shriek followed by the destruction of yet another cup and saucer.

"No, Ma'am, they shouldn't Maddie obediently agreed, she offered that mornings mail to Beatrice and bent down to clear up the broken pieces of china.

"A lady should hold herself with elegance and act with decorum, isn't that right, Maddie?"

"Yes, Ma'am, they should." Giving a respectful nod, she picked up the tea tray and quietly padded across the bedroom, pausing briefly to gather up an item of clothing from the sheepskin rug.

Once out on the galleried landing, with the door shut behind her, Maddie let out a long sigh as she swung the jockstrap over her head like a helicopter blade.

"….. and you definitely ain't no lady, Ma'am!"

"11 seconds, it's holding…" Degsy proffered the fig roll for us all to see, "…that's it, lads and lasses, I've found the perfect dunker."

"Bollocks, the perfect dunker is one you can eat afterwards, that's only clinging on because it's stuffed with what looks like earwax." Bob grimaced.

I filled the kettle up and clicked the switch, busying myself with mugs, teabags and coffee, neatly lining them up on the melamine counter. Waiting for the water to boil, I stared out of the window, their chatter and banter becoming a muted background hum as my thoughts drifted elsewhere. It seemed like only yesterday that I had stood in this spot, staring out of the very same window, watching the rain hit the glass, trees snapping and bending with the wind, knowing my own mum had very little time left. Now I was doing the same again, but for a woman I hardly knew but was bound to me by blood and a sense of loyalty to Mum. Did I really want to be involved in her search for her daughter, who would it benefit? Both of them? One or the other of them or neither? I just didn't know.

"Penny for 'em, Mave." Bob stood behind me. "Not getting into soppy shit, nowt like that, but always here if you need an ear." He patted me on the back. "Now shift yer arse and get that tea made - and if you get chance don't forget to spit in Thrush's mug!"

I pulled a face. "Eeeew gross, I'm sure I can think of something more ladylike to get my own back!" I checked my own mug to make sure there was nothing floating in it, I loved these guys but didn't trust them one iota. Two days ago I'd found a plastic click frog from a Christmas cracker bobbing up and down in my coffee. I sat down next to Petey who, head down, was doodling in his notebook. I checked my watch. Another ten minutes before parade, plenty of time to chill before we all embarked on another ten hours of helping the residents of Westbury to live their lives and wipe their noses.

"So, anyone got anything special planned for the weekend off?" I took a sip of my tea waiting for a barrage of abuse and double entendres. Degsy was the first to offer his plans.

"It's Lil's birthday, so I suppose I'll have to do something or I'll never hear the end of it," he grumbled.

"What are you getting for her?" Mark made a grab for the last gingernut on the plate.

"That's kind of you mate, make me an offer and she's all yours!"

Our laughter was short-lived as Petey's voice cut through the ensuing banter.

"I think my Betty's having an affair."

I was half expecting the proverbial tumbleweed to suddenly appear and roll across the night kitchen, the sudden, shocked silence from us all was deafening. Nobody wanted to be the first to speak.

"Not now son, now's not the time." Bob, in his fatherly way, placed a hand on Petey's shoulder and gave a squeeze. "How about you and me having a pint after work, we can chat then, no interruptions, like?"

Petey nodded.

"Right you shower, parade room… now!" The unusually welcome interruption came from Thrush standing in the doorway, one look at his face and we all knew he was on a mission.

BLUES, TWOS AND BABY SHOES

I stood to make my way through.

"Not you Upton, get your hat, you're on a scene. Get someone to give you a lift, I don't want a car wasted down there." He thrust the print-out at me, leaving me standing in the corridor.

"Right lads, let's get down to business..." throwing his files onto the desk he turned, kicked down on the door stop and forcefully booted the door shut, not even attempting to hide the smirk on his face, "...now that's sorted, we can do what we men do best without the hindrance of women."

Standing on the other side of the closed door, anger bubbling just below the surface, my face flushed and hot, I desperately tried to keep control. One half of me wanted to storm in there and punch his lights out, the other half, my sensible half, told me to bide my time. I gave the door a middle finger salute.

I wouldn't go down without a fight. I hadn't come this far, fought for everything I had achieved for a bitter, nasty man to bully me.

A STITCH IN TIME...

I looked at the clock. 5.30 pm, plenty of time for a soak in the bath. The gorgeous black Karen Millen dress that Joe had bought me, hung from the back of the bedroom door.

Date night!

Ben was having a stop-over with Ella, who had assured me looking after two was no different than looking after one. I laughed and begged to differ, but I wasn't going to look a gift horse in the mouth. After the dreadful couple of days I'd had in work, courtesy of Thrush, this night out was going to be a welcome relief.

"Are you considering a sexy little number underneath that?" Joe angled between me and the wardrobe, hugging me around the waist as he nuzzled into my neck.

"Maybe," I teased, whilst really thinking *how the feck am I going to fit into that without five metres of bloody cling film wrapped tightly around my belly to hold it all in*'. "You'll have to wait, it'll be a surprise," I blagged with a wink. "Where are we going, you haven't told me yet?"

He took my hand and danced me around the bedroom. "Back to the place where I asked you to marry me, thought it would be very romantic and bring back heady memories of our youth and early love."

Jeez, that certainly wasn't how I remembered it.

  BLUES, TWOS AND BABY SHOES

My memory was the gut-churning embarrassment of me getting drunk, falling out of the toilets with my dress tucked into my knickers and the added bonus of several sheets of quilted toilet paper stuck to my bum, trailing behind me. I had been totally convinced Joe was trying to dump me with not an inkling that he was about to propose. Oh well, older and wiser, that sort of shenanigans wouldn't happen now, I'd matured, grown up, I was Mrs Sensible married to Mr Sensible.

Yikes, when did that happen?

I didn't want to be sensible, or boring or anything else that indicated getting old. I wanted to be fun, carefree and sexy.

This definitely called for the Anne Summers collection to come out of mothballs from the back of the wardrobe, hidden for the last god knows how many years. I waited until Joe had disappeared downstairs before bringing out my box of goodies.

Oooh red heart Nipple Tassels with diamantes, I could do that, they'd be fun.

I'd learnt to swing them years ago, I could even do circles and change direction. I put them to one side. Next out of the box was a black PVC all-in-one body suit. I checked the size, it would be a bit of a squeeze, but judging by the lack of give in the shiny material, this little number would certainly hold everything in.

Mmmmm, perfect!

I laid everything I would need onto the bed.

I'd definitely knock him dead with this lot.

I carefully opened the packet containing the tassels and swung them in each hand, the weight of them gave a nice rhythm on the orbit. Chuffed, I peeled back the sticky tape and tested it with my finger. One was good to go, the other had over the years, lost its tackiness, it barely clung to my finger. I had a quick rummage around in our junk drawer.

Eureka! An old tube of false eyelash glue. It was rolled up at the end and a bit congealed around the top, but there was definitely enough in there to do one tassel.

"Joe, I'm just going to have a bath, I'm doing a surprise, so don't go into our bedroom until I'm ready, will you?"

"Nope my little chipmunk, I'll wait down here with bated breath…"

Butterflies danced in my stomach. Joseph Stephen Blackwell you are in for such a treat….

"Would Madam like a drink whilst you are waiting to order?" The maître d' held out a wine list.

"Choose whatever you want Mave, this is our night." Joe's eyes glinted in the ambient glow cast from the rustic branch display between us. Four small tea-light candles sat amongst the twisted twigs and fake moss. The table was beautifully set in a quiet corner of the restaurant. I plumped for a large glass of Merlot, not wanting a repeat of my last visit here when I'd devoured a whole bottle and probably the dregs from Joe's glass too.

"Listen, it's Eternal Flame by The Bangles, I love this song, we danced to that on our wedding night." I gave him a cheeky wink.

A silence fell between us as we excitedly clutched our menu's, reading the gastronomic delights that were on offer.

"I think I'll have the steak, what about you?" he took a sip of his wine.

"Ooooh I think I'll have the same, shall we have a side salad too?"

"Whatever you want, my little love bug, the night is yours." He threw the menu down in front of him, took hold of my hand and romantically gazed into my eyes.

I had to hand it to him, he was pulling out all the stops. I was actually starting to feel quite a warm glow myself but couldn't figure out if it was because of my desire for him or the fact my skin was slowly welding itself to the black PVC bodysuit I'd squeezed into. The bloody nipple tassels weren't helping either, one of the diamantes had swivelled and was digging in. A prick of perspiration began to take hold underneath my fringe.

"You look positively on fire, Mave, you've got a real glow about you tonight." He growled, a grin taking over his whole face.

Jeez, no shit Sherlock, you want to try being encased in something that feels like an industrial fishpond liner, that'll make you glow.... profusely!.

I wriggled, trying move at least some skin to one side to provide a cooling air vent, which only confirmed my fear that the plastic was making me sweat, or is it perspire? That's it, men sweat, but ladies glow.

I was glowing quite a bit now.

Several seconds passed as Joe, still holding my hand, did his best to whisper sweet nothings to me. I sniffed the air.

"Err, Joe...."

"Yes darling."

"Can you smell something burning?"

"Only my desire for you, it'll be my very own eternal flame..."

I sniffed again. "No, don't be daft, I really can smell somethi...."

I squealed as wisps, which quickly became plumes of smoke, rose from his hastily discarded menu and...

Poof!

Flames suddenly began to flicker, higher and higher in the middle of the table.

"Shit Joe, it's the bloody menu, you've set the feckin' menu on fire with the tealights...."

All hell broke loose as the flickering flames spread from the menu, to the tinder dry twigs and fake moss display. I could only watch on in horror as it rippled across the table, igniting the tablecloth and my menu, forcing acrid smoke to curl its way up to the ceiling. A piercing alarm filled the room as the sprinkler system kicked in, showering me, Joe, the Maitre d' and several other diners as I looked on in horror.

Oh God, not again....

Joe shut the front door behind him, grabbing me, he pushed me against the console table and began to kiss my throat, I shivered with excitement. We were bedraggled, wet and cold, but we didn't care. Laughing, we ran like schoolkids upstairs to our bedroom.

"What a night," he breathlessly panted as he flopped onto the bed. "...we were definitely on fire, weren't we?"

I pulled the side zip down on my dress, it was clinging to the bodysuit. "We definitely can't go there again, they were very good about it though, they blamed their rustic display not us." I giggled.

My dress fell to the floor.

Suck it in Mave, suck it in....

I could barely breathe as I flattened out my stomach. "Are you ready for me Joe?"

His eyes almost popped out of his head.

"Oh wow.... just.... oh... come here gorgeous."

I wasn't finished. I had one more trick up my sleeve before he got his hands on me, a trick that would make up for our disastrous meal, one he'd never forget. I pouted and wagged my index finger at him.

"Just a little extra for you my darling..."

Okay, okay it's been thirty years since I'd last shimmied my nellies with something dangling from them, but you never lose it... right?

From a standing start I began to rotate my Anne Summers Red Heart Nipple Tassels, Joe's face was a picture. He was loving it!

"I can make them change direction too, Joe," I whispered, as I clambered onto the bed.

I executed a nifty right to left with each boob and spun them with gusto so they were swinging like a windmill in a gale.... and then to my utter horror, I had a wardrobe malfunction. All stickiness lost, one red heart diamante tassel relinquished its grip, flew off and sped like a bullet across the bed, straight at Joe. He put his hand up to deflect, but it was too little too late.

"Owwwwww Jesus Christ Mave.... me eye, you've taken me eye out..." he wailed as I stood there cringing, half-clad in rolled-down PVC with one tassel still clinging on for dear life, swaying in what was left of my frenzied momentum and one forlorn naked nellie that was hooked over the bedside lamp.

Oh faark!

"So, how did this happen Joe?" The doctor closely examined the cut above Joe's left eye. "I'm afraid you're going to need a couple of stitches in that, hold it together."

I slunk down in the plastic chair, pulling at a piece of cotton on my tracksuit bottoms. This was awful. It was bad enough our night of romance and passion had ended with a half-hearted arson attack on a posh restaurant and a visit to Westbury A&E, but to have Dr Steve Powell on call, was mortifying. We'd both known him for years from our frequent 'on duty' trips with prisoners and victims requiring medical treatment. I looked at him pleadingly.

Please Joe, please don't tell him.

Holding the padding back over his eye, Joe hesitated, his mind ticking over. "Well, it was this…" he held up the rogue nipple tassel in his free hand, the sharp edges of the diamantes glittering in the bright overhead lights. "…diamonds might be a girl's best friend but they certainly weren't mine tonight!" he grimaced.

Steve's eyes widened, a slight smirk playing on his lips. I cringed. "It was an accident, it wasn't on purpose, it just sort of flew off, the sticky stuff was crap…"

"Okay, less said maybe?" he laughed, "I'll sort out getting you stitched Joe, in the meantime, let's have a look at your little predicament shall we, Mavis?"

I stared at Joe. I stared at the floor. I stared at the blue cubicle curtains that wafted as someone walked past. I stared at Steve.

"Mavis, I've seen more boobs and bits than you've had hot dinners, it's my job!"

"I know…but you've never seen mine, that's different, mine are…. well, they're mine," I whined. "Every time I come in here now, you'll look at me and I'll know that you know what they're like."

"I only need to see the one, so flop it out Mavis, let's get this over and done with, I promise I won't laugh!"

"SUPERGLUED!! I can't believe you used bloody *Superglue*, Mave." Joe was crying with laughter. "What on earth possessed you, how painful was that coming off? I've never seen a nipple elongate that much before!" A racking bout of coughing interrupted his snorts of mirth.

I sat in the car wondering if there was anything within reach that I could use on him to match up his other eye. "Oh shut up, don't tell me you've never done anything stupid before….and anyway, it was your fault, you put the bloody tube in our junk drawer, I thought it was my eyelash glue." I snapped. "This is the second time you've accosted my bits with some form of adhesive."

"Oh now we come to it, it's always my fault, you're the one that dolloped big globs of the stuff on it and stuck it on, not me, think you need your eyes testing." He wiped the tears away from his cheeks with the flat of his hand.

I looked at him. His eye was already starting to puff and bruise, a large pad was stuck to his eyebrow. I looked down at myself, bra-less, lopsided and in some considerable pain, my rogue tassels clutched in my hand, one bearing the remnants of encrusted Superglue and what used to be my left nipple, the other, several hairs from Joe's eyebrow.

Jeez, talk about never doing anything that you wouldn't want to explain to a paramedic!

Turning the key in the ignition, I revved the engine. "You never got to see me swing them in opposite directions either…" I pouted, "…and that was my pièce de résistance!"

TOOTSIE

"**G**ood weekend Mave?" Bob rolled his chair backwards towards the filing cabinet, opened the third drawer down and pulled out the battered grey box file.

I rolled the mouse across the pad, watching the curser on the screen play a merry dance, refusing to go where I wanted it to go. I picked it up, rubbed the ball on my palm and tried again. "Don't ask, you really wouldn't want to know." I snorted.

"Ha-ha, THAT good was it?" He winked.

"Nope!"

He dropped the file on his desk, taking the hint that I wasn't about to expand on my weekend adventures, he started sifting through the mountain of paperwork he'd accumulated, leaving me in peace. I opened my emails and groaned. Thrush had me down for Enquiry Office duties.

Mark pushed a mug of tea towards me, gave Bob his coffee then sat down next to me. "We had a go at him you know, Mave, all of us…" he squeezed my shoulder. "…we said it wasn't on him making comments like that and as far as we're concerned, we don't give a shit you're a woman, you do the job as good as the next." He gave me a sympathetic smile.

"Thanks mate, think I'm going to have to watch my back with him." I took a gulp of my tea, it burned slightly as it hit my throat.

"Can't see myself getting back out there for the foreseeable to be honest, if it's not office duties, it's crime scenes, statement taking, which I don't mind doing, but I'd like to get a bit of a look in on my usual role."

He looked crestfallen. "It didn't get us anywhere to be honest, in fact Degsy was the most vocal and he's been shafted with extra crime reports for opening his mouth. You're going to have to take it further if he carries on, you can't let him get away with it."

"I'll see, he might calm down a bit the longer he's here." I wanted to believe that, but all my senses told me he would never change. I couldn't even blame it on him being an old arse and set in his ways, he didn't have much more service than me. He was just a miserable bastard, plain and simple and very much anti-women. I dreaded to think how his wife coped at home.

"Mave."

I looked up to see Jim Shakeshaft, a large file clutched under his arm, a look of frustration etched on his face.

"Looks like we need you, I've cleared it with your Sarge, it's on the DCI's orders. Finish your cuppa and I'll see you in the CID office." He nodded an acknowledgement to Mark and Bob.

"No probs, I'll see you there in five." Inside I was fighting the urge to jump up and punch the air in triumph but seeing Thrush standing directly behind Jim, pulled me up. His scowl said it all.

He'd been outranked by the Detective Chief Inspector!

I didn't bother taking the five minutes I'd promised Jim, I quickly stuffed my briefcase, said a quick 'see ya' to the lads and squeezed past Thrush who was trying to intimidate me by blocking the doorway with his bulk. I used my briefcase as a bumper between me and him, refusing to make eye contact. Taking the back staircase, I was in the CID office in less than two minutes.

DI Shone was taking the briefing, standing to one side, allowing his team to have full visuals on the white board, he commanded attention. The board had been divided into sections, each one displaying an active case. I found a seat at the back and listened intently.

"So, that's it for this morning. There's nothing of major interest to us on the Night Report, DS Shakeshaft has the crime allocation updates for you, so don't forget to pick up a copy before you head out." Roger Shone flicked his hand in dismissal of his troops before heading over to where I'd squirrelled myself.

"Thank you for agreeing to this Mavis, although I don't think the DCI gave you an option did he?" he grinned.

"Not at all Sir, more than happy to help, I take it the 'blackmail' case has reared its head again?"

The DI and Jim exchanged glances, before handing me the file.

"We have a lady downstairs, a Beatrice Higgins, 72-years, she's received correspondence which is a confirmed match to the letters received by Hislop and Flaybrick, the lilac paper is something of a giveaway!"

I nodded, taking the file from him.

The DI continued. "We need you to interview her and take her statement, report back to Jim when you've finished, he'll brief me from there."

"Yes, Sir, will do." I clutched the file to my chest and winced, feeling a stab of tenderness where my tassel had been forcefully removed by the gorgeous Dr Powell.

Yay, go me!

No office duty, a genteel old lady to interview and Thrush having his faced rubbed in it. Today was going to be a good day.

Beatrice Higgins, all 6'2" of her, sat elegantly in the plastic bucket chair in the interview room. Wearing a very expensive camel coat, a shell pink Gucci scarf and a rather large pair of burgundy Carvela court shoes, she occasionally fluttered a crime prevention leaflet in front of her face. I watched her through the small glass divider as she delved into her handbag, pulled out a gold compact and matching lipstick case. She took time and deliberation to apply it perfectly. Chanel Rouge Coco in *Carmen Red*, I was sure of it. I gave her a few more minutes to compose herself. She couldn't be described as a classic beauty, more 1920's silent screen handsome, probably due to the heavy make-up she wore.

"Ms Higgins, I'm Constable Mavis Upton..." I held out my hand in greeting. "...Detective Sergeant Shakeshaft has asked me to speak to you and to take your statement, are you happy to do that?"

She reciprocated, took hold of my hand and squeezed.

Jeez, did that cracking noise come from my fingers or hers?

"Delighted to meet you, Officer, hopefully we can get this done quickly, this is such an embarrassment and inconvenience." She fanned the leaflet again.

"Of course..." I opened the file and took out a photocopy of the letter she had received and pushed it across the table. "...would you mind confirming that this is the letter you received, Ms Higgins."

She looked at it with complete distaste, turning her shoulders slightly to the left, away from it, as though that one action would distance herself from the situation she found herself in. "Yes, yes... that's it. I can't tell you how appalled I am, making threats like that, and for money too, £2,000.00 – it's not a drop in the ocean you know!"

I nodded in agreement. "Now in this letter, there is reference to '*someone liking it hot*'. Can you tell me what this refers to, what it is they know about you that could cause you distress if revealed?"

As her lips met together tightly, forming a thin line, my heart sank. This was going to be another Hislop rather than a Flaybrick. Although Edna had been keen to divulge her early misdemeanours she had still paid up, for what reason, we still didn't know, maybe the Blackmailer had more on her than just her Diamond D'Light days, whereas Cyril had refused point blank to co-operate at all.

Beatrice was on course to be a refusal.

"I'd rather not…" She banged her hand down on the table. "…you don't need to know that, you just need to do your job and get whoever is doing this." The colour flushed across her face.

Oh dear, this was not going to plan.

"Okay, let's take a moment, I don't want to upset you, but I do need to ask these questions if we are to help you…" I indicated to the two mugs of tea I'd brought in with me. "…milk, no sugar."

"Oh my goodness, what's that?" Her index finger shot across the table to point at the ceramic mug.

"It's tea Ms Higgins, like you requested." I gave her a quizzical look.

"I know it's tea, dear - but what is it *sitting* in?"

How anyone could make an everyday word like *sitting* sound disgusting, was beyond me. "It's a mug, a receptacle for fluids… you know, like water, coffee, hot chocolate…err…tea!"

"My dear, a toilet is a receptacle but you wouldn't expect me to drink out of that, now would you?" She tilted her chin upwards as an act of defiance….

….and that's when I saw it!

"She's a man, Jim!" I flipped the file onto his desk. "She's got an Adam's Apple, honestly, she really has."

Jim looked up from the computer screen and turned to face me. "Who's a man?"

"Beatrice Higgins. Don't you see, that's the connection, those are the buzz words in the letter, this one is easier than Hislop's clue. '*Someone likes it hot*' ... that's the exact words so think it through, we've actually got ourselves a real life Tootsie!"

Jim gave no reaction, chewing his pen, he waited for me to expound.

"Helloooooo, the film 'Some Like it Hot', you must have either seen or heard of it, it's a classic!" Exasperated I got my phone out to Google it. "See, it's about men dressing as women, hence Beatrice being a woman...."

"...who is really a man!" he interrupted.

Hallelujah – at last!

"Yep, she's not just an unnaturally tall woman with big feet, she's a naturally tall man with big testicles - in a dress!" Flopping down on the chair next to him, I had to admit I was pretty proud of myself.

"You're having a laugh, a cock in frock!" Dave Aldred arrogantly sauntered across the office. "...and you've got experience of telling the difference how?" he sneered.

"Not that I've got to explain it to you, but yes I have. Joe's cousin, Frank, is a pretty nifty Drag Queen, although I don't think Beatrice is on that level. I actually think she's living her life fully as a woman, she's never going to confirm it though."

Jim shoved his elbows onto his desk and held his head in his hands. "Great, another one bites the dust then? Take it you didn't get a statement?"

"No, she went away to think about it. I went over all the options, but it was no deal. It won't stop us still investigating with what we've got will it?" I hated the idea that there was someone out there who was taking delight in the misery they were causing. "We can't shelve it, the amount has doubled on this one to £2,000.00, what happens if it just keeps getting higher and higher, more and more victims?"

Jim thought for a moment. "We haven't got much to go on, no forensics, no statements; hell, we haven't even got complainants, just 'informants' for want of a better word. Unless you can get someone to start talking, I can't see the D.I keeping this active. We suspect Hislop and Flaybrick have paid up, but that's all we've got, suspicion." He used his hand to squeeze the back of his neck. "Get me proof they've coughed up the money, get at least one of them to make a complaint…." Jim tailed off, frustration clearly getting the better of him.

I took back the file and nodded.

Easier said than done, but I was nothing if not tenacious, and if it got me out of the way of Thrush, even better!

BLUES, TWOS AND BABY SHOES

WEE WILLIE WINKIE

Barnaby sat on the windowsill, the sunshine streamed through the bullseye glass, casting rainbow arcs on the old butcher block table. Cora watched him, the lazy swish of his tail quite mesmerising. She giggled to herself, dropping her glasses to the end of her nose, the knitting needles held in her arthritic fingers clacked together, the *knit one, purl one, knit one* moss stitch growing in multi-colours.

"It's a… oh gosh, what do they call them Barnaby?" She cocked her head to one side, waiting. She knew being a cat, Barnaby could never answer her frequent questions, but the pause would give her time to find the word she was looking for. "That's it…. willy warmer, it's a willy warmer!" Taking the small dressmakers tape measure, she gently patted down her creation.

"Just a little over six inches. I'd say Beatrice Higgins is at least that, don't you?" She giggled again. She had never seen Beatrice's appendage, but if it was as they say and the correlation of either nose or feet size were anything to go by, then she was surely on the right track. "Draw cord or bow, Barnaby?"

Barnaby gave her a deep, meaningful stare of indifference and went back to watching a wood pigeon perched on the shed roof. "Okay, bow it is, right time for a nice cup of tea and a spot of writing." She pushed the two needles into the small ball of wool,

"Hopefully my little gift will be just the nudge Beatrice, or should I say Basil, needs to settle his debt, he does seem to be dragging his shiny Carvela court shoes." She let out another little chuckle.

At this rate, her dream cottage and cat sanctuary hundreds of miles away from Westbury might just become a reality after all.

Lost in thought, I stared from the window onto the communal garden that Agatha shared with the other tenants of Beach Rise apartments. Everything was coming into bloom, the beautiful and plentiful white flowers of the clematis armandii wound themselves around the wooden arbour, falling gently down to drape across the stone water fountain in the middle of the grass. It was such a peaceful place to live. I rinsed the suds from the glass and placed it on the drainer. As if reading my mind, Agatha broke the silence.

"I don't think I like living here Mavis…" Her chin jutted out as she rearranged the flamboyantly coloured silk scarf around her neck. She patted the little brooch down and picked up her cup, her pinky finger hovering out to the side. "…they've got a nasty little boy, Augustus or something like that, he's got that vegetable syndrome that they all go on about."

I finished washing her dishes and dried my hands on the treasured tea towel that she'd 'purloined' on a day trip to Rhyl. It was only when we'd returned home that day had we found it in her handbag, stuffed at the bottom. As Agatha had no money with her, there was only one way she could have obtained it and several other items. "We can never go back there again, you know Agatha?"

"Where?"

"Rhyl, just in case you're recognised and you get locked up for historic shoplifting." I giggled, I was still baffled as to how neither Joe, myself, Ella or Luke had noticed her half-inching in virtually every shop we had gone into throughout the day.

She didn't see the funny side. "It was a ridiculous price anyway, sometimes you have to steal from the rich to feed the poor" she grumbled, taking a bite of the chocolate éclair I'd bought her.

"Ah, I see, so you were going to feed the poor on two KitKats, a packet of Mint Imperials, a dog chew and then wash up after them with the tea towel?" I was just about to giggle when I saw her wince, her eyes pinched shut as she grimaced. "Are you okay, do you need more pain relief?"

She nodded. "Doesn't seem to be touching, some days. I take the bleedin' stuff but I've still got my aches and pains" she shifted in the chair, trying to make herself more comfortable.

Our last visit to the Oncologist had not been a good one, it was only to confirm how far the cancer had spread and to discuss Agatha's options. She had remained steadfast in her wishes and had chosen where and how she wanted to end her days. I hung the tea towel on the radiator and reached for her medication from the cupboard. Tears welled up and slowly plopped down my cheek, I quickly brushed them away with my fingers and spent longer than I should looking for what she needed.

Why am I crying? As awful as it sounds, it's not for Agatha; it's for me. This is making me relive memories of Mum that I'd rather forget…it's just so unfair.

"…but then life is never fair, is it?" Crap, I'd blurted that out aloud instead of just thinking it.

I looked at Agatha. She looked at me.

"No, no it isn't, Mavis, but we work with the hand we're dealt, can't do nothing more than that! Talking of which, any news on your search for my daughter?" She took another sip of tea.

"I'm still trying, I promise but it's not an easy process..." I sat down next to her and took her hand. "...it's the adopted child that has the rights to look for their parents, you sadly don't have the same, but I have started by..."

She quickly interrupted me, waving her hand as though she didn't want to hear any more on the subject. "So, like I was telling you, him next door gets on me nerves, him and his Asparagus Syndrome." She jerked a thumb at the dividing wall, whilst I threatened to lose my poise and snort with laughter. She really was mum and dad rolled into one with more malapropisms than they could manage together, she had taken me from tears to laughter in seconds. If it was a family trait, there was seriously no hope for me.

"Oh he's just a little boy, Agatha, have patience... and it's Asperger's."

"What is?"

"What he's got, Asperger's Syndrome."

"No it isn't, it's Asparagus Syndrome, that's what his mum said he has, so you're wrong!" She defiantly clacked her teeth. "I don't think I'm going to be here for much longer anyway, so he can shout and knock his balls against the wall to his heart's content when I'm six feet under!" she harrumphed.

I didn't know what to say. She was quite stoic about her impending death, having already put her affairs in order, she didn't really do sentimentalities. "Oh I'm sure you'll miss him if he wasn't here, Agatha. Children are the little beacons of youth that keep us on our toes, don't you think?"

She gave me the death stare that she had lately perfected.

"No I bloody won't..." she spat, whilst looking wistfully out of the window onto the garden, "...but I'll definitely miss me flowering clitoris when I go, Mavis."

Sheesh!

Maddie shuffled her feet along the black and white chequered tiles, trying to keep her slippers on her feet. She cursed the effort she had put in to cleaning the entrance hall, far too much of that blasted shine stuff had made it like an ice rink. Regaining her balance, the little top on the china teapot rattled as her tray tilted to one side.

The constant yapping from Hedy the Bichon Frise was driving her insane. "Yap, yap, yap is that all you do?" she bitterly complained as the dog snapped at her ankles. The temptation to give it a nudge with her foot was overwhelming but the last time she'd done that, the bloody thing had clung to her leg humping away performing an unmentionable sex act on her left calf. She shuddered just thinking about it.

Working for Beatrice Higgins was a challenge, no doubt about it, but it was a steady income and a roof over her head. She sighed and began to climb the staircase, her arthritic knees objecting loudly as she made her way to Beatrice's day room.

"Ah, there you are Maddie, time for elevenses already, where do the days go?" She dropped her Parker pen onto the blotter, "Mail too, how exciting." Reaching out for the small jiffy bag that was wedged between the teapot and the milk jug, her beautifully manicured and painted nails picked at the sealed edge. "Feels like a little gift Maddie, maybe from one of my admirers!" she chuckled to herself. Admirers she had, but that was all; her secret made anything else impossible. She slid her hand inside, feeling around.

"Oh my goodness..." She held the rainbow coloured knitted oddment aloft. Pinching it between her fingers, her lips pursed, she read the accompanying typed card.

'Real ladies wear scarves to stop being chilly,
But you my dear Basil need this for your willy..'

***

£2,000.00 by tomorrow or all of Westbury will know
Kindest regards
Celia Fate

"Well I never, Ma'am…" giggled Maddie, temporarily forgetting herself, "…that's definitely something to warm your cock – les!"

SHARTS & FARTS

"Toilet rolls!"

Joe ambled out of the kitchen, pen and paper in his hand and stood by the bottom of the stairs. "What?"

"Bog rolls, we need them, like…err desperately." My voice echoed from the smallest room. I reached across, tearing the small strands of tissue that he had kindly left for me on the brown cardboard tube. "Bleedin' hell, this wouldn't wipe one nostril let alone…."

"Whoa, enough my little dumpling, don't ruin the romance! Do I really need to know exactly what you want to use it for?" he rapped on the other side of the bathroom door, "So, I've got toilet rolls, toothpaste, baked beans, margarine and a couple of those furry things."

"What furry things, I haven't said anything about furry things."

"Yeah, the fruit things."

"Peaches?"

"Yep, that's them, hairy bums as we used to call them when we were kids." He went quiet for a few seconds. "Anything else or will you just grab stuff when you see it?"

"Jeez Joe, can't I have a wee in peace, it's normally only kids who hover around the toilet when Mummy needs to tinkle." Exasperated I yanked my jeans up.

"Okay, don't get your knickers in a twist, kettle's on for a cuppa before you go." He took the stairs two at a time with one resounding thud as he jumped the last two and skidded into the kitchen. Alfie, not to miss out on the fun came hurtling along the hallway barking, followed by Cat, who never did anything more than 'amble' with an air of haughty indifference, as all cats do.

I watched the three of them through the bannisters. My mad family. Ben was having his afternoon nap, but I had no doubt that as he got older, he'd be joining in the melee too.

"How's Agatha?" Joe set a coffee down on the table and pushed a KitKat in front of me.

"Oh, you know, pretty much the same, she is funny though, had me in fits laughing a couple of times. I'm not sure if it's intentional, or if she really doesn't know how hilarious she can be." I split the four wafers into two and took a bite.

Joe nuzzled my neck, stroking my hair. "Actually, that's what I really should have said, I should have asked how you are. I know it's bringing back things you'd rather forget."

I thought about that for a few minutes. Yes, there was stuff with Mum and her passing that I would rather forget, but at the same time remembering was to remember her, even the sad bits. You could never have love without experiencing loss too. They sort of went hand in hand. If you didn't love, then you couldn't experience the pain of loss, because without it, there was no feeling. That also made me think of Agatha and her daughter, wondering what love she would have felt for her tiny baby. I still couldn't comprehend how she must have felt that night when she had left her and walked away, not turning back once.

"Penny for them." He cuddled up to me, swinging his leg across mine.

"Could you have abandoned your own child, Joe, left Ben

somewhere not knowing if anyone would take care of him?" I felt so desperately sad the more I thought about it. Somewhere out there was a girl, well, woman by now, who would always wonder who her real parents were.

"No, of course I couldn't, but then I'm not in the same position that someone who is desperate is, that's what makes the difference. If you've got nowhere to turn, no support, sometimes it's fear." Picking up his mug, he took a slurp of tea. "Now, just imagine what it must have been like in 1955 and in Westbury too, small town, small minds."

1955 – why is that registering somewhere in the depths of my baby brain, beside it being the year Agatha's baby was born?

I pushed the thought to one side. "I've lodged Agatha's details and my contact number with the National Contact Register, it's the only way. Apparently natural parents have no legal right to information on the babies they give up or abandon..." I took another bite of my KitKat and licked the chocolate from my fingers. "... although the Children Act gave adopted kids the right to have access to their original birth certificate, it's not going to help Agatha, as far as I know there never was an original birth certificate." I pulled at a loose thread on my hoodie, twisting it around my finger until the tip turned purple. "I'm still not sure if I'm supposed to report what I know either, I mean, if I did, what good would it do?" I didn't wait for Joe to reply. "I'm never going to find her, am I?"

"Oh, you never know, you just might bump into someone who looks like her..." He pulled a face, pretending to gag. "...blimey, just the mere thought of this world having two Agatha's in it is enough to make you run for the hills!" he chuckled.

Bing-bong…

"Due to a malfunctioning chill system and minor flooding, products in Aisle 9 will be unavailable until further notice. We apologise for any incontinence caused…."

The tannoy screeched again to a background of static and tapping. *"…inconvenience, it says inconvenience …"* a second voice hissed out. More screeching feedback followed before the speakers fell silent.

I caught the eye of two elderly ladies who were loading up their basket with Gordons Gin. A collective eye roll at the faux pas gave us a strange sense of camaraderie in the booze aisle. I grabbed at a couple of bottles of merlot and guiltily hid them underneath the bananas, cabbage and a big bag of sprouts. The last thing I needed was to be judged for enjoying a tipple, sort of like an accusation of being drunk in charge of a shopping trolley and a baby!

"It's not much fun is it sweetheart, I don't like shopping either." I wiped Ben's mouth and tickled his tummy. He giggled, blowing another huge bubble out of his left nostril, the bright overhead lights in the supermarket reflected in his blue eyes. "Just a few more things and then we can be home in time for tea." I'd barely had chance to chuck two bottles of tonic in the trolley, when something wafted upwards, assaulting my nostrils. I sniffed. "Ooops, mister, that stinks, have you got a little bit of wind in that tummy of yours?" I didn't expect a reply, but his expression gave the game away.

Looking along the aisle and seeing the mixed reception to Ben's ready aroma, I put an extra spurt on. Pushing the trolley into the freezer section, I carefully selected my healthy options (a small bag of oven chips instead of a big bag) and a more decadent mahoosive tub of low-fat ice cream. "Moment on the lips, lifetime on the hips," I cooed. Ben kicked his chubby legs and gurgled, as though he understood my predicament.

Ten minutes later, after completing my supermarket sweep, I stood at the checkout waiting to pay. Glancing at my watch, as I silently willed the queue to move a little faster, I noticed Ben had suddenly gone cross-eyed. He stretched his legs, puffed his cheeks out and turned bright pink, a look of pure concentration sweeping over his little face.

"Oh noooooo, Ben - not now!" I squealed as my fellow shoppers in the queue turned to glare at me, but Ben carried on oblivious. He grunted, snorted, grunted a bit more and let rip with the most awful wet bubbly sound. It was barely seconds before his ghastly deposit wafted through the air to assail everyone's nostrils.

What on earth is wrong with this child? Ella was never like this, is it just boys who wee in your face and shit for Britain?

Flustered, embarrassed and uncomfortable from the generalised tutting and disapproving looks, I quickly paid for my shopping, throwing everything at random back into the trolley once it had been scanned through.

"Would you like a......" The cashier, by now a lovely shade of green, began to gag as she wildly pointed to the plastic carriers on the hook, unable to finish her sentence.

I helped her out. "No thank you." Brushing a stray lock of hair behind my ear I blew my cheeks out, "I've actually got my own bags for life..." I stabbed a finger in my face, "... they're here, right under my bloody eyes!" I testily snapped.

Pushing the trolley across the car park, I grabbed my mobile and phoned Joe. Nobody warned me how tiring this would be at my age. I'd left the trolley full of my shopping outside the Baby Change whilst I saw to Ben, only to come out and discover someone had pinched my tub of ice cream and a cauliflower.

He answered on the third ring. "Y…ellow!"

"Joe, can you put the shepherd's pie in the oven, I'm running a bit late, your gorgeous son decided to explode in the middle of Sainsbury's." My breath was coming in sharp rasps as I tried to juggle the trolley that had a mind of its own, hold the phone to my ear and shove the dummy back into Ben's wailing mouth. He hadn't stopped crying since I'd changed him.

"Will do, how much longer do you think you'll be? I could do the veg too if you want?"

"Just getting to the car now, ten minutes tops." I clicked off, "Oh Ben, please, come on sweetheart, we'll be home soon." I scanned the car park as he continued to wail loudly, nothing was consoling him, not even his beloved dodo.

Shit, where had I parked the car!

Row upon row of what seemed like hundreds of cars greeted me. In all honesty, it probably was hundreds of cars, although it hadn't been that busy when I'd arrived. This was all I needed. I stood on tiptoe doing my best meerkat impression.

"Yaaay, here we go, Mummy had a bit of a brain fart there, thought we'd be walking home pushing the trolley with you still in it," I simpered, as my car came into view. Rummaging in my bag, I found my car keys and clicked.

Nothing.

I clicked again.

Still nothing. No flashing lights, no clunking noise as the locking mechanism kicked in. I bashed the key against my palm in the vain hope that action would make a difference.

Nothing. Ben notched it up a level, another decibel and with an added scream at the end of each breath.

I want to cry, sob, weep, disappear into a hole. I am a failure!

BLUES, TWOS AND BABY SHOES

"You okay, love?"

I'd been so immersed in my own small meltdown, I hadn't noticed him. Smartly dressed holding a Tiger Loaf baguette under his arm. Embarrassed, I pushed my hair out of my eyes and tried desperately to look in control. "Erm, it's my key, it's not working, I can't get the door open, nothing's happening."

He looked at Ben and then gave me a sympathetic 'we've all been there' sort of look. Ben responded with another loud wail. "Here, let me have a go, you've got your hands full there" he smiled.

Ten minutes later, apart from Ben having quietened down slightly, emitting only the occasional sob and my Knight in a grey M&S Suite having a droopy baguette, we were still no further along in getting into my car.

"Has this ever happened before?" he raised one eyebrow, Roger Moore style.

"No, never, I can't understand it, maybe it's the battery," I helpfully offered.

He thought for a moment. "Mmmmm, maybe, have you got a spare at home and someone who can bring it for you?" I shrugged, I couldn't engage my brain to remember my own name, let alone think if I'd got a spare somewhere in the depths of the junk drawer at home. I'd have to phone Joe again and ask.

He puzzled a few seconds more before he was joined by two other guys from a nearby van. Another five minutes passed with my Knight in the grey M&S suite, Jack and Graham from Screwfix Direct and another helpful soul, Martin who collected the trollies, all showing their gallantry by looking for various ways to get into my car.

I leant against the rear door, tired, fed up and totally embarrassed. I was a woman who was always in control. I'd broken into vehicles for other people, granted not always gently, there'd been a few smashed side windows and a startled car thief hauled out by his ears over the years, but this was bordering on the ridiculous. I couldn't even open my own bloody car.

How on earth had having Ben turned me into a fluffy-headed, ridiculous caricature of motherhood?

I looked into the back of the car, my mind temporarily wandering. I took in the immaculate interior, the deodoriser smelly in the shape of a tree hanging from the rear-view mirror. I marvelled at the shiatsu beaded cover on the drivers seat. There was something niggling me, something not quite right.

"Oh shit!"

Mister M&S gave a look of concern. "What's the matter, is everything okay?"

I nodded, too dumfounded to trust myself to open my mouth and say anything sensible. I casually peered into the car again, pretending I was fixing my hair in the reflection from the glass.

There was no baby car seat, no cuddly teddy, no blanket, no globby, brown teething rusk smeared on the upholstery, no screwed-up bits of crap, half eaten packets of crisps and a polo mint shoved in the console, in fact nothing of mine at all. Instead, draped across the back seat was a tartan rug, a pair of old wellies and a wicker shopping basket. I furtively edged to the back of the car to check out the registration plate.

Jeez, as if my day could get any worse – this wasn't even my car!

I intently stared at my Knight in the grey M&S suite, Jack and Graham from Screwfix Direct and Martin who collects trollies as they huddled together looking for a solution to my predicament.

I had two choices.

Tell them or.........

Two minutes later, I slowly drove out of the car park, slunk down as far as possible in the seat of my furtively discovered car.

Ben was still howling in the back and my shopping had been hastily chucked into the footwell. I glanced over to where the real owner of the black Qashqai was berating four very bemused men who were clearly trying to explain about the distraught woman with a baby who had just vanished into thin air.

I mean, come on…what are the odds of having two identical cars in the same car park with one of them belonging to a bat-shit crazy lady having a day full of disasters and brain farts?

Actually, no…. you don't have to answer that!

DUCKS AHOY

Petey pulled into the car park at the back of the nick and carefully reversed into the one available space on the back row. It was a squeeze and his nearside wheels bumped up onto the grass verge, tipping his car awkwardly to one side. He turned the engine off and sat in quiet contemplation, musing to himself that Westbury nick building seemed to be on some kind of tilt.

"Oh dear, that could be subsidence or a sink hole opening up." He slowly moved his head to one side until he was happy with the angle. "Ah, that's better!"

He sat for a little while longer thinking about his life. He didn't mind being the brunt of everyone's jokes. He knew that was just banter, part of being in the job, of being in the 'family' and he knew Bob, Degsy, all the lads and Mavis, would walk over hot coals for him if it was needed. But his heart still felt heavy. He picked up the small teddy bear that Betty had given him when he had first joined the police, it always had pride of place on the dashboard, stuck by its fluffy bum with a big blob of blue tack so it didn't fall off. The little navy-blue policeman's helmet was slightly faded on one side by the sun and an unravelled thread hung from the tunic but he didn't care, it meant as much to him today as it had all those years ago.

"I'm just a fuckwit, aren't I, Teddy?" He shook the little bear and pushed his finger at the back to make its head nod. Clearing his throat, he picked a perfect pitch, the type of pitch a teddy bear would have.

'Yes, yes…you're a fuckwit, Petey but I'll always be your friend!'

He gave a thin, wistful smile. He had just given Teddy a voice.

"You know Teddy, the pain in my heart is just a little too much for me on some days, today is one of them." His eyes, magnified by the lenses in his glasses, brimmed and glistened with tears.

'There's always tomorrow, Petey.' Teddy did a little dance across the steering wheel, his furry brown legs kicking from side to side.

"I don't always feel like having a tomorrow, Ted…." he sighed, "…. tomorrows are only good if you can share them with someone who still loves you."

As Petey's tears fell freely, Teddy quietly returned to his spot on the dashboard, settled himself down and took on the vacant brown-eyed stare that he always had.

I spread copies of the three letters out on the desk, my eyes running quickly through each of them in turn.

Flaybrick. She was the first, I made notes.

78 years old b: Poulton Sands, Westbury

Madam of a brothel from the late 1960's to 1987 as Madam Diamond D'Light.

Now Mrs Fine & Upstanding/where does she fit in the community/ on any committees/church/voluntary work?

Serviced some very prominent men/possible hint at police HQ

Money/tax evasion?

Why did she report it, but then pay up?

Refuses to co-operate with investigation

Hislop. I hadn't yet met him, but already I had a feeling he wouldn't be the type of man I'd invite for afternoon tea. Jim had described him as an odious tub of lard.

75 years old b: Aylesborough, Westbury
Letter refers to Easter Surprise in Fifty-five
No known song title/poem – Hislop knows what it means
Negative PNC no known previous convictions
Paid demand?
Refuses to co-operate with investigation

Higgins. Oh dear, where should I start with her/him. I had done some digging and dear old Beatrice was quite the wealthy 'woman' having opened a very exclusive clothes boutique in Westbury in 1985. *Haute Couture by Beatrice* was frequented only by the monied ladies of Cheshire who adored her personal touch and promised assurances that not one lady who graced her premises would ever appear in the same attire as someone else at Chester races. So, what else did I know about Beatrice?

72 years old b: Unknown, arrived in Westbury 1985
Inherited Tinstone Manor as the sole surviving relative of Charles and Prunella Higgins
Wealthy
Lives alone with female companion, Madeline (Maddie) Canterbury

"What's the common denominator, there's got to be something here?" I hadn't said that to anyone in particular, it was an out loud thought which often helped me think.

"Eh?" Bob leant over my shoulder. "What you working on?"

"It's that blackmail job, which isn't really a blackmail job as nobody is making a bloody complaint..." I huffed. "...total lack of co-operation from all of them! There's got to be something that has made them targets. If you were a blackmailer, you wouldn't just pick people at random, it's planned, there's a link somewhere."

I sat back and took a sip of my tea. A storm was brewing and coming in quite quickly by the look of the dark clouds rolling in. Weak diagonal ticks of rain hit the window, pushed by the wind. I watched the tiled roof of the house opposite turn from a dull red to a dismal wet sheen. So much for summer being just around the corner.

"It's their ages!" I squealed, making Bob jump. "They're all born in the 1930's. That and growing up and living in Westbury is what they've all got in common." I was feeling pretty smug with myself. That was a link, albeit a tentative one and at the very least something we could work on as a starting point.

Bob read over my notes. "Very good my little grasshopper, but you're forgetting one thing…"

"What?"

"Beatrice Higgins. You don't know *where* she was born, she only arrived in Westbury in 1985!" He jabbed a finger at the relevant sheet of paper.

I pulled at my ponytail in frustration, tightening the hair bobble. "Feck me."

Degsy broke away from the Beano annual he'd been engrossed with. "I know you're pretty hot Mave, but not right at this moment. Thanks for the offer though." He sniggered.

Before I could reach for something to hit him with, he quickly grabbed the tin tea tray from the side and hit himself over the head with it to save me the bother, the metal clang made me shudder. "Jeez, and you call me bat-shit crazy! DIY masochism does suit you though, I definitely saw a glint of enjoyment in your eyes, maybe one for the every-ready Lillian to incorporate in your nightly shenanigans?"

"Not bloody likely, have you seen her muscles…." he snorted, "…and it wouldn't be an old tin tea tray, it'd be more like the ruddy coffee table."

Knowing Lillian as well as we all did, he wasn't far wrong. I stacked the papers and slipped them back into my file. Whatever I needed to do now would be on my own time, Thrush had put me down for a foot beat in Poulton Sands so that was going to restrict me, unless I could give Cyril Hislop a little visit whilst I was pounding the pavements. Now that was an idea.

"Anyway, back to the job in hand, where was Beatrice Higgins prior to 1985. Where was she born and where did she live before coming here?" I waited. Two very blank, disinterested faces stared back at me.

Jeez, intelligence really is like underwear. Important that you have it, but not necessary that you show it off.

Cyril Hislop lived in an area that had once been well sought after in its day. Now it was run down and bleak. Many of the properties were derelict, their windows boarded up with for sale signs decorating the front gardens, broken, bent and tilted like decaying teeth. There was a general air of sadness, of being forgotten. Families, once their offspring had flown the nest, were left with large Victorian terraces that held too many rooms to keep warm in the winter. A fragmented society had slowly done away with extended families living together, supporting each other.

The rot was on the inside as much as the outside.

Standing in front of 8 Edinburgh Road, I lifted my fingers to touch the tarnished lionhead knocker, the black paint alternatively peeled in parts or had taken on a matt grey bloom with small spores of powdery orange mould nestled in the cracks. I used my thumb and forefinger to knock, the less fingers used the better. I wiped my hand on my trousers waiting for the footsteps to get closer. The door opened barely an inch as one eye peered out.

"Mr Hislop?"

"Who's asking?"

Jeez, me you numpty; the one that's dressed as a police officer!

"I'm Constable Mavis Upton from Westbury Police Station…" I held my warrant card up to the crack in the door, "… I wondered if I could come in and have a chat to you about your recent report?"

He studied me for a moment, tutted and opened the door a little wider. "You're a bit on the short side to be one, aren't you?"

"Oh they let all sorts join now Mr Hislop, I mean look at me, short AND a woman!" I gave him a few seconds for that to sink in, whilst I manoeuvred myself around him and into the hallway. A rumpled red and gold runner covering the original floor tiles elongated towards a door at the far end. 1930's brown woodwork contributed to the dismal feel of the interior, a small scratched console table held a black & white photograph of a pretty young woman in a floral dress, a garish tassel lamp sat next to it, the weak light desperately trying to penetrate the darker corners. The wall held three brass ducks in flight. Duck number one was on course, duck number two was lopsided and sniffing the arse of duck number three above him and in turn duck number three looked as though he was thoroughly enjoying the unnatural attention of Duck number two. I stifled a giggle. Cyril pushed ahead of me, his bulk filling the narrow hallway as he shuffled through the door into the kitchen. I followed him resisting the urge to straighten duck number 2 and destroy the pleasure of duck number three in the process.

"Might as well take a seat, now you're in.." he grunted. "…d'you want a drink or something?" The battered old kettle in his hand clattered as the spout hit the tap.

Looking at the greasy dishes piled on the wooden draining board and the furry culture growing in the bottom of the mug in front of me, I shook my head. "No thank you, I've not long had one before I left the station." That was the favourite little porky we told in any house where the hospitality was kindly offered but the cleanliness screamed for it to be refused.

He jutted his chin in acknowledgement. "So, what d'you want to know then?" Easing himself down, he sat in the armchair in the corner. "And before you ask, I'm not saying nothin' about that letter."

"Why Mr Hislop, what can be more terrible than the act of blackmail itself, surely you want us to catch who is doing this?" My pen was poised over my notebook in anticipation of cajoling him into coming clean, but one look at his face told me otherwise.

"Look, it's like I told that other bloke in your place, it was a joke, a mistake, there weren't nothing in it, so there's nothing to report is there?"

I tried a different tack.

"Do you know a Beatrice Higgins or an Edna Flaybrick, Mr Hislop?"

The colour instantly drained from his face, small beads of sweat began to appear just underneath his nose. I focused on his facial expression, a small, barely perceptible tic touched the corner of his right eye.

"Erm, maybe, well yes…. Edna and me, well we had a bit of a thing years ago…" he mumbled and tailed off, staring out of the kitchen window. "It was before I met my Clementine, I'd much rather forget it, if you don't mind."

BLUES, TWOS AND BABY SHOES

"Do you live alone now?" I changed direction. Sometimes talking about family can temporarily distract before I needed to bring him back on track again.

"Yep, apart from old Tom over there." He pointed to a ragged ginger cat sitting on the windowsill. "Never had no children, couldn't you see, accident on the docks when I was a teenager, affected me… well you know."

I watched him, his eyes focused on a point beyond the glass. Just how many memories were passing through his mind? Where they happy, sad or indifferent. Suddenly remembering the photograph in the hallway and the distinct lack of a feminine touch around his home, I was sure some of those thoughts would touch on grief.

He turned to stare at me, a mixture of mild annoyance and contemplation crossing his face. He took a swig of his tea, scratched under his armpit and pushed his head back to rest on the antimacassar.

"It's okay Mr Hislop, you take your time, I'm a really good listener."

I know
what
you did

DOGTOOTH TREWS
AND TWO NEW CLUES

Bursting through the doors into the CID office, I quickly sought out Jim. "Thanks for clearing it with Thrush for me to come in…" I dragged a chair up to his desk, "…good old Cyril came up trumps, well, at least with something for us to go on." I eagerly waited for Jim's response.

"Mave, unless he or the other two are going to co-operate, we've got no complainants, so if you're going to tell me he's changed his mind, then that's great." he gave a half-hearted thumbs up.

I did my usual and blew my fringe upwards in a full Mexican wave as I prepared myself. "Err, well not exactly, but if I can get enough on what he's given me, then maybe we can push Beatrice to sign on the dotted line, just one of them would be good wouldn't it?"

He pointed to a mountain of files stacked on the corner of his desk. "Look, as much as I love your enthusiasm and dedication, and dare I say it, your pig-headedness, THIS is what we've got on the go. They've all got complainants Mave, they all have something we can at least investigate. This blackmail job is basically just horse-shit without the horse!"

"I know…" I bit the inside of my lip, "…but please just listen to what I've got."

Jim leant back with his hands behind his head. "Bloody hell, you'd persuade the Pope to turn Protestant, go on, I'm all ears."

I took a deep breath. "Right, do you recall Basil Higgins, the son of Charles and Prunella Higgins, they were the big shipping merchants in their day?"

Jim nodded. "Yep, local gossips have always reckoned that's where most of the money came from locally and how Westbury grew, they went into land development too, quite generous to the community by all accounts."

"Well, Basil left Westbury in 1968 after a small scandal involving him being caught in The Blue Dolphin chippy buying a bag of fish & chips dressed in his mum's best frock. Cyril can only assume the embarrassment of it all sent him scuttling to live abroad, either by choice or the family exiled him…" I pinched one of Jim's Polo mints and popped it into my mouth. "… I mean, you can imagine how that would have gone down in the society circles they mixed in, it would have been about as welcome as a wet fart in a lacey thong."

Jim laughed, then grimaced at the thought. "He died though Mave, don't you remember, must have been early 80's some sort of freak accident with a cucumber."

"Oh my god, nooooooooo!" The Polo mint sucked to the back of my throat sending me into a coughing fit. "Oh Jim, don't even go there, surely he could have afforded something more substantial than a cucumber if he was going to indulge in…."

"Why hush your mouth, Baby Jane!" He wagged a finger at me, faking a southern American drawl. "He choked on it, in one of those posh restaurants in Monte Carlo, they'd made fancy shapes out of a large one and it lodged in his throat, apparently."

Suitably chastised, but still finding the whole 'death' of Basil a source of amusement, I ploughed on.

"Well, here's the clincher. According to Cyril, Basil is not dead, he's alive and kicking and living as none other than…. duh, duh, duuuuh…" I gave myself a drum roll on the edge of Jim's desk for dramatic effect. "… Beatrice *'I've got an Adams Apple'* Higgins!" I gave a smug grin. "See, I told you - we had a real live Tootsie in our interview room, and you didn't believe me."

Cora May Spunge checked her reflection in the shop window. Pushing a rogue strand of hair back under her hat, she gave one last glance before going inside. *Peggy Parker Lingerie* had only ever been a distant longing for Cora. Like a kid at Christmas with their nose pressed up against the window of a toy shop, she had coveted the pretty lace underwear and had positively drooled with desire for the bra that had those miracle bits of wire underneath that took boobs from crotch level up to your chin in two seconds flat.

Oh, how wonderful it would be to be perky once again, to bounce and wobble in the fruit and veg aisle at Morrison's whilst doing my weekly shop.

She gave Peggy Parker a genteel smile as she approached the glass counter. Running her fingers across the top, she stopped, pointing to a rather daring little number in a beautiful shade of burgundy.

"May I try that, please?" she felt almost breathless, exhilarated at the prospect of wearing something so decadent against her skin.

Peggy, trying very hard not to look surprised, which was very difficult considering the age of her customer, pointed at the garment again. "This one… are you sure?"

Cora nodded. "Yes, I am quite sure." She watched Peggy slide the silk bodysuit from the drawer and could only marvel at the exquisite detail, the lace edging and the little nip at the front that held a small diamante. Her visit here was twofold. She really did

BLUES, TWOS AND BABY SHOES

want something a little special just for herself, but she also wanted to see the woman who had appeared on page 6 of her *Little Book of Misdeeds, Sins & Mishaps*.

A woman who worked Monday to Friday in her underwear shop, attended church every Sunday, professed to be of kind heart to all and gave what spare time she had on Saturday's to charity. Peggy had every day of the week covered, apart from Wednesday afternoon. Cora smiled to herself.

Oh Peggy, you and your half-day Wednesdays, when you're shamelessly shagging for England with your best friends' husband. Does that come under a 'charitable act', my dear?

Her fingers touched her lips in mock horror at using such a terrible, unladylike term. She'd learnt a lot of new words since obtaining her little book, sometimes she said them out loud, sometimes she just thought them in her head, like now. They did make her feel very alive and decadent, something Harold had never made her feel.

She dipped behind the heavy velvet curtains of the changing room, the metallic swish of the rings on the pole sent shivers down her spine as she closed them behind her. Standing in front of the mirror, the little burgundy number swinging gently from the hook on the wall, Cora slipped out of her black and white dogtooth trews and polyester blouse. She felt like a caterpillar breaking out of its chrysalis ready to become the butterfly she had always wanted to be. Turning her back to the mirror, as she wanted to have the full effect once she was attired, she carefully stepped into the two leg holes and pulled it up slowly. Relishing the feel of the silk as it caressed her skin, she turned to admire herself.

"Oh good grief! My nellies are like headlamps on a Morris Minor!" she gasped to herself, turning every which way to get the full effect on her uplifted boobs. She liked it very, very much.

Smoothing her hands along the bodice, every wrinkled inch of her skin was encased and hidden. The high leg was a bit of a problem, cutting into her thigh ever so slightly but she could excuse that along with the camel toe effect at the front just to have the pert boobs. This was everything she could have asked for.

"Are you okay in there Mrs Spunge?" Peggy's high-pitched, pseudo posh voice cut through her reverie. "Do you need any help?"

She thought for a moment. "Yes actually, I do. How would one go about their toileting needs whilst wearing this?" It was something that had only just crossed her mind, stripping off every time she wanted to have a wee would be such a nuisance.

"Just pull your flaps down…" Peggy helpfully offered from the other side of the curtain.

"My what?" Cora was absolutely horrified. "Aeroplanes have flaps we have, well, I think you'll find the proper word is *labia*…" she almost spat the word out. "Yes, it's called a labia and if you think I'm going to be tugging mine out each time I want a wee AND paying YOU…" she checked the price tag on the strap of the bodysuit before she continued, "…£39.99 for the privilege, you've got another think coming!"

An embarrassed silence followed, before Peggy found the right words to reply.

"No, no, no… it's the flap underneath the crotch area, Mrs Spunge; you just pull it down and undo the little poppers!"

Checking between her legs, Cora found the piece of material that Peggy had described, along with her own aforementioned 'parts' that due to old age and gravity, had ungracefully flopped out either side of the satin crotch anyway, without any need for tugging.

Quickly tucking them back in, she listened to Peggy's sniggers echoing around the shop. Her cheeks flushed hot with humiliation.

Making a mental note, she decided to add another £1,000.00 to her blackmail demand from this dreadful woman for having the sheer audacity to laugh at her!

Joe patted the empty space next to him on our bed. "Bad day?"

I shrugged. "No worse than any other one, I suppose…" I unzipped my SWAT boot and kicked it into the corner, quickly followed by the other one. "…Thrush is desperate to make my life a misery. I don't mind covering the office, foot beat even if it's equally shared and everyone gets to do it, but it's just me. I'm too old in the tooth for this Joe, but I'm not sure where to go from here." I snuggled down next to him, my head resting on his chest.

"Well, two choices really. Either I have a little 'talk' to him or you go to the Inspector." His breathing altered slightly.

I knew without even having to look at him that he was angry. "Nope, not an option, I'm not ruining everything I've worked for by reporting him. You know word gets out and I'd be lucky if anyone would want to work with me again, they'd all be terrified of saying or doing something 'sexist'…." I wriggled my fingers in an air quote, "…and me reporting them, which I wouldn't."

"Mave, there's a difference between banter and bullying, and what he's doing is bullying you purely because he doesn't like women in the job and he likes to look like the big man. Everyone knows what he's like, they'll never turn on you."

I stared at the ceiling. "Maybe not, but I can't take the chance, I'll think of something. Hey, I haven't told you about Beatrice, have I?"

He wrapped his arm around me and nibbled my ear, clearly my tale of Beatrice/Basil was the last thing on his mind. "Nope, but

I've got a feeling you're going to tell me anyway."

I quickly ran through the main body of my visit with Cyril and what I'd updated Jim with. Joe snorted the odd *oooh, yes, no* and *ah* in all the right places as he listened.

"So, he comes back roughly 1985-ish after his mum and dad were killed in that car crash on the Werrington Road, inherits their estate and takes over Tinstone Manor. Now this is where it gets interesting, not sure yet what he is or even if he's actually had a full sex change, but when he does come back to Westbury, he comes back as a woman called Beatrice. He tells everyone locally that he is Basil's cousin and the sole surviving family member because Basil met an untimely end choking on a cucumber whilst in Monte Carlo…" I looked at Joe's face giving the exact same reaction I had done with Jim. I threw my hand up, palm towards him in a staying motion. "…so, he ensconces himself in the community, opens a shop and he's lived happily like that ever since and apart from Cyril, I don't think anyone else has every suspected a thing…… until our blackmailer surfaced."

Silence.

"What do you think, hey? That's got to be what he's being blackmailed about, isn't it?" I caught my breath again, waiting for his reply.

"Yup."

I edged up on my elbows. "Did you know Joe, that husbands only give one-word answers to their wives when they can't be arsed to waste their breath on any more and are probably thinking of leaving them?"

He grinned. "Mmmmm…"

Touché

  BLUES, TWOS AND BABY SHOES

TALKING TO THE DEAD

I helped Agatha on with her Bedouin Birthing blanket and wrapped a lightweight scarf around her neck. Even though it was a pleasant day, she always seemed to feel cold lately. She studied herself in the coat stand mirror, plonking a rather eye-catching, or should I say, eye-gouging vivid green hat on her head. It matched nothing she was wearing, but that only seemed to delight her more.

"Right, I've been in touch with Balm & Potter the funeral directors and they're going to show me their range." She rubbed a little rouge into her cheeks, pinching them between her thumb and index finger, bringing a false flush of health to her face.

"Aggie, is this really what you want, don't you think it's just a little morbid, after all, you're still here and still doing really well?" In all honesty, it was me that was feeling uneasy with this planned jaunt, Agatha was just beside herself with excitement.

She pottered around her flat, gathering her gloves, keys and a clean handkerchief, before making a final check of herself in the mirror again.

"Okey dokey, are we ready?" I unhooked her shopping bag from the back of the door.

"Yes, dear, just let me decompose myself and I'll be good to go..." she took a few deep breaths and nodded. "...yes, I'm altogether now."

"Ah, so lovely to meet you Ms Winterbourne..." Norman Balm held out his unnaturally white and limp hand in greeting, "....and this must be your niece." He gave me a cursory nod.

Agatha, nonplussed by his simpering manner, got straight to the point.

"I need a coffin Mr Balm, not one of your ridiculously over the top ones, I don't need satin, or fancy wood or brass handles, no, I don't need anything like that." She edged towards the first coffin on display, slapped it, rattled it, opened the lid and let it slam down. Norman nearly had an attack of the vapours.

"Please be careful Ms Winterbourne, that one is our SleepWell Double De-luxe model, it's very, very expensive!"

"Pah, sleep well!!!!! When you've checked into the Wooden Waldorf, Mr Balm, what's the likelihood of anyone coming back to complain about the standard of the bed..." she sneered, "...I'm not buying a memory foam mattress you know!"

I felt I should apologise to Norman, but to be honest, I was rather enjoying seeing him squirm. He was such an oily little man.

"Madam, we have some who strongly believe in the resurrection of life, and they will happily choose and fund very handsome caskets for their loved ones." he sniffed, whilst examining the lid of his SleepWell Double De-Luxe coffin for damage or fingerprints.

Agatha was not to be deterred.

"Mmmmmm, yes I've heard of them, Hovis Witnesses they're called, well, whatever floats your boat I suppose." She traced her fingers over the second coffin on the other side of the wall. "I have experience of talking to the dead you know?" She turned and gave Norman one of her steely stares.

Jeez, I think it's time for me to give my fringe a Mexican wave, I

BLUES, TWOS AND BABY SHOES

haven't done one of those for a while!

I blew upwards, my breath giving a slight cooling sensation to my forehead which was becoming decidedly sweaty.

Just choose a feckin' coffin, Agatha for goodness sake...

Norman pulled out his ironed handkerchief from his top pocket and gave his own forehead a quick mop. "Really, is that like a séance or with one of those boards and a glass asking questions?"

Agatha fair bristled with indignation. "A Ouija Board, Mr Balm, is that what you mean?" She flung the tasselled end of her Bedouin Birthing Blanket over her shoulder, "I should think not, Ouija is like texting for dead people.... open to far too many typos, spelling mistakes and misunderstandings! No, I commune directly with the dead, I hear their voices and sometimes I see them."

I could see from Norman's face that he didn't quite know what to say next, so I helped him along. "Mr Balm, do you have anything a little more spiritual, more natural that would be better suited to my Aunt?"

He thought for a few moments. "Well, there is a range in the catalogue, they're eco-friendly, manufactured from willow and such like, you can even get cardboard ones. I don't hold any in stock, but I can show you a photograph." He beckoned us to follow him into the small side office. Pulling out a green and gold leatherbound book, he flicked through the pages, his finger tapped on the *Elfin Willow Weft* casket.

I wouldn't exactly call Agatha elfin-like, but this was more to her taste. "What do you think, Agatha?" I turned to see her reaction, but she wasn't there. "Did she follow us in, Mr Balm?"

Norman looked as puzzled as I did as we retraced our steps back into the main parlour where she had last been.

Bloody hell, this is all I need!

"She's quite a sick woman Mr Balm, she gets confused because of the pain medication she's on, are there any other ways out beside that one over there?" I pointed to the door we had arrived through.

Norman nodded. "There is a door through there, but that's to the laying-out room, surely she won't have gone in there?"

I sighed. "You don't know Auntie Agatha!" I had visions of her sitting amongst Norman's latest delivery of the dead, having an impromptu séance with them. "That woman will be the death of me, I'm sure, what the hell did I do to deserve this?" I tutted loudly.

"I heard that Mavis Upton!"

The disembodied voice filled the room, Norman almost lost his top set of dentures in shock. Frantically, he looked around, the soft, piped-in background music adding to the chilled atmosphere that suddenly swept around us.

He grabbed my arm. "Did you hear that?" His bulbous eyes darted left to right, searching for whatever or whoever was communing with us.

"Aggie, where are you?"

"I'm here…" A soft knocking bounced from the walls.

Norman lost all colour and clung onto the edge of the counter. "In all my years, this has never, ever happened before, are we supposed to knock back?"

"Ooooooh Mr Balm…..oooooooh I can hear you, can you hear me?" the ghostly voice echoed from the far corner.

I snorted.

Oh Agatha, you naughty girl!

Knock, knock, knock….

"Agatha, enough now, you've had your fun, where are you?" I would have loved to have continued with her game, but I didn't want to be partly responsible for Norman's unexpected death due to heart failure.

"I'm in here…"

I followed her voice to a rather cumbersome and over-the-top half-couch oak casket in the far corner, Norman followed behind me as though I was offering him some protection from the spirits of those departed. I pulled open the half-couch top revealing Agatha in sweet repose, her ginger hair splayed out on the oyster satin pillow, hands placed across her chest and a massive impish grin on her face.

"Wouldn't you think they'd have some sort of handle on the inside, I mean, how the hell are you supposed to get out?" she sniffed.

"You're not supposed to, once you're dead, you're dead Aggie! You've snuffed it, curled your toes up, ate dirt, whatever you want to call it, what the hell were you doing in there anyway?" I held her under her arms, to sit her up, whilst at the same time, smacking my shins against a small wooden, three step ladder at the side of the casket.

"I was trying it for size and comfort in the afterlife, what do you think? I'm hardly likely to take it home to replace my single bed, am I?" She heaved herself onto her knees, hitched a leg over the edge, giving poor Norman an eyeful of her lace edged bloomers as she backed down the steps.

I gave him an apologetic look. "I'm sorry Mr Balm, I think my Aunt is trying to have a little fun and adventure before the inevitable."

I watched her twirl around the room, flashes of vibrant colour, clashing materials and bright red hair, like a child that had just discovered magic.

She stopped momentarily, her eyes twinkling. "Oh Mavis, to die would be an awfully big adventure …don't you think?"

I was lost for words.

WHAT KEVIN WANTS
FOR CHRI*TH*MAS...

There are days when laughter does not come easily. Today was one of them. You could cut the atmosphere in the night kitchen with a knife, I don't think I have ever seen so many unhappy faces in one place.

"What's up?" I threw my notebook onto the table along with a packet of digestives and my tie. Dragging one of the chairs out, I squeezed myself in between Bob and Degsy. "Where's Petey?"

"He won't be in today..." Bob pursed his lips together, "...probably not tomorrow either, he's taking a couple of rest days in lieu."

"Shall I play mum?" I held the teapot up. "It'll do him good, he's not been himself lately, maybe we should see if he fancies a night out or something." I busied myself topping up the mugs and spooning sugar in for those that took it.

"Take it you've not heard then?" Degsy broke the silence.

"No, heard what?"

"She's left him, buggered off with Regan Belshaw..." Degsy grabbed the biscuits and tore at the packaging. "...he came home to find her gone. It's killed him Mave, don't think he'll ever be the same."

I didn't know what to say, I was stunned. We had all known about her on and off dalliance with Regan over the years, never had any proof and they'd never been caught in the act, it was just canteen gossip, but we had more than suspected. I looked around the table,

BLUES, TWOS AND BABY SHOES

Degsy, Bob, Mark, Jim... not one of them could meet each other's eye preferring to stare at the cracked and stained melamine. We were as much to blame, we should have done something.

I got up and quietly pushed the door closed. This was going to stay 'in-house'.

"Right, we can sit here all day feeling guilty but that's not going to help Petey, is it? We need a plan."

Mark chucked his briefcase in the boot of the car, checked the tyres and then lifted the bonnet to add a bit of water to the windscreen bottle. "D'you think it'll work?"

I sighed and shrugged. "I don't know, but if we take it in turns to visit, take him out when he's up to it, it'll let him know he's not alone. That's got to count for something, word's out that it's permanent, she's not coming back." Shielding my eyes from the afternoon sun with one hand, I looked up towards the rear windows of the nick. The hairs had prickled up on the back of my neck, giving me a feeling of being watched. I wasn't wrong. Thrush, his nose pushed up against the glass, was staring down from the first-floor window of the Sergeants office, like a buzzard watching its prey. He curled his lip and pointed to his watch. "Think Thrush is trying to tell us to get a move on."

Mark was unimpressed. "Well he can faark right off, I go out in my own time and definitely not before all the checks are made." he turned and snarled up at Thrush. "He needs taking down a peg or two, thinks he's the hard man."

I laughed. "Funnily enough, that's what Joe said about him. At least he couldn't stick me on foot today, being short of drivers, every cloud and all that, hey?"

"Knowing your Joe's fearsome reputation, I'm surprised he hasn't biffed him on the nose by now." He jumped in and started the engine. "D'you think…."

"AR12, AR12… reports are coming in of a disturbance on Borough Road, can you start making, I'll get other patrols to back you up when they come free if they're needed." Heidi cleared the air, waiting for a response.

I picked up. "Yep, will do, it's only two minutes away, any further details?"

"It's Kevin McAlpine again I'm afraid, neighbour states he's, quote, 'off his head and smashing the flat up'…"

Mark flipped the blues and twos on, pulling out in a screech of tyres onto Manor Road. "Any weapons reported, Heidi?"

"Negative."

At least that was something, McAlpine was well known for his love of ornamental machetes, swords and his all-time favourite, a set of nunchucks. Even though I knew it was there, my hand automatically went to check the CS canister on my belt. "This'll be fun, what a way to start a shift rolling around with the delectable Kevin." My stomach did a dry heave as memory served to remind me of the various odours he had a tendency to give off.

"Show us at scene, Mave…" Mark pulled in hard on the left just as an old TV came crashing through the window of the ground floor flat. It landed, with an explosion of leaves and debris, in the garden hedge. "That-a-boy Kevin, always go for the telly first, you absolute bloody melt!"

We gave each other the nod. "Going to be hands-on, he's not going to come quietly." I pushed open the gate to the small front garden, the communal main door was wide open allowing Kevin's dulcet tones to be audible above the banging and crashing coming from inside.

BLUES, TWOS AND BABY SHOES

"Kevin, it's the police, come on, don't be an idiot just come out quietly." I gave Mark a grin. No way was he going to come like a good boy, but you had to have a go at being 'good cop' before wading in. "Heidi..." I clicked my radio and acknowledged her response, "...we're going to need some extra bodies here, can patrols start making?"

"Mave!!!"

I ducked as a rather fetching sequinned covered turquoise ceramic lamp came hurtling through the door. It just missed me, hit the sandstone boundary wall and smashed into pieces on the path.

"You bastard, I feckin' made that lamp meself, it was even on Instagram." The thickly accented voice of Kevin's long-suffering girlfriend filled the hallway. "Yer a fucking knob, you are, yer ma should've swallowed!"

I cringed and pulled a face, Mark just laughed in agreement. "Chantelle, just come out and leave him in there, we'll deal with it." He edged closer to the front door and grabbed her by the arm pulling her outside onto the path. Her hair was plastered to her face, mixed with blood from a cut just above her eye.

"Did he do that?" I quickly pressed a wound pad from my pouch into her hand, indicating for her to stem the flow.

She nodded. "He's got one of his knives too..."

"What is it this time?"

"He's speedballing…. Cocaine." She dabbed her head and checked the pad.

"Mark, we need to go in hard matey, no point in faffing around if he's got a knife." I racked my Casco baton to its full length in preparation. Mark did the same.

"Shit...!"

Before either of us had chance to go in, Kevin came bowling

out, a curved dagger held aloft, his lips pulled back, teeth bared and spittle forming on his lips. With no time to think, any fancy moves taught in training went out of the window as we both jumped on him, knocking him backwards into the garden. I heard a clatter as something metal hit the concrete.

Please God let that be the knife....

Kevin wasn't going to make this easy, his strength was unbelievable, and he clearly wasn't feeling pain as we piled on top of him. He struck his foot out and kicked me in the face, pushing my teeth into my top lip, the metallic tang of blood filled my mouth as my head jerked backwards, smacking into the wall. Stunned, I temporarily lost hold of him. I spat to clear my mouth, anger bubbling in my chest.

He was going to get more than a girlie punch in his hairy chakras by the time I'd finished with him...

Mark had him in a headlock as I twisted myself round to hold his body and legs down. If we could restrain him just long enough until the others arrived, more hands would make getting him cuffed easier. Kevin was having none of it as he bucked, writhed and fought, pulling away from Mark. Hearing klaxons in the distance, I mentally ticked off the seconds as they got closer.

Just a little bit longer, that's all...

Suddenly getting a change of heart, Chantelle took the opportunity to put her two-pennyworth in. "Gerroff him yer bastards, that lads me world, leave 'im alone youse lot..."

If I hadn't been otherwise engaged in flattening Kevin into the grass, I'd have shaken my head and offered her a lesson in English Language and the art of romance.

Suddenly my breath was taken away by the most agonising pain in my undercarriage. "Eeeeeeoooooooowwwww, what the feck is he doing, Mark get him off...."

  BLUES, TWOS AND BABY SHOES

Kevin 'The Twat' McAlpine had sunk his mangy gnashers into my bum. The searing agony radiated outwards, covering the whole of my right butt cheek as he clamped down hard and wouldn't release.

"Mark, Mark, Mark he's biting my arse." I squealed, my voice getting higher and higher the more Kevin bit down on my skin.

Mark sprang into action. "Let go of her.... her.... bottom, you bloody perv..." He grabbed hold of his hair and yanked his head backwards, but Kevin wasn't going to be thwarted. He buried his head further into my bum, his teeth retaining their grip. I screamed. Mark tried again, this time he doubled handed, hair and an ear and two fingers in his nostrils to cause the utmost impact on McAlpine's pain levels. It worked, as Mark and McAlpine tumbled backwards into the flowerbed, my nether regions were dramatically released.

My relief was palpable, both for my poor bum and on seeing the rest of the section arrive in a hail of blues and twos.

Bob was first over the low-level wall, seeing the state of my face, he roared. "Get the bastard in cuffs and in the van."

I scrambled to my feet as McAlpine was overpowered, cuffed and hauled off to the waiting prisoner van, but not before he spat out his words of wisdom.

"You dirthy, thucking thower of filff..."

"Eh, what did he say?" Bob was genuinely interested.

Degsy hauled McAlpine round to face him. "What was that?"

"I thed you dirthy thower of thucking filff, are yoof deaf or thumfink?" He squirmed.

"Ah, I see. Houston, we have a problem..." Degsy doubled up laughing. "...turn around Mave."

With my banged head, split lip and butt cheek glowing and pounding, I grumpily obliged only to be greeted by uncontrollable giggling and lack of sympathy from the lads.

Hanging from the bum of my combat pants, firmly hooked into the newly made holes in the material was a dental bridge holding six manky teeth belonging to Kevin 'The Twat' McAlpine, who now had less teeth than a Halloween pumpkin.

"Hey Kev..." Degsy watched the expression on McAlpine's face. "... here's one for yer. Can you say *Sally is a sheet slitter, she slits sheets?*"

McAlpine thought about it for a moment, sniffed and jerked his head. "Only if her arse givths me my masturbators back!"

Degsy rolled his eyes. "Masticators, Kevin, they're called masticators... although knowing what you and Chantelle get up to at a weekend, nothing would bloody surprise me!"

MORE SECRETS AND LIES

I carefully opened the letter addressed to Agatha. Pulling out the folded paper, I hesitated, taking a quick glance at her as she sat in the chair, lips set firm with her hands in her lap, fingers laced together, staring stoically ahead. It was as though she was afraid to register any emotion.

"I did go back Mavis."

"Go back where?" I sat down next to her and took hold of her hand. It was thin and cold.

"To the picture house. I regretted it immediately, leaving her there, I knew I couldn't keep her, but I wanted to make sure she was safe. She'd already been taken to the Cottage Hospital by then." Her voice tailed off as she took a laboured intake of breath, the tears starting to form in her pale eyes.

I didn't want to speak for fear of interrupting her, she was clearly trying to expunge painful memories. I waited, the wall clock with its intermittent ticking was simultaneously soothing and haunting. She gathered her thoughts before she spoke again. "I waited at the hospital, I told them it was me, it was all such a rush, so much going on, they made me feel so ashamed. I was sent to a mother and baby home…" She wiped her eyes with the cotton handkerchief that was screwed into a ball.

My heart was breaking for her, I could physically feel how

painful it was for her to relive her past.

Her fingers began to pluck at the edge of her cardigan. "They told me I couldn't nurse her, that I shouldn't bond with her, but I did, I loved her. I even gave her a name, I called her Angela." She let out a soft mewling sound as the tears began to fall. "Then one day, about six weeks later, she was gone. I was working the kitchens and when I came back to the nursery, her crib was empty, there was just a faint indent in the blankets where she had been. They'd come and taken her away to her new home, to her new mum and I never saw her again."

"Oh Agatha, I had no idea, I'm so, so sorry..." I put my arms around her to give her a gentle hug. "...I just thought you'd left her and hadn't looked back." I felt dreadful. How many times had I taught others not to assume, not to judge without all the facts, and I had been guilty of just that myself? I had judged Agatha.

She shook her head. "No, sometimes I wish I had, so now you see why it's so important for me to find her. I have to tell her she was loved, that I still love her and to say I'm sorry."

"You will, I'll move heaven and earth for you, I promise. If I can't find her then nobody can, you know I take after Mum for being stubborn, don't you?" I smiled, trying to lighten and encourage but she bit back further tears. She wasn't finished.

"They more or less threw me out the following day. That's how it worked in those places, once the baby has been taken, the welfare of the mum was of no concern to them. I went to the train station and got on the first train that came in, it took me to Blackpool and that's where I started my Gypsy business, didn't come back here for quite a few years. By then it was if it had never happened, as though she had never existed." She waved her hand at the envelope. "Go on, you might as well get it over with."

I opened the letter and read the contents. It just confirmed what

I already knew.

"There's no news I'm afraid, it's just says that your details have been lodged and if the child in question makes contact, they will forward those details on." I paused. "Agatha, who was the father?"

She bit down hard on her bottom lip. "He wasn't a nice man, Mavis, he was the one who forced me to do what I did and all because he'd lied about an accident he'd had…" she took a deep breath. "…he had a fiancée too, went onto marry her a few years later."

I watched the sadness in her eyes as she struggled to compose herself. Time was running out. I knew it and she knew it and something told me that this was one last wish I wasn't going to be able to give her.

"Come on, let's dry those eyes and go on this shopping trip you got me here for, hey?"

She meekly nodded, tucked her handkerchief into her sleeve and picked up her rainbow coloured hippy bag. "… his name was Cyril Hislop, Mavis - and he definitely wasn't a nice man at all!"

My breath caught in my throat as I tried desperately not to show any sort of reaction.

Easter surprise in fifty-five! That's it. Oh what a tangled web we weave!

"Right, here we go, M&S coming up on the right." I held the door open for her, "What is it exactly that you're looking to buy, Agatha?"

"Oh, just something a little special for a special occasion…" She swept ahead of me in a flurry of mismatched colours and materials with those bloody awful T-bar shoes with the Velcro straps slapping on the glossy tiled floor. "A mutant friend of mine and your mums, old Florence from the bakery, said I'd grab a bargain here, they've got a sale on."

"Florence is a *mutual* friend, Agatha." I gave her a kindly smile.

"Oh, is she a mutant friend of yours too? Well I never, small world."

Blimey Mum, she's definitely your sister!

"How about the shoe department first?" I gave a cursory glance at her T-bars. "Shoes always makes a difference to an outfit."

Holding on to the rail in the lift, she tilted her head and stuck out her foot. "There's nothing wrong with these, done me good with every outfit, they seem to go with everything and they're very comfortable." She tipped a toe to admire them. "Don't you like them, Mavis?"

I almost choked trying to force out a lie. "Oh, of course I do, they're absolutely gorgeous, but I was just thinking of something nice to go with your special outfit."

"Well, if you really think so, but it's such a shame to buy new shoes considering where they'll end up, but if you say so…" The lift doors opened, and she was away before I could reply.

She almost glided amongst the rails of clothes, touching fabrics, holding dresses up to the light, actively avoiding anything that didn't display an array of colours like a demented peacock. Every now and then she would find something that tickled her fancy. The *ooohs* and *aahs* indicating that a choice could possibly be made.

"This is it, this is the one…" she held up a bright yellow and emerald green swirl silk trouser suit. "…I want this one!"

Resisting the urge to put my sunglasses on, particularly once she'd chosen a pair of vivid orange sandals to 'compliment' her outfit, I ushered her towards the café. "Time for a coffee and to catch our breath I think."

  BLUES, TWOS AND BABY SHOES

She beamed as she sat down at the table. "I've had a lovely time, thank you for bringing me." She peered into the large M&S bag, examining and coveting her spoils.

"Aggie, I'm curious, what's the special occasion?"

She thought for a moment, offered me a rather breathless sigh and this time, she took *my* hand. "My death of course, Mavis. I'm not going on my last journey without something special to wear for the occasion."

Oh bloody hell…

I didn't think it would happen, or even think it could happen, but in that moment, as the tears stung my eyes, I suddenly realised that somewhere along the way, I'd grown awfully fond of Auntie Agatha.

BOYS WILL BE BOYS

The gentle hum of twenty different conversations hovered over the tables in the canteen. As usual CID were huddled in the far corner near the wall telephone, two spare tables away from uniform who had taken up the three remaining ones near to the serving hatch.

"Morning, love what can I do yer for?" Maggie wiped the stainless-steel servers with her dishcloth, more out of habit than the fact it needed doing.

"Bacon butty please, Maggie and a mug of tea." I handed over the money, waiting whilst she poured from a large industrial tea urn. She banged the mug down on the counter, slopping tea over the sides whilst simultaneously adjusting the pink hairnet on her head.

"I'll give yer a shout when yer butty's ready."

"Thanks, Maggie." I wandered over to where Bob and Degsy were seated. "Morning boys."

"Listen, what d'yer think of this..." Bob pointed a half-eaten breakfast batch at me, drippy egg oozed out of the sides, plopping onto the table. "...see the lass over there working with Maggie?"

I ducked my head down and peered through the hatch. A really pretty, petite girl was busy at one of the food prep stations. "Yep." I wondered where this was going.

"Well, her name's Cheryl and we think she's taken a bit of a shine to our Petey, she's had an extra sausage for him every morning this week AND a bigger helping of beans." Bob jerked his head and popped his eyes in a conspiratorial gesture. "…and that's not a euphemism either!"

Degsy just sniggered.

"Where's Petey now?" The last thing I wanted was for the lads to take the mickey if he wasn't up to taking the banter. He'd come back to work, subdued, but actually stronger than I'd thought he would be. He seemed to have accepted Betty's decision to leave him. Sometimes though, that was when it could be dangerous, when friends and colleagues assume that everything is okay, that the smile has been slapped on and life is good again. We'd all agreed to keep an eye on him just in case.

"He's just gone to get his yoghurt from the fridge in the night kitchen, he's just given us a lecture on healthy eating." Bob smirked as he bit into his batch.

"Bacon butty, get it now before it goes in the bin…" Maggie's rasping voice boomed from the serving hatch. I often wondered if anything ever made it into that mythical bin she'd been screeching about for years. It did make everyone shift their bums at the prospect of losing their breakfast to the cavernous depths of it, though.

Grabbing it from the counter, I turned without looking and almost collided with Petey as he edged his way back into his seat. "Hi Mave, did you enjoy your time off?"

"I did, not too bad, bit up and down with Agatha but it was nice to have some family time, too. Did I miss much here?"

He shook his head. "Not really, ticking over, ticking over." He sat down, spoon poised ready to eat his yoghurt.

I took the chair next to him. "Throw us the brown sauce, Degs."

He obliged, skidding it along the table, it hit my plate and tipped over. "Cheers." Squirting a huge dollop over the bacon I squished the two pieces back together again and was just about to take a bite, when Petey pointed his finger accusingly at me.

"Not good for your health that, Mave, it's real heart attack food, you know." He spooned a dollop of yoghurt into his mouth, savouring the tang. "You should be eating good stuff at your age, setting an example for Benjamin, really you should."

I was lost for words. *At your age! Had he just said, 'at your age'?*

Bob pretended he was looking out of the window, even though he was facing away from me, I just knew he would be trying to control a snort of derision aimed at me.

"I think I've got to be this old Petey even with this type of food, it's only a bacon butty for goodness sake!"

"Ah but it's what it's doing to your heart, processed white bread, fatty bacon AND I know for a fact Maggie fries it rather than grills it. Now take this..." he waved the yoghurt pot at me, "...this is full of goodness, it has tiny minute orgasms, what more could you want?"

That was enough to finish Bob off, he snorted so loudly it made everyone in the canteen go quiet and stare at us. "Petey, mate. I think our Mave would be more impressed with mighty big orgasms if Joe's got anything to do with it!"

Poor Petey turned the colour of the ketchup bottle. "You know what I meant... I...I...didn't.... oh dear!"

As our laughter filled the room, Petey's face broke out into a huge grin which slowly became genuine bellows of his own laughter, his eyes sparkling in fun rather than tears, something he hadn't been able to do for quite some time.

Unseen by us, a pretty young woman dreamily watched him from afar.

Cheryl hung the red checked tea towel on the hook and carefully stacked the mugs in the plastic tray, all the while wondering how she could make this sweet, kindly man notice her.

Beatrice plumped the cushions behind her and smoothed out the counterpane that draped across her duvet as Maddie placed the tray in front of her. "Thank you dear, any mail?"

Maddie shook her head. "Not yet Ma'am." She drifted over to the heavy draped curtains to open them. A stream of sunlight flooded the room, making Beatrice squint. "I've sent word to the village for a fresh delivery of salads and vegetables and the butcher will be making his delivery this afternoon. Is there anything else you require?" She waited, taking on her usual humble stance. How she hated being this subservient but needs must. This was exactly how Beatrice liked her to behave, and Beatrice did put this rather grand roof over her head and paid her wages.

"No, that will be all thank you, Maddie." She flicked the broadsheet newspaper out and began to read the headlines. Hedy, her beloved dog, was curled up beside her.

"Well my little poppet, it's not a very newsworthy day is it?" She thumbed through until she came to the stocks and shares, quickly scanning them, she nodded her head in approval.

Mmmmm, things were on the up, thank goodness.

Haute Couture by Beatrice was really just a little hobby of hers, it kept her mentally agile and gave her an interest. Financially it was merely pocket money in the grand scheme of things. It was well managed by the two girls she had trained herself, which gave her the advantage of only having to go to the boutique if the mood fell upon her. She gave Hedy a tickle under the chin and stared pensively at the portrait of Charles and Prunella on the wall. Not really the best boudoir décor, but she felt she owed it to them to at least acknowledge their contribution to her current wealthy and very comfortable status.

"Status, yes that's the downfall of us all, isn't it, Hedy?" she took a bite of her toast. "I suppose £2,000.00 is mere peanuts to me, but it did gall me so to hand it over."

The plain brown jiffy bag had been left, as instructed, wedged between an old Cosmopolitan magazine, in a bin near the Bowling Green hut in Westbury Park. She had tried to keep watch, but it was competition day and it had been far too busy with the comings and goings of team members and the crowd who had come to watch. In less than five minutes, it had been taken. She had scanned the crowds hoping to pin point a likely candidate but to no avail.

"Do you know, Hedy, one day the world will be more accepting of people like me, I just know it will. I feel such sadness that now is not the time. I could have lost everything, absolutely everything I stand for, if those threats had been carried out."

She picked up the knitted willy warmer from her bedside cabinet, chuckling to herself. "I'll give whoever is doing this their due, they certainly have a sense of humour and a rather over active imagination...." she dangled it between her thumb and forefinger, "...I'm sure my wee appendage unharnessed and unleashed would fit into this with enough room to accommodate Rasputin's legendary third leg as well!"

Beatrice allowed herself a deep, guttural, manly laugh, the type of laugh she hadn't emitted since she had last called herself Basil Higgins.

How's it going chick?" Marion carried on checking her lipstick in the mirror whilst I hastily squeezed behind her and barrelled my way into Trap 2.

"Nightmare, Thrush has had me on foot beat again and I've been desperate for the loo for the last two hours, this is the first chance I've had to come into the nick." I heaved a sigh of relief and rolled my eyes. Since having Ben I'd become spectacularly adept at being a Gusset Gripper. "Hey Maz, what do you know about the new girl in the Canteen, I think Bob said her name was Cheryl."

"Not much really, nice girl, single, bit on the simple side if you get my drift…" She tailed off, the sound of the hand-drier drowning out the possibility of any further conversation.

Clicking the lock, I poked my head out from the cubicle. "Simple! In what way? Simple like dense or simple meaning sweetly innocent."

"The latter, she's just a lovely girl, just hope she doesn't get her head turned by some of the suave bastards in this nick. Why, someone interested?" She smacked her lips together, checking the coverage of her lipstick.

"Well, we think she's a bit hot on our Petey and if the way he looks at her are anything to go by, he feels the same. We could do with fixing something up to get them together." My mind was already racing with ideas.

Maz looked thoughtful as she popped the hairbrush back into her bag. "Mmmm, difficult to know what to do for the best to be honest. Are you sure he's ready?"

I ran my hands under the tap. "Ooh, that's a good point, maybe we could subtly hint until he makes the move himself rather than us setting him up, so he feels in control again."

"Sort of subliminal messages? Great idea, then he can go at his own pace. Best speak to the lads though, just in case their banter starts to put him off." She checked herself again in the mirror.

"Maz, the poor lad is that naïve, nothing seems to register with him, you'd be mistaken in thinking he's got the skin of a rhino..." wiping my hands on my combats, I gave her a conspiratorial grin, "... seriously, the engine's running but there's nobody behind the wheel!"

"Leave it with me chick, I'm sure we can come up with something." She thought for a moment, her hand hovering on the door handle. "Hey, maybe we could put up an OK Cupid poster on the notice board outside the canteen with a thumbnail photo of them both on it, now that'd be a great hint, dead subliminal every time they walk in!"

Oh yeah Maz, subtle as ever!

BLUES, TWOS AND BABY SHOES

IT'S A WOMAN'S WORLD

Junk & Disorderly was a welcoming sight to Cora as she slowly made her way up the High Street. It was nice to get back to a little bit of normality, to serve the public with second hand polyester trews, sandals, threadbare jumpers and dog-eared books with the odd chipped ceramic Scottie dog thrown in. She bent down to pick up a discarded crisp packet, forcing a little burp to unexpectedly escape.

"Oh my, this double life I'm living is playing havoc with my ulcers..." she mused to no one in particular. "...I really must take more care of myself."

It was hardly surprising to find that it was all catching up with her. To the outside world she was just a sweet little old lady, the widow of the late Harold Spunge, who adores cats and knits teapot cosies in her spare time. But then there was the other side to this new Cora May Spunge, the one she had so carefully crafted herself. Oh yes, she was now the wicked, ever so naughty, righter of wrongs, bringer of past sins and misdeeds and wearer of a pretty fine silk body suit with flaps and poppers from Peggy Parkers' Lingerie shop.

She giggled as she pushed open the door, the little bell giving out its unique tinkling sound heralding her arrival.

Edna Flaybrick was cosily ensconced in the book corner which was situated behind the purple rail. She looked up from the paperback she was reading and gave Cora a cursory nod before returning to page 33 of the tattered Mills and Boon she had grabbed from the shelf. Cora knew that Edna would never buy ANY book until she'd found the naughty pages and read them thoroughly to see if they were erotic enough for her taste.

She couldn't resist. "They're like *diamonds* amongst the coal dust aren't they, Edna?" She'd probably overstepped the mark, but it made her tummy flip, just the merest chance that Edna would realise what she knew brought that alive feeling again. It excited her.

Edna's head snapped up, her eyes bore into Cora, who quickly pretended to be re-arranging the clothes on the pink rail. She loved the way each block of rails were divided by the predominant colour of the items hanging from them. She could feel Edna's gaze following her around the shop floor as she fussed, adjusted and flicked through various items of clothing.

"*What* did you just say?" Edna had found her voice and a very cross voice it was too. She put her book down and waited, arms folded.

Cora looked nonplussed. "I said…" she pointed to the book on the counter, "…that is a diamond of a book amongst the coal dust of the other less enjoyable ones. It's just an expression Edna, why?" If she could have taken a more obvious greater glee from this situation, she would have done.

Edna spluttered, setting her lips into a thin line. "Nothing, I just misheard that's all."

The moment was interrupted by Freda bustling in from the store room with a tray of tea and biscuits. "Morning ladies, and what a lovely morning it is." Oblivious to the tense atmosphere between Edna and Cora, she bumbled on. "Shall I play mother?"

Watching the amber liquid pour from the spout of the floral teapot into the delicate cups, Edna vowed she would keep a very close watch on old Cora in the future. Although what a frigid, cat-loving, dried up old prune of a woman could possibly know about her own past life was a mystery.

"Get Upton to come to my office right away." Sergeant Ballcock pushed his pen back into his top pocket and waited for Petey to acknowledge his command. He didn't much care for being on this Section and cared even less for half the crew on it, and in particular this dithering wuss standing in front of him.

In his book this wet behind the ear idiot came only second to Upton at the bottom of the pile. He couldn't abide women taking up a valuable uniform, going around thinking they could do a job that was made for men. He'd broken lesser than her and he was pretty sure she'd crack soon enough.

He sat down at his desk and started stacking the files. She was reputed to be a good typist so this lot would keep her busy, a perfect job for a woman. A laugh bubbled up in this throat but was quickly brought back under control by a knock on the office door.

"Come." He never wasted more words than were necessary.

I pushed open the door and tried to fake a cheery greeting. "Hi Thru...err Sarge, you wanted to see me?"

Faark, that was close, I almost slipped up there.

My heart hammered against my ribs as my palms started to sweat. I wanted to kick myself, I was a grown woman and I was letting this bully turn me into a dithering bloody idiot.

"Mavis, take these. I want all the finalisation reports typed up before scoff time and when you've finished those, I'll have something else for you to do for the rest of the shift."

I looked at his face, he was revelling in this, his slimy grin was getting wider. I took the huge backlog of files from him. "Err will do Sarge, but is there any chance I could do these on handover, I'm doubled crewed with Degsy today and we're the only IR car available for the immediate response jobs?"

"What part of 'do these before scoff' did you not understand, hey?" his voice was measured but angry. He stood up from his desk and closed the office door. "If I say do something, you do it… if I say jump, you pause only to ask, 'how high', got it?"

Taken completely by surprise, I nodded.

"You're a woman, Upton, you don't belong in a job like this…" He sat back down at his desk, pen poised. "…not front line anyway and when you eventually get that fact into your thick skull, then maybe we might get somewhere." He rhythmically tapped his pen on the desk. "You're fit for nothing more than office duties, filing and school crossings. I can and will make life very difficult for you, do I make myself understood?"

I stood looking at him, at first lost for words. He was nothing more than a jerk, a horrible excuse for a human being, or as Degsy would so succinctly put it, he was Twatbadger!

Fuck it!

That had just been the straw that broke the camel's back. I'd had enough, the lost words pushed to the surface and came tumbling out of my mouth.

"I'm glad you closed the door Alan, not just for what you had to say, but for what I'm about to say." My voice quivered, not through fear but through sheer, unbridled anger. I'd called him by his name, not wanting to give him validation by his rank.

Now or never, Mave my girl, go for it!

"How dare you speak to me like that! Sergeant or not, those stripes do not give you the right to treat me, or anyone else like this." I caught my breath, the knot in the pit of my stomach tightened, my heart was pounding. Thrush began to slowly change colour from a mild pink to a florid purple, his eyes almost popping from their sockets.

I couldn't stop, all the frustration and anger was bubbling up. I tore into him, jabbing my finger as I made each point. "I *will* take lawful orders from you and I *will* work to my highest standard; not for you, but for the job, my colleagues and the people out there…" I pointed to the window, "…but I am not prepared to put up with this crap just because you don't like or agree with women in the job. We're here to stay so get used to it. One day you just might need one of us to bail you out of the shit!"

He was leaning so far away from me in his chair, I thought he was going to topple over backwards. His mouth was gaping open like the proverbial fish. "I…I… you…. you can't…."

I didn't give him the chance to speak. I leant in, invading his space. "So, let me make this clear; this is it, one warning and one warning only. It stays here between you and me unless you want to make it otherwise. We work it out, you treat me fairly and we get on, if you can't do that, then the next time you try and make my life a misery, I *will* go to the Inspector. I have all the evidence I need and witnesses to prove any complaint I make about how you treat me. Do I make *myself* understood?"

Thrush, stunned by my unexpected outburst, just nodded.

I dumped the files on his desk. "I'll pick those up at handover and get them done, in the meantime I've got jobs to go to." I slammed the door on my way out.

Only when I'd walked the full length of the corridor and disappeared into the toilets, did I allow myself to breathe. Slumping back against the door, the realisation of what had just happened, hit me.

Shit, shit, shit…. I've done it now!

CALL OF THE WILD

I popped two paracetamols into my mouth and followed up with a slug of water from the plastic bottle to wash them down. The rush of adrenalin in the Sarge's office had given me the mother of all headaches. Holding my hands out in front of me, a slight tremor still ran through my fingers, I'd got myself so worked up, mainly in anger, and now I had the trepidation of wondering how Thrush would follow up on my outburst. I'd either get it in the neck even more or he'd report me, I couldn't see him blithely carrying on as though nothing had happened between us.

I slammed my locker door shut and picked up my hat and briefcase.

Maybe this time next week it'll be my P45 I'll be picking up instead!

"Yo, Mave, control room have just given us a job, sounds like a stinky one…" Degsy stuck his head around the bank of lockers, blowing out his cheeks and holding his nose, "…masks at the ready!"

Although I was glad of the distraction, I groaned. "Maybe we could hijack Petey and send him, he could redeem himself with a real sudden death. What's the score?"

He held up the print-out, scanning the details. "Terrible smell which has got worse the last few weeks, neighbours in the flat next door say it's overpowering."

"Environmental at the Council?" I shoved my stuff on the back seat of the patrol car and jumped in the driver's seat.

"Nah, passed to us as first port of call as always. Probably because occupier's not been seen for a while." He mimicked retching and gagging.

It took less than five minutes to arrive at the Victorian doubled fronted Terraced house. Converted into flats in the late 1970's its grandeur and size had accommodated two ground floor apartments, a further two on the first floor and a large open plan attic flat. The twitch of the net curtain in the bay window, meant our arrival was eagerly anticipated by someone inside. The large glossy red communal front door was flung open before I had a chance to ring any of the bells that stood regimental against the brickwork.

"Oh thank goodness you've come, it's appalling, absolutely appalling... I really don't see why we should have to put up with it." The shrew like appearance of Mrs Dorothy Egerton belied her forceful nature as she continued to rattle on, her voice increasing in volume the more the colourful words to describe her predicament tumbled out. "Ever since we had the heavy rain and flooding, it's got worse. Our cellar has dried out, so it's not us but it still stinks down there and now the whole house is starting to smell." She was quite indignant.

Degsy gave me a dig in the ribs, a cue for me to take the lead.

"Well, we're here to investigate Mrs Egerton, and we will do whatever we can to help." There, that should quell the onslaught, it normally did.

"Well, investigate or not, I'm here to tell you..." The rest of her words were muffled as she disappeared along the small corridor into her flat. She slapped her hand on the first door on the left as she passed it. "...have to keep it shut all the time, it's dreadful I tell you, dreadful; I've even taken to sleeping on the sofa in the back room, it's still bad, but not as bad as in there."

I gave Degsy a sideways glance. Charm and appeasement were not going to work with Dorothy today.

She shuffled into the sitting room waiting for us to catch up with her. The small room was chintz and lace, peppered with china ornaments on every available surface. Two floral wing backed armchairs sat either side of the fireplace, a wicker basket which held needles and wool was nestled at the side of the chair that held her imprint in the cushion, a stuffed sofa had evidence of her sleeping arrangements with a carefully folded duvet on one arm and a pillow on the other. I opened my mouth to speak just as a sudden rancid whiff hit my nostrils.

"You have a lo…. *hwoorf*……"

Degsy looked incredulous and started laughing as I desperately tried to regain my composure. I hadn't retched mid-sentence since I was a probationer. I tried again.

"Mrs Egert…. *hwoorf, hwoorf* … oh dear me… *hwoorf*!" As my eyes began to water and my face flushed to burning point, the stench tentatively reached Degsy's nostrils forcing him to suddenly join me in a similar distress call, until we sounded like two feral cats puking up fur balls in stereo.

Mrs Egerton just looked on in triumph, as though our discomfort justified her demands for our attention. "See, what did I tell you…" she jabbed a finger at the party wall, "…it's coming from him next door. I'm very au fait with death, and THAT…" she stabbed her finger again, almost knocking a porcelain figurine from the mantlepiece "…is the smell of death. Mark my words, he's not only kicked the bloody bucket in that cellar, he's stamped on it as well!"

Bent double outside on the pavement, gulping in a huge lungful of fresh air, we held each other up, crippled half with disgust and half laughter at our ridiculously unprofessional reaction to Dorothy's stinky abode.

"Feck me, if it's that bad *inside* her house, can you imagine what it's going to be like when we go in there?" Degsy caught his breath, shaking his head as he pointed at the house next door.

"Judging by the stench, there's not going to be much to resuscitate either!" I wiped my nose with a tattered tissue I'd found in my trouser pocket. "Right, best battle cry, hold your nose, in we go!" I started up the steps to the front door. It was identical in structure to Dorothy's house, the only difference being, it hadn't been converted and was still one entire house. A voters check gave only one resident, Richard P Swett, who according to Dorothy, in between our bouts of dry barfing, was in his seventies.

"Tell you what, if you go in, I'll nip back to the car and erm… pick up, uh… well, whatever… and I'll tell you what, if it's not in the car, I can whizz back to the nick for you to get whatever it is that we don't have in the car, if you want?" he grinned, looking hopeful.

"Nice try soft lad, I don't think so. If I've got to go in, so have you." I lifted the letterbox and bent down to have a sniff, just to confirm what we already suspected. "Holy shit!" Unexpectedly greeted by a pair of beady eyes on the other side of the slot, I stumbled backwards in surprise, bowling into Degsy. "Someone's in there."

The door creaked open, leaving a gap wide enough for a set of boney fingers to curl around the peeling woodwork. A rush of air brought a blast of putrid odour through the opening.

"Mr Swett?" My voice sound tinny and distant. I cleared my throat and tried again, this time a little more commanding. "Mr Richard Swett?"

He opened the door a little further so that we could see his face, his eyes darting from side to side behind round, dark rimmed glasses. A dim light from the hallway reflected from his polished bald head, tufts of dark hair breaking up the expanse by sprouting out above his ears. Somewhere in the furthest reaches of my memory, I tried to pull out where I knew him from; his familiar face barely registered an acknowledgement of us as his lips set in a thin line.

That's it. It's Reginald Christie! He's the image of Reginald Christie the serial killer.

"Can I help you?" He lisped as his head dropped forward in a slight subservient manner.

Degsy moved in to stand next to me, breathing through his mouth, giving a pretty good impression of Darth Vader, he addressed Mr Swett. "Afternoon Sir, *hhhhhhhaaaaaa…* we're here about the smell *hhhhhoooooo…* I wonder if we could take a look around?"

Mr Swett moved to one side, waving his arm with a flourish to invite us in.

Oh gawd, barf-central; this is going to be horrendous.

"Yes, I must admit it has been a little bit pungent these last few months and I don't even have a very good sense of smell. I haven't a clue what is causing it. You're very welcome to investigate officers." He smiled, not in a nice, welcoming way. It was a simpering, creepy smile.

Just like…….Reginald Christie!

Judging by the look on Degsy's face, he was thinking the exact same thing. Alarm bells were ringing. What on earth were we going to find within the walls of 10 Bridlington Place? What horrors might....

I interrupted my own train of thought by suddenly letting out a squeal, making Degsy almost lose his footing on the vestibule step in shock. "10 Bridlington Place... this is 10 Bridlington Place!!"

Mr Swett peered over his glasses, amused by my reaction to the similarities. "I was in the police many years ago too, my dear..." he pointed to a framed faded photograph hanging against the flocked, damp-stained wallpaper in the hallway. It depicted a middle-aged man in police uniform. I read the inscription underneath. *Special Constable 0030 R Swett 1970-1975*

My skin crawled and my heart beat just that little bit faster as I followed Degsy into the bowels of 10 Bridlington Place.

Bob forked out half of the chicken fried rice onto the plate and dumped a handful of chips on top before pouring the carton of curry over the small mountain he'd made. "Degs, d'you want the rest?"

Degsy, dressed in a white all-in-one prisoner suit, shook his head. He was still green around the gills from our foray into 10 Bridlington Place. "Nah, you're okay mate, couldn't even think of putting anything into me guts just at the moment." He took a large swig of tea, the noise of it hitting his throat gurgled around the night kitchen.

"Mave?"

I looked up from my report. "Yeah, go on then, I think I could manage something now, thanks."

Bob shoved the plastic container towards me. "So, we've heard snippets but what actually went down in the horror house of

Reggie Christie then?" Laughing, he ravenously shoved a large forkful of rice into his mouth.

I looked over to Degsy and gave him a wry smile. "Shall we tell him Degsy, you know, like whilst he's eating?"

Bob looked insulted. "I've been in this job more years than Petey can count up to, d'you not think I've seen, dealt with and heard about every possible way there is to die?"

"Nobody died, Bob." I pinched a chip from the paper in the middle of the table and popped it into my mouth. "It was shit! Straightforward, bog standard; excuse the pun, shit."

Degsy let out a groan and started retching again, scraping back his chair, he quickly vacated the night kitchen, his legs rustling together in the paper suit as he legged it down the corridor. Not meaning to be unsympathetic to his plight, I sniggered as I continued regaling Bob and the rest of the lads with the story. "It would appear our Mr Richard P Swett was a tight arsed miser who thought he was a bit of a dab hand at DIY, so when he fitted his own downstairs bathroom in 1998 he didn't let a little matter of having no direct sewage pipe for the bog stop him in his tracks. So, once he'd found a suitable site in the room for his butt throne and he'd plumbed the water in, he did no more than cut a hole in the floorboards to accommodate it." I pinched another chip and dipped it into what was left of Bob's curry sauce. "He then screwed and sealed an extender pipe on the toilet outlet and shoved it into the hole leading to the cellar, so as far as he was concerned, job done without the need of a qualified plumber."

I could see a few confused faces sitting around the table, forks half-poised as they tried to work out the logistics. "Anyhow, Degsy goes down into the cellar to check and unfortunately confirmed the whole sorry mess by slipping on the stairs and inadvertently taking a little swim in the heady mixture of a DIY cesspit."

Bob looked incredulous. "He did what?"

"Yep, no word of a lie," I howled laughing. "Since 1998 Dick Swett, as we have so affectionately decided to call him, has twice a day been sitting on his throne and shitting directly into his own cellar."

Like the enchanting call of the wild, the distant, muffled, melodic sound of '*hwoorf, hwoorf*' travelled along the corridor from Trap 1 in the gents' toilets as Degsy once again vacated what little was left of his stomach contents.

THE DROP

Cora sat quietly in the shopping mall, enjoying a nice Devon Cream tea. Her dilemma had been strawberry jam first and then the clotted cream, or clotted cream first and then the jam. She had diplomatically solved the problem by cutting the scone in two and decorating each half accordingly. She seemed to vaguely remember somewhere along the line that this was the difference between a Cornish tea and a Devon one.

"See, all those years with Harold hadn't been wasted." She coyly giggled to herself. Harold had been such a stickler for protocol, as far as he'd been concerned, his way had always been the right way to do things. She let a small sigh escape before she took another sip of tea. That had been the problem throughout their marriage, Harold's insistence that he knew better.

She wistfully remembered the day she had opened a letter addressed to her in bold font from Westbury General Hospital. She could still see the typewritten words in her minds-eye, even after all these years. It had invited her for an examination that only ladies have. If she had thought baring her pendulous bosoms to be squashed and prodded by a total stranger was the worst that could happen to her, then she hadn't banked on Harold's reaction when she had told him that she needed a mammogram.

He had immediately insisted she accompany him to Poulton

Sands Haberdashery shop where he would see to her needs.

"…*but Harold, what on earth has a sewing shop got to do with this?*" she had pleaded, but he had refused to be swayed from his mission. Helping her on with her camel hair coat and plonking a hat on her head, he had ushered her through the front door and on to the No. 27 bus. Each time she attempted to discuss the matter with him, he would wave his hand to stay her conversation.

'*Men can be so bloody minded at times!*' she had muttered under her breath as the ding-ding of the Poulton Sands Haberdashery Shop bell greeted them. Marching up to the counter with Cora trailing behind, Harold had doffed his hat to the young shop girl.

"*I have brought my wife here to see a sample of your best stitching, please.*" He had been mightily pleased with himself. "*Her initials are CMS, for Cora May Spunge.*"

She had stood surrounded by colourful wools, cottons and material, embarrassed and a little annoyed at his pompous manner.

"…*what colours shall we have, Cora?*"

At a loss for words, her appointment letter still crumpled in her hand, she had shrugged her shoulders.

Harold gave the shop girl a flirty smile as his green eyes twinkled. "*You see, Cora needs a mammogram, she's had a letter, haven't you, dear?*"

The poor young girl had blushed from the tip of her nose straight down to the low-cut edge of her blouse. Watching the dappled spots of pink spread across her chest, Cora had let out a long sigh.

"*Harold, please!!*" Her voice had been firm but reverent, he was after all, her husband. Taking the hint for once in his life, he had followed his wife outside to be given a lecture on all things wondrously feminine.

They had then spent their entire bus journey home in complete silence, thus giving Harold the chance to contemplate the difference between a fancy monogrammed blazer badge and poor Cora's droopy Elmer Fudd's being crushed in a contraption that was akin to a Russell Hobbs panini maker.

The sudden 'lost child' announcement over the mall tannoy pulled Cora away from her happy reminiscing and quickly back to the task in hand. Chuckling to herself, she popped the last of the scone into her mouth and delicately dabbed at the corners of her mouth with the paper serviette.

Yes, Harold had been such stubborn, difficult man at times, but in a strange way she did still miss him.

So far it had been a no show for Peggy Parker. She checked her watch. She'd give it another ten minutes and if Peggy didn't make the drop, then she would just have to consider upping her game.

No sooner had the idea of turning the thumbscrews on Peggy taken root than the wily old dear appeared from behind a large potted palm next to the bench. Cora discreetly watched from behind her 1977 paperback edition of The Passionate Sinner she had discovered in *Junk & Disorderly*. Peggy was fortunately following the instructions she had given her in the letter but in an over exaggerated stealthy fashion. She sniggered as the fronds from the palm parted revealing Peggy's furtive pink face. With a slight rustle they folded over again, hiding her from view. She appeared seconds later by the bench and sat down, the Debenhams bag she was carrying perched on her knee. She checked inside one last time and discreetly dropped it to the tiled floor between the potted palm and the metal bin. Cora waited until she had left the Mall before making her way to sit on the very bench that Peggy had just seconds before vacated. She bent down, picked up the bag and quickly pushed it to the bottom of her shopping trolley before casually getting up to make her way home.

As the wheels on her trolley trundled and squeaked on the highly polished marble tiles of the Mall floor, she couldn't help but feel a little guilty.

I truly am sorry, Peggy, but needs must; and this takes me one step closer to my dream.

Mentally calculating how many more Westbury residents were the subject of her *Little Book of Misdeeds, Sins & Mishaps* and the amount of money she would need, she could realistically have that dream sooner rather than later.

THE GAMES WE PLAY

Cyril lay on his bed.

If life could give you a chance to consider your indiscretions and misdemeanours before you pegged it, then this was his time to contemplate.

He tried to wriggle his hand through the tight metal of the handcuff. Why he was putting himself through the effort, he didn't know, he'd been like this for hours with no success in extricating himself and no let up from the terrible smell of his new rubber gimp mask that was tightly encasing his head.

His skin had reddened and swollen on both hands but strangely enough the tips of his fingers were unnaturally white. His eyes followed the metal links in between each cuff, that were in turn threaded behind the ornate brass post of his bedhead.

He could hear Thomas purring somewhere in the room. It had been that bastard cat that had got him into this predicament in the first place. Cats and shiny things really don't mix and unfortunately the keys to the handcuffs that had been hanging within reach, were very new and very shiny. Mind you, if he hadn't been such a tight-fisted mingebag and spent some of the money he'd accrued over the years on the services of a real-live woman who catered for his tastes, like old Edna Flaybrick, instead of attempting a do-it-yourself job, he wouldn't now be slowly suffocating to death.

For the first time in his life, Cyril was gradually reaching the conclusion that his current predicament was solely his own fault. He had nobody else to blame.

He pursed his swollen lips, that were just visible through the slit of the rubber.

"I think this is a goodbye from me, Thomas…" his hoarse voice rasped and rattled.

Thomas sat on the bedside cabinet watching his master with an air of curiosity. He had enjoyed knocking the shiny plaything around until with one swipe of his paw, he'd knocked it from the bedhead to the carpet. His amber eyes reflected Cyril in his final throes of life. Feeling totally unperturbed and uninterested in the current state of play, he jumped down onto the bed and nudged the vinyl buttock of his master's playmate. Thomas was a little miffed, normally his master's lap was reserved solely for him. He lifted his paw and sprung out his impressive set of claws and leapt upon the bouncing figure.

Cyril closed his eyes. With his throat constricting and his breath coming in short rasps, he silently hoped his important manly bits would stay intact from Thomas' onslaught, after all, he just might need them in the afterlife. He briefly thought of those waiting to greet him on the other side. His beloved Clementine, would she grace him with her presence to take him over the veil. He thought it highly unlikely, particularly as he had been neither kind in life to her or respectful at her death.

As the darkness enveloped and took him, he suddenly remembered that he would now have to stand in front of St. Peter and those bloody pearly gates wearing exactly what he had expired in and even worse, if the stories were true, he would be wearing it for ever.

A vision of Loretta LoveHoney, pouting, boinging and

bouncing through all eternity whilst permanently attached to his todger filled him with utter horror. Maybe hell would be a better and more entertaining option for him. Well, he'd just have to wait and see which *team* picked him first.

Cyril's eyes fluttered open. He weakly lifted his head to take in the body that had served him fairly well for the last 75 years. If he could have smiled, he would have done.

Closing his eyes again, he took one last, laboured breath before his chest fell still.

Rest in peace, Cyril Albert Monroe Hislop…

… taken by a previously unknown allergic reaction to tight black deviancy masks made of the finest Indonesian rubber!

I puffed out my cheeks in frustration. Telling Joe about my run in with Thrush had been a huge mistake. Joe didn't do forgiveness, and Joe certainly didn't do 'gentle chats' with people that pissed him off either.

"Just drop it, love. I've dealt with it…" I chucked the spoon into the sink, it rattled against the side before wedging itself in the plughole. "…I know you're only trying to protect me, but I've got to stand up for myself, you getting involved is not going to help, is it?" I stood with my hands on my hips, waiting for an acknowledgement from him.

He ran his fingers through his hair and shook his head. "Mave, if it's been this bad for so long, why have you only told me ALL of it now? In this day and age it shouldn't be happening and it's fine for you to say me getting involved isn't going to help; I'm not arsed about that, I just want the bloody satisfaction of smacking him in the face with a cricket bat!"

I took a slurp of my coffee trying to hide a smirk. "Joe, you played for *The Brokebat Mountains* cricket team and never once, in all the years you were with them, did you actually manage to hit the ball?"

"I nearly did, remember that time we played *The Sons of Pitches*…."

"You hit a homing pigeon."

"It got in the way."

"I rest my case!"

"So, he took it well, then?" Bob laughed as he dunked his biscuit in his mug of tea. He checked it for droop. "Mmmm, it would appear a Malted Milk doesn't hold the structural integrity needed to go on our list either!"

I grabbed the last remaining one from the tin and took a bite, waving the half-eaten section at him. "Nope, not good at all, he was pretty pissed to be honest, but then again, I knew he would be, but I couldn't leave him in the dark, just in case I do get any repercussions from it." I'd confided the whole sorry tale to Bob shortly after it had happened, I knew I could trust him with my life and besides, I needed someone to watch my back for me just in case Thrush did decide to get his own back.

"Well, put it this way, I wouldn't fancy getting into a face to face with Joe, his reputation along with his Welsh Death Grip is awesome. Didn't he leave McAlpine dangling three foot off the ground once after that OAP burglary?"

"Erm, yup it's his pet hate, anything to do with stuff against the elderly, it sends him into Incredible Hulk mode. He really is such a gentle guy until he gets his chain yanked."

"…and I've heard you're pretty adept at yanking, Mave!" Degsy spluttered his tea down his shirt, finding his little joke more humorous than we did. He threw his briefcase down onto the table. "Any biscuits left?" Bob hastily brushed the crumbs from his trousers, attempting to hide the evidence of the whole packet he had just devoured, bar the one I'd snaffled.

"Don't be so crude!" I threw the tea towel at him, he caught it and flung it back, it missed me but landed on Bob's head.

"Right, come on, Control Room have given us a job, so straight out from the starting blocks, are you ready?" Degsy jangled the car keys, "I'll drive first half, you can do after scoff, okay?"

I looked at the incident log. "8 Edinburgh Road, that's where Cyril Hislop lives, I've been there before…"

"Yeah, it's the next-door neighbour at 10 reporting, says his cat has been hanging around her house looking for food, which is unusual, milk's on the doorstep and yesterday's newspaper is still dangling out of the letterbox along with today's edition." Degsy gave me THE look. We'd been inundated with sudden puddings lately, if it was dead, ripe and smelly our section got them.

Even though Jim had long since dropped the blackmail investigation through lack of evidence, I often thought of Cyril, Beatrice and Edna. Nothing more had ever been reported, so we could only assume that paying up, which we knew they had done, had appeased the blackmailer and they'd made no more demands to anyone else. It did make me cross to think that they'd got away with it because the others had been unwilling to co-operate, but sometimes we just have to learn to let it go.

"Here we are."

8 Edinburgh Road was no different than the last time I'd been here, apart from more paint had peeled from the front door. Using a key the neighbour at number 10 had provided, we let ourselves in. The tasselled lamp on the console table cast an orange glow into the gloom. It was such a sad, miserable, neglected house.

"It's a bit niffy, hopefully he hasn't been dead too long..." Degsy used his most empathetic and caring voice as he pushed open the first door we came to. "...can't abide smelly ones before scoff."

We decided to split, Degsy taking the upstairs and I took the ground floor. I had a feeling there was a cellar but no way would I be searching that unless we went together. I'd seen the original *Don't Be Afraid of the Dark*, so going down into cellars on my own was a great big, fat no-no. I'd bravely fight anyone who was alive and wanted to have a go, but I didn't do confrontations with ghosts, spooks and creepy things.

"Mave..."

"What?"

"Found him and you won't believe your eyes!"

I looked up the stairwell to see Degsy hanging over the bannister. Whatever was up there clearly wasn't too bad as not much in the smell department had drifted down to where I stood, but he'd already taken on a slight green tinge. I took the stairs two at a time.

"He's in there..." he dry barfed and spluttered. "If you ever get to write that book you keep promising us when you retire, there's definitely a chapter in this one!"

I stood at the bottom of the bed, taking in the vision before me. What on earth was it with the residents of Westbury and their fetishes.

Yep, once again, that's more an observation, than a question.

"Dearie me, Cyril.... whatever possessed you, you silly man!"

I wanted to laugh, but it seemed terribly irreverent to do so. His head encased in a rubber gimp mask, wearing a crotchless PVC body suit, Cyril was handcuffed to the bedhead, his milky eyes just visible through the holes were vacantly staring at the ceiling. A Loretta LoveHoney doll, partially deflated and wobbling in wild abandonment as the slight breeze from the open window blew towards her, was straddling him. Her pouting ruby red lips were open and permanently frozen in surprise.

Jeez, sometimes there really was no dignity in dying.

"We'll have to call it in as a scene, Degs." I made a tentative check for signs of life. Even though I knew it was pointless, I didn't want one of my 'corpses' to suddenly start breathing again in the mortuary throwing everything, including my career, into complete chaos.

Thomas the cat looked on sombrely at the scene unfolding before him, whilst I quietly contemplated the implications of Cyril's demise on poor Aunt Agatha.

THE MOST PERFECT GIFT

"**W**hat do you think, should I tell her, with him being the father of her baby?" I spooned the runny herb sauce over the chicken breasts in the slow cooker. Opening and closing three sets of cupboard doors, I eventually found the pepper mill and gave a couple of vigorous twists to add a bit of flavour. Ella, Luke and Daisy were coming for dinner, Agatha hadn't quite made up her mind if she wanted to come or not, so she was moodily making me beg for her presence.

"Joe!"

"What my little love bug…" he paused momentarily before starting another onslaught, "… bang, bang…. get on your hoss and ride, son!"

Benjamin was squealing in delight, I loved hearing him having fun, although Cowboys and Indians for a baby that hasn't yet quite mastered the art of walking without falling over every two steps, was, I thought, just a little bit premature. The sound of Joe whooping as an Indian brave and galloping around the front room on an imaginary horse was the icing on the cake and suddenly made me realise the game was more for him than Ben.

"Should I tell Agatha about Cyril Hislop, do you think it would just upset her without there being any benefit to it?" I strained to hear his reply above the constant *bang, bang* from his pretend gun. "Cowboys have arrows, Joe!" Now, was it going to be chips or mashed potato? I looked out through the window onto the garden, two wood pigeons were romancing each other in the sycamore tree near to the fence line.

FML, decisions, decisions.

"I wouldn't bother to be honest, she's not seen him for years, what good would it do?" his distant voice was followed up by a loud thump. "You've got me son, right through the heart...... I'm a goner...."

I threw the half-peeled spud back into the bowl and went to check on them. Joe was lying on his front, my best wooden spoon protruding from under his armpit as he writhed on the shagpile rug in the final throes of death, caught off guard by a rogue Cowboy secreted behind the footstool. I could see Benjamin's bright blue eyes over the top of a......

"Jesus Christ, Joe .... where did you get Ben's mask from?"

"Your baby bag, I've got a mask too, it's right dusty in the desert isn't it son?" He gave an added thrust of his legs to add to his dying scene, twisting himself round as Ben giggled. "They had handy bits of sticky stuff each end and little wingy bits in the middle too, like chin straps."

I bent down and ripped it from his face. "Yeeeeeow, Mave, that hurt!" his hand flew up to the side of his cheek.

"They're my sanitary pads you bloody idiot, you've only gone and dressed our son in Always Infinity!"

Poor Ben looked on bemused, the white pad hanging from his cheek, as we both collapsed in a heap laughing.

"Aww well, I suppose I was *ovary*-acting just a little...."

No Joe, just.... no!

BLUES, TWOS AND BABY SHOES

Mother's Day was fast approaching and my heart was feeling heavy. Not just because it brought home to me that Mum was no longer here, I felt that loss every single day, it was just some days were a little more painful than others. This Mother's Day would be more difficult because of Agatha. I had failed to find her daughter and I didn't know if I could soften the day for her by making her an honorary mum within our family, the last time she would have that chance.

There was no denying that I had become increasingly fond of her as the months had progressed, her quirky ways, outrageous dress sense and her fabulous sense of humour had warmed me to her. I really could see what had attracted the men in her youth.

"Penny for them Mum …" Ella handed Daisy to me for a cuddle. It was quite bizarre at times, with us swapping babies to hold. "… the impending Mother's Day is it?"

She knew me so well. "Yep, just wondering what to do about Auntie Agatha and having a few memories of Mum too, not all sad ones though." Daisy's eyes were drooping as she gave a big yawn. "Does she need an afternoon nap, she can always bed down with Ben, he's fast asleep already?"

"Mmmm, good idea."

Leaving Ella to take Daisy upstairs, I put the kettle on and made a couple of rounds of toast ready for when she came back down. Arranging the tray on the coffee table, I threw another couple of logs on the fire, as the weak sun had disappeared behind the clouds, the temperature had dropped too.

"Here you go sweetheart, lots of butter." I passed her the plate as she sank herself into the armchair.

"Gosh Mum, do you remember Nan's buttered crumpets? She always had those on the go when things went tits up, didn't she?"

She bit into the first round and quickly wiped the butter from her chin as it dripped from the crust.

"Yep, she left us so many lovely memories and lots of family 'traditions' to carry on too, buttered crumpets being one of them, but I haven't been to the shops yet, so toast will have to do." I laughed, remembering the time I'd tried to comfort Ella with a plate of crumpets when her and Luke had split up. That had been one of the most inopportune moments to have whipped them out. Mum would have timed it so much better.

"It still makes me howl when I think of you, Michael and Connie participating in your one-upmanship with Nan, you always tried to outdo each other every Christmas and birthday…" She tilted her head, listening out for Daisy. "… not a peep, she must have dropped straight off."

I curled my feet up underneath me. "Blimey, didn't we? I remember one year I made her a unicorn out of a bog roll tube, painted it purple and gave it bright pink pipe cleaner for a horn. Think I was having a Blue Peter moment." I smiled at the memory. "She loved it, said she'd treasure it forever." I passed the plate over to her. "Funny how you can remember things like that, it was for Mother's Day too. To be honest, it was hideous, so she probably got rid of it at the earliest opportunity." Taking a sip of my tea, I clutched the mug tightly to warm my hands.

"Ah, see the handmade stuff is always the best, you kept a lot of my stuff I made you too, didn't you?" She was wholly expectant that I'd give an affirmative answer.

"I did, it's all in the attic in a file next to Mum's box of treasures." I suddenly felt a stab of guilt. How long had that box of Mum's been up there and I'd never opened it. I'd been too afraid to see what it held in case it brought back too many raw memories. She had over the years, like me with Ella, saved a lot of things that must have meant something to her. I pushed the thought to one side.

"I tried to outdo Michael and Connie one year and bought her an awful vivid blue transistor radio to replace her shitty old one …" I took another bite of toast. "…honestly Ella, it was dreadful, really blingy." I smirked, Mum had been the total opposite to Agatha, she didn't do bright colours or anything that had sequins or glitter on.

"Aww I'm sure she loved it."

"Well, she did, until I tried to show her how the concealed telescopic aerial worked, I pushed the button as she was leaning over it and it shot right up her left nostril with some considerable force…" I spluttered tea down my t-shirt and quickly wiped it with my hand "…honestly, if you could have seen her face sitting in A&E with a cotton wool plug stuffed up her nose to stem the bleeding!" I mimicked nose bunging with my finger.

Ella doubled up laughing. "Just console yourself Mum, it couldn't get any worse after that!"

I rolled my eyes as the excruciatingly embarrassing memory of her next Mother's Day gift came flooding back. "Oh but it did, you didn't get to see the M&S belly-button hugger knickers with airflow crotch that I bought her the following year!"

"Noooooooo, why, just why?" Ella's eyes widened in horror.

I shrugged my shoulders. "Safe pressie I suppose, no more trips to A&E. God knows why I thought an airflow crotch would be appreciated though, maybe I thought she could fart in comfort when shopping in Morrisons. Anyway, she just smiled sweetly and said they were gorgeous, but I never saw them hanging on the drier, so she either dumped them or gave them to charity." I pulled a face. "In all those years, I never did find the perfect Mother's Day gift for her."

Ella leant over and gave me a hug. "You probably did, Mum, you just can't remember, that's all."

I loved her eternal optimism and outlook on life.

"It's not the most perfect gift Mum…" I carefully placed the red roses in the bowl and brushed the wet leaves away from the gilded lettering, "…this is all I have to offer now, every Mother's Day will always be the same, just all my love and a bunch of roses from Sainsbury's." I wiped away a tear with the already damp tissue clutched in my hand.

The wind lifted, catching the branches of the trees, letting out a heavy sigh as they bent and snapped back. A purple bow from a floral display rose into the air, it flicked and darted higher and higher until it was out of sight. Looking around the cemetery, I realise I am not alone. Each grave holds the tell-tale signs of a son or daughter visiting their mum.

So many flowers, so many graves, so many lost mums.

"I miss you Mum."

And the wind whispered back.

I miss you too sweetheart.

As dusk descended on the attic, I turned on the overhead light hanging from the rafters, pushing the dusty threads of old cobwebs from my face, I began to lift boxes and files, stacking them to one side.

I know it's here somewhere.

Using my hip to push a larger crate away from the eaves, I found it. Mum's battered box of treasures. Coming home from the cemetery, it had filled my thoughts.

Was this the right time to open it?

I lifted the lid and pushed the cardboard flaps to one side, rocking back on my heels I took a few moments before tentatively peeling back the bubble wrap and peering inside. My heart jumped just a little as I lifted her beloved Theakston's ashtray out and reverently placed it on the floor alongside a plastic bag with a rainbow array of disposable lighters, before delving back inside. There was a drawing that Connie had scribbled for her in the first year of school, a padded card from Michael for her 50th birthday, a newspaper cutting from my award presentation and a souvenir serviette and bar of soap from the posh London hotel we had stayed in on my visit to 10 Downing Street.

Jeez, I seriously hoped she hadn't purloined the Hotel bath towels as souvenirs too!

My fingers brushed against something familiar. Gently holding it in my hand, I lifted it up so the light could catch it.

Oh Mum!

…and there it was.

My unicorn. My beautiful purple 'oonicorn'.

It was squashed, faded and missing half of the pink fluff that made up the pipe cleaner horn, but there was no mistaking it. It was my unicorn and Mum had kept it. Just as she had promised the excitable, eager to please six-year old me…

'*I'll treasure it forever*'

…. and for over 45 years, she had.

A huge lump formed in my throat. My rogue one eye still doing its party trick of crying alone, brimmed with tears. I started to sob. Holding Mum's treasure in my hand, I knew, just as I had on the day I had given it to her in my childish innocence, it was and always would be, *The Most Perfect Gift*.

It had been here all the time.

Grabbing the nearest thing to hand, I used the soft cotton to wipe my eyes and blow my nose. Holding it up to the amber light to check what ghastly deposit I had just snorted on it, I started to laugh....

.... at the rather large pair of M&S knickers complete with Airflow crotch and a price tag that was dangling between my fingers.

WIND IN THE WILLOWS

"**S**he'll be happy there Mave, it's got twenty-four-hour care and it'll take the strain from you." Joe thumped hard with the masher, throwing lumps of potato in the air, splattering them all over the kitchen tiles.

"I know, but if you could have seen her face, she was livid as it wasn't the place she'd planned on going to. You know what's she's like, it wasn't like trying to re-home a cute, cuddly, fluffy kitten..." As if on cue, Cat took the opportunity to filch the sliver of chicken that had dropped on the floor. Alfie looked on in despair. I threw him a piece to make up for his lack of speed and doggie skills. "...we all know Agatha is neither cuddly, cute or indeed fluffy, but she's definitely got claws!" I busied myself draining the veg and then slopped a big lump of butter on top. Checking Joe was still engrossed with his mashed potato and wasn't looking, I added another dollop and quickly riddled it to make it melt quicker.

"Just push her through the doors and stand well back or better still borrow a riot shield from stores," he helpfully offered with a snort.

"Very funny, it's not you that's got to take her in..." I spooned the carrots onto the plates, "...unless Ella can look after Ben and you can come with me."

The kitchen was suddenly enveloped in an eerie silence which a split second later, was broken by the sound of the stainless-steel masher rattling in the pot and Joe nowhere to be seen.

Bastard!

"Come on Agatha." I took her arm and helped her out of my car. She had become so frail and sparrow-like these past weeks, her 'pleasantly plumpty-ness' as she had called it, had gone, the cancer was stealing her bit by bit. It didn't surprise me, after seeing what it had done to Mum, but it saddened me to see her this way, her once vibrantly coloured ginger hair was now washed out and showing grey roots, her unsteady hand had failed to guide her lipstick and she had becoming increasingly more abrasive. I felt a twinge of unexpected love for her, which quickly dissipated with one of her withering looks.

"Feck off Mavis, I can do it myself!" She pulled away from me. "If I'm going to be incarcerated in this shithole, I'll walk myself in under my own steam."

Mmmm, that was the one thing the disease hadn't taken away from her, her occasional acid tongue!

She marched through the double doors of The Weepy Willows Respite home with an air of defiance. I rolled my eyes and sighed. Well, at least she'd got that far. I'd had visions of her clinging on to the door handle of my car like a child who doesn't want to go to school.

Pamela White, Weepy Willows Manager was waiting to usher Agatha into the plush office, eager to make her acquaintance. Offering her a comfortable chair, she poured her a cup of tea and offered her a biscuit. "Well, I think we're going to get along famously, aren't we Agatha?" She expectantly waited for a civil reply.

I had a feeling she'd have a very long wait.

Agatha plucked one biscuit from the plate and placed it on her saucer, her hand snaked out for another one, but Pamela had already returned it to the trolley. She now had her head buried in the file in front of her, pulling a pad to make notes. Peeved, and not to be outdone, Agatha took the opportunity to lean over and grab the plate back. Before I could stop her, she quickly tipped it up, throwing the remaining biscuits into her handbag. I was mortified.

"Agatha, please!" I gave her my best naughty child stare, "...this is for you, don't be rude. I'll still see you virtually every day." I was exasperated and embarrassed.

She curled her lip and harrumphed. "I know when I'm not wanted, I came back here so you could look after me..." She bit into the biscuit, chewed for a few seconds and then pointed her arthritic finger at me. "...and you still haven't found my baby, you promised me!"

Pamela's head jerked up. I quickly utilised every facial expression I could think of to give her the hint that it was a subject best left alone. "It's okay, I'll explain another time, Pam."

She gave me a look of sympathy. "Mavis, please don't worry, my staff are extremely experienced. We really are going to get along fine, aren't we Agatha?" She gave Agatha a look of anticipated mutual understanding. "There's absolutely nothing we can't handle here at Weepy Willows."

I looked at Agatha.

Agatha glared at me.

Uh oh....

Taking out a florescent pink handkerchief from her multi-coloured handbag, Agatha blew her nose, sniffed and grimaced. Tilting to one side in the chair, she lifted her right leg and deliberately forced out a rather loud fart.

"Handle THAT then…" she snorted whilst letting out another rasping bout of flatulence. "…and THAT one too!" She stood up, wafted her hand behind her and gave Pam the middle finger before disappearing through the door.

Pamela stifled a giggle, opening a top transom window to let the air circulate.

"Jeez, see what I mean Pam, I absolutely despair of her, I'm so sorry." I watched her stomp like a petulant child along the corridor in a flurry of pink, purple and yellow, towards the day room.

"She's just a frightened old lady Mavis. They often revert to childhood, it's a scary thing to know you're imminently facing death. there is nothing that she can do that will shock me, I promise." She leant forward and patted my hand.

Somehow, I wasn't as confident in that statement as she was.

BLUES, TWOS AND BABY SHOES

NO MORE...

"**P**oached egg on toast..." Cheryl coyly pushed the plate towards Petey. "...and would you like anything extra?"

Standing behind Petey in the canteen queue, we desperately tried to pretend we were otherwise occupied in selecting rashers of bacon and burnt sausages from Maggie's Tuesday offerings rather than eavesdropping on what we hoped would be their flourishing romance. Bob nudged me.

"See, she's suggesting extra's already, there's no holding her back now!" He covered his mouth with his handkerchief trying to stifle a snort of laughter. "There's me thinking she was sweet and innocent."

Petey glanced over his shoulder, long enough for the bright pink flush, high on his cheeks to have an impact on Degsy. "Bit warm in here is it son?" he playfully teased.

"Leave him be, boys... you'll put him off, there's potential for a little bit more than tea to be brewing, isn't there matey?" I gave him what I thought was a reassuring smile and a small hint. He scrunched his shoulders up to his ears, a bit like a child would do when excited. I leant forward and whispered in his ear. "Go for it, honest Petey, take it from another woman, she really, really likes you."

"D'you really think so, Mave? Oh gosh, how fabulous, what

should I do next?" He clasped his hands together and jiggled.

Jeez, I don't know Petey, what would a man normally do when he fancies someone?

As if reading my mind, Bob jumped in to assist. "Ask her on a date, something simple, a drink or the cinema, nothing too over the top, that's what I'd do if I were 20 years younger anyway." He gave Petey a shove forwards so he was standing face to face with Cheryl, only the formica counter top and a half-filled box of Eccles Cakes between them.

He just stood rooted to the spot, his mouth opening and closing, unable to form any words whatsoever, he was totally in awe of her.

She blushed and prompted him. "Anything else?"

Suddenly he found his voice. "Err, oh yes please…. err, gosh, maybe, or would you… could you, err would you like to…err …. a drink?"

Cheryl looked crestfallen and picked up a clean mug. "Of course, tea or coffee?"

Petey was clearly mortified, his eyes widened and his glasses slipped to the end of his nose. "Oh dear, I need the toilet!"

And with that he disappeared through the double doors and down the corridor, leaving Cheryl holding a mug in one hand and a dishcloth in the other.

Well, that certainly didn't go as planned!

Our mutual sniggers of disbelief were suddenly interrupted by a sombre looking Mark. "Mave, Sarge needs you, vulnerable female job, think you've had dealings with her before…" he gave me the print-out, "…she's 19, he said you'll know the addresses to check."

I looked at the name and nodded.

BLUES, TWOS AND BABY SHOES

I hold her hand. I stroke her cheek. I want to take her in my arms, cuddle her as a mum would, tell her everything is going to be okay, that we'll sort it, that nothing is ever as bad as it seems.

But I can't.

She has already gone.

I won't cry until I get home. I will be professional. I will be caring, I will offer her dignity in her passing, I will stay with her so she will not be alone.

I slowly push the letter she has left into a clear evidence bag. The words, in childish handwriting, just simply say;

'*No more…*'

I don't have to guess or make up reasons.

I know.

Photographs already taken, I pop the plastic bottle and top into another evidence bag, the foil tablet strips in another. Two empty cheap vodka bottles receive the same treatment. Initialled, signed, timed and dated.

The sparse bedsit offers little comfort, just a mattress on the floor where she lies, two black bin bags containing clothes, a cracked plastic chair and a broken mirror propped against the wall. Torn curtains hang limply at the weather stained window, a shaft of sunlight struggles to penetrate the haze drifting in the room, where it can, it meekly illuminates the threadbare carpet.

I know.

I know that once upon a time she was a happy baby. I know that once upon a time she was a mischievous toddler who had a pink pram, a Tiny Tears doll and a cute smile. I know that once upon a time she was a pretty, wilful, intelligent teenager with hopes, dreams and aspirations. I know that once upon a time she was a troubled, sad young woman with demons that couldn't be chased away.

But now she is none of these.

So now I wait.

I wait for her to begin the next part of her journey, and until they come for her, I will sit with her, I will hold her hand, I will let her know she is not alone, until she too is taken, initialled, signed, timed and dated.

I will speak to her family.

I will gently tell them she is not coming home.

And then I will go home to my family. I will count my blessings, I will kiss my son and daughter and I will allow myself to cry for a beautiful life that has been so tragically cut short, and for my own demons...

I am a police officer.

This is what we do.

PUSHING UP DAISIES

I stood in the hallway eyeing up the one striped sock lying in a limp, deathly repose on the bottom stair. Picking it up, I quietly contemplated the benefits of poking my eyes out with a used kebab stick rather than doing the laundry.

"Bastard sock, every bloody time!" I held it between my thumb and forefinger as far away from my nose as I possibly could and took it through to the utility room. The washing machine was already ten minutes into its cycle, so smelly sock would have to wait until next washday. I hurled it across the room just in time for Alfie, thinking it was a game, to jump up and catch it mid-air. He sat there with it dangling from his mouth.

"I'll give you two seconds, old boy and then you'll get the whiff."

Slowly the whites of his eyes became more apparent, his nostrils twitched and his mouth slacked off, letting the sock slowly drop to the floor. Picking it up, I laughed at his facial expression. "Told you, your master ferments these for the utmost impact on wash-day!"

"Did I hear my name being taken in vain?" Joe grabbed me around the waist and planted a sloppy kiss on the end of my nose. Absentmindedly, I rubbed my nose with the one thing that was clutched in my hand, his stinky sock.

"Bleurgh, cheesily disgusting." Pulling my sweatshirt up I made a feeble attempt to wipe my face with the bottom of it. "What's on the agenda today, d'you fancy a pub lunch and a bit of a stroll with Ben and Alfie, get some fresh air?" I looked down at Alfie expecting him to jump with excitement at the prospect of a jaunt to the park, instead he was playing dead on the floor, eyes rolled back and paws in the air. Yanking a clean pair of grundies from the fresh wash pile, I watched the love of my life hold them up to his nose and sniff. What on earth he expected to smell other than fabric conditioner, I had no idea. "Is that just a fetish, or are you trying to tell me something?"

He grinned. "Well in the absence of any of your thongs to sniff Mave, it's a compromise. Seriously though, just making sure they're clean."

"Of course they're bloody clean, I'll have you know…." The phone ringing cut me off in my prime as Joe quickly took the opportunity to skip off to answer it. "Hey, where are you going? I want to nag you a bit more," I teased.

Hanging our work shirts on coat hangers ready for ironing, I listened to his one-sided conversation which so far had consisted of 'yes' and 'no' in equal measures. As long as it wasn't work needing him to come in, I'd be happy. We didn't get many days off together, so this was precious time for us both to spend with Ben.

I heard him replace the telephone and then his footsteps hit the tiled floor in the kitchen. He paused and then continued through to the utility room. Just one look at his face told me something was wrong.

"Mave, it's Pamela from Weepy Willows. She said to tell you it's time…"

"She's very weak, Mavis…" Pamela placed the cup and saucer in front of me. "…the specialist care team have given her morphine and she's comfortable, but we don't think it will be long now, maybe a matter of hours."

I nodded. The room had suddenly become unbearably hot, I shifted uncomfortably in the chair. "Can I stay with her, until… you know…" My voice broke.

"Until the end? Yes, of course you can, you can do whatever you or Agatha would wish, we're here to support you and help with anything you need." She pushed a box of tissues across her desk. I took one and blew my nose.

"I'm sorry Pamela, I thought I could be detached from this, but in all honestly, I've grown so very fond of her." I dabbed the corner of my one festering eye that was doing its party trick. Even after all these years I still found it impossible to initially cry with both eyes.

"If you're ready, I'll take you to her…"

"Morning Cora, how's this lovely day finding you?" Bill Paddington pushed the last packet of Semolina onto the shelf and wiped his hands on the striped apron that covered his portly stomach. Tipping his white hat in greeting, he waited for her to reply. Such a dainty little thing was Cora, always with a ready smile. There was something very pretty and very genteel about her. She fair lit up his little corner shop on her weekly visits.

Thirty-two years he'd been married to Mrs Paddington and he could safely say there was nothing genteel or pretty about that woman. No sooner had the thought danced around his brain, then the image of her invaded his imagination. He shuddered. All 368 pounds of her now dominated his entire life – and his bed, from morning to night, her shrill voice that escaped from her wobbling chins regularly cut him to the bone.

Last night's little escapade in the bedroom had ended with her squealing with laughter '*What's THAT, a bloody TicTac...*' as he'd paraded naked around the bedroom for their bi-yearly liaison. Suitably humiliated, he'd spent the rest of the night in the spare room.

"You tell me, how can any man rise to the occasion and perform after that?" he sighed.

"I beg your pardon?" Cora raised her eyebrows.

Bill fumbled with the stack of newspapers in front of him, straightening the edges, trying to give himself time to cover his gaffe. He couldn't believe he'd blurted that out instead of just thinking it.

Cora turned her back to look at the Knitting Magazines so she could hold back a giggle. She knew exactly what Bill had meant, it was all there in her *Little Book of Misdeeds, Sins & Mishaps.* Bill had regularly shared his marital woes with Edna during their cosy little BDSM sessions in her basement. The thought of him bent over a chaise lounge, tied up like a chunky chicken wearing only his striped apron and the Christmas edition of the Woman's Weekly wedged between his gluteus maximus whilst begging for an extra lashing from Edna's pink feather duster, was just too much for her. She let out a very unladylike snort which she quickly covered up with her gloved hand.

"Is there anything I can get for you, Cora?" Bill knew his manner was simpering but he couldn't stop himself. As much as she fascinated him, she also scared him just a little. There was something else about her he couldn't quite put his finger on.

Cora could see his unease and suddenly felt a small twinge of guilt. Maybe Bill wasn't the best choice this time around, he'd had little enough happiness in his life as it was. She just might pick someone else from her book. Yes, that would be the most Christian thing for her to do. Decision made, she took out her little tapestry purse from her handbag.

"Just a lottery ticket please, Mr Paddington….one of those random number ones." She took several coins in her hand and allowed a slight smile to touch her lips and a glint to sparkle in her eyes. "Oh and a quarter of Mint Imperials and a Woman's Weekly!"

I sat watching her sleep and for the first time I could see Mum in her. Not my vibrant, ridiculously funny Mum, but Mum at the end of her own life. I reached for her hand which was lying across her chest, rising and falling with each laboured breath she took. Her eyes flickered open.

"Oooh Mavis, I'm so glad you could make it…." she whispered. Her eyelids quickly drooped and she fell silent again.

"Don't exhaust yourself Aggie, no need to talk, I'm going nowhere except this chair, okay?" That hit me hard.

I'm going nowhere except this chair….

Hadn't they been the exact same words I'd used with Mum in her final hours? I caught my breath, my throat painfully constricted as a tear slowly escaped. I gave her hand a gentle, reassuring squeeze. Could I really do this again, it was bringing back so many heartbreaking memories but if I didn't, who would? She had no one but me. I'd failed miserably in my search for her daughter, I owed her this at least. Nobody should pass on their own, without someone who loved them to hold their hand, and I did love her, in my own way.

Her eyes slowly opened again, she looked around the room, the dimmed lighting cast a warm glow over her pale face as she struggled to speak. "Well, at least I can say I didn't die a vegetarian Mavis…" She let out a little chuckle. "…I was quite a *goer* in my day, you know, always one for the men." She paused to catch her breath whilst I tried to work out what she meant.

"Come on girl, you must have got that one, my final little joke and you're still trying to work it out!" She began to cough and waved her hand indicating to the glass of water on her bedside cabinet.

I smiled as I held the glass to her lips. She really was a rum one, giving out the gags right to the end. I wondered how many of her past malapropisms had been genuine or if they had just been a wind up.

She became thoughtful. "Don't stop looking for my daughter, will you?"

I shook my head. "Of course not, to the ends of the earth, I promised you that, I'm just so sorry I couldn't find her before…"

She waved her hand. "No regrets, we don't need regrets, you tried and that is what counts." She lay back against the pillow, her eyes searching the room until they settled on the floral curtain at the side of her bed, her face became radiant as she smiled at something unseen by me.

"Josie! Oh Josie, I knew you'd come, we're going to be sisters together again." She held out her hand, as though waiting for someone to take it. "Look Mavis, it's your mum, she's smiling at me, she wants me to go with her…."

I watched the serenity take hold of her. Closing my eyes, I bit back on a myriad of emotions that were threatening to engulf me. Brushing the tears away with my fingertips, I offered a prayer in the hope it would be heard.

Mum, if you are here, please, please let her go peacefully.

Agatha's lips moved in silent conversation as I held my breath,

BLUES, TWOS AND BABY SHOES

too scared to speak or sigh for fear of intrusion. She nodded at her vision and then turned to look at me.

"It's time, I'm ready to go now. Bless you Mavis, you've been an angel..." She raised her hand, touched her lips and blew a kiss....

....and peacefully closed her mischievous blue eyes for the very last time until the sound of the rise and fall of her breath was no more.

As night descended and the stars forced their way through the moon-shadowed clouds, I said my final goodbye to Agatha Hortensia Winterbourne, my ridiculously eccentric, flamboyant, free-spirited, naughty Aunt who even in death had the last laugh by curling up her toes in a pair of vivid purple, green and tangerine spotty socks that peeked out from the bottom of her blanket!

To die would be an awfully big adventure....... PETER PAN
*... but shamelessly plagiarised by **Agatha Hortensia Winterbourne***

THE WILL

A gatha's passing had been well orchestrated by her. She had left strict instructions in her Last Will and Testament as to how she wished her estate to be divided and where her final resting place would be.

"There is to be no church service, cremation will be in an eco-friendly coffin and the ashes to be interred in the Winterbourne family plot." The monotonous voice of Mr Charles Charlesworth of *Charlesworth, Charlesworth & Charlesworth (Solicitors)* informed the small gathering in his mahogany panelled office.

I wriggled in my chair, the leather making a loud squeak. The walls were decorated with certificates and family portraits. I stared at each one in turn. Between 1892 and the present day, not one deviated from the Charles Charlesworth moniker.

Wow, clearly the Charlesworth family struggled when it came to naming generations of their offspring.

Mr Charlesworth continued. "In line with Agatha Hortensia Winterbourne's final instructions, the service will take place tomorrow with no mourners or family, but all are welcome at the internment ..." He ticked the side of the large book in front of him and turned the page. "...right, now down to business. *I devise, bequeath and give my...*"

Joe and Ella joined me in staring open mouthed as Agatha's

final wishes and gifts were bestowed.

I sat looking at the hideous crystal vase that Agatha had, in all kindness, left me, along with a box wrapped in bright yellow tissue paper. I touched the folded corners, ready to open it. Deep down I hoped it would be a link to Mum, or maybe even something to help with the mystery of her long-lost child.

"Mave, Ben's done a stinky..." Joe's frantic sing-song voice cut through my sentimental thoughts, "...think I'm gonna need an extra pair of hands, here!"

I pushed the box to one side and grabbed a clean sleepsuit from the top of the washing basket before sprinting upstairs. Agatha's box would have to wait.

Joe was in the nursery, fingers clamped firmly over his nose. "Bleuuurgh, it's everywhere, it's even gone up his back again!"

Ben, oblivious to the effect he was having on his daddy, was clinging onto the side of the cot, bouncing up and down, giggling. The mustard yellow stain had leaked and spread across his bottom and into a near perfect shape that resembled half of Italy up the back of his Peter Rabbit jumpsuit.

"Is it warm and squidgy my little button?" I cooed, kissing him on the nose, catching a whiff I pulled back.

Sheesh, that was a humdinger.

"He's not arsed, is he? How on earth can you squeeze something like that out and still be smiling?" Joe gagged.

I laughed. "Oh, I don't know, wasn't I smiling after squeezing him out?" I pointed to Ben, who was still happily gurgling away.

Joe grinned.

Twenty minutes later, changed and smelling of baby powder,

Benjamin was gently snoring away in his cot, whilst Joe poured me a glass of wine. "Red okay?"

I plumped the cushion up behind me on the sofa. "Lovely, in fact any colour will do, I'm ready for it, it's been quite a day and I've still got the internment to look forward to." I placed the box on my knee as he handed me the glass.

"I still can't believe how much money she actually had, all squirreled away in investments." He plonked himself down next to me, kicking off his slippers.

I took a gulp of wine and let the burn hit before answering. "I know, over fifty grand in total, once all the shares are realised…. AND she's left it all to the daughter I couldn't find for her." I felt a stab of guilt.

Joe cocked his head to one side, deep in thought. "What'll happen if she's never found?"

"I don't know, there must be something in place, maybe a time limit, then to charity, something like that. I would imagine that's what the solicitor and Executor would deal with." I hooked my finger into the side of the box where the paper had started to rip. "Anyway, let see what we've got here…" I actually felt a little excited at the prospect of what the box contained.

I pulled at the corner, ripping the tissue paper, quickly prising the lid from the box. More tissue paper wrapped the gift inside, plumped and crunched filling the space. A handwritten note sat on top, folded in half. I opened it and began to read it out loud to Joe.

'My dearest Mavis,

I know I have never been an easy woman to get along with, I have caused much mayhem and heartache over the years, not just for my family, but for others too. I suppose I'll get chance to pay for my indiscretions in the next life, but I wanted you to know how sorry I

am. As you grow old, you have the chance to look back on your life and face up to your mistakes.

No doubt I'll get plenty of time to repent mine.

Well Mavis my dear, if you are reading this, then I've tipped up my toes and shuffled off to another place, to have my adventure and dance barefoot, just like your mum.

Love

Agatha

Ps I know how much you admired them, they're yours now...

I stopped reading and slowly peeled back the tissue paper,

....do look after them, won't you?'

I held up my gift from dear Auntie Agatha, the glow from the table lamp catching them in all their glory....

....one pair of hideous tangerine floral T-Bar shoes with curled up Velcro straps!

ARABIAN NIGHTS

"**N**inja mode…."

I'd barely pulled the duvet up to my chin when Joe came hurtling into the bedroom. Flinging his bath towel to one side, he launched himself onto the bed. Anticipating his next madcap move, I stuck my knees up, sending him crashing to the floor.

"Ooooof, bloody hell Mave…" his head appeared over the side of the mattress, "…take it a bit of how's yer father isn't on the menu tonight, or are you just practicing for protective training tomorrow?" He heaved himself up onto the bed, bouncing down next to me. "Go on, just a little kiss, right there." he pointed to his cheek.

I leant in, lips puckered. He turned quickly to catch my lips with his, but badly misjudged his distance and headbutted me instead. "Ah, my little love-spud, a meeting of minds…" he laughed.

I rubbed my forehead. "Yeah, and I felt so alone!"

"You're very prickly tonight, what's up?" he was genuinely concerned.

I punched my pillow, making a dent where I wanted my head to go, and buried myself under the duvet. "Just stuff, sometimes this job gets to me, that's all, you're damned if you do and damned if you don't and I'm tired…" I pouted. "…what I wouldn't do for an exotic holiday in the sun!"

"Don't go anywhere, I'll be back in a minute." He slid from the bed and disappeared onto the landing.

I lay on my back looking at the ceiling. The bumps, bangs and rattles coming from the spare bedroom didn't bode well. What on earth was he doing?

"Joe, be quiet, you'll wake Ben, come back to bed for goodness sake!" No sooner had the words left my lips, when the bedroom door burst open.

"Ah my mysterious Princess. Ahmed finds you most exquisite, but your milky skin desires a touch of sun, no?"

In a flurry of spare bedsheets with a hair band around his head holding one of my best tea towels in place, Arabian Prince Ahmed, aka my idiotic husband Joe, swept across the bedroom with a caged inspection lamp in his hand, which in turn was plugged in to an extension lead trailing from the landing.

"See, sunshine for my beautiful Princess, you may bask and feel sexy, no?" pushing the lamp into my face, almost blinding me with 5 kilowatts of brilliance, he pulled back the duvet, panting in anticipation. "I will ravish your beautiful naked body, I will…fuck me, Mave!!"

"What?"

"THAT… it's something me nan would wear!"

"It's a nightie, I was cold!" I sniffed, trying to pull the duvet back over me.

"Cold! Even Scott of the feckin' Antarctic wouldn't have worn one of them it's a winceyette sack, and what are those on your feet?"

"Bed socks…" Embarrassed, I curled my feet up underneath the winceyette nightie trying to hide them, my mardy lip outdoing even one of Ben's spectacular pouts. "…they were brand new from Agatha's, it seemed such a shame to waste them."

Joe looked bemused and disgusted in equal measure. "She's dead!"

"She wasn't bloody wearing it when she expired for God's sake!" I huffed.

"Well, in that case, don't you think it would be a shame to let this go to waste too?" Writhing his hips, he pointed to the unnatural tent like shape his bedsheet had taken on at the front. Grinning he grabbed at the toe of one bed sock, pulling until it elongated and pinged off my foot, half dragging me to the bottom of the bed.

I laughed, it was hard not to. "Okay my exotic Prince, but don't forget to pull me winceyette nightie down once you've finished!"

"Gird your loins Upton, I'm a coming in…"

I banged my locker door shut and slung my belt over my shoulder. The echoing clangs from other lockers randomly rang out, bouncing between the painted brick walls and the huge metal central heating ducts than ran the length of the ceiling.

"Mornin'…" Bob opened the locker next to mine. I got a faint whiff of sweaty boots and what could distinctly pass for egg butties. He baulked. "Ooops, I side-lined them yesterday for a full English instead." He pinched the wrapped tin foil between his fingers and went in search of a bin.

The locker room clock ticked to 06.25, I checked my watch. "Anyone for toast, I'll set up the tea stuff as soon as I get this lot dumped." Shoving my jacket, briefcase and hat on top of the boxes in the loading bay void, I threw the two packets of Ginger Nuts to Degsy and nipped to the comms room to get my radio.

"1261 to Alpha, test call." I clicked off and waited.

It didn't take long for Heidi to acknowledge. "1261 first class, good morning Mavis."

"Morning Heidi, I'm AR12 refs hopefully at 11." I filled the kettle and sorted out the mugs, Bob had his feet up on the table already reading the local rag whilst happily excavating his left nostril, Petey was buttering the toast with a spoon, don't ask, whilst Degsy was carefully counting the biscuits as he tipped them into the tin. I rolled my eyes.

God, I love this bunch of loons, I really do.

"I've been thinking…." Petey broke the silence.

"Painful was it son?" Bob gave a twitch of a smile to show him it wasn't meant in any other way than banter.

He grinned back and pointed the butter laden spoon at the ceiling. "Yeah, about you know, Cheryl upstairs." A large greasy blob dropped off the spoon and landed on the sleeve of his shirt. "I think she might like me a bit…"

"Err, no shit Sherlock, she's been trying to give you the hint for ages. Think you're going to have to come up with something pretty sharpish before Dave Aldred from the Jacks office starts sniffing around her."

The clatter of the teaspoon hitting the stainless-steel draining board made Degsy jump. A ten second silence followed in which Petey tried to process the advice Bob had just given him. Flustered he eventually spoke.

"Oh dear, I'm not really into stuff like that, why on earth would you do that?" He took his glasses off and wiped them on the tea towel. "I mean, what type of weird person would be turned on by sniffing a woman, that is just so gross…and if Cheryl likes that type of fiveplay, then she's not really for me, is she?"

The night kitchen resonated with collective groans as Bob stood up to offer more worldly advice.

"For feck's sake lad, my eyeballs have just rolled so far back my testicles have had to budge over.... it's slang for showing an interest in someone and just in case you need to know in future, it's foreplay, son, foreplay!"

Petey's eyes once again magnified ten-fold behind his lenses

"Oh...but Bob...I don't play golf and to be honest, I don't think I ever will...."

Jeez, they happily walk among us!

EVERYONE'S A WINNER...

Freda Wainwright carefully picked her way through the window display she had just completed for *Junk & Disorderly*, being careful not to kick the rather fetching plaster bust of Margaret Thatcher. Granted she had already lost the tip of her nose and half an ear by previously unknown means but what was left of old Maggie would surely be an asset for someone's mantelpiece.

Cora stood behind the counter watching Freda with feigned interest. She really was a silly woman at times. The lopsided window doll they had affectionately called *Mannequin Antoinette*, its hand held up in a ridiculous gesture as though a tea tray balanced on its fingers wouldn't go amiss, had been stripped naked by Freda. All the Autumn finery had been consigned to the storeroom to make way for a more festive, wintry display. With that in mind, Freda had decided upon a warming, thermal theme.

"I'll put the kettle on then, shall I?"

Freda looked over from her lofty perch on the window platform. "Oooh yes Cora, thank you, I'm parched. I'll be finished very soon." She went back to arranging and rearranging the clothing she had chosen from stock.

Listening to the water gently bubbling, Cora ticked off the seconds. It was true what they say, a watched pot never boils, but in this case, it was an ancient electric kettle. She counted the white tiles on the splashback in the tiny kitchen. Then she rearranged the sugar cubes from the cracked basin into a nifty wall surrounding the milk jug before finally turning all the cutlery the opposite way up in the drawer.

Blimey, at this rate counting the hairs that had recently begun to sprout on her chin would be a welcome distraction. What was it the youngsters say…Fuck My Life! She of course couldn't say THAT word, but it gave her such a buzz to be able to merely think it.

Finally, the kettle clicked at the same time as Freda called her to come and see the display she had created. "Yes, yes, I'm coming…" Exasperated, she picked up the tray and carried it into the shop.

Freda was standing in triumph, hands on hips, grinning from ear to ear. "Well, what do you think? Doesn't it just scream winter fun with a touch of optimism for Spring?"

Cora put the tray down on the counter and made her way to the door. Viewing it from outside would give a better perspective, it would be the first thing that potential customers would see.

"Oh, bloody hell, Freda!" her hand shot to cover her mouth, the naughty word having slipped out quite loudly.

Freda popped her head around the front door. "She's playing in the snow, I found a catapult in one of those bags and an all-in-one winter suit, although it is really a bit on the thin side."

Mannequin Antoinette stood frozen in time, a rather fetching red jockstrap dangling from the delicately poised fingers of her left hand and a fake snowball made from cotton wool in the other, whilst being clad in what was, to Cora's knowledge, the contents of a donated bag from the estate of the recently deceased Thomas Pumpkin Esquire. Thomas' slightly stained Balbriggan long suit underwear with buttoned back-trap hung from *Mannequin Antoinette's* shapeless form giving her an eerie likeness to Albert

Steptoe from the telly. As a final flourish and a nod to Spring, Freda had inserted a plastic daffodil in her wig.

Aware of the sniggers from passing shoppers, Cora hastily ushered Freda inside, diverting to the window display on route to the counter to make a grab for the jockstrap. *Mannequin Antoinette* wobbled slightly before she gave up her treasure. She seriously didn't have the energy or the inclination to do anything about the rest of the attire until after her cup of tea.

The little bell jingled heralding a customer. Cora looked up to see Edna manoeuvring her ample bosoms between the rails. "Morning ladies…" she cheerfully offered, which was unusual for Edna as she was more likely to wither the testicles on a stray dog than greet you with a modicum of charm. "…any new books in?"

"Two lots in bags over there, help yourself." Cora took a sip of her tea whilst discreetly watching Edna from the corner of her eye. She still had little pangs of guilt each time she saw her, and Beatrice and Peggy too. She had never felt guilt or sympathy over Cyril, he had always been a horrible little man. If there was any justice in the world, he would now be toasting his toes in front of the Devil's fireplace. She'd been a little remiss of late with her epistles of want to the rest of the characters in her *Little Book of Misdeeds, Sins & Mishaps.* She really needed to get a move on, attack it with gusto or else at this rate she'd be at least a 102 years-old before she'd gathered enough money together for her much-needed cottage and Cat Sanctuary.

"I'll take these…" Edna dropped three paperbacks on the counter. "…don't suppose you've heard the news yet, it's been on the radio and Peggy Parker said the TV cameras would be coming to Westbury too." Seeing the blank looks on Freda and Cora's faces, she fair bristled with glee. For once, she knew something they didn't.

Cora was loath to have to ask and give her the satisfaction, but curiosity was getting the better of her. "Heard what?"

"Lottery winner! Someone's won the big one, it was sold by Paddington's corner shop, they've traced it to there and it's not been claimed!" Edna looked positively fit to burst. "So, someone in Westbury is very, very wealthy." She gave Cora and Freda time to digest her exciting news before breathlessly adding, "So ladies, one of us could be in line for a sugar daddy at some point if they come forward to claim it!" She winked and then jauntily disappeared through the door, the bell tinkling loudly as she closed it.

Cora's heart did a little jump and a flutter. She'd brought a lottery ticket at Paddington's ages ago, hadn't she? Why should Edna automatically assume it was a man who had won. She hadn't even thought to check hers, in fact she didn't even know where she had put it.

Oh my goodness, what would the chances be that it was hers?

"Barnaby, where are you Barnaby?" Cora slammed the front door shut behind her. Leaning against it, feeling the worn wood against her palms, she measured her breathing. If she could have broken into a run, rather than a half-hearted trot with her handbag slapping against her thigh and her stockings wrinkling to her ankles to get home quickly, she would have done.

"Ah, there you are, I suppose you've been sleeping all morning, have you?" She bent down and tickled behind his ears. Barnaby obliged with one of his figure-of-eight leg rubs. "Well, you'll never guess what Barnaby, something happened today, someone, somewhere in this village has won the lottery, what do you think of that?" As usual she didn't expect Barnaby to suddenly develop a talent for speaking, but talking to him as though he could answer, made it less obvious that she was all alone in her little abode.

Barnaby prowled over to the cupboard that held his cat biscuits and sat down, on guard. She knew he would now alternate between soft mews and glacial stares until she gave in and filled his bowl. "In a minute, have patience, I have something very, very important to do…"

Rushing along the narrow hallway, she almost knocked poor Harold off the console table as her hip brushed the aged wood. The photograph tottered sideways and collapsed backwards, Harold's eyes stared at the ceiling, just as they had that fateful day when he had rudely shuffled off this mortal coil.

Giggling, she looked down on him from over the top of the bannister. "Except this time dear Harold, I don't have to endure your vibrating toothbrush and the sight of your floppy…" She bent her little finger and wiggled it to show him exactly what she thought of his manhood.

She didn't even attempt to right poor Harold before she eased herself up the flight of stairs and almost skipped along the landing into her bedroom.

Flinging open the wardrobe door, she disappeared into its depths before a myriad of coloured handbags sailed through the air, landing on the bed, the dressing table and the floor.

The search had begun……

AUNTIE AGATHA'S
FINAL RESTING PLACE

The brittle wind whistled across the gravestones, I shuddered, pulling the collar of my coat further up over my ears, hunkering my hands down into my pockets. Stamping my feet trying to bring some warmth back to my toes, I kept my eye on the far side of the cemetery, waiting for the cortege to arrive. It was quite depressing being the sole mourner for poor Agatha. Joe hadn't been able to get time off work and Ella was looking after Benjamin for me. I had put a piece in the Westbury Globe, hoping to attract any friends she had left from her past but judging by the distinct lack of anyone else in attendance, I had to accept it was just me.

I checked my watch. 10.45 am. Taking the opportunity of my early arrival, I made my way through the plots to the far side, where Mum was. Here, exposed, the wind caught the fallen leaves whipping them into a frenzy, spiralling them up into the air before dropping them in a random flurry as it temporarily abated. I brushed away the wet leaves that had stuck to her stone. I hated to see her name obscured. To me, if her name couldn't be seen, then it would feel as though she had never existed.

"I suppose Agatha is with you now, Mum ... well that's if she didn't pull the short straw because of her decadent life and end up down there." I exaggeratedly pointed to the ground. "I'm sorry I couldn't find her daughter, I did try."

I waited for her reply, my mind forging the words, my heart giving them feeling.

Oh Mavis, I had no idea at all, I just thought she was going through an early mental pause and then she disappeared....

I laughed. Yes, that's exactly what she would have said.

I checked my watch again, the second hand ticking away. 11am came and went with still no sign of Agatha's cortege.

I looked up, black clouds had begun to roll across the sky, casting shadows over the vast cemetery. Well, I suppose being late for your own funeral would suit Agatha and her scatty ways down to the ground. I broke off one of the white roses from the posy I'd brought with me for Agatha and placed it in Mum's rose bowl. Standing up, I brushed the flecks of moss from the bottom of my coat.

Suddenly in the distance a vision caught my eye.

"Ooops, looks like it's time to go, Mum. I'll pop by next week.... I might even wear Agatha's gift, that should give you a laugh!"

I turned to pick my way along the path back to the main cemetery gates. Hurrying through the graves and tombstones towards me, cassock billowing in the wind was the Reverend Pitchford, closely followed by the diocese Gravedigger, his trusty spade held upright against his shoulder and following them was Norman Balm, the Undertaker.

Norman reverently held a fine oak casket in which I assumed Auntie Agatha was currently residing having already been 'bonfired' in her eco-friendly willow coffin the week before. I checked my watch. 11.15 am. It was going to be a late start. Holding my hand out, I felt the first drop of rain.

Reverend Pitchford hastily brushed down his one strand of remaining hair that had been thrown off course by the savage wind, he straightened his cassock, wiped a large dewdrop from his nose and nodded a greeting to me. "My apologies dear, I'm unfortunately running a little late this morning." He blew his nose with gusto and pushed his handkerchief into a hidden pocket. "Norman, I feel we must proceed with despatching Ms Winterbourne with speed as I have another internment to officiate and I am already late."

Norman nodded in agreement, pressing forward, the Gravedigger began pointing wildly into the distance. "It be right yonder, the Winterbourne plot..." his gnarled finger jabbed at the air.

The wind was whipping up a storm, howling as it hit the headstones, finding direction around them, swirling as it met the next barrier, bouncing everything in its path. The three of them set off at a fair pace, robes flapping in the wind, with me frantically trying to keep up with them. After much swerving through the stones we eventually stood huddled together, the Reverend, the Undertaker, the Gravedigger and me, around a small hole that had already been excavated in anticipation of receiving the late Agatha Hortensia Winterbourne.

I felt a pang of sadness, sadness at her passing and sadness at the bleakness of the day.

Poor Agatha, she had always been such a vibrant, flamboyant bright soul and today was the opposite, so very dark and grey.

I watched as she was unceremoniously lowered into the ground whilst Reverend Pitchford gave a few words of blessing and offerance.

"Forasmuch as it hath pleased Almighty God of his great mercy to take unto himself the soul of our dear sister here departed..."

I glanced at the large, encrusted gravestone marking Agatha's final resting place. In gothic letters, aged with moss and grime it proclaimed....

IN LOVING MEMORY
OF
ERNEST CHARLES WORTHINGTON
1889 TO 1946

~ ** ~

WORTHINGTON.... nooooo, that's not right!!

As the seconds ticked by, with Reverend Pitchford still beseeching The Lord to take good care of Agatha, I wrestled with the awful knowledge that some dreadful mistake had been made. I looked down at the small hole, the casket sitting snug as I tapped the Norman on the shoulder.

"Pssst..."

He gave me a look of contempt as I wildly pointed at the hole in the ground. "...it's the wrong plot," I whispered, as the Reverend droned on and on.

Norman Balm looked at the stone, looked back at me and swiftly tapped the gravedigger across the back of his head with his prayer book, whilst also pointing wildly. The gravedigger took out a battered old plot map. As he unfolded it, the howling wind whipping the corners, he let out a low moan. "It's 19c, Winterbournes plot is on ruddy 19c. We should be over yonder..." his gnarled finger made the second appearance of the day pointing to the other side of the cemetery.

Reverend Pitchford faltered long enough for this little gem of information to sink in as Norman and the gravedigger frantically looked around the vast expanse.

Windswept, cold and verging on a fit of the giggles, I looked down into the hole that now contained the dusty remains of both poor Agatha AND Ernest Worthington.

How wonderfully fitting that this lapse in direction by the gravedigger had given Agatha the chance for one last time to be laid by a man.

Now that did make me involuntarily laugh out loud. I cupped my hands over my mouth and pretended to have a coughing fit to cover it up. Reverend Pitchford, who had clearly embraced the view that the 'show must go on', continued to ramble away as Norman ushered and pushed him away from the plot. The Gravedigger hastily retrieved Agatha from the hole and inclusive of soil, worms and a clod of grass, he unceremoniously plonked her into my arms leaving me to watch in utter disbelief as the Reverend raced across the cemetery, cassock billowing in the wind, closely followed by Norman with his Book of Prayer wedged under his left armpit and the Gravedigger with his trusty spade holding up the rear.

Running after them, I could feel poor Agatha's remains shifting from side to side as I hurdled gravestones and dodged trees. By the time I caught up with them a new hole had already been hastily dug on Plot 19c. "What on earth is going on?" My voice came out in rasps between bouts of heavy breathing. "This is just awful!"

Without even bothering to reply, Norman wrenched the small casket from my hands and shoved Agatha into the ground with very little consideration. Reverend Pitchford offered three terse lines of blessing, wiped his nose, shook my hand and turned on his heels and fled.

I watched him disappearing through the trees to the main gate, cassock still blowing and strands of hair flailing, with Norman in tow, leaving me in the company of the gravedigger and what was left of Agatha shoved and half-buried in the small hole.

"You're not going to leave her like that are you?" I squeaked, the wind buffeted my hair, flicking it into my face and mouth. He cocked his head to one side and studied the hole.

"Eh lass, it just needs a bit of a backfill, that's all…"

The rain that had been threatening to break through since I had first arrived, began to fall in large plops as he furiously began to shovel the soil on top of Agatha. He reverently replaced the square of grass and then, much to my horror, began to jump up and down on it with his muddy boots, shouting into the wind whilst spraying spit all over my jacket.

"Eeeeh, there yer are love, that'll do reet nicely, once settled yer'll never know she's even been 'ere…"

Jeez, Agatha Hortensia Winterbourne… peacefully at rest with Nana and Granddad.

I think!

A BIRD IN THE HAND

The thundering sound of SWAT boots on the blue marbled lino, followed by the fire doors bursting open with such force they hit the wall behind them, along with our radios simultaneously blaring, sent my adrenaline rushing.

A knot formed in my stomach.

"It's a Con requires, emergency radio activation...." Degsy flew along the corridor following the others. Already the sirens could be heard coming from the back yard as the patrol cars, tyres squealing, roared through the barrier. "It's Thrush but we don't know where he is."

Christ, that's the worst words you can hear... location unknown.

"Patrols we have a track on the AS11 vehicle, it's Dock Road near to the Launceston Warehouses..." Heidi's voice had gone up several octaves, but this time we all knew it had been influenced by the call and that her calm manner was being challenged. "...can first at scene update?" No reply was expected as her fingers deftly clicked over the keyboard, noting the incident log with each call sign attending.

"AS11, AS11...." Heidi paused, desperately hoping for a response. "7832, 7832 are you receiving?"

The radios were open, the lack of response and the dead air that came from the handsets pushed the adrenaline further. I barely paused at the junction, giving a mumbled thanks to myself that the roads were quiet as I screeched out onto Werrington Road.

"AS11, AS11…" Heidi tried again.

For fecks sake Thrush, answer your bloody radio you numpty!

Within minutes, our call signs were being shouted up as we each arrived at Launceston Warehouse complex. A vast dockland area that had been broken down into smaller units over the years, housing everything from engineering works, motor mechanics, Double Glazing businesses to Mad Max's Café and overnight parking which serviced the HGV'S on their way to the Belfast ferry.

"1261 at scene…" I'd followed Bob and Degsy who were already out of their car, their Maglite beams sweeping across the frontage of the imposing buildings. Thrush's car sat abandoned on the cobbles with no sign of him. Cavernous openings, rigid with gantries broke the solidity of the brickwork, channelling the eye through to the docks behind. The moon caught and shimmered on the dark waters giving an eerie feel to what in daylight, was normally a bustling industrial area.

"Christ, we could be here all night, there's got to be in excess of a hundred units down here, he could be anywhere." Bob edged inside the first section, lighting up the communal area. Several roller shutter doors to individual workshops lined either side. "AR12…"

"Go ahead Bob…" Heidi waited.

"His vehicles here, it's unlocked and so far, no sign of him. We could be chasing our own tails unless we work out a search pattern." He checked the door on the Sarge's vehicle and shone his torch inside. "There's ten warehouses that are split into smaller units, if one patrol takes a warehouse each and we systematically search, that way we won't be falling over each other or missing an area out." Bob clicked off, gathering his thoughts before continuing. "Can you get everyone down here to RV outside Warehouse 8, Heidi, we can direct from here."

"Force Incident Manager agrees Bob, patrols please make to Warehouse 8, AS11 vehicle has been located there." Heidi acknowledged each call sign again.

Bob counted everyone off, he would take Warehouse 8 with Degsy, I got Warehouse 6 with Petey, the others would work the remaining units.

"Right guys, spread out, let's find him pronto."

"Feck me, Mave it's bloody dark in here isn't it?" Petey's hushed voice echoed from the far side of the Warehouse. "Wonder if it's haunted, you know, long dead pirates or something, like that Jack Sparrow fella!"

Jesus, some mothers do really have 'em...and Petey's mother was one of them!

"That's why you've got a torch, numpty, use it!" I tried to sound jokey with him, but it came out quite abrupt, I immediately felt awful. "Sorry, Petey, let's just concentrate on the job in hand, hey? Take it slowly, check the doors to each one, even the roller shutters, see if there are any signs of a break, maybe that's what Thrush was down here for."

I felt ahead of me with my feet, the cobbles were also laid inside, making it difficult not to stumble every now and then.

Claaaang....

BLUES, TWOS AND BABY SHOES

"What the hell!" The metallic sound resonated around the massive void.

"I'm okay!" Petey's high pitched, childlike voice broke out of the darkness. "I just banged me head on something." His footsteps became quieter as he moved further away to start his side from the bottom end of the building.

My first three units were secure, the roller shutters tightly down, no bends, kinks or movement in them. I moved onto the fourth unit, Phillips Aluminium Extrusions. Rollers were also intact, my torch swept along the wall, picking out a second smaller door to the unit, the mangled and bunched metal at the bottom made my heart thud.

"Petey…" I hissed into the darkness. I knew the chances of him hearing me were practically zilch. I waited. Nothing. I clicked my radio, keeping my voice down. "1261, warehouse 6, I've found a break." I knelt down and looked underneath. A faint glow from the orange night security light in the far corner of the building picked up a flash of white slumped to one side, a pale face suddenly broke out of the darkness.

"Shit…." I pulled back, edging to one side, trying to give myself time to think. Not only was Thrush lying there in a state of semi-collapse, whoever he'd disturbed was still in there with him.

Think Mavis, think….do I stay here and wait for back up or do I go in?

The decision was made for me. Two loud bangs followed by a groan. I took another look. He was now standing over Thrush, holding a long metal pole aloft, Thrush held a hand to his head, a black liquid seeped through his fingers.

"1261, I'm going in, unit 6D…." I silently rolled under the shutters and inched behind a large crate, hunkering down.

I had to play this right, if I didn't, it would be both of us down.

"Have a go, would yer, hard man?" The dark figure circled around Thrush, who was cowering on the floor. "Come on, let's see you give it out now, hero." He smacked the pole against the palm of his hand. Thrush didn't react.

How many ways could this go? How many options have I got? I could surprise him, rack my Casco and jump him. CS gas? No, enclosed space, it'll affect me. Straightforward fists, kicking, whatever it takes….

"Lost yer fight, have yer, Sarge… come on, one more little go, for old times' sake." The figure leant in towards Thrush, mocking him.

Hold on. My head is swimming, I'm clutching at something in the back of my mind…. that's it, I know that voice.

"JACKSON!!" I stood up and burst out from behind the crate, screaming at him like his mam used to, only I didn't have a fag hanging out of my mouth and half a can of Stella dribbled down my front. "Put that down right now, you naughty boy!"

Flummoxed, Jackson Paul Kenwright almost wet himself on the spot, he tugged at his haphazard balaclava. "Fuck me, Miss Mavis, you put the shits up me then!" His eyes bulged, his lips pulled back to show his teeth in an act of contrition. He quickly studied the three-foot aluminium pole in his right hand, a look of confusion playing across his face. "Shit, I don't know where that came from…." He exaggeratedly pointed at Thrush who was still slumped on the floor, "…he must have planted it on me, honest, swear down miss!"

He quickly dropped it to the floor with a clatter.

I felt for my handcuffs, unclipped them. "There's no walking away from this Jackson, you know that don't you?"

His eyes went from Thrush, to me, to the jemmied door, bouncing on his heels.

"Don't, just don't…" I held the cuffs towards him. "…you'll have to go through me Jackson, and it won't end well. Either I'll hurt you very badly, which I don't really want to do, or worse still, you'll hurt me very badly, which I know you don't want to do, isn't that right?"

I seriously hoped I was right, this bluff could quickly go tits up!

He grunted and looked at the floor, still leaking tension from every point of his body.

"I won't go down without a fight, Jackson, I promise you that. You know I won't and I always keep my word." I steeled myself, not breaking eye contact. The tension in my jaw was starting to hurt as I clenched my teeth.

He suddenly relaxed but I still held my breath, still held his gaze. "Aww miss, you know I respect yer, wouldn't hurt youse ever, like…" He held both hands out. "…go 'ed then, I surrender." Decision made, he seemed calmer. "Can I just tell youse like, I never done that to his head, swear down, I think the soft bastard fell over trying to run away from me!"

Relief washed over me as I clicked the handcuffs into place, and also a terrible urge to giggle, a vision of Thrush trying to leg it and going arse over tit in the process. "Right Jacko, you do not have to say anything but it may harm your defence…."

Thrush staggered to his feet, keeping his distance, a look of incredulity on his face, waiting as I finished the caution. Suddenly he made a half-hearted lunge at Jackson, fist clenched. I moved swiftly between them. "That's enough Sarge…." I nodded towards the red flashing light in the corner. "CCTV…"

His lips, thin and tight barely opened. Blood trickled down his face and dripped onto his shirt. He could barely contain his anger.

"Any reply to the caution, Jackson?" I waited.

"Only to that bastard there." He jerked his head towards Thrush,

"I always said we'd meet again, I'll probably go down for this but it was worth every minute..." He nodded to himself, a reassurance that he was happy with. "... and d'yer think the chippy will still be open on the way in Miss Mavis, I'm bloody starving!" he grinned.

"Mave, you okay?" the breathless voice of Bob cut the tension as he crawled underneath the roller door, pulling it up as far as the damage would allow, Degsy followed him in and from the sound of shouts, boot stomping and yelling, the rest of the section were closely following up on the rear.

I nodded, grateful to be unscathed and in one piece. "Let's just get him in, I couldn't half do with a cuppa after all that too..." I grinned, "...and maybe a biscuit or two if anyone's offering!"

Degsy patted me on the back, and slyly brought his knee up to give me a friendly dead leg. I shoved him back knocking him into one of the nearby crates. "Don't mess with the girlie ninja, lads..." I winked at Bob, "... it often doesn't end well, does it Sarge?"

For the first time ever in his career, Sergeant Alan 'Thrush' 'Cockbollocks' Ballcock couldn't think of anything to say.

Result!

LAUREL & HARDY

Shift work had the advantage that you never had a Monday to hate. You could either hate every other day of the week too, or just hate a particular shift. I loved nights and lates, as there was always plenty going on, but I absolutely loathed early shift.

Like today.

Lying in bed waiting for the alarm clock to go off, I contemplated the day ahead. A 5a.m get up and a ten-hour shift to look forward to and the joys of having Thrush as my Sergeant. Admittedly so far, nothing had come of my outburst or the warehouse incident, he'd stopped putting me on foot beat and to a degree, left me alone but the atmosphere between us was decidedly tense and frosty. The others had noticed the shift in dynamics between us, but I chose not to share what had gone on that fateful night. As long as Thrush kept his side of the bargain, I would keep mine.

That thought had barely left my head, when the intermittent shriek of the alarm filled the bedroom. I slammed my hand across it to find the button and shut it up.

"Morning pumpkin…" Joe's disembodied voice from under the duvet grunted a greeting before he turned over and went back to sleep.

I gave him a kiss on his shoulder, threw the duvet back and jumped out of bed – only to find that for the first time in my life, something other than my feet had hit the carpet first. Sleeping butt naked had given my boobs the chance to unfurl themselves and dangle tantalisingly at belly button level before dropping to the floor. I forlornly looked at them; even a pair of pyjamas wouldn't have harnessed them enough to stop them from thudding to the floor like two potatoes in a pair of elastic compression tights.

Jeez, gravity at its finest.

Distraught, I dragged them along the beige shagpile towards the bathroom, narrowly avoiding Joe's boots that had been hastily kicked off the night before. Bemoaning double nipple burn from the carpet; I just counted myself lucky that I hadn't smacked them into the wrought iron candle holder on the landing.

Sitting like a rag doll on our low-level budget bog, trying to summon up the energy to get into the shower, my once pert nellies rolled out to comfortably drape themselves across my upper thighs.

Overnight I seem to grown old – Mother Nature has given me a kick in the ass and I want to cry.

I propped my chin on my hand and nudged my right nellie out of the way so I could rest my elbow. No amount of budget cosmetics or cover-ups from the cheap store could rectify this travesty! After my accidental carpet glue incident with Joe and the woefully inadequate regrowth in the months that followed, I'd almost resorted to purchasing a merkin from *Discount Dollies* in town, such was my desperation to retain my youth. They were available in three sizes, four fancy shapes, two hair densities and five different colours. I'll admit, I was tempted but knowing my luck, the glue would have been crap and Joe would have ended up wearing it on his chin when he took on a bit of energetic muff-diving.

I sniggered at the mere thought of him clean shaven one minute and then coming up for air with a fully-grown beard.

Bizarrely enough, now I came to think of it, I had suddenly become very adept at sprouting hair in other random areas, mainly on my top lip according to Ella, who accused me of trying to electrocute her when I'd given her a kiss goodbye. Brushing my teeth, I consoled myself with the fact that at least nature hadn't combined the two by giving me hairy nipples.

Then again, on closer inspection I could be wrong.

Plucking at the fine fluff adorning them, I gave a sigh of relief. Carpet fibres. I offer up a half-hearted thank you to God. Although what a man would understand about despair, old age and hairy nipples is beyond me!

I nimbly took two stairs at a time in silent ninja mode so I wouldn't wake Ben up. My joints creaked as I neared the bottom and then unexpectedly gave up the ghost sending me skidding down the last two steps on my bum, just like I had on my wedding day, only that time it was the fault of a pair of rogue stilettos and not arthritic kneecaps.

Promising myself an extra gym session each week to try and stave off my rapidly encroaching old age, I grabbed my car keys and set off for work.

"Yo, Mave...."

I stopped halfway up the back staircase and peered over the handrail to see Bob on the flight below, waving a torn scrap of paper.

"Urgent message for you, can you go to the CID office? Jim wants to see you asap."

"Yep, no problem, can you let Thrush know where I've gone, don't want him thinking I'm skiving." Diverting to the next floor up, barely a minute had passed before I was standing by Jim's desk.

It was like the Marie Celeste, every desk was vacant, paperwork, coffee and much coveted biscuits were abandoned, computer monitors left flickering on the last input that had been brought up. The Jackson file for the burglary at Phillips Aluminium Extrusions was open on Jim's desk, all our statements were stacked and sorted, paperclips keeping them tidy. I quickly sifted through until I got to Thrush's statement. We all knew he'd bulled himself up on his confrontation with Jackson, making himself out to be the hero. He really was a prize melt with his macho image, still as long as he left me alone, I wasn't going to blow him up. My thoughts were suddenly interrupted by muffled raucous laughter coming from the Incident Room behind the large blue bi-fold doors at the far end of the room.

The doors parted slightly making the gentle hum of conversation drift towards me. Jim squeezed through and quickly shut them behind him. "Mave, thanks for coming up so quickly, I need you to see something before I ask you a couple of questions." He turned and jerked his head, beckoning me to join him in the Incident Room. "It's the CCTV footage from the Warehouse job."

Edging my way between the chairs that were already taken, I sat towards the back as the large white screen held a frozen frame of Thrush in all his glory. It was like an afternoon matinee at the local cinema, I was half expecting someone to start passing the popcorn around. Jim sat next to me and leant in. "It won't be long before this gets around the nick, but because you were there, I wanted you to see it first. It would seem our delightful Sergeant Ballcock hasn't been totally honest about his bravery that night!" The smirk on his face gave me a hint of what was to come.

As the previously frozen image came to life, I could only look on in awe edged with a grateful feeling of karma as Thrush, cowering in terror, pranced across the screen. Like a black and white movie before talkies were invented, he held his hands up in a show of surrender, the night camera picked out his eyes making them eerily shine from the grainy images. Jackson moved in from the right of the picture, fumbling around in the dark, arms ahead of him feeling the way, aware someone was in front of him but clearly restricted in vision as his balaclava had dropped down over his eyes. The pair of them took on the persona of Laurel & Hardy in a slapstick sketch as they danced around each other in a circle. Thrush suddenly made a run for it without realising a dropped metal duct pipe was fixed to the ceiling at perfect head height right in front of him. The momentum of his flight helped the pipe to take him swiftly out, his legs swept up underneath him as his head snapped back, the force of his spectacular *Kirby Kiss* with metal threw him to the ground, where he remained motionless.

A cheer went up in the room.

"Feck me, what an own goal, couldn't have happened to a nicer fella!" Dave Aldred sarcastically offered.

The recording continued. Jackson hastily rearranged his balaclava and grabbed at the aluminium pole, he smacked out with it twice, but missed Thrush by a mile, hitting the stacked crates instead….and then I came running in, pointing and wagging my finger at Jackson like a very cross school ma'am. More snorts of laughter filled the room.

"Bleedin' hell, Mave comes to the rescue and nags him into surrender!" Dave was now giving a running commentary as Jackson dropped the pole. "Hey, up…Thrush is coming in for the kill…no….no…. wait a minute…"

Another resounding cheer went up as I stepped between Jackson and Thrush.

"Oh look, Thrush's mummy has jumped in to save the day." Another off the cuff from Dave.

Freezing the recording, Jim touched my shoulder. "Nice job Mave, you did really well there, it could have got nasty. How do you feel now you've seen it?"

I looked at the image still on the screen. Thrush and Jackson together and me with my back to the camera. Even in the poor light it was blatantly obvious as it almost filled the entire screen, a beacon in the darkness, there in all its glory. Rather than revel in my starring role or focus on the action, I felt a sense of despair. It was all I could see.

Somehow, without knowing it, I had managed to cultivate a humongous bum to go with my hairy nipples, droopy boobs and arthritic knees.

"How do I feel now I've seen it?" I muttered under my breath...
Bloody mortified!

BONUS BALLS & BISCUITS

It wasn't an attack of the vapours, it wasn't the early signs of a stroke…it was pure unadulterated euphoria.

Cora sat at her little desk and pushed her pale blue Smith Corona typewriter to one side, the crumpled lottery ticket she had purchased at Paddington's all those months ago, clutched in her hand. Trembling she opened the Westbury Gazette, licked her middle finger, and quickly flicked through the pages until she found what she was looking for.

"Oh my goodness, it's definitely the right date. My, my Barnaby, what is a lady to do? Deep breaths I think, deep breaths." She set about a form of meditation, her eyes closed as she gently rocked backwards and forwards in her chair. Her eyes shot open. "Right, it's now or never."

8   *She ticked the newspaper.*

17   *Another one.*

22   *She ticked that one too.*

9   *Oh my goodness.*

36   *Palpitations.*

41   *The bonus ball……*

She checked the numbers again, her breath coming in short, sharp rasps as Barnaby looked on with an air of curiosity. He had never seen his mistress this excited not even when Troy Tremble the odd job man from the next village had come to trim her Convolvulus Silver Bush.

"Five and the bonus ball, Barnaby, five and the bonus ball…."

The Stupendous Ms Spunge of 27 Lavender Lane, Westbury was now a Millionaire.

She jumped up from her chair and proceeded to dance around the small room. A lap of honour was very much on the cards until she unexpectedly did an excitable little lady wee in her Peggy Parker silk bodysuit with popper flaps. At any other time she would have been mortified, she would have fretted over the rusting of her gusset studs, but not now. They could rust to their hearts content down there, she now had enough money to buy lots of Peggy Parker silk underwear… and a yearly supply of Tena Lady to boot!

"Flapjacks!" Bob sat back in his chair, hands behind his head, his right leg forming a V-shape over his left leg.

"Custard Creams." That offering was from Degsy.

"Ginger Nuts!" Mark sniggered.

"We're talking biscuits here, not Chief Inspector Ronnie Barnett's colourful nether regions!"

I gave Bob a dirty look.

"What?" he held up his hands in feigned innocence. "Come on Mave, bit of humour hey? Actually, talking of which, rumour has it that Thrush is going to throw his hand in, take early retirement after the embarrassment of that Warehouse job, now that's something to have a laugh about."

I underlined the date in my pocket notebook. "Yep, that would be a bonus, but when, that's the big question, that job was forever

BLUES, TWOS AND BABY SHOES

ago and he's still here?"

"Actually, as of yesterday, troops!" Sergeant Beryl Scully, all 6'1" of her, was framed in the doorway, waving a large packet of Digestives. "So, who's playing mother?" she nodded at the tea tray in the middle of the table.

"Yay, Sargie you're back!" Petey literally couldn't contain himself, I half expected him to do a circuit around the parade room table in pure unadulterated glee.

If I'd had a hard time with Thrush, so had Petey. His had been compounded by what had happened at home, so even coming to work had been no relief when Thrush started on him. Whereas our teasing was in humour and affectionate, Thrush had been downright cruel and Bob had diplomatically stepped in on a couple of occasions. I felt a sense of relief too. Now we could get back to normal, or as normal as this job ever is.

Beryl thumped her files down on the desk and skitted the biscuits across to Degsy. "Keep them out of Bob's reach, I want them to last at least two parades!" she laughed. "Right, listen up troops, parade on…"

The grins plastered on our faces and the sense of relief in our eyes, were proof of a once again, happy Section.

"Are you going first or second jockey on this one?" I checked the CCTV evidence and the statement from the store detective, along with the list of high value recovered goods. A pissed overnighter in custody for theft was now sober enough to be interviewed. I looked at the details on the board.

Degsy shrugged. "You go lead, I'll just chip in when needed and I'll do all the exhibits."

"You know who it is, don't you? It's Uncle Fester!" I rolled my eyes. "Didn't take him long to start grafting again after getting out of Walton, did it?" I started off along the corridor to the interview rooms, keying in the security number on the pad. The door clicked open.

"He's declined a brief, so fingers crossed it's going to be a straight cough, mind you, CCTV has got him bang at it, no way he'll wriggle out of this one." Degsy pushed the door open to the interview room, hitting us with an overpowering smell of stale booze, underarm sweat and farts. Dave, the custody assistant, was flushing various shades of green as he stood watch over Fester, waiting our arrival.

Barry Francis Kewley sat in the corner, leaning on the table looking very hung over. He wasn't the brightest crayon in the box so to add the effects of alcohol to his brain was a slam dunk for an interesting interview. Leaving us to it, Dave eagerly left the room.

"Right Barry, you remember me, Mavis Upton, this is my colleague Constable Derek Legge, we'll be interviewing you over…."

Degsy nudged me in the ribs, cutting me short. He leant in and whispered.

"Cliff Richard songs…"

"What?"

"It's a sort of Cliffy type of day, don't you think?" he grinned.

I didn't think, I just wanted to get on with it and get out of the smallest room in the world and Fester's festering odours. I popped my eyes at him, giving him fair warning before pressing record and going through the taped interview Aide-Memoire and caution. "Okay, Barry, you understand what you have been arrested for, now let's take you back to 13.20 hours yesterday, you were in Appliance & PC Global, 236 Market Street, Westbury with a female companion…"

Degsy interrupted. "Is she a bit of a *Living Doll*, Barry?"

I paused, pen between my teeth, wondering where the hell this was going.

Barry nodded. "Yes, but this shit's got nuffink to do with her, it was all me."

"Ah, so she's not a *Devil Woman* then, hey Barry?" Degsy, in all seriousness shuffled his papers and didn't even make eye contact.

"No, she's banging, told yer, it was all down to me, I took all that stuff, don't be trying to drag 'er into it."

I pursed my lips and pinched them shut between my teeth, trying not to smile. "Okay, let's get back on track, in the statement I have here…" I shot Degs a glance whilst trying not to snigger as I went through the statement, all the time Kewley was nodding in agreement.

"So, there is nothing in the store detective's statement that you disagree with, Barry?" I waited for his response. He nodded. "You'll have to verbally say it Barry, for the benefit of the tape."

He cleared his throat. "Yeah, everyfink in there is right, I did all of that."

"*Congratulations*, Barry it's good to accept your guilt…" Degsy smirked. "… keeping your girl out of it means you won't end up a *Bachelor Boy*, that's for sure." He quickly licked his index finger and chalked a number 4 in the air.

I stifled a giggle whilst Kewley looked on baffled. "Well, I suppose you can't say *We Don't Talk Anymore* because we are, we're having a nice chat and I'm sure this will go well for you when you get to court, Barry." I was surprised that I'd got away with that one. Degsy looked impressed as I continued. "Get yourself sorted and when you come out, you can have a bit of a *Summer Holiday*."

That was the icing on the cake for Degsy, he completely lost it, tears streaming down his face from silent laughing so the tape wouldn't pick up his guffaws.

Promising myself that I'd give him a dead leg once we'd cleared the Custody Suite, I completed the interview without any further Cliffy-type interruptions from him and began to sign and seal the tapes. "Just here, Barry." I gave him the pen and pointed to where his signature was needed.

He looked at the pen, turned it around in his hand, examined the nib and quickly scrawled his moniker. Sagely nodding as the penny finally dropped, he pointed to Degsy. "I got it you know, took me a bit but nuffink gets past this ace brain…" He animatedly tapped his own head. "…but I really fink Delilah was his most boss one, though!"

Jeez, 'It's Not Unusual' to have a brain that doesn't quite fire on all cylinders, either Barry!

TYING UP LOOSE ENDS

Maddie made a discreet shove with her foot towards Hedy, as she bent down to pick up the mail from the tiled floor of the entrance hall. She straightened herself up, pushed her knuckles into the small of her back and stretched. The dog had already managed to puncture several envelopes with its little yellow teeth, goodness knows what Beatrice would say. She quickly shuffled through them, sorting them into stacks, household bills, *Haute Couture* business correspondence and then personal letters to Beatrice, apart from one. A bulky, well-padded jiffy bag with a typed label but no postage stamps or franking marks. Intrigued, she slotted it between the teapot and the milk jug on the tray and started to climb the stairs.

"Morning ma'am." She dropped the legs on the tray and waited for Beatrice to sit up and rearrange the bedcovers. "It's a lovely morning, shall I open the drapes?"

Beatrice regally waved her hand. "Of course, let the light shine forth Maddie. What have we got for breakfast today?" She lifted the stainless-steel plate cover to reveal lightly scrambled eggs, two rashers of grilled bacon and a small triangle of wholemeal toast. "Ooh, and what have we here?" Her long red fingernails plucked at the jiffy bag, bringing it to eye level she read the label.

"Err, that will be all, thank you Maddie, I'll call if I need anything else."

Maddie cursed under her breath. She had so hoped to remain whilst Beatrice opened the package. Reluctantly she left the room, closing the door with a gentle click. Beatrice waited until she could hear Maddie's footsteps making their way down the sweeping staircase before she slipped the breadknife under the flap and pulled. A lavender letter was wrapped around a bundle of £50 notes.

Beatrice,

Please find enclosed your £2,000.00 and my humblest apologies. I am besides myself with guilt at my actions. It was cruel and unwarranted.

May I wish you every happiness in whatever form you wish to live your life but if I can offer some words of advice and comfort, don't buy your underwear from Peggy Parkers Lingerie as her silk bodysuits with popper flaps will cause untold damage if you bend over and get your ging gang goolies caught in them.

Kind regards

Celia Fate

Maddie stood at the bottom of the staircase, duster in hand, listening to Beatrice's deep masculine laughter resonate throughout the vast upper rooms of Tinstone Manor, bouncing from the walls and beyond.

Peggy Parker flipped open the metal lid of her letterbox and pulled out her mail. Juggling two bags of shopping and a plastic tub of daffodils for her front garden, she slipped her key in the front door lock and let herself in.

BLUES, TWOS AND BABY SHOES

A nice cup of tea and a custard tart were the order of the day after battling the old dears in Morrisons. She threw the two letters and a jiffy bag on the kitchen worktop and hung her keys on the little hook on her notice board.

Filling the kettle she set out her cup and saucer and a small side plate. Bill would be paying his regular Wednesday visit later in the afternoon, so she would save one for him. Her stomach gave a little flip of anticipation. Dragging her unharnessed nellies across the memory foam mattress whilst pleasuring him was something she looked forward to every week.

It was only when she sat down after putting her shopping away some twenty-minutes later, did she open her mail. Tipping the jiffy bag upside down, she shook it.

A lavender letter, and a bundle of £50 notes dropped onto the table.

Peggy,

Please find enclosed your £2,000.00 and my humblest apologies. I am besides myself with guilt at my actions. It was cruel and unwarranted.

May I wish you every happiness in however you decided to live your life, but if I can offer some words of advice and comfort. Three inches fully erect isn't really the national average, I think Mr Bill Casterman, husband of your best friend, Yvonne Casterman, has been embellishing his prowess as a lover.

Kind regards,

Celia Fate

Ps It's called the Karma Sutra, he can't even get that right. Korma is a curry sauce and sultanas are dried up grapes!

Peggy read and re-read the letter, the money scattered across the table where it had fallen. Suddenly her exciting Wednesdays with Bill, didn't feel so special or erotic anymore.

Edna Flaybrick finished reading her latest *Junk & Disorderly* acquisition. This one had been a page turner and had reminded her of her own heady days of hedonistic pleasures. She'd suddenly become all-aglow and tingly. Easing herself up from the armchair, she picked up the Order of Service that she had saved from old Cyril Hislop's funeral a few months back. His smug, fat face peered out from the scroll artwork on the front page.

She found herself laughing again. Cyril's casket had been carried into Westbury St. Nicholas church to the strains of Frank Sinatra's *I Did It My Way,* which, judging by the rumours circulating the village, was pretty apt and bloody hilarious considering he'd been found suffocated by his own weird fetishes.

So, with Cyril AND Agatha Winterbourne dead, their secret would probably die too, and their child spared the knowledge of what dreadful parents they would have been. Her letterbox rattled, heralding the delivery of the lunchtime post. She checked her watch, it was a little late today, but that was Frank for you, too much chatter and gossip always made him late on his rounds. She popped her reading glasses on and made her way into the hallway, the sound of her mule slippers slapping on the quarry tiles, becoming muted as they reached the tufted runner.

She tilted her head on seeing the padded jiffy bag lying on the mat. Bruno, her chocolate Labrador, snuffed his nose at it, pushing it towards her.

"Well, well, well, what have we here Bruno, Mummy hasn't ordered anything from Ann Summers lately, so what do we think

  BLUES, TWOS AND BABY SHOES

it is?" she bent down to pick it up. It didn't buzz, vibrate or wobble, so it definitely wasn't from her dear friend, Ann. She smirked as she ripped the corner and looked inside.

"Oh my, Bruno…." Hastily making her way back to her comfy armchair, she sat down, a bundle of £20 notes on her knee and a typewritten lavender letter in her hand. She dropped her glasses to the end of her nose.

Edna,

Please find enclosed your £1,000.00 and my humblest apologies. I am beside myself with guilt at my actions. It was cruel and unwarranted.

May I wish you every happiness in however you decided to live your life, hanging from a pole, handcuffed to a bedhead or thrashing the local gentlemen with your pink feather duster. But can I also offer some words of advice and comfort.

It might be a good idea in future to close your curtains on Wednesdays. Troy Tremble is a mere boy, and as handy as he may be for gardening or window cleaning, you pleasuring yourself with a Rampant Rabbit whilst reading your latest steamy paperback is not something he should be subjected to.

Kind regards

Celia Fate

Ps Peggy Parker Lingerie has silk bodysuits with quick release popper flaps and they're now available in fat bird sizes too. Thought you might be interested.

Edna stifled a giggle. She'd been called some things in her time, but *fat bird* had never been one of them. She reclined in her chair, smiling at the thought of Troy Tremble, catching her unawares. Glancing at the calendar on the wall, she hurriedly made her way upstairs to get changed into something a little more…. appropriate.

Her recently purchased Peggy Parker silk bodysuit with quick release popper flaps in a svelte size 26 would fit the bill perfectly.

Edna did so love her Wednesdays.

Eleanor Jones sat down at her desk, flicked through her diary, rearranged her pen pot, straightened her ruler and checked the stapler for staples. She twiddled her thumbs, checked out the cobwebs hanging from the ceiling, readjusted her thermal socks and stamped her feet on the tatty carpet tiles.

She was bloody freezing.

Saving pennies was top of her agenda for The Westbury Women Refuge. The last thing she wanted to do was turn up the heating to indulge her own comforts rather than have the money spent on the families that desperately needed her help. She pulled the latest file from the tray.

'Sarah X, two children under 5-years and a six-week-old baby. Historical and recent domestic abuse'

She sat back in her chair and sighed. Can you imagine being so terrified you have to flee in the middle of the night with only the clothes you are wearing, and that had been nightwear, bloodied from the beating Sarah had taken. Thank God she had though. Eleanor was under no illusion that this case could have so easily ended in tragedy.

Funds were low, two raisers had been planned, but that wouldn't help her out of the situation the refuge faced now. She pushed her hands through her hair, tucking the strands behind her ears before

BLUES, TWOS AND BABY SHOES

she reached for that mornings mail. Bills, bills and more bills, but she knew she couldn't put off opening them. True to form, the electric and gas bills were the first two, followed by a 'provisions' invoice from the local supermarket. They were good, giving her food and baby stuff on tick at a discounted rate, but their bill still needed paying.

Her hand automatically reached out for the next letter. Her fingers touched the very large padded jiffy bag. Addressed, but no postage so it had been hand delivered. She picked at the edge with her nail, peeling it open. Instead of plunging her hand into the depths, she carefully shook the contents out onto her desk. Her heart missed a beat as several wads of money, held together by currency straps, scattered across her desk. She opened the lavender letter and began to read.

Dear Eleanor,

Recently a local gentleman passed away in unexpected circumstances. Before his death I came into possession of £1,000.00 of his money. Sadly he expired before I had chance to pay it back after coming into a little windfall myself.

I know he hadn't quite lived his life to the best, so I am absolutely sure that he would have wanted to make amends in some form and what better way than to donate his money to your wonderful cause.

I have added a little extra myself too, my way of saying thank you.

Kind regards

Celia Fate

Eleanor sat for a few seconds, mouth open wide as she tried to process the words she had just read whilst at the same time counting each currency strap with the amount of money it bound.

"£10,000..." she squealed, almost choking on her own excitement, "... we've got £10,000 for the refuge!" Desperate to share their good fortune, tears streaming down her cheeks, her heart bursting with happiness, she rushed into the corridor in search of her colleagues.

BLUES, TWOS AND BABY SHOES

A FOOL'S ERRAND

"**B**udge along a bit…." Ella positioned herself next to me, Daisy was happily gurgling, head snuggled into her shoulder. "…Luke, you stand here." She grabbed him by the sleeve of his T-shirt and pulled him towards her. He grinned, slipping his arm around her as she repositioned Daisy to face the front.

"Family photo!!" Joe exuberantly declared from behind the camera and tripod he was setting up with a delay timer. "If you all just shift slightly that way…" he artistically swept his hand to the right, "…yep, yep that's it, the fireplace makes a nice backdrop."

"Jeez Joe, you're not David Bailey, it's a simple photo of us all together." I laughed, whilst picking a blob of gravy and mash from my top, sprayed courtesy of Ben, who hadn't quite mastered the art of eating and sneezing simultaneously. "Come on spud." He held out his arms for me to pick him up. Holding him close to me, I had a quick mummy-sniff of his hair and kissed the top of his head.

"Right, on the count of two, I'll shout cheese, run and take my place and it'll automatically take our picture, okay?" Joe was beside himself with excitement. "One…. Two…" He bounced towards us, vaulting the pouffe and hastily slotting himself in next to me.

Whoomf!

"That should be a good one, our first all-together family photo."

He eagerly checked the image that had just been taken. "Oh bloody hell, that damned dog!"

"What's Alfie got to do with it?" I walked over to have a look as Joe turned the camera screen towards me. Granted we looked a fine bunch of misfits, all grinning inanely with startled eyes, but the icing on the cake was Alfie in the background, dragging his arse across the carpet. Funnily enough, he too had a startled 'caught in the act' expression.

"Sorry folks, we'll have to go again." He reset the camera. "Okay, positions please!"

We stood there, Joe, me, Ben, Ella, Luke and Daisy grinning like idiots as they seconds ticked by.

"Dust hang on, only de a sssecond…" Joe tried to talk through a cheesy grin and clenched teeth.

More seconds passed and apart from Ben letting out a fart which rattled against my arm and Daisy elongating a dribble onto Luke's jeans, nothing else happened.

"Bugger!" Joe vaulted the pouffe and….. *whoomf*…the flash activated.

"Shit!" He started messing with the camera, resetting it. "Okay, same as before, take three.."

He ran back and positioned himself, cheesy grins on standby, we all posed for the camera. The old mantle clock ticked like a metronome in the background, the only sound that was breaking the silence as we waited, until suddenly a little voice gurgled;

"Shit…."

Whoomf.

And there was our family photo, one that in all truth summed us up as a family. Alfie having a second stab at itching his arse by dragging it along on the knobbly Berber carpet in front of us and our horrified faces as Ben decided to utter his first words.

BLUES, TWOS AND BABY SHOES

Not mummy or daddy, or dog or cat, but the all-encompassing, descriptive word of '*shit*'!

"Good weekend?" Beryl took the chair next to me in the Cons Writing room, "Mint Imperial?" She offered the open packet. I gratefully took one, glad of the distraction from the crime report I was writing off.

"Cheers, Sarge. Yep, it was lovely, Ella and Luke came over with Daisy for Sunday lunch and we had a bit of a family photo session..." I sniggered. "...and Ben said his first words, too."

It was funny, and probably very fitting that the son of two police officers would choose that word to be his first, as most descriptives used by cops are combinations of it, for example *shit magnet, crock of shit, shitbag, shitweasel, oh shit*... the list is endless. On the other hand I felt a little sad too, my son hadn't said 'Mumma' or 'Mummy' first, not like Ella had. Crunching my Mint Imperial, I regaled Beryl with the story.

"Oh Mave, that's hilarious, but as you say, that photo will forever sum you all up as a family, far better than a stiff, posed one." She grabbed the file I was working on, glancing over the tick boxes that had been completed. "Now, down to brass tacks; Petey!"

I looked puzzled. "What about Petey?"

"Well, two things actually, firstly there's a position coming up as a Schools Officer, I...err, we think that it would be an ideal role for him, because let's be honest, Response isn't really his thing is it, he's been increasingly more unhappy over the last few months, what do you think?"

I puffed out my cheeks. I loved Petey, I loved his daft ways, he was part of us, our Section. Yes, granted he always seemed to faark everything up, but his heart was in the right place, he always gave a hundred percent, even if ninety-eight percent of it was a failure.

"Gosh, hard one, I'd hate to lose him from the Section, and so would the other lads, but at the end of the day, it's what's right for him, if that's something he would love to do, then I'd say go for it. He can only say no." I pushed the paper through the green tag and flatted it down. "So, what's the second one?"

"Cheryl in the canteen. We really do need to play cupid here, Mave. It's obvious she adores him and he clearly likes her and he's far too slow on the uptake. I think they need a little push, don't you?"

I plonked the tea tray down on the parade room table, the mugs clattered together, Bob's personalised mug with *'I see Guilty People'* toppled from the stack and rolled across the surface. Degsy caught it before it disappeared over the side.

"Oooh close call Mave, if you'd broken that he'd have your guts for garters."

I shrugged. "Have you seen the state of it? It's got more chips on it than you get with battered cod in the canteen!" I started pouring the milk, waiting for the pot to brew. "Oh, talking of which, Petey, the Sarge gave me this to give you." I handed over the small brown envelope, bearing one word in Beryl's handwriting.

He stared at it, turned it over and seeing it was sealed, he held it up. "Is it just to go to the canteen, what's it for?"

"I don't know, probably something to do with ordering the ambient meals for the Custody Suite, Sarge said to wait for a reply and then come back here. If you hurry up and go now, your cuppa will be waiting when you get down."

He eagerly nodded and disappeared into the corridor.

"There's something going on here, I can smell a set up a mile off." Bob clipped his tie into place and sat down. "What's it say? It's not one of those *'I'm a very shy young police officer, can I have a packet of Durex'* notes that we used to send the proby's to the chemist with, is it?"

"Mmmmm, well you're not far out Bob, it actually says *'I really like you, but I'm too shy to ask myself, but would you like to go out for a drink or maybe the cinema.'* He'll give it to Cheryl, she'll open it, read it and bingo, we've played matchmaker. There's no way she'll turn him down, she fancies him as much as he fancies her." I sat back in triumph, chuffed at how me, Beryl and Marion had come up with such a stonkingly great idea.

"Cheryl's not in today." Mark helpfully offered through a mouthful of biscuit crumbs.

"What?"

"I said Cheryl's not in today, she told me yesterday she'd booked the day off, something to do with the dentist."

"Oh crap, don't just sit there, we've got to stop him!" I dropped the teaspoon and spun round, making for the door, just as Petey, bemused and confused returned to the parade room. "Oh Petey, that was quick, erm the envelope, have you still got it?"

He stood shell-shocked and silent.

"Petey, the envelope?" I held out my hand.

"I handed it in like you said to do..." he looked from me, to Bob, to Degsy and back to me. "....and I waited for a reply too."

"Oh no, who did you give it to?" I visibly cringed.

A sudden tic twitched at the corner of his eye. "The only person that was in there, our Maggie. She got all excited and said she'd love to. Jeez, Mave, I've got a date with Maggie and she's old enough to be me bloody Nan!"

Oh faark.

IT'S A GAY DAY...

Four people.

Four Westbury residents who had nothing in common, save for their complicated past and present lives and a little old lady who had desperately wished for something other than her ordinary, mind-blowingly bloody boring life...

....and a discarded book that had been rediscovered.

Cora cut a strange, solitary figure as she slowly ambled along the aptly named Angels Lane making her way to the cemetery. Her floral coat and jaunty hat with cornflower blue flowers gave her a touch of colour. She had tied up her loose ends and now she just needed to speak to Harold. She pushed the old arched gate, listening to it creak as it afforded her entrance to where he lay. She had something very special to show him, and it wasn't her Peggy Parker Silk Bodysuit, that was for sure, she certainly didn't fancy raising Harold from the dead.

That thought made her chuckle, nothing she had done in over forty years of marriage had raised so much as a flicker from him, not even his legendary vibrating electric toothbrush had enjoyed success, if his final repose was anything to go by.

She sat down on the bench that was next to Harold's polished black granite stone, her wicker basket at her side. She bent forward, placing the daffodils in the plastic pot.

"Well, Harold this is a turn up for the books. Me sitting here and you having no choice but to listen to me." She snapped the stem of one daffodil so that it matched the height of the others. "You can't run off to your study now to smoke your pipe and read your *magazines!*" She spat the last word out as she picked up the leather-bound notebook, embossed with flowers and wrapped with a blue velvet bow, from her basket.

"You see, Harold, this is my *Little Book of Misdeeds, Sins & Mishaps...*" she waved it at his grave, giving herself a little flush of satisfaction. "...I have had such fun reading about the exploits of our friends and neighbours. Such shocks I've had, I can tell you." She placed it beside her whilst she wrapped the flower paper into a ball and popped it into her basket ready to put in the bin.

"But do you know what the biggest shock of all was Harold?"

She paused, as though he would suddenly reply. "No? Well, let me tell you then. The biggest shock of all was finding a page that was dedicated to YOU, my dear, yes a whole page."

Cora stood up. She felt more confident being able to tower over him. "It said '*Harold Spunge is in the closet*'. Well, it took me some time to figure that one out, I mean we didn't have one did we? We had a bow fronted armoire wardrobe, but no closet..." She shook her head at her own ignorance.

The arched gate creaked open, Cora paused in her revelation to Harold, although in truth it wasn't a revelation to him at all, he already knew what he was. She waited until she was alone again.

"So, Harold Clarence Spunge, my rather deceased husband, secret *Friend of Dorothy* and receiver of swollen goods, who incidentally didn't die wondering..." she grabbed the estate agent's brochure and waved it directly over his headstone, taunting him, "...this my dearest, is goodbye." She folded the brochure, which had a colourful photo of a thatched cottage gracing the front page, tenderly placed it back into her basket and rummaged around for what was to come next. Blowing him a kiss, in one final act of defiance, she dropped Harold's legacies onto his grave.

As she walked away she smiled. A song thrush on a nearby branch had taken to serenading her with its beautiful distinctive voice….. accompanied by the buzz of Harold's vibrating toothbrush as it rattled against the glistening green stones and a dogeared copy of The Gay Times.

Clutching her *Little Book of Misdeeds, Sins & Mishaps*, she jauntily skipped to the other side of the cemetery. She had one more errand to carry out before she disappeared to embrace her new life. It was fitting, in her humble opinion, for the book to be returned to its rightful owner, the creator, the one who had first turned the pages and penned the words. She had included her own little addendum inside the front cover, just so the blame for her money-making scheme didn't rest on the shoulders of the original author, after all, how were they to know their diary would fall into her hands. It was only right and proper that she should tell the truth and shoulder the blame as her alter ego.

Cora reverently placed it upon the grave stone and took a bow. The wickedly naughty *Ms Celia Fate* was no more….

…and The Stupendous Ms Spunge was now free.

FRIENDS AND FAMILY

"I do love our little chats." Marion ripped open the pack of biscuits and shook them out onto the plate. "Still keeping off the extras, Mave?"

I nodded and grinned, wiping my fingers across my lips trying to hide the crumbs from the one I'd purloined whilst her back had been turned. "Yup, well sort of, you know what it's like at our age!" I gave my thigh a vigorous slap.

Blimey, gone were the days when only lean muscle gave resistance, all I got back now was a tsunami of wobbling cellulite.

As if reading my mind, she wagged her finger at me. "We've earned our wrinkles, flabby bits and creaking joints, it's the lives that we have lived well." She dunked the oatie and held it up, waiting for the droop. It didn't disappoint, lasting all of three seconds before it plopped onto the table.

We both burst out laughing.

"Bloody hell, how many years is it now that we've been looking for the perfect dunker? Seriously, I don't think there is such a thing, I'm inclined to just *dunk it & trunk it* these days." I popped what was left of the second biscuit into my mouth, attempted to feel guilty for a nanosecond, thought better of it and reached for another one. "Think Petey and Cheryl are going to be a long-term project…" I rolled my eyes, "…what a farce that was!"

Marion opened the window, letting in a stream of warm air. It had been one of the sunniest days of Spring so far, everything was starting to bud and bloom. It always gave a spark of hope and happiness, made getting up early a whole lot easier in the mornings.

"Yep, I was the one that had to go and break it gently to Maggie that he had the hots for Cheryl, not her." She smirked at the memory of Maggie's dejected face, fag dangling out of the corner of her mouth, hairnet awry.

I took a swig of coffee and quickly wished I'd taken the little bag out first as the corner bobbed up my left nostril. "Bleurgh, whoever thought up coffee bags didn't have anything better to do, it's disgusting! Got anything special planned for the weekend?"

"Not really, Kevin, my brother is coming up next weekend, so I've taken a bit of leave for then, so I'll more than likely just do a bit of a spring clean ready for when he arrives."

In the absence of finding a spoon, I swilled the teapot trying to agitate the teabags. "Are you close to your brother Maz?" The tea was still weak as it poured out of the spout, I took the lid off and jabbed inside with a knife.

She sighed, pulling her bottom lip over her top one. "Well, sort of. We get on when we're together, but it's not like maybe it would have been if we'd been blood related. He was adopted by Mum and Dad and I think he's always had a bit of a chip on his shoulder because of that."

Pushing the mug towards her, I sat down. "Gosh lovely, I didn't know you had experience of adoption, I've been working on something similar for quite a while now, not that I've got anywhere with it, and probably won't to be honest."

She took a sip and bit into her biscuit. "I thought I'd told you. Funny, I suppose because I've lived with it all my life it's not something I ever really discuss anymore, there's not much point.

What's your link with it?"

Shoving my feet up onto the chair, I checked my watch. "It was Auntie Agatha; the wily old goat had a bit of a chequered past which included an illegitimate baby that she gave up for adoption. She was devastated and wanted me to find the baby before she died so she could make things right, show the love she had, explain that it wasn't her choice." I stared wistfully through the window, watching a robin hop from branch to branch, tilting its head as though it was listening to our conversation. "It's all a bit late really, now that she's gone, but I've still been trying though, just in case. You never know, they might get in touch one day."

"Aww, at least she loved her baby and gave it up for adoption so it would at least have a chance of a family and a......"

The sudden abrupt ending to her sentence made me turn to look at her. Her bottom lip wobbled, dimples appeared in her chin as her eyes glistened. She cleared her throat trying to keep whatever was going to bubble up in its place, she failed miserably, the first tear trickling down her cheek.

I jumped up and put my arm around her, hugging her to me. "Oh Maz, what on earth's the matter, is it something I said, I'm so, so sorry, forget I mentioned anything."

She took a few minutes to regain her composure before she replied. "Mave, it's me that should be saying sorry, sorry because you've lost someone and sorry because I'm weeping and snotting all over you, I'm just very emotional at the moment." She wiped the shoulder of my shirt, attempting a weak smile. "The truth is, it wasn't just Kevin that was adopted, I was too, but from different orphanages. Even after all these years, it still hurts, I will always have a sense of rejection and hearing you talk about Agatha.... well, it's just I've never known why I wasn't wanted or where I'm supposed to belong."

BLUES, TWOS AND BABY SHOES

She was looking to me for reassurance, validation, something. I wasn't sure what. She waited for me to make a response. I quickly ran through so many trite replies that I could give, but none of them would hold sincerity. Marion was not just my work colleague, she was my friend, she had lived my life with me, the ups, the downs the laughter and sadness over the years. I owed her more than meaningless words.

"You must have been loved so very much, you were offered for adoption and you were *chosen* from all those babies by your mum and dad. You.... you must...." I hesitated, I was lost not knowing where to go from here, wishing I hadn't touched on the subject in the first place. I'd opened a Pandoras box and I couldn't get the emotionally tarnished lid back on again.

She rested her hand on mine. "No Mave, you don't understand. I was abandoned, I was a foundling, not wanted, not loved. I was discarded by the one person who should have loved me and protected me, my real mother." She dipped into her shirt pocket and pulled out a black leather wallet, opening it up, she reverently took a small piece of paper that was sandwiched between the compartments. "When Mum died, I found this in the drawer of an old desk in the attic, it was attached to my adoption papers." Placing it on the table she used her fingers to gently spread out the creases so I could read the yellowing newspaper cutting.

"This is me. THIS is where I came from."

As I focused on the headline, an icy chill swept over me.

WINTER GARDENS BABY ABANDONED
'Only hours old, the child had been found by Norma Pattinson, 19-years, who worked the ticket box at The Winter Gardens, Alderney Road, Westbury.'

I struggled to catch my breath, my heart racing, thumping against my ribs as I frantically processed what she had just shown me. What am I supposed to do? Say nothing, go home and talk it over with Joe first, try and find out more or just blurt it out.

Think Mavis, think!

I know I resemble a big fat goldfish with my mouth wide open unable to form words. I want to cry, or maybe laugh at the sheer ridiculousness of it all. How close I had been to finding her, all this time she had been right here.

"Maz, are you sure this is you?" I hesitated, not wanting to upset her even more.

She wiped her eyes with a piece of kitchen roll, before sitting back down next to me. "I'm such a wuss, look at me at my age, whinging like a big kid." She defiantly grabbed another biscuit. "No wonder us woman have big bums, we see comfort in biscuits and chocolate." She forced a smile. "I just wish I knew why, that's all I've ever wanted, even if she didn't want to see me, at least then I would know for sure. I actually originate from Westbury but didn't know that until I was in my thirties, by then I'd married and been living back here for years anyway."

This was my chance. "Did you ever try to contact the authorities and see if your birth mother had been in touch to try and find you?"

She shook her head, another small tear trickled from the corner of her eye, making a track down her cheek. "No, what would be the point, if she hadn't been looking for me, then it would have hurt even more and besides which, you've only got to read that clipping, she abandoned me so why would she come back to find me."

"It can only work from your side, Maz. Birth parents can leave their details but they would never be allowed any information about the child they gave up unless that child in later life agreed to them being told..." I held her hand, giving it a gentle squeeze. "...and there's another thing too, how do you know that she abandoned you?"

A smile touched her lips. "Feck me, Mave and there's me thinking you were the smart one, err …. Hellooooo!" She jabbed the newspaper clipping that was still sitting between us. "This is a bit of a feck off clue matey! You forget your shopping bag in Morrisons, or leave your coat in the pub, jeez, even *you* have been known to forget your knickers and have gone commando… but you don't bloody go out and drop the baby off in a cinema and forget to go back for it. I was abandoned, pure and simple."

I laughed. "What are you talking about, I am smart, I almost made CID, if I'd developed a set of bollocks and a hairy top lip, that desk in the corner would've been mine instead of Dave Aldred's."

That lightened the mood. She began to giggle. "Mave, being your best mate and all that, is it in order to point out…" she prodded my top lip with her finger, "…that you do actually sport quite an impressive tash as it is!" She slapped the table hard, snorting in amusement which then developed into a coughing fit, followed by another bout of crying.

It's strange how laughter and tears are so closely linked as emotions.

I waited for it to abate before I spoke. Pushing my own copy of the newspaper clipping towards her, I waited for her to register what it was.

"Maz, you're not only my mate…. it would appear, if I've got this right, that you're also my cousin." Once again, I held my breath waiting for her response. She looked at the cutting, then to

BLUES, TWOS AND BABY SHOES

me and then back to the cutting again. Pushing her piece forward so they sat together side by side, she seemed mesmerised by them.

"I don't understand, why have you got this too?" Her fingers traced across the paper.

"This was Agatha's, she gave it to me to help find her child, this is what happened to her new-born baby. I think… in fact I'm almost sure that *you* are Agatha's daughter, she went back for you, Maz, she really did love you."

Marion's lips silently mouthed the words of the newspaper article, even though she knew they were the same, word for word. The very same words she had read over and over again, year after year, but she had to check, she had to make sure.

"This is Agatha…." I pushed the small photograph of her that I kept with the clipping, across the table. Marion's fingers tentatively touched it, gently stroking the smiling, vibrant face.

Her voice broke. "This is my mum?"

I nodded.

Marion gazed at her friend sitting opposite her, her gossip buddy, her off the wall, reckless, feckless, funny, kind and lunatic mate, Mavis Upton.

After all this time, could she really dare to belong? She thought her heart would burst. As the tears once again welled up in her eyes, she broke down and wept.

For the mum she never had the chance to know, to forgive and to maybe even love - for the lost years, for family.

A MOTHER'S LOVE

I sat crossed legged in front of Mum's grave. The sunlight caught the water drops on the black granite so they gave the appearance of translucent pearls shimmering in the slight breeze.

"It's yellow roses today Mum, they looked so pretty in the shop." I fussed a little bit more with their display, ensuring they were all equal height. I loved this time of the year in the churchyard, everything was green and lush, the birds enjoying the high branches of the trees, their individual songs battling for supremacy. I slipped my shoes off and scrunched my toes in the thick grass.

"Right, where to begin…" I tipped my head back, the sun dancing across my face. "…I'm having a crisis Mum, I don't know what to do for the best." I waited just in case she wanted to reply but my imaginary voice wasn't giving anything away, so I continued with my tale of woe.

"I don't think I can carry on with shift work, it's killing me, I get so tired and stressed out. I think I'm losing out on my time with Ben too, he's not going to be little forever and I'll never get this time again." I could feel Larry the Lump welling up in my throat. "I just seem to see so little of him, Mum. Me and Joe work it well between us, but more often than not he's in bed when I get home and then I'm gone again before he wakes up. I don't feel like a proper mum, I'm spectacularly failing at it. I think I'm going to have some tough decisions to make about my career."

The first tear threatened to spill over, I indignantly brushed it away with the heel of my hand before it got chance. I checked my palm for black smudges, grateful for waterproof mascara.

"….and I've got a cousin, I found Agatha's daughter, she was there all the time, my best work buddy, Marion. How's that for spooky? There's a lot of explaining and sorting out to do, but we'll get there. She's got a nice little nest egg coming her way too." A wood pigeon swooped low, dropping a feather before it disappeared into a tree. I watched the single feather sweep from side to side, getting lower and lower. "I have decided not to tell her who her dad was, I can't see anything to be gained by it. Joe thinks the same too, we've only got Agatha's word for it anyway, there's no evidence to prove he was."

The breeze rustled the leaves, a whisper of a voice.

'Oh Mavis, that was the trouble with Agatha, no matter how hard she tried, she just couldn't be monotonous with any man….'

I smiled to myself, although I still had difficult choices to make, once I'd had my imaginary conversations with her, things always seemed a little brighter. "Right, I'm off to put some flowers down for Agatha, see you soon Mum." I stood up and blew and kiss.

Agatha's plot was a brisk walk away from Mum's and in less than two minutes, I was standing before her headstone. The inscription that she'd insisted upon was picked out in gold leaf.

AGATHA HORTENSIA WINTERBOURNE
(PSYCHIC MEDIUM)
'I DEFINITELY DIDN'T SEE THAT COMING'
1938 ~ 2011

~*~

Humour to the last, I loved her for it. Although she had frustrated the life out of me at times, I actually did miss her. I pushed the colourful bunch of meadow flowers I'd picked from my garden into the empty vase and rearranged the flowers.

"I found her Agatha, I found your daughter, but if you're in the afterlife you so strongly believed in, then you'll already know that. Her name is Marion and she knows you loved her, you can rest easy now." I did the same as I always did with Mum, I waited.

'The whole sorry saga has been an absolute transvestite, Mavis, it really has...'

The leaves fluttered their applause for Agatha Hortensia Winterbourne's very last malapropism and a saga that had been a very real, very emotional travesty!

I felt an inner peace, the first time it had touched me for many months, laying Agatha's ghosts to rest would hopefully lay mine. Standing up to leave, my foot caught the vase, knocking it on its side, the flowers tipping out. As I bent down to pick it up, my fingers touched a small notebook that had been dropped between the vase and the headstone.

I held the leather-bound booklet in my hand. Intricately embossed with flowers and with a blue velvet string wrapped around it, tied into a bow.

I tentatively pulled on the loop, the cord fell away, I opened the first page and began to read Auntie Agatha's distinctive, neat, elegant handwriting.

1. Edna Flaybrick aka Madam Diamond D'light, brothel, tax evasion, Assistant Chief Constable, Mayor Anderson, Councillor Brent...

"Oh faark ... Agatha, really?"
I definitely didn't see THAT coming!

A NEW LIFE

Cora stood at the garden gate, the early morning sunshine kissed her skin and warmed her bones. Barnaby, who had very quickly adapted to his new surroundings, appeared spasmodically between the copious shrubs and meadow flowers that she delighted in.

Honeysuckle Cottage had been purchased with the proceeds of her little windfall and it was everything she had spent her entire life wishing for. She had a wonderful garden with an orchard, which was perfect for her several rescue cats, who sat like rare fruits amongst the branches on sunny days, a small vegetable plot and a stream that trickled its beautiful melody as it lazily swept over rocks and stones underneath her kitchen window. Washing up had gone from being a chore to being a delight, she had even spotted a Kingfisher during her first week here.

Yes, everything was just picture perfect.

Westbury and its curious inhabitants were many, many miles away and a thing of the past along with the life she had lived for more years than she cared to remember. She allowed herself a little smile, wondering if Edna was still reading her ridiculous steamy charity shop books, whilst Peggy dragged her droopy nellies over her memory foam mattress to pleasure Bill every Wednesday. And then there was Beatrice. She had quite a soft spot for Beatrice, but the thought of her inadvertently allowing her Adams Apple and testicles to wobble manically in the local Co-op when ordering her weekly shop brought Cora to tears of laughter.

She giggled as she collected her mail from the cute post box mounted on a tree stump, giving Mrs Jones from the cottage opposite a little wave as she came out to collect her milk from the doorstep.

"Lovely morning, Mrs Jones," Cora intelligently observed.

"Yn wir, bore da I chi hefyd, Mrs Spunge." Aelwen Jones kindly observed.

The little Welsh village that she had chosen as her place of retreat was just perfect. She was already on good terms with so many of the local residents, who had brought her delightful sponge cakes along with home-made jams and marmalades when she had first arrived.

"Come Barnaby, time for breakfast…" She made her way into the slate tiled hallway, pausing to admire Harold's photograph which now had pride of place on the large welsh dresser. She took it in her hands "…good morning dear, and what a beautiful morning it is… or should I say what a gay day because of course, you'd know all about that, won't you?" She wiped the glass with the hem of her pinny before placing it back on the shelf. "You know Harold, I would have understood, we can't help who we are or who we want to love. I'm angry with you because you took away my life in order for you to live a life that was a lie." She wiped a small tear away from the corner of her eye, mourning the children that were stolen from her because of Harold's ways. Barnaby completed his usual figure of eight around her leg, letting her know his needs were greater than her pique.

"Okay, I get the message, come on, kitty, kitty, kitties…." Her shrill voice filled the kitchen, as she tapped the side of the pottery bowls with a fork.

Her life here was good, she wouldn't allow Harold's ghost to haunt her any longer, she had her dream cottage, her cats and her new neighbours with jam, marmalade and cake. What more could she possibly want?

"...and I've still got enough money to see us through, haven't I, Barnaby?" She prepped her teapot and put the kettle on to boil. "Mind you, even if I do get a little over indulgent and find myself short of a bob or two, there's always the lovely residents and new neighbours of Piddling Bach village..."

Barnaby looked at her quizzically as she poured the milk into the china cup. "...well, they do so like to gossip about each other over their Bara Brith, don't they?"

The mischievous gleam in the eyes of the Stupendous Cora May Spunge was savoured only by her beloved cat Barnaby and the piercing glare from Harold's photo on his lofty perch in the hallway, as she sat down to open her mail.

"Right, let's see who is corresponding with us today, shall we?" She took a sip of her tea and allowed the cup to rattle back in the saucer as she picked up the first missive. Her lips silently mouthing the words as she read. "Oh dearie me..."

The lavender notepaper lay on the table next to the torn, unstamped envelope, Cora's hand stayed in shock and mild amusement. "Well, that wasn't quite the ending I had in mind at all for this story, Barnaby..." The realisation that her monetary fortune may not be forever had just hit Cora May Spunge like a two-ton sledgehammer to the back of the head. "...it looks like I'll be reluctantly sharing it with an old friend."

If Cora had known how to do air quotes with her fingers, she would have happily wiggled them around the word 'friend'.

In the silence that followed, as she digested what she had just read, the ridiculous irony of her situation forced a giggle to erupt, which then gave way to a bout of very unladylike guffaws of genuine mirth as she slapped the table.

Cora's laughter drifted out through the open kitchen window, sailed across the cottage garden and over the wall until it reached the ears of the ample figure standing by the gate.

Wearing a large straw sun hat that obscured her face, the woman listened intently, nodded her head and smiled a smile of triumph. Comfort in her dotage was now assured and best of all, she was already toying with the idea of *Madam Diamond D'light* coming out of retirement should she become bored in this little Welsh backwater. After all, her pink feather duster hadn't thrashed a decent rump in months.

Ambling off along the picturesque lane on her bunioned feet, Edna Flaybrick couldn't help but laugh too.

The Blackmailer had just been blackmailed!

I wriggled trying to get comfortable again. Elbowing the squishy cushion, I shoved it back into the snug between the arm and the button back of the sofa and jiggled a bit more until I'd found my perfect position. Alfie buffed his snout against my hand, turned three circles – he never ever did more than three – before settling himself down in the crook of my legs. The warmth from his body seeped into my pyjama bottoms. I turned back to page 2 of the little book I'd found in the churchyard. I needed to read this one again.

'*Cyril Hislop. Liar, cheat, thief, bully, father of my daughter. Insurance pay out, false claim for an accident in 1953, claims permanent erectile disfunction*'

Agatha's handwriting flowed across the page in black ink until underneath in red, highlighted with several asterisks, she had made an addition.

'*Unless it was the miraculous conception and I don't remember getting a visit from an angel - it worked well enough to give me a baby (17th April 1955)*'

I took another large slug of wine and dropped my head back, staring at the ceiling watching the reflected light from the flames of the fire dance across the plaster and beams, I sighed. Everything I could possibly need to know about the three blackmail jobs, Flaybrick, Hislop and Higgins, was all there between the pages. Additional notes in another style of handwriting indicated that there had been more who had been subjected to a dreadful 'letter', in particular Peggy, owner of Peggy Parker Lingerie in the village.

"Well that's me stuffed, Alfie, I'll never be able to darken her doorstep again knowing what I know now about her and her little liaisons..." I cringed. Her Wednesday afternoon beau was not someone you would automatically consider for swinging around the stanchions of a four-poster bed or shaking your flaps at from a Peggy Parker silk body suit.

So many skeletons, so much heartache and deceit – it was all there in those pages. Lives that had been lived for pleasure and gain with no thought of the pain it would cause or the fragile webs that had been woven.

I closed the book. What to do now? The postscript inside in that different style of writing had taken responsibility, the monies we suspected had been handed over had, according to the pseudonym of *Celia Fate*, been repaid.

Considering what I was about to do, I would have to trust that.

Apart from the deceased Cyril Hislop and his fake insurance claim, there had been no crimes within those pages, just desperately sad characters of a cheap village soap opera, that only Agatha the author, *Celia Fate*, the blackmailer and Mavis Upton the wife and mum, were privy to.

There was no Constable 1261 Mavis Upton, ace police driver, apprehender of naughty people, lover of crisps (any flavour) and hater of big knickers to consider in this awful mess. Sometimes we have to just follow our heart and our conscience.

I stoked the fire; glowing red embers broke apart from the partially burnt logs. I let the poker drop with a clang onto the brick hearth.

The book made a gentle thud as it hit the glowing logs, sparks flared up, swaying in a little dance as they sought the draught from the chimney. I watched as the flames flickered and caught hold, embracing the leather, curling the blue velvet tie, as it was consumed first.

"It's the right thing to do, Alfie ..."

THE FINALE

Dressed smartly for the occasion, I tottered out of the Waterfront Museum toilets on my court shoe heels and checked my watch. Plenty of time, even my nifty detour to the nearest little girls' room after a huge mug of tea in the café hadn't eaten up the extra hour I'd allowed myself.

Breathe Mavis, breathe!

I desperately need some fresh air.

The double doors silently opened as the breeze from the River Mersey pushed in bringing with it the smell of salt and diesel from the ferry terminal. It caught my hair, whipping it across my face as I stepped outside. White clouds scooted across the blue sky, the sun dipping in and out throwing its warmth onto pavements, benches and the dockland cobbles.

I found a bench and sat down, quietly contemplating the choices I have, no longer the thirty-something naïve woman who sat in this exact same spot all those years ago, waiting to go for an interview to join her dream job in the Police. The woman who dyed her hair specially, and whose collar and cuffs didn't match in colour. I smile as I remember Mum's horror when she thought I had worn a grubby blouse for the occasion rather than its true meaning.

So, where do I go from here?

Is it the end of an era, or do I push on, work towards pastures new?

The sun lit up the front of Police Headquarters, the red façade overlooking Albert Dock brightened, before fading back with the passing of a cloud. The magnificent Liver Bird looked down on me as my bottom lip gave a little wobble just as good old Larry the Lump formed in my throat, making it almost impossible to swallow.

I have to accept I have grown old, as we all do. I can still just about chase the naughty boys and climb up walls after them, but these days I struggle to get down on the other side without dislocating a knee cap, giving myself a double hernia or succumbing to an accidental Tena Lady moment. Is it time to move over, make way for the youngsters who are full of the enthusiasm and passion I still possess, but have the added bonus of agility and better bladder control?

Maybe.... maybe not!

'*What a pity that youth should be wasted on the young...*'

I love that quote, it sums up everything about life. When we are young we have our health and vibrancy, we are carefree. Later a thirst for knowledge and a desire to succeed creeps in and in time we sacrifice that health and vibrancy to achieve those goals, to prove our abilities.... and once we have achieved them and hold the knowledge we so eagerly sought, we are seen as too old, depleted and surplus to requirements.

I try to shake off the feeling of sadness that is weighing heavy on me. I should be happy celebrating an achievement, not mourn the passing of my own youth.

Today I will receive an Award for Outstanding Contribution in Policing and a Commendation for Bravery.

But inside I don't feel very brave or very outstanding. I am just a woman who had a passion to make things right. A woman who knew that by becoming a Police Officer she was never going to change the world, but if she worked hard and took the time to care, then maybe she could make a difference. I think that is my greatest achievement; I did make a difference. That was all I ever wanted, from being a little girl who read Enid Blyton's Famous Five to who I am now.

A seagull soared inland on an unseen thermal, and just as quickly swept back out towards the water. I watch until it disappears, prevaricating, holding back, not wanting to take the next step.

I suppose inside I am still that child.

I start to walk towards Headquarters, ready for my moment, ready to make some tough decisions, but instead my head suddenly snaps up, alert.

"Stop him, he's stolen my bag…. somebody please, help, help.."

The high-pitched scream hit my ears at roughly the same time as a shaven-headed muppet barrelled in front of me, a tan leather handbag clutched to his chest, his Lacoste tracky top flailing in the wind and his pants hanging from a very unattractive, partially bare arse.

In a split second I take it all in, I can see the woman, her face screwed up, her mouth open, a feral wail permeating the air, bystanders in slow motion, car horns, engine noise and muppet boy almost tripping over his feet as he heads towards the alley with his ill-gotten gains. I'm already wired, adrenalin pumping, I'm not put out to grass just yet.

Tally-ho Constable Mavis Upton…….

I race after him dragging several sheets of the Museum's finest quality bog paper behind me, firmly attached to the heel of my shoe. It quickly flits through my mind that for the last twenty minutes I must have been sweeping Liverpool's pavements with budget two-ply and nobody had thought to point it out to me.

Ah, c'est la vie...

I close in on him, my heels clattering on the concrete and cobbles before I manage to execute a quick, swift kick between his legs, and he's down.

Yay, go me......

Resisting the urge to do a lap of honour around the Liver Building, I straddle him, pressing my forearm into the side of his face, holding him down. He bucks and writhes, trying to escape, but I won't give in, I'm using every ounce of strength I have to keep him pinned down. I curse what I'm wearing, there's no give in a pencil pleat skirt or support in a Gossard Wonder Bra. The skirt hem cuts into my thigh as it rides up and the more effort I put into my method of restraint, the more my post-baby droopy nellies want to escape and give muppet boy a slap around the chops.

Something rips.

Oh shit!

"Stop fighting, I'm a police officer, stop resisting!" I shout the words, but it's more lip service than anything else as I know it won't have any impact. I can hear sirens in the distance followed by boots scuffling on the pavement and the static of radios as the troops pile in to help.

"Bleedin' hell, I'd know that bum anywhere ..." Danny Hodges, my old classmate from our heady early days at the police training centre, towered over me, "...and *thongs* at your age, for fucks sake Mave, really?

Embarrassment is written all over my face as I frantically try to adopt a more feminine position, lying legs akimbo on the pavement, whilst the clicking of mobile phones taking photographs of the unfolding excitement, fills the air. My knees are grazed and bloody and I've lost a shoe.

Jeez, who the hell did I piss off today to deserve this?

"Here y'go." Danny held out his hand to help me up. "The lads will take him in and no doubt you and your derriere will be in tonight's Liverpool Echo!" He jerked his head towards our audience of sightseers and cameras.

I visibly cringed and gave him my best mischief grin, happy to see him again after so many years but wishing it was under better circumstances and with a bit more dignity. Scraping my remaining shoe on the pavement to dislodge the toilet paper, I ran my hands over the back of my skirt to smooth it down and retain at least some decorum. "Way to go Dan, how did…." My eyes widened in horror as my fingers snagged in a gigantic hole ripped from zip to hem, the two pieces of material flapping in the breeze either side of my barely covered bum cheeks. "…oh bloody hell, nooooo, so that's how you knew what I was wearing!"

I screwed up my mouth and wrinkled my nose Elvis style, holding my hands up in resignation as Danny roared with laughter.

Sheesh!

So you see, I was never going to go out quietly, well-behaved and ordinary.

I was, as I will always be (with *polyester thong* on show to the whole world) …

Mavis Jane (Blackwell) Upton.

Mum

Wife

Police Officer

Colleague

Idiot

Feckwit

Melt
Friend
Bad-ass cousin…
…and total bloody shit-magnet!

THE END
…or is it?…

BLUES, TWOS AND BABY SHOES

I know
what
you did

ACKNOWLEDGEMENTS

I've had the most amazing beginning to my writing career, courtesy of my brilliant Publisher (still love saying that), my fantastic family and all the wonderful readers, book bloggers and my new found Twitter and Facebook buddies. It's special and it's fun when you are sharing your scribblings with people that mean something to you, so I am grateful to be able to have the chance to say thank you.

Firstly to Matthew Smith, the heart and soul of Urbane Publications, who probably rolls his eyes and sighs when another 'Ginamail' comes pinging into his inbox suggesting all sorts of off the wall ideas ranging from Extra Large Thongs, to Doughnuts, Drag Queens and scruffy, mad-eyed storks. Matthew, thank you. Thank you for giving me such an amazing chance, thank you for putting up with me and my quirky ways and most of all, thank you for believing in me. Without you there would be no Mavis, no thongs and no ridiculous escapades.

Where would Mavis be without the fabulous actor and playwright Lynne Fitzgerald bringing her to life. It's not just your incredible talent at character reading and comic timing Lynne, it is being mates, 'turning right with Johnny' and the fact you still haven't forgiven me for 'Sheridan Bloody Smith'. I will blush and howl with laughter every time I hear her name. Thank you my lovely, you have my undying admiration and friendship.

I very quickly found out how amazing book bloggers and readers are. There are too many to mention individually, and I would hate to miss someone out, so this is a collective 'thank you'. A bit like a group hug. As writers, where would we be without them? Our words wouldn't be heard, our stories wouldn't be told, they would lie dormant on paper or screen, meaningless. They only come alive because people read them, discuss them, promote them and enjoy them. This is a humongous thank you to you all, for your encouragement, support and words of advice.

To my cousin Del Willden, aka Beverly Macca. Del, I know we're family and part of the Marriott Mafia, but even so, you go above and beyond. What would Mavis do without you? Thank you from the bottom of my heart.

Gosh, Lorraine Kelly, where do I start and is it really okay to fangirl at my age? My hand shook like crazy signing Mavis's first two adventures to her with 'lots of love' and several smackeroo kisses. I absolutely adore Lorraine, so you can imagine the loud squealing that came from our house when she so very kindly gave me her words for the cover of Blues, Twos.

Mòran taing, Lorraine.

I'm over the moon to have Shaun McKenna bringing one of my characters to life again at the Waterstones Liverpool One launch for Blues, Twos. Hold on to your padded bras once again for the amazing Shaun (stage name Lady Seanne) as Beatrice. Thank you so much, Shaun, you are one of life's so very lovely and genuine people.

For Gavin Brace, an old colleague who went on to pastures new in the South Australia Police. Gav, thank you for your assistance with the welsh dialect and for the fantastic photos of your brilliant colleagues in the SA Support Unit with Mavis's thongs! A special mention to Kev T Brown my Twitter buddy from the IOM, his late night message gave me the idea for the title of Mavis's third adventure. I promise, the bag of crisps will be yours one day! To Sarah Lynwode (Hughes) my funny, smiley friend. I owe you so much, you took a chance on me, an unknown writer. I wish you every success with Thingio Events, you deserve nothing less.

I could never forget my very handsome, debonair brother, Andy Dawson - for no other reason than being handsome, debonair and of course, my brother. Love you Bro.

To my beautiful daughter Emma. You are my sunshine, I'm so very blessed to have you in my life, thank you for always being there for me.

And last but definitely not least, my gorgeous, funny husband John, the love of my life, my bodyguard, chauffeur and real life SatNav, the man who makes me laugh every single day. Your burning desire to make me happy is truly admirable much the same as when you set fire to the menu in that posh restaurant! Without you there would be no Joe, no love life for Mavis and no wonderful stories to tell and I'd still be driving around various parts of the UK panic struck and lost. I love you to the moon and back.

Gina x

Gina was born during the not-so-swinging 50s to a mum who frequently abandoned her in a pram outside Woolworths and a dad who, after two pints of beer, could play a mean Boogie Woogie on the piano in the front room of their 3-bed semi on the Wirral. Being the less adventurous of three children, she remains there to this day – apart from a long weekend in Bognor Regis in 1982.

Her teenage years were filled with angst, a CSE in Arithmetic, pimples, PLJ juice, Barry White and rather large knickers until she suddenly and mysteriously slimmed down in her twenties. Marriage and motherhood ensued, quickly followed by divorce in her early thirties and a desperate need for a career and some form of financial support for herself and her daughter.

Trundling a bicycle along a leafy path one wintry day, a lifelong passion to be a police officer gave her simultaneously an epiphany and fond memories of her favourite author Enid Blyton and moments of solving mysteries. And thus began an enjoyable and fulfilling career with Merseyside Police. On reaching an age most women lie about, she quickly adapted to retirement by utilising her policing skills to chase after two granddaughters, two dogs and one previously used, but still in excellent condition, husband.

Having said goodbye to what had been a huge part of her life, she suddenly had another wonderful epiphany. This time it was to put pen to paper to write a book based on her experiences as a police officer. Lying in bed one night staring at the ceiling and contemplating life as she knew it, Gina's alter-ego, Mavis Upton was born, ready to star in a humorous and sometimes poignant look at the life, loves and career of an everyday girl who followed a dream and embarked upon a search for the missing piece of her childhood.

*Will have you laughing out loud and is hugely entertaining.
This is a book that oozes charisma and character, one you will
not be able to put down.*
Nikki's Books4U

Hilarious ... real life and so touching, a fabulous read!
Christina Green

Laugh out loud brilliance, so witty and cleverly written.
Samantha Magson

Hilarious! It's true, everyone needs Mavis in their life.
Sherrie Hewson, actor, broadcaster and novelist

URBANE

Urbane Publications is dedicated to developing new author voices, and publishing fiction and non-fiction that challenges, thrills and fascinates.

From page-turning novels to innovative reference books, our goal is to publish what YOU want to read.

Find out more at
urbanepublications.com